It is the autumn of 1999. A year has passed since Lucy Darby's unexpected death, leaving her husband David and son Whitley to mend the gaping hole in their lives. David, a trauma-site cleanup technician, spends his nights expunging the violent remains of strangers, helping their families to move on, though he is unable to do the same. Whitley–an 11 year-old social pariah known simply as The Kid–hasn't spoken since his mother's death. Instead, he communicates through a growing collection of notebooks, living in a safer world of his own silent imagining.

As the impending arrival of Y2K casts a shadow of uncertainty around them, their own precarious reality begins to implode. Questions pertaining to the events of Lucy's death begin to haunt David, while The Kid, who still believes his mother is alive, enlists the help of his small group of misfit friends to bring her back. As David continues to lose his grip on reality and The Kid's sense of urgency grows, they begin to uncover truths that will force them to confront their deepest fears about each other and the wounded family they are trying desperately to save.

Also by Scott O'Connor

*Among Wolves*, a novella

# UNTOUCHABLE

# untouchable

A NOVEL

SCOTT O'CONNOR

TYRUS
BOOKS

Published by
TYRUS BOOKS
1213 N. Sherman Ave. #306
Madison, WI 53704
www.tyrusbooks.com

Library of Congress Cataloging-In-Publication Data has been applied for.

15 12 13 12 11 1 2 3 4 5 6 7 8 9 10

978-1-935562-38-2 (hardcover)
978-1-935562-50-4 (paperback)

For Karen

one

They come in the abandoned hour of the night, moving through quiet arterial streets, empty intersections, past gated storefronts and darkened windows, homeless men curled into bus stop shelters, prostitutes walking the desolate concrete stretches.

They come in a pair of white Ford Econolines, identical vans, flanks unmarked, windowless and blank. They sit parallel at stoplights and the drivers raise their eyebrows at each other and yawn, sip coffee from Styrofoam cups, roll forward when the lights change, toward the motel, the apartment complex, the house in the hills.

There is always someone waiting when they arrive, someone standing in the driveway or doorway, looking more than a little shell-shocked, still not quite able to believe what they've seen, that what has happened has actually happened. The police have left, the coroner's people have left, but someone slipped them a business card on the way out, passed along a company name and phone number and told them to call and wait. Mothers, husbands, wives, motel night clerks, apartment managers, security guards. Whoever was unfortunate enough to be the one to open the door, to walk into the room and see something they will never forget.

They weren't going to call the number. There was a moment after all the noise and commotion, after the police and the coroner's people left, when the person waiting in the doorway was alone in the new silence of the place, just outside the room, a moment where they thought they could handle it themselves, thought they could take care of things quickly and efficiently, that it would be the right thing to do for their son or husband or tenant or employer. That it would be unpleasant but possible. But then they remembered the sight and the smell and the profane mess, the horror of the thing, and they dialed the number on the card and spoke to a sweet-sounding old woman who took their information and told them that help was on the way.

The white vans pull to the curb, engines cooling, ticking in the stillness.

Two men get out of the first van, stretching and yawning in the bad light. These are not the kind of men the person in the doorway expected. The person in the doorway is not sure what kind of men they expected, but these are not those men. One of the men is tall, buzz cut, with full sleeves of multicolored tattoos. The other is short and gym-built, with a thinning cap of flaming orange hair. These are rough-looking men, truckers or sailors, heavy-lifters, men who look like they're in the habit of breaking things, dropping things, banging around in small rooms. They do not seem equipped for the subtlety and reverence required for the task at hand. The grandmother on the phone had used the term *technicians*, had said that she was sending a *crew of technicians*, but these men do not appear to have the degree of precision that the term implies, the level of scientific expertise.

The person in the doorway considers redialing the number on the card, canceling the job, dealing with this themselves. But then there is the memory, that first moment when they opened the door and came upon the scene in the room, the unspeakable thing. So they do nothing, they hold the business card and wait as the men move to the backs of the vans and pull out their equipment, red plastic buckets, squeeze bottles and spray cans, wire brushes and putty knives, roll after roll of paper towels.

Another man, the driver of the second van, steps down onto the sidewalk. He approaches the person in the doorway, walking slowly, head down. He is terrifically fat. He has a graying ponytail that stretches down between his shoulder blades and a thick, bushy mustache that turns up at the ends. There is a name for this type of mustache, an antiquated style, but the name escapes the person waiting. Remembering it seems important, suddenly, proving that they are still capable of simple acts, putting names to things. It seems like this would restore a level of normalcy to the night, having a name for it, that style of mustache. But the term is just out of reach and they are left at a loss, again.

The two men at the vans are pulling on blue paper body suits, they are pulling on rubber gloves. They are duct taping each other's suit sleeves closed around the gloves. They are pulling safety goggles out of the vans, plastic-and-rubber respiration masks, a box of disposable surgical booties. More duct tape for the pant cuffs of their suits, a man standing on one leg, balancing with a hand against the side of a van while the other rolls the tape around his ankles.

They look like something out of an old science-fiction movie. Moonmen. They look like moonmen.

The fat man approaches, the fat man arrives. He is even bigger up close, towering, damp-browed, breathing heavily from the short walk. He smells of cigarettes and coffee. He looks down at the scuffed toes of his work boots. He is about to speak and the person in the doorway has absolutely no idea what he is going to say, what anyone could possibly say on this night, standing outside after the police and coroner's people have gone, after the facts have been given and recorded, the known details. The person has no idea what's left, what words would still have a shred of relevance, what words wouldn't fail, utterly.

The fat man nods and looks up and speaks in a low, rich rumble. What he says is, *I'm very sorry for your loss.*

And maybe this is the moment when the person in the doorway cries or screams or lets loose a fusillade of vulgarities, a seething mass of profanity and loss. Maybe this is the moment where the person falls to their knees, dissolving into guilt, sobbing convulsively, and has to be helped up by the fat man, held under the elbows and lifted, gently. Maybe this is the moment when the person hits the fat man, when they punch the fat man in the chest, just to put a physical action to the feeling, just to strike some kind of blow. Maybe this is the moment when they speak in tongues, when they resurrect a primal language, finding comfort in the acceptance of extreme things, babbling in God's own voice. Or maybe this is the moment when they say nothing, when they stand silent, when the weight of the thing that has happened finally settles upon them, and they sag a little, in the shoulders and knees, the smallest thing, the way they will sag from now on, the way they will carry this night in their bodies from this moment forward, and maybe this is their only response to what the fat man says.

The moonmen pass inside, carrying their equipment. Their blue paper suits crinkle and shush. The fat man stays for a few minutes, and maybe he says something else and maybe he doesn't. Maybe he just stands and waits as the person in the doorway gets used to the sagging weight, their new posture, the slight adjustment in bearing. Then the fat man returns to the vans and pulls on his own moonman suit, gathers the equipment the others have laid out for him, passes by the person in the doorway and enters the motel or apartment or house in the hills.

And maybe this is when it comes to them, when it arrives unexpectedly, the lost identifier. Maybe this is when they remember. The name of the thing. The fat man's facial hair. Maybe it comes to them then, just like that, a gift.

Handlebar mustache. The name of the thing is handlebar mustache.

David Darby hauled his gear down the narrow hallway and up the stairs to the fourth and top floor. Jerry Roistler followed half a flight behind. They set their buckets down outside the numbered door and waited. Bob Lewis was downstairs speaking with the person who'd been waiting when they arrived. The apartment manager, Darby guessed, a harried-looking man with a gold hoop dangling from one ear. Bob would get whatever information he felt necessary for the job, probably more than he needed, then he'd come up and look at the room and give the manager an estimate, a timeframe for completion.

Darby could already smell the job on the other side of the door. The room had sat for a while. A week, he guessed, maybe longer.

Roistler winced at the smell, pulled on his respiration mask.

"What do you think, Tattooed Lady?" Roistler said, voice muffled by the mask. "Vectors or no vectors?"

"Not interested."

"Five bucks says vectors."

"No interest."

"With that smell, five bucks says *mucho* vectors." Roistler worked his knuckles, his neck and shoulders, an irritating sequence of fire-cracker pops. Darby ignored him, listened to the stairs groan as Bob lumbered up to the top.

"Apartment manager was in Reno for a week," Bob said. He pulled a loose strand of tobacco from his mustache. "Came back to a phone full of messages about the smell."

"Nobody called the cops?" Roistler said.

"Older people in the building, mostly. Keep to themselves. Nobody called anybody until it was time to complain about the smell."

Bob pulled on his mask, lifted the instant camera out of his bucket, unlocked the door with a ring of keys the manager had given him. He would take a picture of the room before they started work, what they called the *Before* photo. He stepped into the doorway, filling the frame.

"Studio apartment," Bob said. "One main room, small kitchen off one side, smaller bathroom off the other."

He lifted the camera to his eye, snapped a picture. The light of the flash echoed back out into the hallway. The print slid from the face of the camera, slowly developing. Bob pulled the print, shook it with his free hand. Darby strapped on his safety goggles, picked up his equipment and entered the room.

The trick of the job is to forget what had happened. The trick of the job is to acquire as little information as possible about the site, the former occupants, the current occupants, the thing that happened there, and then to forget that information. Not to see the big picture, the whole story. There is no big picture, there is no whole story. There are only details that need to be sprayed, scrubbed, bagged, disposed of.

The trick of the job is to use an alternate vocabulary for these details, a list of terms developed over the years by the technicians, sanitized for their own protection. Once inside the room, there is no blood, or skin, or hair, or teeth, or chunks of brain, heart, lung, stomach. There is no evidence of violent death, self-inflicted or otherwise. There is no detritus of a human body left to decompose for days or weeks. There is only fluid and matter; there are only spots, stains, leakage.

The trick of the job is not to listen to the people who are waiting in the doorway, in the driveway, in the parking lot when the vans arrive. Often they will have a lot to say, a lot to explain. It is important to understand what those people do not: that there is nothing to explain. There is just fluid and matter. There are just spots and stains. There is only a mess that needs to be cleaned up.

Remember those things, understand those things, and the job is possible. The room can be cleaned, finished, set right. Remember those things and the picture taken once the job is complete, the *After* photograph, will show evidence that the trick is more than a trick. It will show what has been achieved through hours of spraying and scrubbing and scraping and bagging, what future occupants of the site will believe, safe and unsuspecting. That the trick of the job is now the new truth of the room:

Nothing happened.

The recliner would have to be disposed of. That much was immediately clear. The recliner was a lost cause, soaked in fluids and studded with matter. Once Bob came back up from the manager's office, they'd need to wrap it and carry it down to the vans. After the cleanup was complete, they'd drive it to the disposal facility with the other red biohazard bags full of all the other things they couldn't salvage, contaminated items that were impossible to clean.

The carpeting around the recliner was dark with dried splotches, stipples trailing out toward the wall a few feet behind. Darby pulled a spray bottle from his bucket, squirted the liquefying enzyme across the first splotch, softening the dried fluid, creating a low mist around the recliner. He gave it a few seconds to burble and hiss, then pulled a fistful of paper towels from a roll and soaked up as much as the towels would hold. He red-bagged the towels and sprayed the next splotch.

Roistler came into the apartment carrying the fogging machine. He closed the door behind him and shut all the windows, sealing them in. He set the machine down in the middle of the room. The fogger would flatten all smell in the room, years of cologne and cooking and cigarettes and a week's worth of fluid and matter sitting in the heat. It also helped with the flies, though it didn't do much about the vectors.

Roistler had been right. There were *mucho* vectors. Flies gathered almost immediately at a job site, and given enough time, flies laid eggs that became vectors and vectors multiplied at an alarming rate, squirming around in any fluid and matter they could find. A week was more than enough time for a complete generation of vectors, maybe two.

Roistler flipped a switch on the fogger and the machine jumped to life. Darby could feel its low rumble in his knees, vibrating through the floor. The machine chugged and pumped, releasing a thin white mist in a steady stream. Roistler said something Darby couldn't hear, then laughed at his own joke.

Darby sprayed another splotch at the foot of the recliner, tore more paper towels from the roll, scooped the softened fluid. There were sharp shards of broken glass near the toe of his work boot, the remains of a shattered vodka bottle. There was another empty bottle on the TV, a third lying on its side on the bed. Darby caught himself, stopped himself from looking around the room. He narrowed his vision, refocused on the recliner.

"Darby," Roistler said. "Look at this."

Roistler was standing at the bookshelves on the other side of the room, inspecting picture frames and detective paperbacks, anything that could have been hit with flying fluid or matter.

"Darby, look." Roistler raised his voice to be heard over the fogger, through the hood of Darby's suit. He was holding something between his thumb and forefinger, dangling it for Darby to see.

Darby didn't look. He nodded like he'd looked, nodded and grunted loudly as a false confirmation that he'd looked, because sometimes that was enough, sometimes that satisfied Roistler and he'd get back to work without any further conversation.

"Darby, look. You're not looking."

Darby didn't look. He nodded and grunted and scooped the last of the fluid from the carpeting. It wasn't going to be enough. The carpeting would have to be disposed of. He picked a scoring razor out of his bucket and started cutting the carpet into record album-sized squares, pulling the squares loose, stuffing them into a red biohazard bag.

It was already hot in the room. Darby sweated in his suit, used his forearm to lift his goggles a half inch from his face, clear the condensation.

There was a large, shrieking splash of fluid on the wall behind the recliner. Above the fluid was a fist-sized hole that had contained the discharge of the weapon used. The discharge would have been taken by the cops, but there would still be other things in that hole, things that clung to the discharge as it made its way from the recliner to the wall.

Darby pulled a plastic dustpan from his bucket, sprayed the stain on the wall with disinfectant and held the pan underneath to catch the fluid as it ran. The disappearing stain revealed more matter stuck to the white paint, little wads of what could easily be mistaken for colorless chewing gum. Darby kept the dustpan pressed to the wall with one hand, tore paper towels with the other, picked the matter from the wall. Sprayed the entire area again, wiping it clean.

He carried a short stepladder in from the hall, climbed up to the hole, sprayed disinfectant and shone a flashlight around inside. Tough to see what the situation was. He grabbed a wad of paper towels and pushed his hand into the hole. Came away with enough on his towel to repeat the process a few more times.

Roistler stopped talking. Bob was back in the doorway. Darby tilted his head toward the recliner and Bob nodded. They tore long sheets of black plastic from a four-foot roll and wrapped the recliner, Bob rocking the chair one way and then the other while Darby pulled the plastic tight. They each took an end and carried it out of the room, down the hallway to the staircase, the gaps under the doorways shadowed as they passed, eyeholes darkening, a few doors cracking open along the way, braver souls, long faces peeking out, older men and women, mostly alone, one per room, nightshirts and pajamas, woken by the sirens and the sounds of people and equipment trampling through the building, fearstruck now by the two moonmen. They pinched their noses when they saw the recliner. The recliner didn't carry much of an odor, but they saw the hoods and the masks and a chair bound in plastic and thought that it must smell, assumed that it must stink like cellophane-wrapped meat gone bad.

Down the stairs, third floor, second floor, the recliner heavy from the liquid weight it carried. They stopped at each landing for Bob to regain his breath. Finally they were out the front door of the building into the early light, the sun-gathering haze. Bob wedged a wooden block into the doorway to keep it from shutting, locking them out. Darby covered the floor of the first van with a large sheet of plastic and they lifted the recliner up and in.

They peeled off their gloves, pulled back their hoods, took off their goggles and masks. Breathed deeply. Traffic was starting to thicken on the freeway overpass a block away, headlights and taillights in the gloom. Bob readjusted his ponytail up under his hair net, pulled the tape from his wrists, rolled his sleeves to get some air on his skin. His moonman suits were special-ordered for his size. One of Roistler's favorite jokes was to open a new shipment of suits at the garage, rummage through the box and announce that the supplier had refused to make Bob-sized suits any more, that the techs would have to sew two large suits together to make new Bob-sized suits.

Bob looked at his watch. "What do you think? Three hours? Four? We're back at the garage by ten?"

Darby nodded. He looked up at the apartment building, a gray stucco slab, counted up, counted back, looking for the light, the closed windows of the room.

"Which is it?" Bob said. "Three or four?"

"Three."

"Fifteen bucks on three?"

"Sure."

"Dinner on three?"

"Sure."

Bob tapped his watch, marking the time. He pulled two new pairs of gloves from a toolbox, handed one pair to Darby. He closed up the van and Darby kicked the wooden block loose from the front door of the building as they went back inside.

Darby stood in the center of the room, pulled off his goggles and mask, pulled back his hood. The cleanup was complete. Roistler was hauling out the last of the redbags and equipment; Bob was settling the paperwork with the apartment manager downstairs.

Midmorning light through the windows, soft orange and yellow. Citrus light. The beginning of another hot day in a string of them. Too warm for this late into October. He tore the duct tape from his wrists, retrieved the camera from where Bob had left it on the table by the TV.

The room had no smell, thanks to the fogger. There was a blank spot where any smell should be.

Darby lifted the camera to his eye, stepped back toward the door, getting as much of the room in frame as he could. There was a small, hard knot behind the bridge of his nose, the kernel of a headache that spread quickly out toward his temples, the back of his skull. A rushing in his ears, a loud white noise that threatened to fill the room. This had been happening for a while now, this feeling that came upon him when he was making his final check of a site. A nagging disquiet. The feeling that the room was unfinished.

He looked for something they had missed, some detail that would be discovered in days or weeks, after the carpeting had been replaced, after the wall had been patched and repainted, a telltale sign that would betray the secret of what had happened here. There was nothing. The room was clean, the job was done.

He tried to shake the headache. He held his breath to steady his hands and snapped the picture. The room flashed white.

The Kid woke in the gray pre-dawn, a sinking in the pit of his stomach, that familiar leaden feeling. He rolled over and looked at his alarm clock. He had beaten it again, had snapped awake first. The clock was a ballgame giveaway, Dodger blue, with glow-in-the-dark hands, and in a few minutes it would sound out the national anthem in bleeps and buzzes to start the day. The Kid tried to remember the dream he'd just woken from, tried to catch the last quickly-shrinking remnants, a dream where he and his dad were on the road, moving across the map, chasing someone, but the dream was fading fast, pulling off and away. He sat up in bed, shaking off sleep. He remembered where he was, how things really were. No dream, just morning. That familiar leaden feeling.

It was the autumn before the end of the world. There was a special segment on the news every night devoted to this. The woman who hosted the segment said that now was the time to stockpile bottled water and canned food, first-aid supplies, a battery-operated flashlight and radio, batteries, clean underwear, any necessary prescription medication. Two or three months worth of all of these things, the woman said, though The Kid wondered what would happen after that, after two or three months had come and gone and it was still the end of the world.

In the bathroom he peed, flushed, continued peeing, watching it swirl in the bowl. Downstairs, he sat at the kitchen table in his underpants, feet dangling, crunching cereal. The light grew slowly through the back window. He heard the alarm clock bleep to life, the first notes of the anthem. He let it play while he ate his breakfast, reading the side of the cereal box, the nutrition information, the long list of unpronounceable ingredients.

Almost every night, The Kid watched the end-of-the-world segment on the news, took notes, made lists. His dad usually watched
the segment with him, but they hadn't bought any canned goods
yet, any extra batteries. It was already the middle of October, sixth
grade was already a month and a half old, and The Kid didn't think
they were even close to being ready for what could happen on New
Year's Eve.

He finished his cereal, rinsed his bowl in the sink. Took the vita-
min that his dad had set out for him on the countertop, swallowed
it dry.

At school, The Kid had overheard other kids talking worst-case
scenarios. What about weapons? Wouldn't they need weapons for
when the American system broke down and everybody started killing everybody else? This was a big deal to some of the boys in The
Kid's grade. At recess, the boys played like the end of the world was
already happening, like it had arrived early. They broke into separate
classroom tribes and raided each other's side of the playground to
loot supplies and capture prisoners for slaves. The Kid stayed away
from this type of game. He was a magnet for trouble regardless of
what was being played, but this type of game was an especially bad
idea. This type of game was asking for it. At recess, he sat with his
friend Matthew Crump at a picnic table near the playground aides,
heavyset mothers from the neighborhood who didn't move too
quickly when there was a problem, which is why it was important to
sit close by. They might not bother to cross the entire playground to
pull a pile of kids off him, but at least they'd shout a couple of warnings to keep them back if he was sitting a few yards away.

The end of the world had a sinister-sounding robot name that
gave The Kid a bad little thrill when he thought about it. *Y2K.* He
liked the name, despite what it meant, that all the machines and
computers would go haywire, planes falling out of the sky, missiles
launching from secret hatches in cornfields, streaking out over the
plains, across the ocean, going that way, coming this way, landing
on whoever was unlucky enough to be standing in the wrong place
at the wrong time. He liked the feeling of the name when it sat in

his head, though he worried that just thinking it long enough might actually trigger it, might become its actual cause.

He got dressed and brushed his teeth, scrubbing as hard as he could. He pulled his face into a smile, looked in the mirror. Bright red strands of blood across his gums. He gargled with the astringent green mouthwash, the big plastic bottle so heavy he could barely lift it to his mouth. He counted thirty seconds like it said on the label, swishing all the time, then spat into the sink. Filled his mouth a second time, swished, spat. Gasped from the spearmint burn. Opened his mouth and stuck out his tongue, looked in the mirror for anything strange, anything suspicious. He didn't want to carry any offensive odors, bad-breath germs, didn't want to give the kids at school any more reasons for name-calling, nose-holding.

The leaden feeling grew, roiled in his belly.

The Kid stood in the bathroom, stood in his bedroom, stood back in his parents' old bedroom, looked out the windows at the front yard, the back yard, the broad side of the brick apartment building next door. A few weeks before, his dad had installed metal security bars on all the windows in the house, even the windows upstairs. He'd climbed to the top of a ladder and bolted the bars into the wooden window casings. The Kid stood down at the bottom of the ladder, watching, using his hand to shield his eyes from the sun. The bars were to keep people out of the house when his dad had to work at night, the people who ran through the narrow alleyway alongside the house, the people who yelled at each other out on the street, the people who spray-painted glossy hieroglyphics across garages, sidewalks, the side of the apartment building next door, tagging anything that couldn't move out of the way. The Kid didn't like the bars. They kept people out, but what if somebody got in? Then it would be harder to escape, harder to run. What if he came home from school and his dad had already gone to work and someone had found a way into the house, was hiding in a closet, waiting for The Kid? Then he'd be trapped. The Kid didn't like the bars.

He sat on the couch in the living room, pointed the remote control at the TV, rewound the tape in the VCR. His dad taped the late-night talk shows for him every night. Every morning The Kid watched the tape, studying the delivery of the hosts during their opening monologues, analyzing their gestures, their facial expressions, the nuances of their interviewing techniques. The way they led their celebrity guests away from boring stories, back toward the jokes, the perfectly-timed punchlines. He watched certain parts over and over, rewinding and replaying the tape, pantomiming the hosts' rhythms, mimicking their timing, taking notes in his notebook. This was something he had always done with his mom in the time before school. His mom had gone to school at the same time as The Kid in the mornings, catching the bus at the corner that took her to the high school on the other side of the city. She'd taught history to eleventh and twelfth graders, big kids. The Kid and his mom used to sit on the couch, watching the tape until it was time to leave. Sometimes they talked so much about what they saw that they had to stop the tape and watch the rest of the shows when they both got home in the afternoon. Now it didn't take very long at all to watch. Now The Kid was usually done watching the tape with time to spare.

He lay down on the floor of his room and reached under his bed, pulled out the calendar he kept there. This was the last thing he did every morning before leaving the house, marking the calendar with the secret symbol, an arrow pointing to the right, one in each square for each day his mom had been gone. The arrows didn't mean anything on their own. He just used arrows instead of X's so his dad wouldn't know what he was doing, so his dad wouldn't feel bad for what The Kid was keeping track of.

He drew an arrow in the previous day's square, then looked back through the pages of the calendar, arrows in each square back to the beginning of the year. There was another calendar under his bed from the year before, and it had arrows in each square back to nearly this same time, both calendars making almost a full year's worth of arrows.

His dad had left The Kid's brown bag lunch on the kitchen counter, peanut butter on white bread. The Kid slid his lunch into

his backpack, slid his notebook and pencil inside, hoisted the backpack over his shoulders. He unlocked the locks on the front door,
top to bottom: chain, deadbolt, knob-lock, deadbolt. Stood behind
the steel screen security door his dad had installed at the same time
as the bars on the windows. Almost fully light outside. He pressed
his nose to the cool mesh, looked out at the short, scrubby front
yard, the sidewalk and the street beyond. Kids from his school were
already passing by the front fence, shoving and joking, readjusting
their backpacks, laughing, snapping gum.

The Kid stood at the door, debating. What if he didn't go? How
long would it take the adults at the school to find out? What would
happen? What if he went somewhere else instead? What if he went
out the door and just started walking in the other direction? Twenty
miles to the ocean, that's what his dad told him once. Twenty miles.
How long would it take him to walk? What would he do when he
got there? He thought about the dream he'd had, what he could
remember of it, the feeling of being somewhere else, moving across
the map in another direction.

He stood at the door, debating. The feeling in his belly was at
its worst now, this moment at the door every morning, when he felt
there was a decision he could make.

He opened the security door, stepped out onto the porch,
relocked all the locks with his key. Not today. Twenty miles was too
far. He headed out onto the sidewalk, into the ramshackle procession
of kids, head down, moving quickly, up the slow hill toward school.

Here he comes, Whitley Earl Darby, commonly known as The
Kid, big head, big feet, spindly body, the whole contraption threatening to tip over at any moment as he navigated the buckled sidewalk, readjusted the weight of his overlarge backpack. Here comes
The Kid, make room, make way. Don't get too close. Known to have
germs, cooties, bad breath, B.O. Known to be diseased, known to be
contagious. Known as Whitley to only a very few: Miss Ramirez, his
teacher; Mr. Bettemit, the vice-principal; Mr. Bromwell, the school

counselor. Known to everyone else by his preferred name, his alter ego. Known to everyone else as The Kid.

His neighborhood was at the eastern end of Sunset Boulevard, Los Angeles, California, the United States of America, Western Hemisphere, Planet Earth. Not too far from Dodger Stadium. This was only one part of the city. The city was big. There was a whole other part of the city a half hour drive to the west, maybe a forty-five minute drive, where the ocean was, where the movie stars and talk-show hosts lived. The Kid had been there a few times. His mom had taken him to the beach a couple of times each summer. They'd looked for seashells in the sand and ridden the giant Ferris Wheel at the end of the long wooden pier.

The other kids were some distance ahead of The Kid, some distance behind, over on the opposite sidewalk. The other kids ignored him, which was okay, which was fine, which was preferable to the alternative.

Everything in his neighborhood was crooked. Everything bent away from everything else at different angles—the outside walls of houses, the iron-barred fences around the front yards, the street lights, the telephone poles, the sickly palm trees that shot up through the overhanging mess of telephone wires. He noticed these things as he walked, and when he thought something was particularly interesting he made a note in his notebook.

He looked at the paintings on the walls, the murals that he passed. They had learned about murals in school the year before. They were all over the neighborhood, painted on the sides of buildings, across the lengths of freeway underpasses, along the cinder-block walls sloping down from the side streets toward Sunset. They'd learned that in ancient times murals were a way of sharing news, of telling other people what was going on. This was before TV or radio stations or the Internet. People painted murals to show other people what was happening, what they should be aware of. These murals were newer than those murals, but they were probably still way older than The Kid.

He stopped in the tunnel under the Sunset Boulevard bridge, looked at the mural on the wall above. It was a painting of the city, the tall downtown buildings jumbled along streets that rolled like waves. Behind it all was a giant brown-skinned woman, smiling, holding her arms out like she was about to hug the city or maybe the person walking by the mural. A big golden sun glowed from behind her hair, lighting the sky above and the buildings below.

The Kid didn't know what news this mural imparted, what it was trying to say, but he liked the drawing. He liked imagining someone up on a ladder under the bridge, painting the scene to be found and looked at years later by pedestrians and passing drivers and kids on their way to school.

Echoes jumped along the walls and ceiling of the tunnel, the sound of cars speeding by, the shouts and laughter of the other kids horsing around on the opposite sidewalk. There was even more graffiti covering the mural than there had been the day before, creeping across the painting, choking the woman and the buildings. The graffiti was written in dripping spray paint or fat magic marker, black mostly, but some red and yellow and green, people's nicknames, gang tags, bad words, arrows pointing this way and that, arrows leading toward something, away from something, secret messages to other graffiti writers: go here, meet here, hide here.

The Kid was worried that someday he'd come by on his way to school and the mural would be completely covered with tags, suffocated under all that paint and marker. He was worried that someday he'd come by here as an adult and wouldn't even remember what the mural had looked like, the thing he'd seen so many times. The news someone was trying to share. All that work would be gone, forgotten.

He started drawing the mural in his notebook. He tried to get the woman's face right, her warm smile; tried to draw the bend of her arms correctly. Cars whizzed by on the street behind him. He drew the downtown buildings, the rolling streets. He was rushing, eventually just sketching the outlines of things, because there was no way he could draw it all in the time before school, but at least he could get some of it down, finish the rest later on his way home.

It was quiet under the bridge. The traffic had come and gone, the other kids were all well out of sight. He'd lost track of time. He closed his notebook and hurried out of the tunnel, backpack bouncing as he ran, finally reaching the front gates of the school. The other students were streaming in, hundreds of them, pushing and shoving to get inside. The gates looked like open jaws, eating kids. The feeling in his stomach returned with a vengeance. He usually tried to get into his classroom before everyone else so he could take his seat safely, but he'd lost track of time and now he'd just have to hope for the best, he'd just have to brave it, so he put his head down and clutched his notebook and ran into the middle of the crowd, deflecting punches and shoves, pushes, kicks, finally breaking through the other side, sprinting full-tilt into the building and down the hall.

They entered a room never sure what they would find, prepared for the worst. This is what they trained for, Friday afternoons at the Everclean garage in Glendale, once a month, once every six months, whenever the state safety reps came down from Sacramento and stood sweating in the heat in their dark suits, watching the techs work through simulated clean-ups on the set Bob and Darby had built in the parking lot, a mock motel room, a floor and three plywood walls, open to the sky. The techs had arranged an assortment of thrift store furniture inside, two twin beds and a night table, a broken TV on a thick oak dresser. They'd hung curtains over the window holes, tacked strips of mismatched carpeting to the floor. Somewhere along the line, someone had procured some authentic motel room art, Bob probably, blurry pastel watercolors of seascapes and sand dunes in chipped wooden frames, and these were hung on the walls over the bed and dresser.

They rehearsed using different props, set pieces they'd constructed, a narrow air duct they could crawl into, a short staircase leading nowhere. Every job was dangerous, potentially. Every room contained invisible pathogens, some air-borne, some fluid-borne, some deadly, some merely unpleasant. Herpes Simplex Type 1, Herpes Simplex Type 2; Hepatitis A, B, C; Trichophyton; Giardia; Human Immunodeficiency Virus; Escherichia coli; Campylobacter; Staph; Strep. The names cycled through Darby's head at a job site. The list of potential miseries. The respirator masks and rubber gloves and Tyvek body suits were protection against the list, although there were hidden dangers at every site, rusty nails and broken glass and pinprick syringes discovered under mattresses, in dark corners.

They worked through every eventuality on the set in the parking lot—natural expiration, accidental expiration, murder two, murder three—though suicides accounted for maybe eight jobs out of ten.

Bob and Javier Molina, a friend from his old neighborhood, had started Everclean ten years before in Molina's mother's garage. Molina handled the business end while Bob handled the cleanups. Things had gone well. It turned out there was a need for their particular services. The company had grown to include Darby and Roistler, Mrs. Fowler in the dispatch office, the two vans and enough equipment to warrant the Glendale garage.

The garage sat near the end of a dry, sun-exposed industrial strip, amid long, flat, stucco-and-cinderblock warehouses and machine shops, a small salvage yard, a couple of empty, trash-strewn lots wrapped in chain-link. Behind the garage, on the other side of a high fence, was the long drop-off into the concrete trough of the Los Angeles River. The river was dry most of the year, just shallow pools of oily water around swollen trash bags and discarded shopping carts. A chain of small islands stretched off to the west, each maybe thirty or forty feet of high weeds and brush. There were homeless encampments clustered along the islands, and at night the techs could see the flickers of cigarette lighters and cooking fires, shadows jumping along the river's graffiti-striped walls.

Bob maneuvered the van into the garage and Darby climbed up into the back, emptying out the equipment, spraying the walls and floor with disinfectant. The phone rang in the dispatch office. Darby could hear Mrs. Fowler's sunny sing-song answer, *Good morning, thank you for calling Everclean.*

There was a waiting area at the other end of the garage, a couple of chairs, a coffee maker, a table with a spread of muscle car magazines, a TV on a metal stand. The TV showed a live news shot from some outlying location, a brown, bleak place, dust and long sky, a low ridge of mountains in the distance. The camera zoomed in on a large barn without windows or a visible door, then pulled back to reveal a pair of smaller buildings, a garage, a water tank, all behind a high deer fence topped with concertina wire.

"Where is that?" Bob said, squinting at the screen from halfway across the garage. "The Tehachapis? Looks like the Tehachapi Mountains."

Roistler stood in front of the TV, head forward to hear the low volume. "Some kind of survivalist group," he said. "Been living there for a few weeks. They're going to wait out the Millennium Bug."

"Where is that?" Bob said. "Roistler, turn up the goddamn sound."

A female reporter was now in the shot, holding a microphone, standing in front of a satellite news van.

"Twenty-five, thirty people," Roistler said, relaying what he heard. "They all met in an online message board. These reporters found their web site."

"Can you please turn up the goddamn sound?" Bob said.

Darby hopped down out of the van, still shaking the last of the headache from the job site. He patted his waist, his belt. His cell phone was gone. He kept the phone in a leather holster clipped to his belt, set to vibrate in case The Kid needed to reach him. The entire holster was gone. He checked the front of the van, under the seat, behind the seat. He tried to remember if he'd had the phone with him when he'd left the house the night before, if he'd clipped the holster to his belt next to his Everclean pager, if he'd had it in his hand when he stood in The Kid's bedroom doorway, watching him sleep.

Molina came out into the garage from his office, looked at the TV. He pulled at the collar of his white dress shirt, too tight around his wide neck. A bird's claw tattoo poked out from under his cuff, the man that the businessman had once been showing through a little.

"Have you seen this?" Roistler said. "Tell me you've put a bid in on this."

"There's nothing to bid on," Molina said. "Nothing's happened."

"Give them a call. Get us on a list. Someone's starting a list, government bids."

"Roistler, they can't take bids on something that hasn't happened."

"Big job," Roistler said. "That's going to be a big job."

The Kid had convinced Darby to buy the cell phone, had come up with an entire system for its usage. Darby hadn't wanted to leave The Kid alone in the house when he went out on night jobs, but The Kid didn't want to stay with anyone else, so one evening, nine or ten months before, The Kid laid his cell phone plan out for Darby on the front porch. The plan took up an entire two-page spread in his note-book—diagrams, arrows, the whole nine yards. Darby would buy a phone and subscribe to one of the monthly calling plans The Kid saw advertised during the late-night talk shows. The Kid would be the only person with the phone number. If there were any problems at night while Darby was at work, The Kid would call Darby and relay a series of dot-dash-dot bleeps using the keypad of the kitchen phone. Morse Code. Bob had bought The Kid a book on Morse Code for his birthday that year, and this had sparked his whole idea. In his notebook, he'd copied over a few phrases he thought he'd be using in his transmissions to Darby: *Help, Come at once. What is your position? Calling for assistance. S.O.S.*

Darby stood in the middle of the garage, scanning the cement 'floor. No sign of the phone or the holster.

"Here you go, *jefe*." Bob handed Molina the paperwork from the cleanup. He turned up the volume on the TV, pulled a three-ring binder down from the shelf above the set, slid the *Before* and *After* photos into a plastic sheet at the back. These were the sales binders, the case study binders. Molina would sit in his office with potential clients, property managers and county administrators and represen-tatives of hotel chains, and take them on a tour through the binders, a pictorial history of Everclean cleanups, selling them of the need to plan for the unthinkable. He showed them the Polaroids of how the rooms looked before the techs got to work and waited as they flinched, as they turned their heads or covered their mouths, as their faces blanched, as their lunches rose. He always made sure they'd eaten well before they sat with the binders, a rich and heavy meal on the company credit card, a visceral reminder of how unequipped they'd be to deal with something like this. When he was sure he had their attention, he showed them the next set of pictures, the *After* photos, the disappearing act, the rooms good as new. That was how clients were acquired, contracts were signed. An ad in the yel-low pages, word-of-mouth from cops and EMTs, a binder full of Polaroids.

"They've come from all over the country," the TV reporter said. "Single people, couples, possibly entire families now living in this compound at the foot of the Tehachapi Mountains."

"I knew it," Bob said. "Used to camp up there."

"I'm sorry," Mrs. Fowler said into the phone. She had one finger pressed into her open ear. "I can't hear you. There's a TV here that's turned up too high." She slid the plexiglass window between the dispatch office and the garage shut.

"What are you looking for?" Molina said. He'd turned from the TV, was watching Darby scan the floor.

"Lost my phone."

"Check the vans," Roistler said.

"Already did."

"Call," Bob said, shouting over the TV.

"What's that?"

"Call your number from the office, listen for the ring."

"Bob," Roistler said. "You are a goddamn genius."

Bob poured himself a cup of coffee, flipped Roistler the bird.

Darby went around into the dispatch office. Mrs. Fowler was off the phone, had her reading glasses perched back up on her nose, her face pressed into a paperback romance. Darby slid open the window, shouted out into the garage.

"It's set to vibrate, so we have to cut the noise."

Bob turned down the TV. Darby dialed the secret number. Mrs. Fowler lifted her nose out of the book and they all kept still, listening for the sound of the phone.

"I think it's lost," Roistler said, finally. "I haven't felt a single vibration."

They stood against the wall in the school courtyard, backs against the brick, boys only. The girls were somewhere else, playing soccer, running relay races. The boys lined up according to height and The Kid generally ended up at the short end of the spectrum, next to Matthew Crump, the shortest of them all. It didn't really matter where he stood to start the game though, because after a few throws everything shifted and reshuffled as boys ducked and jumped and got hit and fell out of line and The Kid always found himself smack dab in the middle of the line of fire.

The boys with the ball were always gunning for The Kid. Brian and Razz were their names. Brian was from another sixth grade class. Razz was from The Kid's class, though he really should have been up in seventh grade. His real name wasn't Razz, it was Ramón, but Razz was his tagging name, the name he used when he was spray-painting on walls around the neighborhood. His older brother was in a gang, that's what the other kids said, and Razz would be in the gang, too, in another year or so, which is why he kept his head shaved down to the scalp and wore his clothes as baggy as he could without getting sent home from school. Brian was tall and blond, a real athlete, always won the relay races and push-up contests in P.E. class. He had a throwing arm like a big league pitcher. Whenever Brian had the dodgeball, girls came over from whatever they were doing to watch him throw and cheer him on and giggle to each other about how strong he was.

The dodgeball was hollow, red rubber, basketball-sized, and when it bounced off the wall behind the boys' heads it made a loud, vibrating punching sound, and when it bounced off the boys themselves it made the same sound and hurt like heck.

Brian and Razz found The Kid wherever he stood in line. They were helped by other boys who stood next to The Kid and held his arms so he couldn't duck or jump or fall out; not even surrender, not even quit.

The line winnowed down as boys fell out or got hit. Matthew Crump fell out, Little Rey Lugo got beaned in the stomach and stumbled forward from the wall, clutching his middle like all of his guts were going to spill out. The Kid got hit right above his left eye, but there was a rule someone had made that if you got hit in the head it didn't count toward elimination, you had to stay in the line, so over the course of a game The Kid could get hit in the head six or seven times and he just had to stand there while the other kids got hit in the stomach or shoulder or fell out.

The Kid adjusted his notebook, made sure it was safe where he always kept it during P.E., tucked into the waistband of his shorts, covered by his t-shirt.

The rule about getting hit in the head was not an official rule, was not spelled out by the P.E. teacher when he ran down the instructions for the boys before the game began, but the P.E. teacher was over on the other side of the courtyard anyway, supervising the girls' relay race and talking to Miss Ramirez, telling her his loud, dumb jokes, so the made-up rule about getting hit in the head was in play and strictly enforced.

One by one, the other boys were eliminated. After they got hit or fell out they became spectators, standing in loose groups behind Brian and Razz, watching the game. The Kid could feel the cold-slap sting in the places where the ball had hit him. Cheeks, forehead, chin, neck. Brian stood fifteen feet away, dribbling the ball, planning his next throw. The Kid tried to avoid eye contact with Brian, tried not to antagonize him, get him angry.

Brian made a few quick stutter steps toward The Kid and fired the ball. It slammed into the right side of The Kid's head, bounced off and away into the courtyard. Cheers from the other boys. Someone ran to retrieve the ball. The Kid stumbled, woozy, but he stayed upright, kept his hands at his sides. It was important not to cry, not to show that the ball hurt, although of course everyone knew that it hurt, could see that it hurt. Crying or covering up would only make things worse in the long run. The Kid knew this from experience. So he stood as straight as he could after getting hit, kept his head up, his hands at his sides, ready for the next throw.

Brian did his stutter step and hurled the ball again, his face twisting with the effort. The Kid ducked but still got hit, this time in the forehead. More cheering from the boys as the ball bounced out in a long, high arc.

The Kid watched the P.E. teacher's back, hoping that he'd turn around, see that it was just The Kid left against the wall and blow his whistle, stop the game. But the P.E. teacher was busy yelling at Michelle Melendez, who all the kids called Michelle Mustache. Michelle was tall and fat and had dark hair on her upper lip, and she never hustled or ran or even seemed to care in P.E. class or in school in general, for that matter. The P.E. teacher was yelling at her because she was refusing to run during the relay race. She was just grabbing the baton from the girl who passed off to her and then walking her leg of the race in her heavy, rolling swagger, shoving the baton hard at the next girl on the team when she reached the end.

Brian stepped and threw, hitting The Kid squarely on the nose. The sting was bad enough to make The Kid's eyes fill, to blur his vision for a few seconds. Hoots and hollers from the crowd of boys. Was his nose broken? He felt it with his hand. It didn't seem like there was any blood. Someone ran to retrieve the ball for Brian. When The Kid's eyes cleared, he looked for Matthew in the crowd, Matthew's round head, Matthew's black face among the brown and white faces. The Kid had dinner at the Crumps' house once a week, had what Mr. Crump called a *standing invitation*, and tonight was that night. Mrs. Crump always made meatloaf or shepherd's pie or ground chuck casserole, something thick and hard to digest, but at least it was homemade, it was a break from the frozen pizzas his dad made, the takeout Chinese food, the drive-thru windows they visited.

The Kid couldn't find Matthew in the crowd and this made him worried, both because some kids could have dragged Matthew back out of sight to do bad things to him but also because it was good to see his friend standing there during the dodgeball game, it was reassuring to think that there'd be something after this, dinner at the Crump's house and making comic books up in Matthew's bedroom.

Brian stepped and threw, hitting The Kid in the side of the neck. Stepped and threw, hitting The Kid in the throat. Stepped and threw, hitting The Kid in the mouth to a thrilled round of *Oooooos* from the other boys. Every time The Kid got hit, the boys closed tighter around the scene, this secret thing, blocking it from outside view. Brian jogged in place, impatient for someone to retrieve the ball so he could throw again.

The Kid tasted something in his mouth, hot salt and battery tang. Blood between his teeth. The freshness of the mouthwash was gone. He worried that the blood in his mouth would give him bad breath, would give the kids in class something to complain to Miss Ramirez about. But he worried more about spitting it out, a red blotch on the concrete, showing Brian and the others this inside thing. He worried more about what the sight of blood would do to the crowd of boys.

He finally found Matthew, standing on the other side of the courtyard talking urgently with Miss Ramirez and the P.E. teacher. The P.E. teacher turned and saw the crowd of boys and The Kid alone against the wall and blew his whistle. When the crowd didn't budge he blew it again, louder this time, the whistle screaming over the noise in the courtyard, and the boys started to disperse, reluctantly, the edges of the crowd dissolving first, pulling away from the heart of the group, making their way inside to the locker room. Brian held fast at the center, though, bouncing his weight from leg to leg, gripping the ball, readying for one last throw.

The whistle had blown. The game was over, technically. The Kid no longer had to stand against the bricks waiting to get hit with the ball. The game was over, officially. He could walk away from the wall and the game.

Brian made a last stutter step and threw at The Kid but The Kid ducked away from the wall and the ball *ka-rannge*d off the bricks, bouncing far out into the yard. Some of the other boys laughed at the missed shot, hooted at Brian for missing The Kid with his final throw.

The Kid had made a mistake. He knew this immediately. The whistle had blown, he was following the rules, but he had made a bad mistake. Brian was still standing where he'd thrown the ball, fifteen feet from The Kid, murder in his eyes. A bad, stupid mistake. He should have stayed against the wall for that last throw, let the ball bounce off his face or the side of his head one more time. What difference would it have made? But now he knew that what happened next in the locker room with Brian and Razz and whoever else would be much worse.

Brian joined the jumbled line filing into the school, giving one last slanty look over his shoulder at The Kid. The P.E. teacher herded the rest of the boys inside, Matthew sticking close by him for protection. The Kid stood at the wall until everyone was gone, until even the girls had passed, Miss Ramirez and Michelle Mustache, everybody. Waited until the courtyard was empty before spitting a thin stream down to the cement. A shocking, scary thing to see, a bright red splat by his sneaker, part of The Kid's insides left out there on the ground. He nudged the splat with his toe and spread it out across the ground, erasing it from sight.

The graffiti had appeared sometime during the night, sprayed across the sidewalk in front of the house, a long string of challenges and curse words. Darby scratched at the dried paint with the toe of his work boot. The Kid had certainly seen it on his way to school, had probably already copied it into his notebook, minus the curses. He wondered if The Kid had heard it being sprayed, if he'd been woken by the *shht-shht* of the aerosol can in the night.

The security bars weren't enough. He'd have to figure out something else, some other way to keep The Kid safe at night.

He swung open the gate, got back into the pickup, pulled up the short cement driveway and parked in front of the garage, just beside the house. The house was small, fifty or sixty years old, sunbeaten and sagging. The clapboard, sky blue when they'd bought the place, had faded to gray, worn to white in places. The roof and windows and front porch all slumped a little, gravity tugging, all things Darby needed to fix, all things he had neglected, the exception being the new security bars, the steel door, gleaming incongruously in the bright sun. Lucy would have hated the bars, would have said that treating their neighbors like criminals would only encourage them to behave like criminals. But Lucy wasn't there now and The Kid stayed alone two or three nights a week and Darby had to make sure he was safe in the house.

He splashed concrete cleaner across the sidewalk, waited for it to soak, sprayed the graffiti away with the hose.

He moved through the house, turning out lights. The Kid was a notorious light fiend. Darby walked from room to room, flipping switches. He looked for the cell phone without luck. He stood in the hot shower and scrubbed the feel of the job from his skin, the recliner and the carpeting and the hole in the wall. He pulled clean clothes from the dresser in the dark bedroom behind the kitchen, their old bedroom, all the shades drawn, the room undisturbed for a year. He was in there just long enough to get his clothes, get out. He dressed in the kitchen, washed The Kid's cereal bowl, set it to dry on the counter.

Sometimes after overnight jobs he went to a diner with Bob, ate breakfast. They'd sit in a booth, bleary, overtired, plates of sausage and eggs on the table, so wired from the job and all the coffee they'd drunk that they ordered more coffee just to help bring them down, to soften the edge of the morning. Sometimes when Bob was too tired to come along, Darby went to a diner alone, sat in a booth, letting his body adjust to the light, the movement of a normal day beginning around him.

Without the cell phone, he'd had to come straight home. There was always a good chance that The Kid would call from the school therapist's office, transmit a coded message, and now that the cell phone was apparently lost, Darby would have to listen for the home phone, The Kid's Plan B.

He made himself a bologna sandwich, drank one of the squeezable juice bags he packed in The Kid's lunch every night. Stood in the kitchen, out on the front porch.

He was almost completely deaf in his right ear. The net result of a fight years ago outside a bowling alley in Carson. Sometimes he could plug his good ear and still hear muffled voices, the buzzing of loud machinery. Sometimes he got vibrations, echoes. Sometimes in quiet moments he heard what sounded like bells, early morning, the middle of the night, a faraway ring. A little eerie, a little disconcerting. He used to tell Lucy when he was hearing it, sitting at the kitchen table, or on the couch in the living room. He'd stick his finger in his good ear and look up, away, listening. She'd stop talking to listen along with him.

There it is, he'd say. Can you hear that? There it is.

Out in the pickup, he rolled down the windows, stretched out across the front seat. It was a blocky hulk of a truck, a 1972 Chevy

Cheyenne Super he'd bought fifteen years back. It still had its original green and white two-tone paint job, marred here and there by dings and dents and spiderweb patches of rust. The stereo hadn't worked in a decade, but he kept a transistor radio up on the dash, murmuring low. Political talk, religious talk, financial talk, sports talk. The subject didn't matter, just the sound of someone's voice while he tried to sleep. Light and heat gathered around the day. He dozed fitfully for a while, half-listening to the radio, jerked awake by dogs barking, cars backfiring, blasts of hot air sighs from buses stopping down at the corner. He'd once been a prodigious sleeper. They had to literally drag him out of bed on Saturday mornings, regardless of whether or not there had been a job the night before. Head under the pillow, sheets pulled tight around his body, a great bear in hibernation. Lucy and The Kid would each grab an arm and pull, groaning with the exertion. The Kid would snap on the overhead light to help the cause, Darby burrowing deeper, dead weight, The Kid lowering his face to Darby's, checking for signs of life. The Kid's Saturday morning breath, chocolaty cereal and cold milk. Lucy pulling one way, The Kid pulling the other, both of them straining, laughing at the massive struggle.

From his low angle in the cab, Darby could see the wide brim of the postman's straw hat through the back windshield. The hat coming up the driveway, crossing toward the house, disappearing. The thump of mail tossed onto the front porch. The hat crossing back past the pickup, down the driveway, disappearing again.

He gave up on sleep, pulled on his boots and climbed down out of the truck. His knees and wrists were sore from scrubbing at the job site. He flipped through the bundle of mail on the porch. At the bottom of the stack was a plain white envelope, addressed to Darby in Mrs. Fowler's immaculate script. Inside was another, smaller envelope, addressed to *Tall Technician With Tattoos* in care of the Everclean garage. Darby turned over the envelope, looked at the return address. Hacienda Heights. He tried to remember the job. Two or three weeks back, a large sunflower yellow house across from a church; a tiny, older Asian woman waiting at the door when they arrived. Bob had taken her into the kitchen while Darby and Roistler went upstairs, hauling their gear.

Inside the envelope was a note card, a single line written across its face in a birdlike scrawl, the time and effort it took to shape the letters apparent in the labored precision of the handwriting.

*I thank you for doing what I could not.*

Cards arrived every few weeks, once a month, maybe, forwarded from the garage to the techs by Mrs. Fowler. People at job sites didn't know the techs' names, so they sent the cards addressed to *Heavyset Man With Handlebar Mustache* or *Shorter Red-Hair Muscle Man.* Their Native American names, Bob called them. Darby was *Tattooed Technician With The Blue Eyes.* Darby was *Shaved-head Technician Who Looked Like My Son.*

The cards came weeks after a job, sometimes months after, sometimes years. They came at holidays, Christmas and Easter and days significant only to the sender, birthdays, anniversaries. Sometimes they came on the anniversary of the job itself, and then they came every year on that date. *We will never forget what you did for us.* They gave phone numbers, email addresses, websites where they'd set up online memorials to the departed. Sometimes they asked questions, wanted to know if the techs had families, if they'd experienced similar tragedies. Darby never answered the cards. He didn't think Bob or Roistler answered their cards, either. Only Mrs. Fowler responded, replying to the cards that were addressed to the company as a whole, a few lines on Everclean stationary, short passages from the Bible or inspirational verses from her book of famous quotations.

Darby stood in the back of the house, a corner of the laundry room Lucy had jokingly referred to as her office. A green metal desk they'd bought at a yard sale sat under shelves of teacher guides and textbooks, a bulletin board covered with yellow sticky notes and her class rosters from the previous year. There was a snapshot tacked to the corkboard, Darby and The Kid sitting at the picnic table on the back porch, The Kid's birthday party from a few years before. A couple of other kids standing in the shot, The Kid's friend Matthew and some boys from younger grades Lucy had managed to rope in to the party. There was an empty space beside the photo on the corkboard, where two other photos had once been tacked. There was an empty tea mug on the desk, a short stack of ungraded essays. A thin film of dust covered everything. He hadn't touched her desk in a year.

There was nothing in the house. He'd thought that there would be, somehow. He'd imagined that the place where they'd lived would have something more to it after one of them was gone. But there was nothing. Wood and windows, carpeting, furniture, pictures, frames. A place of objects, materials. There were no ghosts. Her absence was a blank space, nothing more.

He stood on the back porch, in the living room, The Kid's bedroom. He stood at her desk with his hands at his sides, still holding the note from the woman in Hacienda Heights.

The phone rang in the kitchen. He answered it, expecting the dot-dash-dot bleeps of The Kid's Morse code, hearing instead the cigarette-roughened voice of the middle school's vice-principal telling him there had been more trouble, telling him that he needed to come and pick up his boy.

The Kid waited. He looked at the wall clock above the part in Mr. Bromwell's hair and tried to gauge the amount of time it would take his dad to get from the house to the school. He had to keep reconfiguring his answer because his dad hadn't arrived yet. His calculations were off or maybe his dad had gotten into some terrible crash, the pickup wrapped around a tree or a telephone pole, his dad launched through the windshield, head first. A reporter on TV once said that 25% of all fatal car accidents happen within a mile of home. This was about the distance from their house to the school. That meant that if three other people left their neighborhood at the same time his dad had left to come pick up The Kid, one of them would be in a fatal car accident. The Kid pictured his dad shot like a spear through the windshield, glass shattering around him, sailing straight as an arrow, arms at his sides, flying over honking traffic, drop-jawed pedestrians.

Mr. Bromwell's office was a windowless room beside the nurse's office. There was the desk and Mr. Bromwell's chair and a chair for a visitor. Mr. Bromwell's chair had wheels and reclined a little when he pushed back in his seat; the visitor's chair did neither. The office was so small that it seemed likely Mr. Bromwell could touch both walls if he stretched his long arms out to either side, but The Kid had never actually seen Mr. Bromwell do that.

There was a phone on Mr. Bromwell's desk, a blotter covered with yellow sticky notes, a small picture in a metal frame of Mr. Bromwell's wife and two sons. There was a wooden coat tree in the back corner, hung with running shorts and a t-shirt. There was a pair of running shoes on the floor beside the tree, tongues and laces spread wide, insoles up and out, airing, because in addition to being the school counselor, Mr. Bromwell was also the track & field coach.

The clothes The Kid was wearing were too big. The pants itched. After the incident in the locker room, the nurse had given him pants and a shirt and socks from the lost-and-found box, but the clothes were for a bigger kid, and the pants felt like wool.

"I don't really want a name, Whitley," Mr. Bromwell said. "A name does us no good. We're looking at a pattern of behavior. There are reasons why this happened. There are reasons why you are sitting here and not another student."

The Kid had an appointment with Mr. Bromwell on Monday, Wednesday and Friday afternoons, after lunch. He'd had these appointments for almost a year now. He came from the cafeteria and sat in the visitor's chair, sneakers dangling six inches above the floor. Mr. Bromwell sat on the other side of the desk, underneath the clock, and drummed the eraser tip of his pencil against his blotter and asked questions for The Kid to answer in his notebook. The questions weren't about specific things that had happened to The Kid, incidents in the classroom or the locker room, but about why The Kid thought these things were happening to him, what The Kid thought he was doing to make these things happen. Mr. Bromwell would ask a question and then push back in his chair and stretch his legs out under his desk so that the tips of his shoes touched the feet of The Kid's chair. Or sometimes he'd ask a question and then get up and stand next to the coat tree and pull his ankle up behind his back, stretching his leg muscles. There were posters tacked to the walls of the office, bright color pictures of waterfalls and mountain ranges with sayings underneath about hard work and endurance and determination. Mr. Bromwell liked to talk about these things, about being strong, being tough mentally and physically. He liked to talk about *Responsibility For Our Actions*, which meant that sometimes when other kids did bad things to The Kid, it was actually The Kid's fault.

"Can you think of a reason," Mr. Bromwell said, "why something like this would happen to you and not to another student?" He stood and held onto the coat rack with one hand, pulling his ankle back behind him with the other, watching The Kid, waiting for an answer.

It was known to The Kid's teacher and all the other teachers that The Kid could visit Mr. Bromwell any time he needed to. This was a special arrangement, owing to The Kid's circumstances. It was also known that The Kid could be sent to Mr. Bromwell's office if something bad happened, if he locked himself in a stall in the bathroom and refused to come out, or if something like this happened, an incident in the locker room. The Kid didn't like going to Mr. Bromwell's office, didn't like all the questions, but at least he could use the phone, could call his dad's cell phone and send a Morse Code message. This usually made him feel a little better, even if he wasn't calling for his dad to come pick him up and take him home. Just sending the message made him feel better, receiving his dad's coded reply from somewhere in the city, knowing that his dad wasn't so far away, that they were in contact somehow.

The Kid looked at the clock, thought of his dad and three other neighbors leaving their street at the same time, three cars and the pickup, 25% of them involved in fatal accidents.

It was always the moment between taking off his gym clothes and putting on his school clothes when bad things happened. An especially vulnerable moment. The Kid tried to change as quickly as possible, tried to minimize the length of time he was standing in the locker room in only his underpants, because that seemed to incite some of the other kids. But he wasn't always fast enough, and this time his gym clothes were stolen as soon as he took them off, grabbed by one of the dodgeball boys who ran back toward the showers, waving The Kid's shorts like a captured flag. The Kid didn't even bother to run after him; he knew that would just be asking for trouble. He would think of some excuse to tell his dad for needing new gym clothes. He'd lost them, they'd gotten muddy, something that wouldn't make him sound like such a wimp. He wouldn't let his dad pay for the new clothes. He would pay for them with his own allowance money. He didn't want his dad to have to pay for the fact that he was weak, the fact that he couldn't stop the other kids from stealing his things.

The Kid could smell it even before he'd opened the door of his gym locker. Strong pee. Morning pee. He opened his locker and the stench socked him in the nose. Boys around him made gagging noises, plugged their nostrils and backed away from The Kid's locker. The Kid looked inside. His school clothes were dark with it, his pants and shirt and socks. His backpack was dark with it. The smell was overpowering. On the other side of the lockers, Razz and some other boys were laughing, even though they couldn't see what happened. They knew what had happened, they'd been waiting for it. Some other boys made retching sounds, mimed throwing up into a garbage can. The Kid looked for Matthew and found him over at the other end of a wooden bench, tying his shoes, staring hard at the laces, trying to pretend he didn't hear or see or smell anything.

The Kid felt someone standing right behind him. He turned and Brian was there, towering over him.

Mr. Bromwell dropped his leg to the floor, lifted his other leg by the ankle and pulled it tight behind his back. He looked at The Kid, looked at The Kid's notebook. Waited.

The Kid knew he could give the answer Mr. Bromwell wanted, the answer that would explain everything, why bad things happened to The Kid, why The Kid was like he was. He knew that if he told this, Mr. Bromwell could maybe even get the other kids to leave him alone, to let him be. But The Kid also knew that once you told a secret it was loose in the world, it was a wild thing.

The Kid picked up his pencil, stared at the blank page.

Brian Bromwell was a good six inches taller than The Kid, long and lean like his father, packed with wiry muscle. It was impossible to get away from him, impossible to run faster or break free when Brian pinned him to the sidewalk and dangled long, glistening strings of saliva from his bottom lip, squeezing The Kid's face with one strong hand, prying open The Kid's mouth, trying to get the spit to fall in. Sometimes The Kid was able to clench his jaw tight and Brian's spit landed on his cheek or in his eye. But sometimes Brian got a thumb wedged inside and was able to get The Kid's mouth open and the spit fell right into the back of The Kid's throat.

Or sometimes worse things happened, things like this, the smell of strong pee in the locker room.

Brian had smiled at The Kid, a nasty slash of a smile, then he moved away, turned the corner into the next row of lockers. More laughter from the boys on that side. The bell rang and the locker room emptied. The Kid looked for Matthew, but Matthew had already gone. The Kid stood there in his underpants, looking at the wet clothes in his locker, frozen, unsure what to do.

"Whitley?" Mr. Bromwell pulled his ankle tight alongside his waist. He was watching The Kid, still waiting for an answer.

Brian once told The Kid that Mondays, Wednesdays and Fridays were his favorite days of the week because at dinner those nights his father would tell Mrs. Bromwell and Brian and his brother everything The Kid had written in his notebook during their session at school. Brian said that at dinner those nights the whole Bromwell family would laugh and laugh at all the secrets The Kid told their father.

The Kid closed his notebook, returned it to his backpack. Mr. Bromwell dropped his leg, frowned.

The phone on the desk rang, a single red light flashing along with the sound. Mr. Bromwell answered, shook his head, hung up the phone.

"Your father's here," he said. "We'll talk more about this on Wednesday."

The janitor came out to the curb in front of the school, a tall, bearded black man with a blue bandana wrapped around the top of his head. He leaned his elbow into the passenger window of the pickup.

"You the father?"

Darby nodded.

"He wet his pants," the janitor said. He was holding an empty paper cup, tapping it lightly against the door of the pickup as he talked. Darby had never seen him before, figured he was new to the school. Most everyone there knew Darby by sight due to his frequent visits.

"Vice-principal told me he wet his pants and put them back in his gym locker and then didn't know what to do about it," the janitor said.

"Who found him?"

"I found him. Standing there in his briefs." The janitor dug into his back pocket, pulled out a tobacco tin, wedged a plug between his gum and lower lip, worked it in tight. "I went and got the vice-principal because your son had a look on his face like he wasn't going to move from that spot without some assistance."

"Did he say he wet his pants?"

"He didn't say anything."

The janitor lifted the cup to his lips, spat, rearranged the tobacco plug with the tip of his tongue.

"When does he talk?" the janitor said.

"He doesn't."

"Is he mute?"

"He made a conscious decision," Darby said. "He made a conscious decision not to talk."

"How long's it been?"

"Ten months. Eleven months."

The janitor spat into his cup, whistled long and low, impressed.

The Kid emerged from the front doors of the school. He was wearing clothes two sizes too big, stepping on his pant cuffs as he walked. He carried a plastic shopping bag in one hand, filled with his books and folders. In the other hand he carried his backpack, filled with what Darby assumed were the clothes the vice-principal had described on the phone as *urine-soaked*.

The janitor pulled the rest of his plug from his mouth, dropped it into the cup. He knocked twice on the door of the pickup by way of signing off and headed in toward the school. He nodded to The Kid as they passed.

The Kid reached the passenger window of the pickup, held up his backpack.

"You wet your pants?" Darby said.

The Kid shook his head.

"Then let's get rid of them."

They walked to a dumpster at the far end of the parking lot. Darby lifted the lid and The Kid tossed the backpack up, missing the shot. Picked it up and tried again. Picked it up and tried again, finally getting the pack up and over.

The Kid pulled his notebook and pencil out of the plastic bag, wrote a line and held it up for Darby to see.

*How much do they cost?*

"Don't worry about the money, Kid."

*I'll pay for new clothes. The backpack.*

"Don't worry about the money. The money's not a big deal."

Darby found a hose attached to the side of a small utility building, rinsed The Kid's hands, rinsed his own. The Kid tucked his notebook under his arm to keep it from getting wet. They dried their hands on the fronts of their pants.

"Whose clothes are those?" Darby said.

*Lost and found.*

"They look like they itch."

*They do.*

"You want to tell me what happened?"

The Kid ignored the question, stared at his hands.

"I'm not mad, Kid."

The Kid nodded.

"But if you don't tell me what happened, I can't help."

The Kid turned to a new page in his notebook, wrote a line, held it up for Darby.

*Loose lips sink ships.*

"I'm serious, Kid."

*So am I.*

They went to the drive-thru of a hamburger place on Beverly Avenue for lunch, sat in the pickup in the parking lot with their burgers and fries. They ate fast food three or four times a week, ordered pizza or take-out for most of their other meals. The Kid was still toothpick-skinny, but Darby was starting to feel it in his gut, in his thighs, his shirts and jeans tight across his added weight. He knew their eating habits weren't great, but he wasn't much of a cook. That had been Lucy's department, whipping around the kitchen, humming along with the country station on the countertop radio, slicing, chopping, pots and pans clanging, steam rising, smells forming, basil, oregano, garlic, onions, the aroma drifting out into the rest of the house, onto the front porch, drawing Darby and The Kid to the table where she'd turn from the oven and present the finished dish with a little flourish, *violá*, a magic show performed nightly.

In the last year, Darby had only attempted dinner once or twice, failing miserably, ham-fisted, inexpert at that particular job. Now they sat in fast food parking lots, ordered takeout.

The Kid set his notebook on his lap, flipped back toward the front of the book, pages from the beginning of September, hand-drawn scorecards from the final month of the Dodgers' disappointing season. Darby looked over The Kid's shoulder at the grids, the tiny diamonds, the lists of hitters and pitchers in The Kid's rushed capital letters. This was something he'd taught The Kid, almost a year ago now. This was how he had taught The Kid to communicate once it was clear that The Kid was no longer going to talk.

It hadn't seemed like much at first, but he wasn't really noticing much at the time. Molina had told him to take a couple of weeks off from work, and The Kid was out of school. An excused absence, bereavement leave. It was probably a couple of days before he really noticed that The Kid's silence was something more than quiet sadness. That The Kid's silence was a deliberate thing.

He'd thought it would go away on its own. He'd thought that The Kid would get tired of the effort, that one night he would pick The Kid up at the Crump's after dinner and The Kid would start talking in the pickup on the ride home, chirping away, just like before. But days went by, then a week. The Kid went back to school and nothing changed. The fifth-grade teacher sent him to see the school therapist once a week, then twice a week, then three times a week, but nothing changed.

A month into it, Darby stopped at the drugstore on his way home from work and bought the first notebook, a standard-issue black and white composition book. That night he sat The Kid down in the living room and dug through Lucy's boxes of videotapes, ballgames she'd recorded, something to watch in the off-season when she was in serious withdrawal. He found a home game from a couple of seasons before, Dodgers-Padres, and as the lineups were announced, Darby drew a grid across the first two pages of the notebook, drew tiny diamonds in the squares, filled in the batting order, the pitching matchup, just like Lucy had showed him years earlier on their second or third date, when she'd told him that she watched or listened to every game the Dodgers played, something she'd done since she was a girl, and that she taped the games when she couldn't watch or listen live. She told Darby that she rarely went to the stadium to see a game, maybe once or twice a season, though she loved the atmosphere, the history of the place. She preferred watching or listening at home, without all the people, the noise, the distractions. It was hard to concentrate in the stands, she said. It was hard to really see the game when you were actually there. Then she had showed him the binders on the bedroom shelves of her apartment. Each binder was full of hole-punched scorecards, 162 a calendar year, plus postseason games if things had gone the team's way. Each binder was labeled on its spine in black magic marker, one for every season since 1969.

They played the videotape and Darby showed The Kid the shorthand for the movement of the game, how to fill in the frames with base hits and ground outs, runs batted in, the advance of runners around the diamond toward home. He showed The Kid the numerical designations for each defensive position, the fly ball out to left field recorded as F7, the grounder to short tossed to second and thrown to first marked as a 6-4-3 double play.

The Kid took to it quickly. He appreciated the logic, the consideration required, the concentrated pace of the game. His mother's son. They watched more tapes over the course of the winter, one or two games a night when Darby's pager didn't buzz with a work call. Neither of them were sleeping much. The Kid got better at it, faster, keeping up with the games in real time, no longer needing to rewind and re-examine a play. The Kid took pride in his scorecards, getting the details right. Darby could see that he liked having a permanent record of the thing at the end of a game, a narrative in secret code. Darby asked questions during the commercial breaks instead of fast-forwarding, questions about the players, the teams, the division standings, the league leaders in various categories, and The Kid began answering in his notebook, true to form, always a show-off when he'd learned something new. He answered with numbers he'd copied down from on-screen graphics, batting averages and slugging percentages, runs allowed against left-handed batters, right-handed batters, the statistical inner engine of the game, the hard facts that represented the intangibles, the simplest, most difficult thing. Hitting a ball with a bat. And this was how The Kid learned to communicate again, game by game, tape by tape, sitting with Darby on the living room couch, answering questions about a prerecorded baseball season while the night deepened around them.

The school said that as long as The Kid got his work done, as long as he wasn't a distraction to the other students, he could communicate in the notebook until he was ready to speak. This was fine, they said. This was okay for a while.

One notebook turned to two. Two turned to three. Three turned to the shelf Darby put up in The Kid's bedroom, now ten notebooks long.

Darby finished his burger, wadded up the wrapper, stuffed it into the empty food bag. The Kid turned back to the pages he'd been using that morning. Darby could see a drawing of what looked like city buildings, a woman towering over them, arms spread wide.

*Why didn't you answer the cell phone?* The Kid wrote.

"It's been temporarily misplaced."

*It's lost?*

"It's been misplaced. I'll find it, Kid. Don't worry."

He should have done more. He knew this. He should have pushed harder, should have taken The Kid to a doctor, someone other than the school therapist. His inaction had only added to the problem, had made permanent what might just have been temporary at the time. The notebooks only solidified The Kid's silence, reinforced his resolve. He should have done more. The silence was so deep now, so entrenched, that Darby didn't have a clue what else he could do about it.

He collected The Kid's burger wrapper, his empty soda cup, stuffed it all into the food bag. Leaned out the window, tossed the bag into a nearby garbage can.

"If you give me the kids' names," Darby said, "I can stop this from happening."

The Kid shook his head, kept his eyes on the scorecard. Darby started the pickup, put the truck in gear and pulled out of the parking lot toward home.

They crouched behind the large plastic garbage bins in the Crump's backyard, listening for approaching footsteps, scanning the area for signs of trouble. When they were sure the coast was clear, Matthew counted to three and The Kid helped him lift one of the bins and move it over half a foot on the grass.

It was getting dark, would be time for dinner soon. A light switched on in the kitchen window at the back of the house, just a few feet away. The Kid could see Mrs. Crump passing back and forth as she set the table. They waited for her to pass again, then moved the garbage bin over another half-foot.

"I was supposed to throw them away," Matthew whispered, "but I couldn't do it. If they're just going to be destroyed then I'd rather you had them."

There was a small stack of comic books set into the mud where the plastic bin had been. Five issues of *Captain America*, the numbers on the covers all in order. An entire storyline hidden under the garbage.

"My parents asked me where Captain America got his powers," Matthew said. "They asked me if he got his powers from God. I told them he got his powers from the army. That he was injected with the Super-Soldier Serum during World War II." He peeled the comics out of the mud, rubbed the covers and spines clean with his hands. His skin was blacker even than his father's and mother's, but his palms and fingertips were lighter, almost pink. "My father didn't believe a character could get those kinds of powers from the U.S. Government. He said that if Captain America didn't get his powers from God, then he must have gotten them from the devil. And if that was the case, then there was no place for these books in our house."

Matthew flipped through the comics, lingering on some of the more exciting panels, fights and chase scenes. The Kid kept watching the kitchen window, expecting Mr. Crump's stone face to appear any second, catching them in the act.

They didn't talk about what had happened in the locker room. They never talked about the incidents. Incidents had happened before, would happen again. They never talked about Matthew crying in class or other kids telling The Kid that he had bad breath or B.O. It was like if they said it out loud then that would confirm it, it had to be true, the other kids were right. So they never repeated what was said to them, and when one of them was being picked on at their lunch table the other looked away, pretended he didn't see, didn't hear. It was important to have at least one person not witness what was going on.

Matthew was only one spot above The Kid in the eyes of the other kids at school, only one rung above the absolute bottom. Or maybe The Kid was actually one rung above the absolute bottom, which would be Michelle Mustache, who the other kids hated as much as they hated The Kid, but on top of that she was also a girl. Either way, The Kid knew that if he weren't around, Matthew would be the one with all the incidents. The Kid knew that Matthew knew this as well. They'd been friends for as long as he could remember, but sometimes The Kid wondered if Matthew only stayed friends with him because of this. Because without The Kid it would be Matthew standing there in the locker room looking at his wet clothes.

Matthew held the comics out for The Kid. "I'm giving them to you to take home for safekeeping."

The Kid reached for the comics, but Matthew held them back, fixed The Kid with a serious look.

"But only on one condition," he said. "That I can come over to your house and look at them any time I want."

That sounded reasonable. The Kid nodded in agreement.

"You've got to promise officially," Matthew said.

The Kid opened his notebook to a blank page, wrote quickly across the top.

*I promise.*

Matthew read the line, looked back at the covers of the comics. He finally nodded, handed the stack to The Kid. The Kid slid the comics under the waistband of his pants, tucked his shirt in over the tops.

"You should write down where I'd hidden the comics," Matthew said. "So you'll know where to hide them again if you need to."

The Kid opened his notebook, wrote, *Under a garbage can* on the next blank line.

They pulled the garbage bin back into place and snuck back around to the front door, into the soft, carpeted calm of the house.

Matthew's father sat in his armchair in the living room, reading the newspaper. Mr. Crump was a big bald man, an accountant for an insurance company downtown. The Kid had never seen him without a dark suit and tie, even on weekends. Matthew had a couple of dark suits, too, hanging upstairs in his bedroom closet. He wore a suit and tie to church, to bible meetings. He also wore these suits when he and his parents went out in the mornings and knocked on people's doors, told them about their church, invited them to come along.

The living room was ringed with high wooden shelves packed with encyclopedias and bibles and other religious volumes. An electric organ sat in the corner, sheet music open on top, hymns to the Lord. There was no TV in the living room, in the entire house. Matthew's father said that they didn't need a TV. They had books, they had the electric organ.

The Kid could hear Matthew's mother's kitchen radio set low to a religious station, organ music and a pastor's deep voice. Mrs. Crump moved through the kitchen like a bird, cautious and precise, setting out silverware, folding napkins, humming along with the radio.

There was still time before dinner, so they went upstairs and sat on the floor of Matthew's bedroom with the big blank sheets of paper Mr. Crump brought home from work. The sheets were big enough that when a few pages were folded in half, it was the perfect size for a comic book. The Kid wanted to work on a new issue of the comic that he and Matthew had made for the last couple of years,

*Extraordinary Adventures.* A new issue every month, maybe every two months if they were really busy with homework. They each wrote and drew their own stories, one or two per issue. Superhero stories, outer-space stories, cowboy stories, war stories—anything, really, the only rule was that the stories had to be extraordinary. No boring stories, no stories about people doing normal things.

The star of most of The Kid's stories was Smooshie Smith, Talk Show Host of the Future. Smooshie was the most popular talk show host in the history of TV because he had a time machine that let him go back and forth through the years and interview all sorts of people. He interviewed cowboys in the Western stories, soldiers in the war stories, aliens in the outer-space stories. Sometime he got caught up in battles and fights, but mostly he stuck to broadcasting his highly-rated show from different points in the timeline of the universe.

For the first issue of *Extraordinary Adventures* back in fourth grade, The Kid's mom made copies of the original comic at her school. Then The Kid and Matthew sold as many as they could to other kids for fifty cents each and used the money to make copies of the next issue at the print shop on Vermont Avenue. With the money from that issue, they paid for the copies of the next issue, and so on. That was how it worked. Ten or twelve pages, usually, per issue. Black and white drawings because color copies were too expensive.

Since that first issue, they'd sold fewer copies of the comic. More kids didn't like The Kid, didn't want to buy the comic. The Kid had always been picked on, had always been smaller than the other kids, not as tough as the other kids, but things got really bad in fourth grade. A girl in his class said that The Kid's breath stank. She may have been right, The Kid didn't know. It shouldn't have been a big deal, plenty of kids' breath stank, but it stuck to The Kid. Someone told someone and someone told someone else and before The Kid knew it almost every day some kid was telling him that his breath stank. And then his armpits. And then his hair. They said that he was contagious. They didn't want to touch anything that The Kid had touched. It grew like a weed, this idea of The Kid as an awful thing. It tangled around everyone and everything.

Around that time, his class had done a history unit where they learned about people in India who were so despised that they couldn't even be brushed up against, could barely be looked at. That was where the name came from, the untouchables, the name for The Kid and Matthew and Michelle Mustache. Things got so bad that for the last issue of the comic they'd made, right at the end of the last school year, they'd only sold one copy. The rest were under The Kid's bed, or boxed up in the garage back at the house, hidden away, embarrassing, a failed thing.

He'd tried to keep it from his mom and dad. He was ashamed of this, the way other kids thought about him. He didn't want the germ of the idea to be planted with his parents, that he was dirty, that he was contagious. He was afraid that they would start to think this, too.

Of course his mom got it out of him. She noticed all the unsold comics, his increasing fear about going to school. He finally told her what was happening. She talked to his teacher and the principal of his school, but that only made things worse, really, only made the other kids angry about being lectured to. He pleaded with her not to say anything else, just to leave it alone, let it go away on its own.

But it didn't go away. It had only gotten worse since his mom had been gone.

Matthew didn't want to work on a new issue of the comic before dinner. He didn't see the point. No one would buy it anyway. He said that instead he had a superhero scene he'd been thinking about, that he'd come up with a good idea, but he'd have to tell it to The Kid and The Kid would have to draw it because he wasn't allowed to draw superheroes anymore. The Kid adjusted the *Captain America* comics in his waistband, made sure they were still covered by his shirt. Got a blank sheet of the big paper, a couple of colored pencils, started drawing the scene as Matthew told it.

There was a giant robot that was trying to destroy Los Angeles. It was a robot the government had made to pick up trash, but it had gone haywire when all the computers went berserk on New Year's Eve, and now it was trying to destroy the city. The robot had big metal jaws with broken-glass teeth that it was supposed to use to eat garbage but now used to eat people. Matthew had The Kid draw a panel where the robot was walking through the downtown buildings, scooping up businessmen in its iron fist and biting them in half as other businessmen ran around screaming and waving their arms.

In the second panel, a superhero team arrived. This was the team's last fight. They would have to give up their powers once they defeated the robot, because they'd found out that their powers were a gift from the Devil and not a gift from God, as they'd originally thought. They were pretty sad about giving up their powers, but they'd all banded together one last time to try to save the city.

The Kid drew a panel where the robot had reached their middle school. Kids poured from the doors, screaming as the robot crushed the building with its giant metal boots. The Kid gave each classmate an exaggerated distinguishing feature that made Matthew laugh and nod with approval. Brian Bromwell was flexing bulging muscles, Razz was wearing baggy pants ten sizes too big, Michelle Mustache had a real mustache, a dark brick of hair on her upper lip.

Matthew had the idea that he and The Kid should be two of the superheroes, that they should each have their own costume and power. The Kid drew Matthew flying into the scene, drew his oval head, his big round eyes. Drew him wearing gloves and boots and a long blue cape.

"What superpower do you think I'm going to pick?" Matthew said.

The Kid shrugged.

"Guess."

The Kid found a blank corner of the page. *Super strength*, he wrote.

"Heat vision," Matthew said. "And cold vision. One in each eye. That way I can melt things or freeze them in a block of ice."

The Kid colored one of Matthew's superhero eyes red, colored the other one blue. He finished drawing Matthew's costume, decorated half with flames, half with icicles.

"But before I attack the robot," Matthew said. "I shoot my

beams at some of the other kids. The kids we don't hate so much are getting frozen with my cold vision, but the kids we really hate are getting melted with my heat vision."

The Kid drew cold beams shooting out of Matthew's blue eye, ending in an icy cube around some of the kids who didn't give them such a hard time. He drew shiver lines wiggling out from their bodies, tiny puffs of frozen breath coming from their mouths.

"Now draw the others," Matthew said. He was sitting on his heels, starting to rock with excitement. "Draw the others getting melted."

The Kid drew a blast of heat vision shooting from Matthew's red eye, then a ring of fire burning on the ground around Brian and Razz's feet. He drew shaded tendrils of gray steam rising from the tops of their heads, big beads of sweat leaping from their brows. Then he went to work on their faces, distorting their eyes and noses, stretching their features, melting their skin in the heat. The more he drew, the more he wanted to draw, the more gruesome detail he wanted to add. He drew blood pouring from their eyes, bile oozing from their mouths. He set their clothes and hair on fire, opened their bellies to spill their guts.

The Kid stopped, finally, put the pencils down. He and Matthew looked at the drawing. A riot of colors, filling the entire page. They could hardly make out the individual figures in the gory mess. The only character who could be easily identified was the superhero Matthew, standing in the middle of the scene, causing the carnage, cold and heat beams shooting from his eyes.

"Now draw yourself in there," Matthew said, breathing hard from the excitement of the scene. "Draw yourself using your power for the last time."

The Kid leaned back into the page, drew a tiny gray figure way up in the corner, a red cape fluttering behind.

"What's your power?" Matthew said, rocking back and forth. "What do you do?"

The Kid didn't answer. He kept drawing, sketching skinny arms reaching out from his sides, skinny legs stretching out behind, the superhero Kid soaring, passing the puffy clouds, leaving the scene, flying away out of the picture.

S ea green light in the fish fry on Alvarado Street. Darby and Bob sat in their booth by the window, looking out into the dark parking lot. A knot of people stood at the curb waiting for the bus, women in nurse's scrubs, men with toolboxes and lunch pails, slump-shouldered, the fatigue evident in their bodies.

Bob was laying waste to a large basket of fish sticks and tater tots. Darby picked at his filet, the greasy roll wrapped in a page of car ads from the morning's paper. There was a TV on a high shelf behind the counter. Darby could see its reflection in the window, a news report on the survivalist group up north, the same footage from earlier in the day, a long-lens shot of the buildings behind the high fence.

"He wanted to haggle about the price," Bob said. "That room was a heavyweight job and he wanted to haggle about the price." He dunked a fish stick into one of the cups of tartar sauce, tossed it back into his mouth. "I told him that if he wanted to haggle, I had twenty-five biohazard bags full of he-knows-what that I was willing to dump back up in that room, just give me the word."

They had dinner on the nights The Kid was over at the Crumps', usually in the same booth at the same fish fry. Bob was always eager to have a meal away from home. After a couple of marriages and head-case girlfriends, Bob had lived for the past few years with his elderly Aunt Rhoda in her claustrophobic old house in Boyle Heights. He took care of her as best he could, though there was nothing really wrong with her but old age. She never left the living room, the couch in the living room, where she slept, where she watched game shows and the daily *Mass for Shut-ins*.

"I don't mind the cleanups," Bob said. "The fluids and matter and all of that shit. It's listening and talking to those people that wears me down."

A bus pulled up to the curb. The group at the corner climbed aboard, leaving the stop empty. Darby scratched at his hand, a small scab on the black-script W above the knuckle of his index finger.

Bob coughed into a napkin, wiped his mouth. "How's my guy?" he said.

"I had to pick him up at school again today."

"What happened?"

"Somebody pissed on his clothes."

Bob shook his head. "Don't let them fuck with him, David."

"I know."

"You think they're little kids so, so what, what's the worst they can do."

"I know what they can do."

"Get on the horn to their parents. Call their fathers. A phone call to the father yields fearsome results."

"He won't say who's doing it."

"Find out. Get a name and make a call. I'm telling you. These little kids can be fucking animals." Bob tossed his napkin on top of his empty plate, let out a rolling belch.

A waitress came by with the check, set it on the table. Bob slid the check toward Darby.

"This is yours."

"How do you figure?"

"The job took four hours this morning," Bob said. "You bet dinner on three."

The sleigh bells over the door jangled. Two young Mexican girls came inside, selling tissue paper flowers from an emptied coffee can. Bob signaled to them, dug into the back pocket of his jeans for his wallet.

"I'll get one for Rhoda," he said. "A souvenir from the outside world."

He accepted a flower from the smaller of the girls, passed her a dollar bill, smiled.

"*Gracias, mijita,*" he said.

Darby picked The Kid up at the Crumps' and they drove home

in silence. At the house, they pulled the trash and recycle bins out to the curb. Garbage night. Something caught Darby's eye out on the sidewalk, some movement under the twin holes set into the manhole cover. A trick of the streetlight maybe, something reflected. He saw it again, called The Kid over. The Kid crouched down next to the cover, looked into the holes. Put his ear to the metal, listening. Stood up and shook his head. He didn't notice anything.

Darby still had remnants of the feeling from the job site that morning, the headache, the nagging tug. While The Kid got ready for bed, he sat on the living room couch with his eyes closed, pressing the heels of his hands to his temples.

The Kid came back downstairs in his Dodger pajamas. He stood in the kitchen for a moment, head down, taking deep breaths, composing his thoughts. Darby never knew if The Kid was nervous before he started, before he stepped through the threshold into the living room. Didn't know if The Kid's imaginary audience caused actual stage fright.

The Kid hosted a nightly talk show called *It's That Kid!* He'd done this for a couple of years running. It was a highly successful show. It lasted about ten minutes—fifteen if The Kid had a particularly intriguing guest. He'd come up with the show as something to cheer Lucy up during the baseball off-season. Every night before bed, back when he was talking, he'd burst from the kitchen with a full-face smile and launch into his opening monologue, a few bits cribbed from the taped real-life shows he'd watched that morning before school, jokes he'd heard around the neighborhood, some real groaners from his book of knock-knock gags. Then he'd give a little intro where he told the audience about that night's guest, their history and accomplishments. His guests were usually celebrities, sports figures, world leaders, people The Kid had seen on TV or heard about in school. Sometimes they were long dead; sometimes they were fictional. Past presidents were recurring guests, superheroes from his favorite comics, members of Dodger teams Lucy had told him about, men who played long before The Kid was born. The guest would come out and The Kid would stand politely while they waved to the audience, basking in the applause. Thank you, no, please, no, this is too much. The Kid sat on the other end of the couch from Lucy. His imaginary guest sat in the empty armchair a few feet away. The Kid asked questions about the guest's current projects and past accomplishments, then answered in the closest thing he could approximate to the guest's voice. The voice never sounded anything like the guest's actual voice, but The Kid didn't bill himself as an impressionist. He'd ask a question and alternate between his impression of the guest's response and his reactions as host. When the guest told a joke, The Kid would laugh his ridiculous horse laugh, snorting and rocking like this was the funniest thing he'd ever heard, egging on the audience, finally taking a minute to pull himself together before moving forward with the next question.

When there was a particularly important or interesting guest, The Kid taped the show with a small cassette recorder Bob had given him for Christmas one year, using the microphone to interview his guests and deliver the opening monologue. When the tapes were full, Lucy marked them with the guests' names and the dates of their original broadcast, and The Kid kept them in a shoebox up in his room. This allowed him to air occasional reruns, play a tape instead of a live show on nights when he didn't feel like interviewing a new guest or when he wanted to revisit an especially successful episode. Lucy made requests sometimes, asked The Kid to replay a show with a guest she liked, a funny monologue she remembered. The Kid opened each pre-recorded show with a brief announcement to the audience, slightly apologetic for not having a live show to offer.

*It's That Kid!* had been the highlight of their night. Lucy would grade papers on the end of the couch, glasses slipping down the bridge of her nose, sipping a glass of wine, smiling at The Kid's bad jokes, his ridiculous impressions. Darby would sit in the chair in front of the TV, looking at that morning's paper, drinking his coffee, watching his wife, watching his son, their day ending, his just about to begin.

The show had changed in the last year. Now The Kid wrote the questions in his notebook, listened as the guests answered from the empty chair in a voice only he could hear. Darby had to sit beside The Kid on the couch and read the notebook to follow the half of the show that was available. The Kid no longer performed the monologue at the beginning, or made the flattering introductions. It was too much to write. The shows were no longer recorded, of course. The tape recorder and cassettes had been packed away in the garage.

The Kid's guest that night was an artist of some kind, a painter. From what Darby could gather from the notebook, the artist painted murals under bridges. The Kid was asking him if he was worried that his murals were going to disappear under all the graffiti that was happening. If he was worried that one day he would walk under a bridge and find that his work was gone.

When the show was finished, The Kid thanked the painter, walked him off stage, giving a last wave to the audience. Darby followed upstairs. The Kid got into bed, switched off his light, set his notebook and pencil on the bedside table. Darby leaned down and kissed The Kid's high forehead, whispered what Lucy had always whispered when she tucked The Kid into bed.

"Congratulations on a good show, Kid."

It didn't sound the same coming from Darby. He knew it, was sure The Kid knew it. But he said it anyway, every night. Congratulations on a good show, Kid.

He sat back down in the living room, flipped channels on the TV. It didn't take long to find him, selling a steam-cleaning mop on one of the higher-numbered stations. Sometimes it was the mop, sometimes it was the car-finish repair kit. Sometimes it was the weight-loss program, two books and a series of videotapes. Earl Patrick, Lucy's father, gone for almost a year and a half but still haunting the outer reaches of late-night TV.

Darby kept the sound off, watched Earl's demonstration of the mop on a tiled kitchen floor. Lucy had looked more like her mother than her father, but she had his physicality, the strong, deliberate presence in rooms. Earl pushing a mop across a TV studio set; Lucy walking up and down the rows of desks in her classroom. Darby pictured her there clearly: insistent, determined, the students listening with varying degrees of interest, restlessness, teenage boredom. It is a day toward the beginning of November, a little less than a year ago. They are nearing the end of the unit on the 1960s, so she's talking about Robert Kennedy and his run for the Democratic Nomination in '68, his swing through California, his visit with César Chávez in the San Joaquin Valley, the famous photo, the two men sitting side-by side in a soybean field. A lesson he'd heard many times in various forms as she talked to herself in the kitchen, back at her desk. He pictured her asking questions in the classroom, looking to see if anyone remembered details from the lessons she gave the week before, poll numbers, troop levels, dates of sit-ins and marches.

She reaches the front of the classroom, stops, turns, asks a question, waits for an answer. Gets an answer, the wrong one. Waits again. Gets another answer, the right one, smiles, nods, keeps smiling, keeps nodding, too long, something strange happening, the students starting to notice, even the ones paying the minimum amount of attention. Lucy at the front of the room, smiling and nodding stupidly, stuck in some broken-record loop.

A student at the back of the class says, "Mrs. Darby," a concerned note in her voice, and then Lucy falls, heavily, without her arms to soften the impact, face-first on the floor.

Shocked cries in the classroom, students standing, the scraping of desk legs across tile. She is well-liked, not that it matters, not that any person falling in such a way wouldn't provoke a similar reaction, but she is well-liked, patient and wise and funny with these kids, not the best students in the world, and she's one of the few teachers who treats them like they still matter, like they still have a chance, and there's a rush to the front of the room, some screams, a crowding around her body, everyone afraid to touch her. Face down, fluid pooling out from under her nose and mouth.

The student who finally reaches for her is tall and solid, a football player on the varsity squad, one of a few in the class. It's a Friday, a game day, so he's dressed for the occasion in a crisp white button-down shirt. There is a brief discussion over whether or not she should be moved, but he acts before any conclusion is reached. He rolls her over, gently, and the students gasp at the first sight of her face. The football player slides his arms under her, unafraid or unconcerned with the fluid, and then he lifts her, getting to his feet, her weight not much of a burden to him, cradling her in his arms. Another student opens the door and the football player carries her out into the hallway. A few students run ahead to the nurse, but the others follow the football player, a careful parade down the hallway, the boy's white shirt wet and red now, Lucy's head resting against his chest. Through the halls to the office where the nurse waits with the phone receiver in her hand, an ambulance on its way.

Darby could never picture the football player's face. It was just a blur above the boy's game day dress shirt, the red stain spreading across the starched white as he carried Lucy down the hall.

The doorbell had rung and Darby had opened the door to find two cops standing on the porch, hats in their hands. He'd stood in the kitchen for a long time after they left, before The Kid got home from school, trying to figure out what he was going to tell The Kid, how he was going to say it. Unable to move. The clock on the microwave gaining minutes, a rain shower coming and going, the light outside shifting and fading. That endless afternoon. At some point, he noticed The Kid standing in the living room, watching him. At some point, The Kid asked him what was wrong.

He told The Kid the story. Lucy falling in the classroom, her students rushing to her side, the football player carrying her down the hall. He left out some details, possibly added others. It was hard to remember, exactly, what he'd said. If he'd talked about her face hitting the floor, if he'd talked about the fluid on the boy's shirt. He hoped not, he hoped he'd spared The Kid those things, but it was hard to remember.

He'd only repeated the story a couple of times, to Bob, to Lucy's friend Amanda, and once, the day after, over the phone to Lucy's mother in Chicago. That was it. The story was sealed, finished, never repeated. But most nights in the quiet house it visited him. He couldn't shake it. He imagined the look in her eyes before she fell, her cheek on the cold tile floor.

Darby wondered what he had said. The football player. If he'd said anything as he carried her down the hall. If she had said anything, if she had been conscious at all.

He felt like he was still inside that moment, after the cops had left, before The Kid got home from school. Like nothing had happened since then. Like that afternoon had never really ended.

He turned off the TV and went out onto the sidewalk to get some air. He heard sirens in the distance, fire trucks, ambulances. There was an orange smear just above the rooftops to the east, gray smoke rising against the black sky. A quick movement caught his eye and he looked down at the cement, the cracks and crevices, the buckling sidewalk beneath his boots, and it was there that he saw it again, beneath the two holes in the manhole cover, some trick of the light, the glow of the fire reflected, maybe, something flashing through the holes from the space below.

It was there and then it was gone.

The Kid was in and out of sleep. It was like that most nights. His dad would tuck him into bed and go back downstairs to the TV playing low in the living room or out to the pickup, the radio playing low in the night. The Kid would drift, dozing, trying to stay awake to hear the important things, the buzz of the pager signaling that his dad had to go to work, and the other sound, the sound he'd waited to hear for almost a year now.

His dad had a job where he helped people after something bad happened to their family. That was how The Kid's mom had explained it once, although his dad wasn't a doctor and he wasn't a cop. The Kid imagined his dad like a character in a comic book, a detective or government agent who showed up after a villain had committed a crime. He didn't have any superpowers, but he used his brains, he used his wits to figure out what had happened and how to fix what had gone wrong.

The pager buzzed when somebody needed help. The pager was his dad's signal device. One o'clock in the morning, two o'clock, The Kid would hear it buzz, hear his dad gathering his change of clothes and thermos of coffee, hear him coming back up to The Kid's bedroom to stand over the bed. The Kid pretended he was asleep during all of this. He closed his eyes and made his breathing slow and deep. The Kid had seen superheroes do this in a couple of comics, pretending they were sleeping or dead. Batman knew how to do this, Green Arrow, Captain America. Lower your heart rate, calm your breathing. The Kid learned from their techniques, pretended he was asleep while his dad stood over his bed with his hand resting lightly on The Kid's forehead.

Sometimes his dad left for work before the pager even buzzed, and this was how The Kid knew that his dad did have a kind of superpower, an intuition that he was needed somewhere in the city, a sense that someone out there needed help.

His dad got postcards sometimes. The Kid saw them when he brought in the mail. He'd gotten used to opening the mail that wasn't addressed to him in the month after his mom had gone. So many cards had come from teachers at his mom's school, parents of her students, old friends from back when she was a kid. His dad didn't open them so The Kid opened them all, and that was how he knew that his dad got postcards from different people all over the city that said, *Thank you,* or, *God bless you,* or, *You did the impossible for us.* These cards were from people his dad had helped, the people he went to when his pager buzzed in the night.

The Kid drifted, dozing, half hearing things, sirens and car horns, engines gunning down the street, the rhythmic beating of police helicopters passing overhead, and then something would bring him back, a bus backfiring, a dog barking, some loud, sharp noise, and he would wake in a panic, afraid he'd missed it, the other sound he was waiting for.

He didn't believe his dad, the story his dad had told him that day, about his mom falling over in front of her class. The Kid had never heard of a mom just dying like that. He had heard of dads dying, even knew a couple of kids in school whose dads had died. They'd been hurt at work or shot or killed in a car crash. This was the way some dads died. But moms didn't die that way, as far as he knew. What moms did sometimes was leave. They got sick of kids and dads and they walked out the door and left. This had happened to Little Rey Lugo. His mom had left a couple of times. Once she was gone for over a month. The other kids in school said that she had another family, another husband and kids way out west by the beach. They said that when she got sick of Rey and his dad she went to live with her other family. The kids said that her other family was probably rich and lived in a bigger house.

This is what The Kid thought had happened with his mom. Something similar. Maybe she didn't have another family, another husband and son, maybe she didn't have a big house by the beach, but she had left, she'd gone to school that day and hadn't come back.

He'd heard his mom and dad arguing sometimes, whispering in the night down in their old bedroom or out in the living room when The Kid was supposed to be asleep. He'd heard his mom crying sometimes after an argument, and even sometimes when The Kid's dad wasn't there. Just standing in the kitchen in the afternoon while The Kid ate his after-school snack, talking to The Kid one minute and then quiet the next. The Kid would look over and see her crying. He'd look over while they were watching the talk show tape in the morning sometimes and see her crying then, too, just watching TV and crying silently. When he asked her what was wrong, she said that she didn't know, that she just felt bad. She said that she didn't know what was wrong.

The Kid suspected what was wrong. She was disgusted by The Kid, the fact that The Kid smelled bad, that he had B.O. and bad breath. She was embarrassed by The Kid, the things people said about him, all of The Kid's problems at school. That's why she'd left. He had made her sick and sad. That's why his dad lied about what had happened. To protect The Kid's feelings.

She was out there, somewhere. Sad, maybe alone, maybe crying. The Kid kept an eye out for her whenever he went anywhere. This is why he paid such close attention when he was walking around the neighborhood. When he came home from school, he looked for her in the windows of the house. He walked through the front door hoping she'd be standing there in the kitchen, smiling at him, opening her arms. She'd see how clean he was now, how long he brushed his teeth for, how long he swished the mouthwash, how hard he scrubbed in the shower, how much deodorant he used. His dad would come in from the pickup and apologize for the fights they'd had. She'd see how much they missed her and decide to stay home, decide that she was happy here, that this was where she belonged.

The Kid's dad slept out in the pickup instead of in the old bedroom. One night, not long after his mom had left, The Kid heard something outside and went to his window and saw his dad down in the pickup, listening to the radio. It happened every night after that. His dad usually left one of the truck windows open for a while, until the night got too cold, and on nights when The Kid had his bedroom window open he could hear the radio from down in the truck. His dad listened to talk shows, people talking about sports or the news or taking calls with listeners' questions about health problems or real estate. The Kid didn't know what his dad's interest was in any of this stuff, but that's what he listened to. Sometimes The Kid would stand at his window, looking down on his dad in the glow from the streetlight, watching his dad sitting, watching his dad lying across the front seat. He wasn't sure how much sleep his dad got. Some mornings The Kid woke up and went outside to find the windows of the truck rolled up, foggy with his dad's breath, the radio still playing. The Kid would knock on the pickup's window so his dad would wake up and start the day.

The Kid knew why his dad was sleeping out there, though his dad never told him. The Kid just knew. It was the same reason that The Kid tried to stay awake all night. His dad was waiting for The Kid's mom, too. His dad was keeping watch, just like The Kid.

For weeks after she was gone The Kid would come home from school and find flowers and cards waiting on the front porch. The Kid felt bad that people had spent money on those things, wondered how mad those people would be if they found out it was all a lie. His dad never brought the flowers and cards inside. They just kind of piled up and then one day they were all gone. He didn't know what his dad had done with them. Maybe his dad was ashamed, too, ashamed of lying to save The Kid's feelings and then all those people went to all that trouble to send flowers and cards.

Every week for a while, Amanda had come by with dinner in Tupperware containers for The Kid and his dad. Chicken and cheese enchiladas, green corn tamales. The Kid felt bad about this, too, but the dinner was always good, better than the drive-thrus they went to, so he didn't feel too bad. Amanda had been friends with his mom back before he was born, back even before his mom and dad had met. She brought the dinners for a while, and then she stopped. The Kid didn't know why. At one point she just stopped and then they didn't see Amanda at all anymore.

The flowers and cards hadn't come for a long time, but his dad
still got the postcards. Whenever The Kid felt angry that his dad
hadn't been able to stop his mom from leaving, he read the postcards
waiting on the porch, thought of all the other people his dad had
helped.

The only person The Kid had told about his suspicion was
Matthew, about a week or so after his mom had gone. He couldn't
hold the secret anymore. It was too much for him. He was afraid he
was going to blurt it out in school and get his dad in trouble. He felt
like it was going to burst through his chest, like it was going to jump
up out of his mouth into the quiet of the classroom. After school
one day, up in Matthew's bedroom, he told Matthew the story his
dad had told him, and then he told Matthew why he thought it was
a lie. Matthew agreed that this was a definite possibility. Matthew
could picture The Kid's mom leaving like Rey Lugo's mom had left.
This wasn't unheard of. Matthew promised not to tell anyone else the
truth. He swore on a Bible, which The Kid knew meant Matthew
was serious.

Matthew told him what he could do to bring his mom back.
He could make a Covenant. A Covenant was when you made a deal
with God. How it worked was you gave something up, something
that was important to you, something that was hard to go without.
You sacrificed something and stuck to it, and what you asked God
for in return would come true. Matthew said that this happened all
the time. It usually happened with little things, stupid things, lost
homework or lost pets, but it could happen with big things, too. Lost
mothers. But this would mean a bigger sacrifice. Matthew said that if
The Kid wanted this big thing, if he wanted his mom to come back
from wherever she was, then he'd have to sacrifice something that
would be very hard to live without.

The Kid thought for a while, and then he decided. He wouldn't
talk. He knew that if he sacrificed talking, he would never grow up
to be a real talk show host, that he'd never broadcast *It's That Kid!*
on actual TV. It would always only be a made-up show. He thought
about what it would be like to never talk for the rest of his life. He

tried to picture himself as an adult, at his dad's age, walking around not talking. It was a scary thought, but he would do it if it meant that his mom would come back.

The Kid didn't know much about God. He'd never gone to church except on Christmas Eve with his mom a few times. All he knew about God was what he'd seen on TV and heard from Matthew. He hoped that this didn't matter to God, hoped that God would accept The Kid's sacrifice even though The Kid didn't know too much about him.

He'd knelt on the hard wood floor of Matthew's bedroom and followed the instructions Matthew gave. He closed his eyes, clasped his hands, repeated after his friend. The words of the Covenant. When Matthew stopped talking, The Kid was supposed to tell God what he promised to give up. Matthew stopped talking and there was a hole in the room, a pause, and then The Kid said the words, offered his sacrifice, and when he was done talking he closed his mouth and didn't talk again.

It had gotten easier after a while, after his dad bought him the first notebook, after he'd learned to write fast, learned to think quick. He still even hosted the talk show, although it wasn't quite as good, wasn't quite the same. He knew this. But nothing was really quite the same.

The Kid had kept his end of the deal for a year now. Matthew said to be patient, but The Kid didn't know how long he would have to wait, or if something else was required for the Covenant, if there was something else he needed to do.

He lay in bed and listened in the night, waited for the sound of his dad's pager, for the other sound. He heard sirens instead, fire trucks from far away, getting closer. He went to his window, looked through the bars. He saw his dad out on the sidewalk, looking down at the manhole cover. There was a flickering orange glow a few neighborhoods over, on the other side of Sunset Boulevard. Something on fire. The Kid could even smell it, burning wood, deep and dusky. He watched the glow, listened to the sirens getting closer. He watched until the glow went away, until the fire was put out, until he could barely stay awake any longer, fading at the window, fighting it but fading, and then it felt like he was being carried, someone in the room, maybe, a shadow of a person, it felt like he was flying, back into bed somehow and mad at himself for being so weak, unable to stop from falling asleep before he could hear the sound of his dad's pager or the other sound, the one he was really waiting for, the sound of the front door opening and his mom coming home.

two

The Kid stood outside Mr. Bromwell's office, on time for his appointment but waiting, listing to the murmur of Mr. Bromwell's voice on the other side of the door, talking on the phone. He had all his stuff in a brown paper supermarket bag, his notebook and pencils and schoolbooks. The bag was only temporary, was only to make do until he and his dad could go shopping for a new backpack.

"Hey, Kid."

The Kid turned and there was Michelle Mustache, coming slowly down the hall, what looked like cherry fruit juice staining her upper lip, making her nickname seem even truer than usual.

"You waiting for the shrink?" she said.

The Kid nodded.

"What do you talk about in there?"

The Kid shrugged. He didn't feel like getting into a whole conversation.

"Did you see the fire last night?" she said.

The Kid shook his head.

"I did. It was a white house right down the street. I went out and watched it burn, watched the firemen shooting water. The news trucks were there. That woman from Channel Two was there, standing at the corner talking on TV. I saw the whole thing. I watched it in real life and then I watched it on TV. Then this morning I saw the house on the way to school. Completely burned. It looks like a tooth with a cavity. No one lived. The person who was in the house died in the fire."

The Kid took his notebook out of the grocery bag.

*How do you know that?*

Michelle coughed loudly, didn't cover her mouth, letting the cough fly out into the hallway. It looked to The Kid like she didn't feel the need to answer his question. She had been there, The Kid hadn't. She knew what she knew.

"Are you and Matthew still making that comic book?"

The Kid nodded.

"It's been a long time since the last one came out. How long's it been?"

*A couple of months.*

"Why's it taking so long?"

The Kid shrugged, didn't bother writing the obvious answer: *What's the point?*

"I thought it was pretty good," Michelle said. "Not as good as a real comic, but it was pretty good to read sometimes."

Michelle smelled bad, even from that distance. Like fruit that was too ripe. Michelle had B.O. and bad breath, but the other kids rarely made fun of her for it. She was too big, too wild, too mean.

"I go in and see Dr. Bromwell, too," she said. "Twice a week. Tuesday and Thursdays, right after lunch. I bet you didn't know that."

The Kid knew that. He'd gone down to Mr. Bromwell's office on those days to call his dad and found the door closed, heard Michelle's deep voice on the other side.

"We talk about my real dad," Michelle said. "He lives in Minneapolis, Minnesota. Minneapolis and St. Paul, those are the twin cities. He moved out there a few years ago because he hates my mom. He took a bus out there, I think. He didn't take the car, because my mom's still got it. My mom's boyfriend takes it to go buy beer. I tell Dr. Bromwell about how when I save up enough money I'm going to take a bus to Minneapolis to live with my real dad."

*He's not a doctor.*

"Who?"

*Mr. Bromwell. He's just a Mr.*

"He's a doctor. He's like the nurse, except he's even higher up than the nurse. He's got diplomas on the wall."

*I think he's just a Mr.*

"If he isn't a doctor, then why the fuck do we go talk to him, Kid? Why the fuck would they send us here?"

Michelle's face went red, redder than her fruit juice mustache. She got angry so fast. The Kid closed his notebook. He didn't want to make her any angrier.

"Whatever, Kid," Michelle said. "He is who he is. You don't have to tell me what you talk about in there. I don't really give a fuck."

She shoved off past him, swaying down the hallway, walking with that bad-guy shoulder roll. The Kid wondered if she had a hall pass. Thought that the answer was probably no.

Rhonda Sizemore was the prettiest girl in sixth grade, maybe even the whole school. She had clear blue eyes and long blond hair and nice clothes, fancy clothes. The kids who were her friends were like celebrities and the kids who weren't her friends wanted really badly to be her friends.

The Kid was not one of her friends. No way, no how. She looked at The Kid like he was something she'd stepped in, like he was something stuck to the bottom of her shoe.

Rhonda had drawn a picture of The Kid sitting in a garbage can with squiggly fume-lines flying out from his tongue and under his arms. In the picture, he was holding his notebook open to a page that said, *I Stink*. Rhonda had given the picture to the girl who sat in front of her and that girl had passed it to the girl in front of her and so on. The drawing went around the room during Independent Reading Time, while Miss Ramirez graded quiz papers at her desk.

The Kid saw the drawing because it was passed down his row, and when it reached his desk there was really no way to pass it around him. The kid in front just passed it back to The Kid. When The Kid had the drawing in his hands he wanted to tear it up, but Razz grabbed the back of The Kid's seat and shook his desk and whispered *Come on, come on*, until The Kid passed it over his shoulder.

There was a new girl in class. The Kid hadn't even noticed her. She must have arrived while he was in Mr. Bromwell's office. When

Independent Reading Time was over, Miss Ramirez called her up in front of the dry-erase board and introduced her to everyone. The Kid didn't hear her name. He was watching the drawing make its sneaky way around the room.

The new girl was small and pale and incredibly skinny. She wore a plastic barrette in her blond hair, a little blue flower. She said she had moved to Los Angeles from Arizona. She said her father was in the military. The class began introducing itself, one kid at a time, and after each kid the new girl said, *Hello*, and then that kid's name.

The Kid knew where Arizona was, but he'd never been there, and he wondered if everyone in Arizona looked like her, sun-kissed and slight.

"Hello, Rhonda Sizemore," the new girl said.

The Kid wished he'd held onto the drawing. He didn't want the new girl to see it. He thought that this was someone who didn't know anything about him, who didn't know how disgusting he was. He thought that if he could get a hold of the drawing again, he could maybe keep her from seeing it and thinking those things about him.

"Hello, Matthew Crump," the new girl said.

Arizona, The Kid thought. That should be the new girl's name. He thought of the desert, bright white sun, clean sand stretching to each horizon. Images from a cowboy comic he'd once read. A new place, it seemed like. No buildings, no people. A place where nobody knew anything about anybody.

The drawing was making another circuit, moving from desk to desk every time Miss Ramirez looked at Arizona instead of the rest of the class. When it reached The Kid he grabbed onto it, folded it once, twice, three times into a small, tight rectangle. Razz shook the back of The Kid's seat again, Come on, Come on, and when The Kid didn't pass it back he heard other kids whispering too, Come on, Come one, Razz whispering the loudest, an undisguised threat in his voice.

It was The Kid's turn to say his name, so Miss Ramirez said, *Whitley Darby*, to keep things moving along, to avoid the awkward delay of The Kid writing in his notebook and holding it up for the new girl to see. The other kids laughed, but The Kid was grateful that she'd saved him the embarrassment of explaining the notebook to a new person.

The Kid's desk was really shaking now, Razz trying to jar The Kid loose so he'd drop the drawing. The Kid didn't want the new girl to see the drawing, but he couldn't think of a place he could hide it. The shaking got worse, *Come on, Come on*, and when he felt the kicks starting, the kicks trying to knock over his chair, he folded the paper again, *Come on, Come on*, making it as small as he could and then he popped the drawing into his mouth, chewing fast. The kids around him erupted in angry yells, drawing a stern look from Miss Ramirez. Razz giving him a final hard kick. The Kid swallowed.

"Hello, Whitley Darby," the new girl said.

The Kid took different routes home from school, alternate routes, attempts to confuse the enemy, to get home without incident. He had four of these routes, one for each of the first four days of the week. He followed them in sequence. On Fridays, he went back to the Monday route, which meant that the next week he would start with the previous Tuesday's route, and so on. He kept track of all of it in his notebook. It was a complex safety system. Sometimes it worked, sometimes it didn't. Sometimes he turned a corner and there they were, Razz and Brian Bromwell, waiting for him.

Sometimes The Kid came up with different routes when an incident had occurred, or when there was something he wanted to see. Then he would take another way home, *circuitous*, his mom's word, meaning a route that went way out of its way to get him home. This was one of those days. He made a new route through the neighborhood where the fire had been. He wanted to see what all the commotion had been about, the sirens and the glow in the sky. He wanted to see if Michelle's story was true, wanted to see what was left of the house after the fire.

At the traffic signal at the top of the hill he took a left and doubled back, away from Sunset, the opposite way from the way home, down the hill along the cinderblock wall at the backside of the strip mall. High up on the wall were signs for the donut shop, the nail salon, and then the main store, *Gift 2000*, where they sold a little of everything, school supplies and cleaning supplies and boxes of cereal with brands The Kid had never heard of. Everything in the store was supposed to cost 97 cents. The store used to be called *97¢ Gift*, but they'd recently changed the name and hung new signs on the outside of the building in anticipation of the new year. The Kid thought that was just as well, because *97¢ Gift* was misleading. After tax, everything in the store actually cost $1.04.

It was hot again, bright afternoon sun in his eyes. A rickety van rumbled by, what Michelle Mustache called a roach coach. There were placards on the side of the van with a menu in Spanish, pictures of tacos, burritos, tostadas, hand-drawn logos for soft drinks and juices. The vans stopped at construction sites at break times, and workers lined up to buy breakfast and lunch from the back. Michelle said that she bought food from roach coaches all the time. She said that the tostadas were really good, you just had to be careful that you knew what you were biting into.

There was a large cardboard box on the sidewalk halfway down the hill, the box for some sort of major appliance, a stove or a giant-screen TV. Two dirty, shoeless feet were sticking out. The Kid almost stopped to check if the person was okay, but then he heard snoring from inside the box, so he moved quickly away.

Every few seconds he checked back over his shoulder, half-expecting Brian to be gaining ground at a full sprint, impossible to outrun, to get away from. He scanned the street ahead of him, the corners of houses and apartment buildings, ready to change direction and run like heck if need be. When he saw something that he wanted to write down in his notebook, he stepped off the sidewalk and crouched down between cars in a driveway to hide while he was most vulnerable, while his eyes were on the page.

He walked down the final slope onto the street where he figured the fire had taken place. He wasn't exactly sure what he had expected, but this wasn't it. No fire trucks, no police cars, no dead bodies, no smoking craters. The street looked the same as it had ever

looked, small houses in ramshackle rows stretching out to the base
of the next hill, cars and trucks parked at the curbs, dogs sleeping
on porches. Like nothing had ever happened. It didn't seem likely
that he'd gone down the wrong street. He had a very keen sense of
direction. He continued along, looking for any evidence of what had
happened the night before.

He smelled it before he saw it. Charred wood and stale smoke,
like the morning after a barbeque. It was a small house near the end
of the street, wedged in tight between two larger houses. One level,
maybe a few tiny rooms. There was a cement porch in front and two
thin strips of concrete running through the dirt at the side of the
house to function as a driveway. The Kid couldn't remember ever
noticing the house before, couldn't remember what it had looked
like before this.

The house was burned to a crisp. The two front windows were
nothing more than ragged black holes, the wood frames blown out
around the edges. Whole sections of the low roof had collapsed, and
long fingers of black sear-stain shot out of the holes and down the
front and sides of the house. The walls and roof were soaked from
the fire hoses, the wood still wet even in the afternoon heat. It looked
like a piece of soggy charcoal in the shape of a house. The Kid held
his nose. The closer he got, the more powerful the smell was.

He didn't know if there had ever been grass in the small patch of
front yard or if the grass had burned up or what. It was just dirt now,
rutted with tire tracks and boot-prints, slithery snake trails from fire
hoses. There was a big plastic garbage bin overturned in the front
yard, melted almost perfectly in half. The front door of the house
was missing, maybe burned down or kicked in by the firefighters,
but there was a heavy steel security door still in place, closed tight.
It looked ridiculous with the blown-out windows and the holes in
the roof. Who would want to break into the house now? The Kid
thought of somebody closing the security door when they left, a
policeman or fireman, which he guessed made sense. What did you
do when you were the last person to leave somebody's house, even if
it had burned down? You closed the door behind you.

The houses on the street were so close together that it was hard to believe the entire block hadn't caught fire, that the flames hadn't leapt across the street, shot out up the hill toward Sunset, toward The Kid's house. The Kid tried to imagine the scene as Michelle had described it, the satellite trucks, the newswoman from Channel Two. It seemed impossible that the fire had been contained in such a small space.

No one had survived. The Kid knew this. Michelle had been right. No other conclusion could be drawn by looking at the house. Someone had been inside and hadn't gotten out. He just had to look at the house to know.

He wondered what would happen to the house next. Somebody would come and tear it down, he guessed. Bulldozers, dump trucks, men with shovels. They'd knock over what was left, haul it away. Spread new dirt across the lot, build another house. Once the smell was gone, once the people on the street had moved away or died, no one would know the house had even been here. No one would know what had happened, what had been left.

He looked around to make sure that no one was watching, then he stepped to the side of the house, placed his hand against the outside wall. He wasn't sure why he was doing this, what he expected. What he thought it would feel like. It was strange, what it felt like. It felt like a body, like a human being, like a person's side, their ribcage, breathing slowly, in and out, settling down after something scary, something awful. It felt soft, it felt fragile. It felt warm.

Midnight in Van Nuys. The flat, still depths of the San Fernando Valley. They drove the vans down the narrow aisles of a vast public storage facility, between rows of low, identical garages, their headlights sweeping across the steel doors, gravel crunching under their tires, deeper in, down rows with more garages, through long stretches of darkness between security lights, peering out the vans' windows, looking for numbers above the doors. Bob was in the first van, following a makeshift map Mrs. Fowler had drawn on the work order, as per the caller's directions. Darby and Roistler were in the second van, trailing close behind.

Their headlights found him standing in front of a garage door in the middle of a row, smoking a cigarette, coughing into the crook of his elbow. Young guy, dark-featured and heavy-lidded, wearing a baggy gray jogging suit, a thick gold chain around his neck, a Yankees ball cap pulled low over his eyes. He did this weird thing where he slapped the hood of each van as it came to a stop in front of the garage, a quick blast with the heel of his hand as if he were congratulating them for winning a race.

"It's about fucking time," he said. "How long have I been standing here? Two hours, at least."

Bob checked the work order on his clipboard, turned his wrist to look at his watch. "You Tino?"

"You Bob?"

"Forty-seven minutes," Bob said. "Call placed to our dispatcher just after eleven pm."

"Look, Bob, give me a break, okay? I've been standing out here for I don't know how long with this fucking *thing* back there in the unit."

"The coroner didn't take the body?"

"The coroner took the body, Bob, but there's still a hell of a lot of him in there." Tino tossed his cigarette, knelt down next to the padlock on the door. "I locked it back up," he said. "I locked it back up, and then I thought, Why am I locking it back up? That mess isn't going anywhere on its own."

"Have you been in contact with the owner of the facility?" Bob said.

"The owner of the facility's my father. The owner of the facility's on vacation. Cops wanted to know that, too. *Can we get in contact with the owner of the facility?*" Tino unlatched the padlock, pulled it from the door. "I told them to come back in a week, he'll be here. In the meantime I've got to get this shit cleaned up. I said, What do I do? Go get a mop? The cops said, *Try the Yellow Pages. Contaminated Waste Disposal.* I thought they were fucking joking with me. Then I saw your ad."

Tino lifted the garage door, flipped on the overhead light, covered his nose with the sleeve of his jogging suit. Bob stepped inside the unit. Within a few seconds, Darby could see the flash of the Polaroid.

"The coroner said it happened a week ago, at least," Tino said. "Told me before he even saw the body."

"Thank you," Bob said. "That's fine."

"He said he could tell by looking at the flies. He could tell by looking at the number of maggots, at the generations of maggots, if you can believe that shit."

"That's fine," Bob said. "That's all the information we'll need."

They suited up and walked through the site. There were two connected units, and there had been some movement back and forth. Things had spread, dripped, dragged. The units were set up as an apartment almost, a living room with a thrift store couch and coffee table and TV, a bedroom with a small army cot, an exercise bike, throw rugs on the cement floor. Tino said this happened sometimes, even though it was against the rules of the facility. People came to live, quietly, kicked out by their wives or landlords. They set their stuff up in their units and went on with their lives, went to work, went to the gym, came back here to watch TV and sleep. Tino said it wasn't common, but it wasn't exactly uncommon, either.

They started with the second unit, the bedroom. Bob turned on the TV, all night news, something to drown out the spraying and scrubbing and Roistler's incessant chatter. There was more footage of the Tehachapi compound, a shaky, long-range shot of a pair of sheriff's deputies walking the dirt road up to the fence, speaking with two men on the other side. After a minute the camera moved away from the conversation, panning the compound, searching the spaces between structures, hastily focusing and unfocusing, looking for something more interesting, finally coming to rest on a spot beside one of the smaller buildings, a swing set and slide, a short row of childrens' bicycles.

Tino paced outside the unit while they worked, in and out of the glow of a security light, kicking the gravel, chain smoking, talking loudly on his cell phone about what he'd found.

At about four in the morning, they took a meal break, got breakfast at a diner near the freeway onramp. Bob and Roistler debated the Tehachapi situation, armchair quarterbacking the authorities' next move. Roistler said they should just leave the survivalists alone, they had rights, let them do what they wanted. Bob said that was all well and good, but he'd seen the TV shots of the bikes and if it turned out that kids were inside the compound then the state was going to get involved, there were no two ways around it.

Darby half-listened to the debate, ate his pancakes, sipped his coffee. Barely any traffic outside, just a few headlights on the freeway. This was the time of night he'd often come home to find Lucy sitting at the kitchen table, unable to sleep. She'd have made instant coffee, standing by the stove, ready to pull the pot before it whistled so as not to wake The Kid. She wrote out lesson plans or read a magazine or just sat at the table, hands around the warm mug, waiting for him to get home.

They'd sit and talk in low tones, in whispers. She'd ask him about the night, about everything other than the details of the job, about

Bob and Roistler and Molina, the whole strange crew. About where
he'd been, out in the sleeping city. There wasn't a part of town he
hadn't been to, a neighborhood he didn't know. His easy intimacy
with the place fascinated her. She still felt like a visitor after a decade
and a half, still got turned around in the stretching maze of streets
and freeways, kept a gaggle of maps in her purse, stopped and asked
for directions more often than she liked to admit. The names of
surrounding towns still sounded beautiful to her Midwestern ears,
exotic and bright: La Mirada, La Cañada, Montebello.

She talked about everything other than why she wasn't able to
sleep. She didn't like to recount the dreams that had woken her, the
thoughts that kept her up. At the kitchen table she wanted to be
distracted. She wanted him to talk, to guide them both to morning,
to sunrise and safety, the start of a normal day. He'd ask what was
bothering her and she'd shake her head, smile tightly, request a story
about the desert, another of his stories about growing up in what she
thought was the strangest place of all.

He'd tell her about the one-gas-station-town, the dusty trailer
park, the freezing nights, the daytime heat so unrelenting he'd had
to wear gloves to open the tin mailbox at the end of the road. He'd
tell her about the sight of vacationing families on their way to Vegas,
motoring through town without slowing, without so much as a look
out their windows. About the brave few who pulled over to the side
of the road to admire the heat, stepping out of their air-conditioned
station wagons just long enough to snap a quick picture of the bleak
Martian landscape, the mirages in the dips in the asphalt that shim-
mered like standing water. He'd tell her about the mysterious blue
mountains in the distance, an hour's hike away, the borax mines
and relay antennae. The abandoned Air Force base where he and
his friends hopped the fence and rode their bikes up and down the
crumbling cement stairwells. Hours spent this way, entire days, skipping school, exploring the vacated barracks, looking for rattlesnakes
and scorpions, drinking pilfered booze, smoking contraband Kools.

He'd tell her about his grandmother, Eustice, a tough, leathery
old bird who drank too much, smoked too much, carried a wireless

radio everywhere, room to room in the trailer, out to visit at neighboring trailers, out in the car, to the grocery store ten miles east,
always tuned to the Country & Western station out of Barstow,
humming along with Waylon Jennings, Jim Reeves, Patsy Cline.
About her insuperable pride, how she made every repair to the trailer
herself, every repair to their rusted-out Dodge Dart, repairs to all
the neighbors' places. How she shepherded him in one end of childhood and out the other in relative safety, with a minimum of broken
bones, no head trauma, no time in juvenile hall.

There was no father. There was no mother. He had no memory
of either. When Lucy pressed a little, he told her of the two short,
sun-streaked flashes he still had, the only recall, two hot desert afternoons when he was five, six years old.

The first, of a tall man with calloused hands, a mustache and
mirrored sunglasses. He wore army boots caked with old mud. The
rough feel of the man's hand on the back of Darby's neck. The man
leans down and says something in Darby's ear. The smell of cigarettes
on his breath, his teeth yellow and broken. There was no memory of
the man's voice. He's there and then he's gone.

The second flash, at the diner on the other side of the road from
the trailer park. Darby sitting in a booth with a woman in a white
halter-top and blue jeans. She's smoking instead of eating, filling the
plastic ashtray on the table while she picks at a plate of fat yellow
French fries. She wears her sunglasses inside the diner. There are little
cuts on her hands, scars and scabs on her forearms. The red polish on
her fingernails is chipped. Darby eats a bowl of Frosted Flakes and
milk. The Frosted Flakes came in a fist-sized single-serving box that
was an exact replica of a real-sized box. The waitress brought the box
and a cup of milk to the table and Darby was amazed by this. He
looks at the box more than he looks at the woman beside him. The
woman looks like an old photograph of his grandmother that hangs
in the front room of the trailer. His grandmother as a young woman.
She talks non-stop in a voice that's a smoother, higher version of his
grandmother's gravelly twang.

After he finishes his cereal, they walk back across the road. The
woman holds Darby's hand as they cross. She goes inside the trailer to

use the bathroom and has another argument with his grandmother. Darby sits on the bumper of the woman's brown Camaro, looking at the miniature cereal box he has kept, this amazing thing, pretending that it's a normal-sized box and he's a giant. How big his hands look. After a while, the woman comes out of the trailer, angrily wiping at her eyes under the sunglasses. She lifts Darby off the bumper, sets him down on the trailer's front steps, drives away in the Camaro, wheels spitting sand as she pulls out of the driveway and off down the road.

That was it. That's all there was. Not memories, really, just flashes of heat and dust, light reflecting in sunglass lenses, cereal and cold milk. Lucy would ask if he was curious at all, if he ever wondered about the rest of it, and he had to admit that he was, curious and angry and a little sad, but there was nothing he could do about it, there was nothing to look for, nothing left behind. Except for the cereal box. He kept the cereal box all throughout his childhood, kept it as a teenager, took it with him when he finally drove west into the city. It sat in the bottom of his toolbox, filled with a small block of wood so the sides wouldn't get crushed under the weight of the tools piled on top. One night he brought it out to the kitchen table. Lucy held the box, smiled slowly at the outdated package design, the thought of Darby as a little boy holding the box years ago.

That's it, he'd said. That's all there is. It's not a memory. It's just a cereal box.

She smiled like she didn't quite believe him.

They both wished like hell for a cigarette on nights like that, just one. They thought about how good it would feel to stand on the porch in the cool air, passing it back and forth, hands touching at the warm exchange. They hadn't smoked since Lucy got pregnant with The Kid, but it still pulled at them on nights like that, nights with long whispered stories and instant coffee at the kitchen table. They came close to giving in, talked resentfully about ease and convenience, the insidious temptation of 24-hour gas stations. They rushed to change the subject, to get the delicious thought out of their heads.

Some nights Lucy would tell him about Chicago, her parent's
house in the northwest suburbs. About going to the sets of her
father's early infomercials, a warehouse in Skokie converted to a bar-
gain-basement soundstage. About the visits from the IRS, the FTC,
other government agencies, local and federal, about the constantly
shifting corporate names, front companies, holding companies, the
late night phone threats from irate customers, husbands of customers, husbands of secretaries and call center operators. The evenings
her mother sat expressionless at the dining room table with glass after
glass of white wine, Lucy's father doing battle on the phone in the
other room, his voice rising and falling, bellowed threats and hushed
whispers. Her mother's thin fingers finding the stem of the glass, lifting the glass to her lips.

She'd tell Darby about Wrigley Field with her father, Dodgers-
Cubs games, great seats procured from some business contact, field
level, eight or ten rows back from the visitor's dugout. Two Dodger
rooters among the Ron Santo and Fergie Jenkins fans, hooted at
for their ball caps, their cheers for the opposing team. Her father
recognized in later years, when she was twelve, thirteen. Her father
known by name to many of the fans around them, Earl Patrick, the
late-night TV sales guy, or known to some as the snake-oil man, the
confidence man, the huckster. Earl sucking in the warm greetings
and bristling at the insults, skin as thin as a Cubs lead in the bottom
of the eighth. He had dreams of throwing out the first pitch, of being
asked to partake in the ceremony; he had a wild imagination which
he shared with her in the moments between the pitcher's windup
and delivery to the plate, the runner taking a short lead off first, the
pauses, the breath in the game. He had dreams of national celebrity,
of respect, of finally being appreciated as a visionary of the future of
televised commerce, moving Lucy and her mother to Los Angeles to
produce legit television, situation comedies and hour-long dramas,
awards shows, variety specials. He kept a color postcard tacked to the
wall of his office in Skokie: Sunset Boulevard circa 1970, gleaming
headlights and taillights, theatre marquees, yellow spotlight beams
crossing the night sky. This was the dream. Between pitches, he

leaned over and shared it with her in a conspiratorial hush that sent a chill from her tailbone to the nape of her neck. Her father's beery whisper in her ear. This was the dream, he'd say, and it was within reach. A few more years here and then they'd take off west. They'd all live happily ever after, Lucy and her mother and the great Earl Patrick. No more angry phone calls, no more insulting greetings at ball games from mouth-breathing drunks, just swimming pools and sunburn, everybody happy, everybody getting what they deserved.

The sun would start to show out the kitchen windows, the morning finally arrived, and Lucy would sip her coffee and Darby would ask again what the dreams were about, the dreams that made it impossible for her to sleep. She'd give her small, deflecting smile and shake her head and say that they were nothing. They were about nothing. They were about baseball.

Bob paid their bill at the diner, the result of some previous lost bet with Roistler. They drove back to the storage facility. There was a good deal of fluid sprayed around the first unit, the living room. The couch had to be disposed of, a pair of rugs, piles of newspapers and magazines, freestanding racks of clothes. Darby worked on his knees on the cement floor, spraying and scrubbing underneath crates and boxes, into cracks and crevices where fluids had spread and dried. The day grew, lengthened, the sun pouring into the unit through the open doors, the heat getting bad, worse. Game shows played on the TV. Tino returned in a fresh red jogging suit, a matching Cardinals ball cap, resumed pacing outside the unit, smoking and talking on his cell phone.

About noon, the wife arrived.

Roistler noticed it first, an angry female voice outside the unit. He whistled until he got Darby's attention, nodded toward the doorway. Bob was out at the vans, loading up for a run to the disposal site. There was a woman out there with him, petite, short-haired, dressed like she was on her way to work, a prim suit with a pleated gray skirt. She was yelling at Bob, jabbing her finger at his chest.

Bob listened, nodded, moved slowly back toward the doorway, positioning himself between the woman and the unit. Tino paced in the background, eyes on the situation, whispering excitedly into his phone, a hand covering his mouth for privacy.

The woman gasped for breath as her voice rose. It had taken the police this long to find her, she said. It had taken her this long to find the storage facility, to find Van Nuys. They weren't from there, her and her husband. They were from Costa Mesa, an hour and a half away. She'd driven up alone, as soon as the police had given her a location, even though they had told her not to come.

Bob pulled back his hood, removed his goggles and mask. He listened and nodded, kept himself between the woman and the unit.

Darby tried to ignore her. This was Bob's job. Bob would handle it. Darby moved deeper into the corner. Some fluid had spread under the couch, drying on the concrete, filling the cracks. He sprayed the area, watched the enzyme bubbling.

The noise from the TV was gone, suddenly. Roistler had turned it off so he could hear the conversation outside. Darby waved his hand, trying to get him to turn it back on, snapping his fingers ineffectively in the rubber gloves. Roistler ignored him, watching the woman, crying now, hysterical, jabbing her finger at Bob's chest.

"We're not at liberty to discuss that, ma'am," Bob said. "That's something you should discuss with the police."

"The police said it was some sort of knife."

"We're not at liberty to discuss that."

"The police said it was some sort of large knife but I want to know for sure. You have to understand that."

"Yes, ma'am."

"I have to know if it was a knife from our home. If he took a knife with him when he left. If he intended to do this all along."

Darby focused on his immediate area, the cracks beneath the couch, scooped up the liquefied fluid with a fistful of paper towels.

"You can't keep me out," the woman said.

"I can't let you in, ma'am."

"The police said he was living here. Is that true? Why would he live here?"

Darby moved deeper into the corner. This was Bob's job. Bob would handle it. He sprayed another crack in the floor, coughed into his mask. It felt like there was something caught in his throat.

"Who else is in there?" the woman said.

"Ma'am, if you'd just go back to your car."

"I heard someone else in there. I heard someone cough." Her voice gone ragged, shrill.

Darby coughed again. There was something stuck in his throat, a little piece of something, a speck, a fleck. It was next to impossible that a contaminant could pass through the mask. The mask was thick rubber and plastic. He coughed again. It had to be a piece of the mask, a little speck of plastic or rubber that he'd inhaled.

"Who else is in there?" The wife was almost screaming now.

"We have a team of technicians, ma'am," Bob said. "We're trained to deal with situations like this."

And then she was past him; then she was inside. She ducked under Bob's arm, pushed past, punched, kicked, something. She stood in the center of the unit, between Darby and Roistler, looking at what was left, what was yet to be cleaned up, the fluid and matter and dead vectors and these men in their masks and moonmen suits, one standing not far from her, watching, one kneeling in the corner, clutching a handful of red-soaked paper towels, turning as if caught, as if discovered doing something unspeakable.

She put her hand over her mouth. "Oh you cocksuckers," she said. "Oh you dirty cocksuckers."

Bob was at her side, had her arm, leading her back out of the unit. She was sobbing and he had his arm around her shoulders, was saying something to her, low and soothing, steering her back out into the fresh air, the sunlight. Tino had dropped his cell phone in the gravel, was watching incredulously, his hands up at the sides of his head, pulling at his ball cap.

They could hear the woman wailing now, the familiar soul-deep keen, a sound they'd heard a hundred times, the call of inarticulate loss.

Darby coughed again. It was still caught in his throat, a speck, a fleck. He coughed into the mask, trying to get it loose, get it out.

Once the woman's moan had faded, Roistler poked his head out the door, looked one way, the other.

"Where's Bob?"

Darby tossed his redbag into the center of the room with the others, pulled off his gloves and goggles, turned up the volume of the TV as he exited the unit. Tino was still outside the door, trying to fit his cell phone back together, the battery and the miniature antennae. A trail of dust from the woman's car stretched down to the end of the gravel row. Bob was nowhere to be seen.

It was the high heat of the day. The sun pounded Darby's forehead, the back of his neck. He walked down the gravel drive to a narrow shady space between the buildings. He heard something from the other end of the space, gagging sounds, coughing. He followed the sounds, gravel crunching under his boots, through to the other side, the back of the storage unit, bright sun again, where he found Bob doubled over by the fence, retching into a patch of high weeds.

"Christ, what the hell did I eat?" Bob spoke between heaves, gasping for air. A long strand of saliva dangled from his lower lip.

"Let's go," Darby said. He put a hand on Bob's arm. "Let's go. Let's get back to work. It's over."

"Something didn't agree with me." Bob sounded a little wild, spitting into the brush. "What the hell did I eat?"

"It's over," Darby said. He struggled to pull Bob to his feet, steer him back around toward the storage unit. "Let's get back to work. It's over and done."

He stood alone in the second unit, the bedroom. Bob and Roistler were out packing the vans. He held the camera, tried to shake the woman's voice from his head, the look on her face when she'd seen what they were doing. He lifted the camera to his eye, looked through the viewfinder at the unit. Just some boxes left, some crates that had escaped the mess. The frame of the cot, the exercise bike. The room was clean. The job was finished.

He coughed again, that fleck still in his throat. He looked through the camera, tried to shake the woman's voice. Coughed again. The woman's voice folded into his familiar headache, the behind-the-eyes knot, and then came the white-noise rushing in his ears, spreading into the entire storage unit, the only sound in the vacuum of the room, a tremendous noise, almost deafening.

It was a man's gold wedding ring, sitting on one of the boxes in the far corner of the unit. He hadn't noticed it before. It had escaped the splatter and spray. He tried to ignore it. The room was finished. He wanted to leave, go home. He wanted to take a shower; he wanted to sleep. He looked through the viewfinder. It felt like his eardrums would split, the rushing was so loud. The ring sat on a box in the corner of the camera frame. He couldn't take the picture. He couldn't take the picture as long as the ring remained. The ring was proof of the room before they'd come. The ring left the room unfinished. He could barely think, the noise was so loud. He would give the ring to Tino. He would take the ring back to Everclean. He coughed, trying to dislodge the speck from his throat.

It was there, in his hand. He was standing on the other side of the room, near the boxes, and the ring was in the palm of his hand, cool against his skin. He would give the ring to Tino or bring the ring back to Everclean. Or he could take the ring. The ring would be safe with him. He would find a safe place to keep it. Something like this could be easily lost, thrown away. Something like this held meaning for someone and should be kept safe.

The silence of the room screamed in his ears. The ring was in his hand and then the ring was in his pocket. He was standing back in the doorway between the units and the ring was in his pocket and the rushing in his ears ceased. It was there and then it was gone. The room empty of all sound. He looked through the viewfinder. The room had settled. The room was finished, the room was complete.

He snapped the picture and the unit flashed white.

Finally, just before lunch, Miss Ramirez told the class about the plans for Halloween. They'd been waiting for this information for a long time. Over the last couple of weeks, whenever someone had asked what was happening for Halloween, Miss Ramirez told them they had to wait, Halloween was still a long way off, they had plenty to accomplish before then. The kids were worried; the kids were unsure. They didn't know if there would be any Halloween festivities in sixth grade, didn't know if that stuff was just for elementary school kids. They worried and they didn't know if they should be worrying, if those were little kid things to do, both dressing up for Halloween and worrying about whether or not they were dressing up for Halloween.

They were going to dress up. This was the news from Miss Ramirez. There was an eruption of relieved, joyous applause in the classroom. The Kid clapped, too, clapped right along with the other kids. He looked over and saw Arizona clapping and smiling. This was the news they'd been waiting for. There was going to be a party in the classroom. They'd need to bring twenty-two Halloween cards to the party, one for each student in the class, not counting themselves. In the card, they should write one thing they appreciated about the classmate the card was intended for. The Kid wrote this in his notebook. *22 Halloween Cards.* Then he crossed out the *22* and wrote *23* because Miss Ramirez hadn't included herself in the total and The Kid thought she'd probably feel bad if she didn't get any cards.

There was still some residual clapping as they lined up to go outside for lunch. The Kid rushed to his spot at the front of the line, right near the door, just behind where Miss Ramirez would stand when she led them out to the courtyard. If he didn't get that first spot in line, he was invariably shoved toward the rear, where Razz flicked his ears and spat on the back of his neck all the way out to the picnic tables.

The line was a crooked mess, surging back and forth, the kids all jazzed up about the Halloween news. The Kid kept getting crushed against the door, so he opened it and stepped out into the hallway to give the line some room, and that was how he saw Little Rey Lugo walking slowly down the hallway, alone.

Rey didn't look okay. He was holding a large cardboard bathroom pass and walking unsteadily toward The Kid, listing toward the left side of the hallway. There was something wrong. He was looking at something at the other end of the hall with a weird, spacey expression on his face, like he couldn't believe what he was seeing.

The rest of the class was still jostling for position back inside the classroom. It was just The Kid and Rey in the hall. The Kid turned to look behind him, to see what Rey was staring at with that strange expression on his face. There was nothing there. The hall was empty. When The Kid turned back, Rey's crooked walk had him brushing right up against the lockers, still staring at something down the hall, his mouth hanging slack, his eyes open wide.

He looked like he was in a trance.

The Kid turned back to the classroom doorway. Miss Ramirez was way at the end of the line, reprimanding Razz for something. The Kid waved his arms to get her attention. The girls in the front of the line plugged their noses and stepped back at the smell that was released when The Kid lifted his arms. He ignored them, kept waving to get Miss Ramirez to look his way. Rey was still walking toward him, mouth hanging open. The Kid started clapping his hands. He didn't know what else to do. He had to get Miss Ramirez's attention. The kids in line looked at him like he was crazy, like maybe he was still clapping for the news about the Halloween party. Miss Ramirez turned from where she was scolding Razz and said, "Whitley, enough, please," her voice frustrated and sharp. Rey was still coming. The Kid stopped clapping and started knocking on the door as loud as he could to get Miss Ramirez's attention. The girls at the front of the line stepped back even further, looking at The Kid like he had really lost it. Miss Ramirez turned from Razz again, narrowing her eyes. "Whitley, I've said that's enough." She turned back to Razz. The Kid didn't know what else to do. Rey was walking almost directly into the wall now. He looked sick. He looked scared. The Kid had an idea, and before he could decide whether it was a good idea or a bad one, he grabbed Norma Valenzuela's arm, leaned in close and breathed in her face. A full blast of hot bad breath germs. Norma screamed. Miss Ramirez turned from Razz and marched to the front of the line, eyes burning at The Kid. When she got to him, he turned and pointed down the hall, stopping her in her tracks when she saw Rey and the look on his face.

"Rey?" she said. "Rey, are you all right?"

Rey stopped walking. Or, actually, he stopped moving forward but his feet kept walking in place. It was the strangest thing to watch. Rey kept looking at whatever he was looking at down the hall, walking in place.

"Rey," Miss Ramirez said. "Rey, look at me."

Rey turned his head at the sound of her voice. He looked at Miss Ramirez the same way he had looked at the invisible thing behind The Kid. Amazed. Then he lifted his skinny arms, held out his hands and threw up into them.

Norma Valenzuela screamed again. Rey kept throwing up, a long, steady flow coursing over his hands, splattering on the tile floor. Miss Ramirez ran over to him, waved back at the kids in line, told them to go out to the yard. Most of the kids turned and ran, heaving and gagging at the sight of Rey throwing up. The Kid stayed behind, watched as Miss Ramirez led Rey back down the hallway toward the nurse's office, Rey still holding the bathroom pass, his hands and shirt covered with throw-up, that look still on his face, like he couldn't believe what he was seeing.

The Kid and Matthew sat at a lunch table out under the pavilion. The Kid was reading one of the *Captain America* comics Matthew had given him for safekeeping, writing a description of each page in his notebook so Matthew could still follow the story even though he wasn't allowed to look at the comic.

"It's stupid when everybody gets so excited," Matthew said. "When everybody claps for something dumb like that."

The Kid knew that Matthew was upset because he wasn't allowed to dress up for Halloween. It was against his religion. When they were littler kids, Matthew used to beg his father every year to let him dress up and go trick-or-treating with The Kid. His father never gave in. The last few years Matthew hadn't even bothered asking. Instead, he just told The Kid how stupid the whole thing was, that it was a demonic ritual anyway, that he could care less whether he got to dress up or not.

"Look at that," Matthew said. "There's a police car and an ambulance here."

Matthew was right. A squad car and a bright white ambulance were on the other side of the fence, parked by the flagpole at the front of the school. A couple of policemen were walking toward the front doors, hitching their belts up on their waists.

"What do you think happened?" Matthew said.

The Kid shrugged.

Matthew took a pull on his juice box. "I think they're arresting Rey Lugo for throwing up in the hall."

The Kid heard someone approaching from behind, running fast across the asphalt toward the table. He stashed the comic in his grocery bag, watched Matthew's face to gauge the level of fear, to see if it was Razz or Brian running at their table to attack. But Matthew just looked confused, like he couldn't figure out why whoever was running toward their table was running toward their table.

The Kid braced himself, turned. It was the new girl, Arizona. She sat down next to The Kid and smiled.

"Hi," she said.

Matthew and The Kid said nothing.

"Is anybody sitting here?" she said.

The Kid shook his head.

"They said that you never talk," she said to The Kid. "They said that you only write things in a notebook and that you never say anything out loud. Is that true?"

"It's true," Matthew said.

"Is something wrong with your voice?" she said to The Kid.

The Kid shook his head, getting embarrassed suddenly, going red and hot in the ears.

"Then why can't you talk?" she said.

*It's a conscious decision.*

She leaned in to read the line he'd written, brought her head back to look at the whole notebook.

"How full is it?"

The Kid flipped through the previous pages, three-quarters of the notebook, all of them covered with writing and drawings.

"Is that the only notebook?"

The Kid shook his head.

"How many are there?"

"A bunch," Matthew said. "Probably a thousand."

"I don't believe you."

"Then maybe like a hundred and fifty. Maybe two hundred."

*Ten,* The Kid wrote.

"How long has it been since you've talked?" she said.

"Twenty years," Matthew said. "He's older than he looks."

"I'm asking him."

Matthew made a face and looked away, out at some kids playing kickball on the other side of the yard.

*About a year,* The Kid wrote. *A year almost exactly.*

"That's a long time," she said.

The Kid shrugged.

"Why did you stop talking?"

The Kid didn't answer. He sat and looked at his brown paper grocery bag, the name of the supermarket printed across its front. He waited through questions like that. He'd learned that he could wait a long time, longer than anyone else. He could outlast the question.

"It's a secret," Matthew said, still looking out at the game.

"Do you know the secret?"

"Of course I know the secret. I'm the one who told him how to do it."

Arizona looked at The Kid. "If I ask you a question, will you answer with the notebook?"

"Of course he'll answer with the notebook," Matthew said. "How else would he answer?"

"I mean answer with something you've already written. Something from before in the book."

The Kid shrugged, nodded.

She smiled. "What's your name?"

The Kid flipped pages, settled on one. Held it up, pointed to the relevant line. Matthew leaned over the table to see.

*Captain America.*

Arizona laughed. It was a nice laugh, warm and surprisingly deep.

"Where do you live?" she said.

The Kid flipped, settled on a page.

*Under a garbage can.*

"That's true," Matthew said. "His house is falling apart."

She laughed again, and Matthew laughed, too.

The Kid liked this, making her laugh. He wanted to ask her some questions. He wanted to ask her about her old hometown, what it was like out there, what the people there were like. If they were all like her. But that wasn't the game. He wasn't supposed to write anything new and he didn't want to scare her away.

"Ask something else," Matthew said.

Arizona looked at the notebook, looked at The Kid. Didn't flinch from sitting that close to him, didn't seem to mind the smell.

"Someday will you tell me the secret?" she said. "If we're friends long enough?"

Matthew looked at The Kid. The Kid kept his eyes down in the notebook, flipped pages.

"No, he won't," Matthew said.

"I'm asking him."

"You won't be friends long enough," Matthew said. "You'd have to be friends a long time for him to tell you and you won't be friends that long."

"Why not?"

"Because you won't. No one's friends with us but us."

Arizona kept looking at The Kid. "I want him to answer."

"He can't," Matthew said. "If he tells you the secret, it won't be a secret anymore."

"I want him to answer."

The Kid found a page, a line he'd already written, turned the notebook for her to see. Watched her face, her expression falling, disappointed as she read.

*Loose lips sink ships.*

He called Bob and Bob came. That day, after the cops left, after he'd stood in the kitchen for he didn't know how long, after he'd told The Kid the story of what had happened to Lucy, he called Bob. He didn't remember what he told Bob on the phone, most likely a leaner version of what he'd told The Kid: Lucy fell in her classroom; Lucy's gone. He didn't know who else to call. Over the next few days he'd call Amanda, he'd call Lucy's mother in Chicago. Over the next week he'd find cards and letters and flowers on the front porch. The Crumps would pay their respects, offer to help any way they could. Amanda would bring lunch; Amanda would bring dinner. Amanda would arrange a memorial service at her church. Darby would take The Kid to the mall and buy him a new black suit for the service, too long in the arms, too long in the legs. But that afternoon, that evening, he would do only two things: tell The Kid the story of what had happened, and call Bob.

Bob came and stood on the porch on the other side of the screen door and listened to what Darby said. His hair was pulled back in a loose, greasy ponytail, dangling from under the back of his black cowboy hat.

When Darby was finished, Bob asked how The Kid was, and Darby said that he was upstairs, he was up in his room drawing his comic. Bob nodded, like this was a good enough answer to his question. It was a hot night, still humid after the earlier rain, and Bob wiped moisture from his eyebrows with his fingertips. He kept nodding, slowly. The familiar response from job sites, from parking lots and doorways and living rooms. Bob nodding slowly, waiting for whoever had met them at the door to tell him more or tell him nothing or start screaming or sobbing or laughing, the whole litany of reactions they had encountered over the years. Bob's response honed to that simple, measured movement.

The Kid heard Bob's voice and came downstairs. Bob looked at The Kid through the screen door and then he looked back down at his boots and Darby could see Bob's nod dissolving into gulping sobs, saw Bob trying to hold them in for his sake, for The Kid's sake, trying to swallow them down, keep them back, but it was no use, Bob's great shoulders heaving, and then a sound escaped his mouth, a strange squeak, wholly out of proportion to Bob's size, and Darby took the handle of the screen door, gripped the handle like he was going to open the door, like he was stepping out onto the porch to put a hand on his friend's shoulder, but he realized that he was gripping the handle to hold the door shut, to keep this outside, Bob's bulk shaking, his face wet, The Kid watching from the foot of the stairs and Darby holding the screen door closed, the muscles straining in his forearm, keeping Bob safely out of the house.

They stayed like that until it passed. A minute, five minutes, Bob finally gulping air, shaking his head and blinking, pulling himself together, embarrassed, apologetic. It was another minute before Darby's fingers relaxed on the door handle, before he could be sure it was over. Before he stepped away from the door and let Bob in.

The ring was in his pocket. He kept touching its shape through the denim of his jeans to convince himself that he had really taken it, that it was really there.

He stopped at a cell phone store on Sunset and bought a new phone. He had lunch at a hot dog stand. He couldn't stop thinking about the ring. He had taken this thing. He had taken this thing to keep it safe. He placed the ring in the pickup's glove compartment, closed the hatch.

He crouched down on the sidewalk in front of the house, peered through the holes in the manhole cover. He waited, eye pressed to the hole, but whatever was down there was quiet now. Whatever was down there was waiting him out.

He pulled the garage doors open to a wall of boxes, crates of books, a crowding of old furniture. Broken long-necked lamps, a couple of small tables. The Kid's crib, a rocking chair. Lucy could never throw anything away. He dragged stacks of boxes out into the driveway, clearing a narrow path. There was a workbench at the back of the garage, with drawers he'd built when they first bought the house. The ring would be safe there, hidden. He dragged box after box, clearing a path, wiping the sweat from his eyes.

Halfway through, he found a box marked *Extraordinary*. These were the comic books that The Kid made with Matthew. On top of that box was an unmarked shoebox. Darby lifted the lid. Inside was The Kid's tape recorder, a row of cassettes of *It's That Kid!* episodes. Lucy's cursive labeling on the paper cards in the cassette cases, the thin loops at the tops of the letters, the words slanting gently to the right. He felt weak at the sight, the forgotten familiarity of her handwriting.

There were other, unlabeled tapes in the box. The Kid had carried the recorder around with him for the better part of a year, taping everything, anyone he came into contact with. Darby lifted an unmarked cassette out of its case, slid it into the slot in the recorder.

It was his voice that came forth from the machine, Darby's voice explaining the process of replacing the pickup's battery. He remembered this, an afternoon last summer, bending under the hood of the truck, The Kid standing beside him in the driveway, holding the microphone as high as he could reach. The Kid had been quizzing Darby about things he knew how to fix, had asked Darby to explain how to pump a bicycle tire, how to unclog the kitchen sink, how to change the battery in the pickup.

Darby ejected the tape, set it aside, pulled another out of the box.

The batteries in the cassette player were going. The tape started slowly, smeared sound, finally getting up to speed. Street noise, a bus approaching, stopping, pulling away in a roar. A dog barking in the distance. A woman speaking quickly in Spanish, walking by the microphone, in and then out of range. The Kid on his way to school, maybe, the sounds of his travels, or just standing at the corner with his recorder one afternoon, holding the microphone out to everything that passed.

There was a break in the tape, an abrupt patch of silence, then some muffled fumbling. The Kid turning the microphone back on. And then it was there in the garage. Darby hadn't quite expected that sound. He wasn't sure what he had expected. He knew that he would hear it if he played those tapes, but it still shocked him. It filled the garage, overloud, the volume too high. The Kid's volume, always talking too loud.

"This is Whitley Darby," The Kid said. "Also known as The Kid."

Darby couldn't breathe. He'd forgotten. He hadn't realized that he'd forgotten the sound of The Kid's voice.

"Tonight I'm turning the show over to a very special guest host, a person who needs no introduction."

More fumbling, the microphone being passed. The motor of the recorder whirring in the garage and whirring on the playback of the tape, over a year in the past.

"This is Lucy Darby," Lucy said. "Honored to be filling in for Whitley on this installment of his popular and long-running show."

Darby sat. His knees just buckled or he sat on the box behind him, his weight pushing in the top, the sides. Her voice in the garage, speaking clearly, carefully into the microphone. Her teacher's voice, enunciating every word.

"Today we're turning the microphone back on our esteemed host," she said. "We're going to give our audience a chance to learn more about him, his likes and dislikes, what makes him tick. Thank you for this opportunity, Whitley."

"You're welcome."

"Am I allowed to ask any question?"

"You are."

"Nothing is off limits?"

"Fire away."

"Good. Okay. How long have you been hosting this show?"

"A couple of years."

"And before that, what was your occupation?"

"I was just a normal kid."

"What were your interests?"

"Talk shows. Comic books."

"And now?"

"And now, what?"

"What are your interests now?"

"Talk shows. Comic books."

Darby tried to picture where they had been when this was recorded. Sitting in the living room, maybe, or out on the front porch. There was an end-of-day quality to the sound, a hushed ambient tone, a sleepy softness to their voices. Evening, then. Darby out at a job. The Kid in his pajamas, maybe, just out of the tub, teeth brushed, hair combed, fingertips pruned from the bathwater, sitting with his mother on the top step of the porch, passing the microphone back and forth.

Lucy's voice again. "Where can we find you most days?"

"Mrs. Heredia's fifth grade class, first row, front seat."

"What kind of student are you?"

"About average."

"Is there room for improvement?"

"Probably."

"How's Ms. Heredia?"

"Mrs. Heredia."

"Actually, it's Ms."

"She's pretty nice."

"She's a good teacher?"

"She's pretty good."

"And what's next for you, Whitley? Once the show runs its course. Once you're grown up."

"I haven't thought that far ahead."

"You haven't?"

"Maybe I'd like to do what Matthew's dad does."

"What does Matthew's dad do?"

"He wears a suit."

"How about your dad?"

"He helps people. He helps people for work."

"Have you ever seen him wear a suit?"

"No. Have you?"

"Once," she said, the edges of her voice turning up in a smile. "I've only seen that once."

Darby sat in the garage, the machine in his hands, his body shaking. He listened until the tape ran out, and then he listened to the dead air hiss at the end of the tape, the sound of the blank space and that ringing in his bad ear, bells in the quiet afternoon.

"Kid, you got any scars?" Michelle said.

The Kid thought about it, shook his head. No, he didn't have any scars.

"I do," Michelle said. "I've got some cool fucking scars."

They were standing in a cluttered aisle of *Gift 2000*, looking at the packages of greeting cards. Fifteen to a pack, twenty-five to a pack, cards that said Thank you or *Get Well Soon* or *I'm Sorry for Your Loss*. The Kid remembered that last card, remembered a number of these exact cards from people who'd believed his dad about his mom dying. They'd come in the mail along with the thank-you cards his dad got from the people he'd helped at his job.

Michelle had been waiting for him at the end of the school day. The Kid had come through the front gate a few steps behind the big wave of other kids, hoping to duck down the street without anyone seeing which way he'd gone, but as soon as he turned down the sidewalk he heard Michelle calling, "Hey, Kid," and the next thing he knew they were walking up the hill together toward Sunset, right behind the crowd.

"This one's from punching a wall." Michelle said. She made a fist and shoved it toward The Kid. There was a rough red scrape across her knuckles that looked pretty recent.

*That's not a scar.*

"The fuck you mean?"

*It's a scrape.*

"It's a scrape. What do you know? It'll be a scar pretty soon."

She turned her arm over, showing The Kid a cluster of pink bumps climbing her forearm. "Hot fat," she said. "I dropped a piece of chicken into the fryer at home and it sprayed up all over my arm. I didn't scream or cry or anything. Even my mom's boyfriend was impressed." She held her arm under The Kid's nose, looking hard at him while he looked at the bumps, daring him to dismiss them.

"You think that's a real scar?" Michelle said.

The Kid nodded. That was a real scar.

He knew that being seen leaving school with Michelle only made him seem worse than he already was. But it also meant that Brian and Razz would probably leave him alone, that he might get home without an incident. They never said it, but The Kid knew Brian and Razz were afraid of Michelle, afraid of her size, of the viciousness she'd shown a few times in fights in the schoolyard with other kids, both girls and boys. In those fights she'd had to be pulled off the other kids by two or three teachers plus the P.E. teacher. Even then it was tough for them to get her off the other kids, to get her away. The Kid remembered standing against the dodgeball wall with Matthew, watching four teachers drag her across the schoolyard while she kicked and screamed curse words, the veins in her neck bulging, her face stretched and ferocious.

A box of superhero Halloween cards caught The Kid's eye. Superman, Batman, Green Lantern, running and flying, holding jack-o-lanterns and sacks of candy. The cards had messages on the front like, *You're Super* and *I'm Glad You're on My Team*. The Kid thought that the boys in his class would appreciate those cards, but he wondered if there were enough Wonder Woman cards in the box for the girls.

"Here," Michelle said. "This one's good." She pulled the collar of her t-shirt away from her neck. There were three deep brown scratches running down past where The Kid could see.

"We used to have a cat and we all hated it except my little sisters," she said. "My mom said she was going to put the cat outside and let it run away but my sisters would bitch and moan, so she wouldn't do it. One day when my mom and her boyfriend weren't home, I carried the cat outside to let it go. My sisters came out too, bitching and crying at me not to do it. I tried to throw the cat out onto the sidewalk but it grabbed onto my neck and wouldn't let go. It just fucking dug in. I pulled it off, but it ran back into our building, back to our apartment. My sisters didn't even care I got hurt, they were so happy the cat wasn't lost." She pulled her t-shirt back up. "That's a good scar. Right, Kid?"

The Kid nodded. It was a good scar.

"Ask me where that cat is now."

*Where's the cat now?*

"All I can say is he got permanently lost. All I can say is that little fucker won't be scratching anybody anymore."

The Kid had just enough money for the superhero cards. He thought that maybe buying them would be worth it, that maybe really good Halloween cards would change other kids' opinions of him.

"Come here," Michelle said. "Come close to see this one."

The Kid didn't move, so Michelle took a step toward him, turning in even though there were no other customers in the store. She pulled her t-shirt out of her jeans, up over her belly. There were little red burns, eight of them, nine of them, angry red and brown circles across the flab on the left side of her stomach.

*What are they?*

"You don't smoke cigarettes, so you wouldn't know."

*How did it happen?*

"It wasn't an accident, that's for fucking sure."

*Who did it?*

"That's a good question," she said. "You'll have to figure it out. Who smokes cigarettes in my house? I'll give you a hint. It's not my little sisters. It's not my mom."

The Kid didn't know what to say, just stood staring at the bottom of her shirt, picturing the burns on her stomach underneath, how they'd gotten there.

"Take a step back already, Kid," she said. "Jesus. What are we, married?" She pulled her shirt back down, tucked it into her jeans.

The Kid moved away, trying not to think about the burns. He looked again at the superhero card box, wondering if they were worth the money.

"We can give you a scar, if you want one," Michelle said. "Something that'll keep those assholes away from you. If you had a badass scar, those guys would probably think twice about fucking with you."

The Kid wondered if this was true. If a scar would make Brian and Razz think that he was more like Michelle, more likely to get uncontrollable in a fight. Or maybe it would just make him uglier, and then even Matthew wouldn't want to be friends with him, then Arizona would keep away.

"Right across the face," Michelle said. "A big cut past your eye and down your cheek. A pirate slash." She pointed a finger at The Kid's face and mimicked the path of a knife, slicing from his forehead to his chin.

The Kid shook his head. He didn't want a scar. Not yet. He looked to the other side of the aisle, saw stacks of orange and black construction paper on the shelf, next to the glue sticks and magic markers. Office supplies. He had an idea. He knew what he could do, what would be better than the box of superhero cards.

"If you had a scar, you could wear an eye patch," Michelle said. "That would be totally badass."

He remembered his mom making valentines for her class once, a couple of years before. His mom's students were probably too old to exchange valentines, but she'd sat at the kitchen table the night before with construction paper and glue and made them anyway. She'd written a little note to each student and The Kid asked her to read each note to him as she finished it. The Kid tried to picture each student by the words of encouragement his mom had written about them, the things she complimented them on. Someone had a nice smile or was a thorough reader or always came to class prepared. And The Kid remembered thinking that when he was an older kid he would probably like to get something like that from his teacher, even if he was supposed to be too old for it. Just a little note of encouragement, something unexpected, something handmade that his teacher had drawn at her kitchen table the night before. He thought he would appreciate the time that had been spent.

It seemed like it would be difficult, making 22 cards. Twenty-three counting Miss Ramirez. But maybe he could do it. He was a pretty good artist. If he ran out of ideas for the cards, he could copy pictures from his *Extraordinary Adventures* comics, the ones nobody bought. He could trace the pictures and write things he liked about each student in the word balloons coming from his characters' mouths, Smooshie Smith and his talk show guests.

"It would keep people away," Michelle said. She made a slicing sound as she drew another slash in the air across The Kid's face. "Nobody'd come near you with a badass scar."

The Kid put the box of superhero cards back on the shelf and added up the cost of the construction paper and a couple of those magic markers, making sure to include the tax in his calculations. He figured he had just enough, figured he'd just make it under budget, and wouldn't she like this, his mom, wouldn't she think this was a good idea.

He made a new route home from *Gift 2000*, one that would take him past the burned house. He wanted to see what they had done with it, to see how quickly they'd torn it down, removed the debris, maybe even started building again.

He didn't tell Michelle where he was going. They parted ways in the strip mall parking lot and The Kid waited for her to walk out of sight before he doubled back down the hill, into the neighborhood of the burned house.

The house was still standing. The Kid was surprised. From a distance, it looked the same as it had before. The smell still hung in the air, old smoke and burnt wood, getting stronger the closer he got. He didn't even notice what was new until he was standing right in the front yard.

There was a bright red sign nailed to the front wall of the house, black block lettering that said, *Peligro! No Traspasar!* But beside the sign was something else. A wing, the wing of a giant hawk or eagle or something, drawn on the wall in white chalk to look like it was floating out of the front door. A single feather falling from the wing to the porch below.

He stood in the yard, looked at the wing. Who had drawn it? When? The Kid moved closer. It was a very good drawing. There was shading and texture along the wing. It really looked like it was made of feathers, like it had drifted out the front door and was floating gently to the porch.

The front security door was open. Just a half inch, but definitely open. He didn't remember it being open before. Maybe whoever had drawn the wing had gone inside the house. Maybe whoever had drawn the wing was still in there.

He knew that he should go home. His dad wouldn't be happy if he knew The Kid was here. He was supposed to go home directly after school, unless he went to Matthew's house, in which case he was supposed to call the cell phone, leave a message in Morse code. But the cell phone was lost, so really, what could he do?

The sign on the house was there for a reason. No Traspasar! This was a dangerous place. The roof could cave in, the floor could cave in. The sign was there for a reason.

The Kid stepped up onto the front porch. The wood was soft beneath his sneakers. It felt like it could give way at any minute. He moved with his arms out, like a tightrope walker. He kept his weight on the backs of his feet, so as not to put too much pressure on the boards too quickly, another trick he'd learned from comic books. The Flash running on water, keeping his balance and controlling his weight as he zoomed across the face of the ocean.

He made it to the door. The smell was incredibly strong. He covered his nose with the sleeve of his shirt. It felt like there was still heat coming from the house, a low-grade burn, but he knew that was just his imagination, he knew he was just making that up.

From this close he could really see the shading in the chalk wing, the detail. The kind of drawing he could never get right. A beautiful drawing, a slow drawing. It looked like real feathers.

He put his hand on the door, pulled slowly. It didn't make a sound. No creak, no groan, nothing. It just opened. Too dark inside to see. The Kid took a step over into the front room. The smoke smell was awful. His eyes watered in the dark. He plugged his nose, covered his mouth, but it was too much. He backed out onto the porch, took a big gulp of air, wiped his eyes, coughed the smoke smell from his nose and throat.

It was dinnertime when he got home, the sky behind the house turning a deep orange. The garage door was open and there were boxes out all over the driveway. His dad was sleeping in the pickup, stretched across the entire length of the seat, his head sticking out one window and his socked feet sticking out the other. His face twitched a little as he slept. His whole body twitched a little.

The radio was playing on the dashboard, an excited, high-voiced man talking about something that was happening north of the city, something with people and a barn and the police and news vans. The man said that this was just another sign, this was just more proof of what was coming for Y2K.

His dad's big red toolbox was in the bed of the pickup. The toolbox was rusted in spots, the red paint chipped away to reveal the gray metal beneath. The Kid lifted the top. All sorts of things inside. Hammers, wrenches, screwdrivers. An old, faded miniature cereal box with a block of wood stuck inside. A paper facemask like the kind he saw old people wearing sometimes to protect themselves from the bad air. The mask had an elastic strap that you pulled over the back of your head to keep the mask over your nose and mouth. The Kid put the mask into his grocery bag. It would come in handy if he went back to the burned house. There was a pair of plastic goggles in the toolbox. The rubber strap was loose, but they still fit on The Kid's big head when he tried them. He put the glasses in his grocery bag, too.

He looked inside the driver's side window. His dad's socked feet rested right near The Kid's face. Hot and smelly in the pickup. His dad's undershirt was too tight, stained yellow in the armpits. The Kid's mom had always bought his dad new undershirts when the old ones got like that, but since his mom had been gone his dad just wore the same old undershirts. The Kid liked when the undershirts were too old, when the fabric was thin, because then he could see all of his dad's tattoos underneath.

On his dad's left shoulder was a picture of The Kid's great-grand-mother, his dad's grandmother, who had raised his dad out in the desert east of Los Angeles, somewhere on the way to Las Vegas. The Kid didn't know exactly where. He'd never been there, had never met his great-grandmother. She'd died before The Kid was born. The portrait was a gray-toned drawing of her face, copied from an old photograph. She was a young woman in the portrait, wavy-haired, soft-featured. Her lips were set in a tight, thin line, her gray eyes looked straight ahead. She was very serious about posing for this picture. Her name and a date were written below the portrait in black script: *Eustice Darby, 1922.* His dad had told The Kid that the date was when the original picture had been taken at a portrait studio in Reno, Nevada. He told The Kid that Eustice Darby had been twenty years old when the picture was taken and that was a big deal back then, getting your picture taken, which was why she looked so serious. She didn't want to screw it up.

His dad had gotten the tattoo after his grandmother died. The Kid didn't know how long after, but he didn't think it was a year. A year seemed like too long to wait to do something like that, to get a drawing of someone on your skin after they died.

The bottom of the portrait drifted away in ghost-like wisps. Just below, a long, winding snake stretched down his dad's bicep, flicking his tongue at an unrolled scroll that said, *Don't Tread.* There was sand from the desert sliding out of the snake's mouth, down past his dad's elbow, with all sorts of desert creatures twirling in the fall: a taran-tula, a scorpion, a coyote, tumbling down to his dad's forearm, where brick buildings sprouted, alleyways and phone lines, crooked streets with trash cans and a shining Cadillac and a police car. There were howling dogs and broken bottles. There was a pretty woman with fire-red hair and big boobs under her sweater sitting on the hood of a flame-painted hot rod. There was a yellow moon overhead, about mid-forearm, swollen and cratered. The sand from above just grit in the air down there, shining in the moonlight.

His dad rolled over on the seat, resettled.

Tumbling blue waves ran down the length of his dad's other arm. The waves were drawn to look like woodcuts, like they were constructed from the same material as the two boats that tossed atop them, one at the shoulder, the other down lower at the elbow. The boat at the shoulder was a great, fierce pirate ship, its Jolly Roger flag flapping in the wind. There was a scruffy black crow sitting on the front railing of the ship holding a whiskey bottle with *XX* written on the label. The crow had little bubbles popping over his head and a couple of those same X's for eyes. Orange-yellow flames shot from the mouths of a row of cannons poking through the prow. Two cannonballs had just been fired, arcing through the air toward the second ship, curving down the slope of his dad's shoulder, leaving a trail of swirling smoke in their wake. The second ship was a small rowboat, trying to get away, banking around his dad's elbow to the other side of his arm in an effort to avoid the oncoming cannonballs. Two sailors paddled furiously, their sad boat tossing dangerously in the churning waves. The rowboat had sprung a leak. A geyser of blue woodcut water shot up from boat's middle, raining back down on the two desperate figures. Alarmed exclamation points hung above their heads. They couldn't believe their bad luck. It seemed only a matter of time before the cannonballs caught up, before they were sunk.

Below the waves were three letters written on his dad's knuckles in a real fancy, flourishing script, like something a king would write. These were The Kid's initials. His dad had gotten that tattoo when The Kid was born. The Kid was glad his name was on the pirate arm, rather than the desert arm. The cool blue arm, rather than the hot brown arm.

The Kid always puzzled over the tattoos, tried to fit the pieces together, tried to unlock the mysteries, secrets, codes. The Kid felt that he could learn everything there was to know about his dad by studying the drawings on his skin. His dad had told him stories about the tattoos, how and when he'd gotten them. The Kid had heard the stories many times. Sometimes the stories changed. Sometimes they were completely different each time his dad told them.

His dad was looking at him from the other end of the truck with sleepy eyes, a sad smile. His dad always looked disappointed now when he woke up and saw just The Kid there, like he was expecting something else, something more.

"Hi, Kid," his dad said.

The Kid waved.

"I got a new cell phone. It has a different number, though. We're going to have to memorize a new number."

The Kid nodded. He could do that, as long as everything else stayed the same, the contact plan, the Morse Code messages. He could memorize a new number as long as that was the only thing that changed.

His dad sat upright, turned down the radio, pulled on his boots.

"Are you hungry?" he said. "I'm hungry. Let's go out and get a new backpack, something to eat."

The mall was packed. Darby kept close to The Kid as they moved through the crowd. The Kid knew the layout far better than Darby, so he led the way, pulling them toward the shoe store where he could look at the backpacks.

Darby hated the mall. The endless circling for a space in the parking garage, the noise, the crush of people. He'd asked The Kid where they should go to shop and The Kid wrote, *The Mall*. When he'd asked The Kid if there was another option, The Kid wrote, *Not that I know about.*

Darby had worked a job here once, a few years back. The stock room in the men's department of one of the anchor stores. They'd had to work fast, overnight, trying to save as much of the merchandise as possible, finishing the cleanup before the employees arrived in the morning and the store opened for the day, before the first customers came through the doors.

At the shoe store, The Kid found the rack of backpacks, tried a couple on. He walked back and forth across the crowded floor with each one, testing its fit and weight, looking straight ahead as he walked, briskly, stiff-jointed, a rehearsal for the way he walked to school, avoiding all the other kids. After a couple of attempts, he found a backpack that felt right, a blue and white model, Dodger colors. It was one of the smaller backpacks, but it still looked ridiculously large strapped to The Kid's spindly frame.

Darby watched The Kid's sneakers as he tested the backpacks. They were last year's sneakers, scuffed and worn, probably too small for his feet. They hadn't gone back-to-school shopping at the end of the summer. Darby hadn't even thought of it. He'd forgotten that this was one of his responsibilities now.

They stood in the center of the store, looked at the walls covered with sneakers, all the new makes and models. They waited for a couple of seats to open up, waited for a salesman to come over and measure The Kid's feet. It turned out that The Kid needed a full size bigger than he was wearing. The salesman squeezed back through the crowd, into the stockroom to get a box in The Kid's new size.

"What do you think?" Darby said. "So far, so good?"

The Kid nodded, adjusted the straps of the new backpack.

It was still there, in the back of his throat. The speck, the fleck. Darby stepped out into the mall, keeping The Kid in his sight, found a trash can beside a wooden bench. Spat into the can, cleared his throat, spat again. No good. It was still there, lodged, a piece of the respiration mask, a tiny piece of rubber or plastic. Or something worse, maybe, something from the job site that had slipped through. Darby spat again. Still no luck. He thought about the ring, still in the glove compartment of the pickup. He still had to clear out the rest of the garage, get the ring into a drawer at the back.

A woman and a girl were standing by Darby's vacated seat when he returned, a mother and daughter, white, blond, the girl about The Kid's age. The mother was blandly pretty, heavily made-up. Darby motioned to his chair, offering the seat. The woman nudged her daughter forward, but the girl stood firm, shaking her head. She tugged on her mother's shirt to get her ear, whispered something below the noise of the store. The mother looked at The Kid and then at Darby. She gave a phony little smile. They didn't want the seat. Darby hoped that maybe it was the tattoos, that the girl was scared of the tattoos, but when he looked at The Kid's face it was obvious that he knew the girl, that he was the reason she was refusing the chair. The girl stood behind her mother, looked at The Kid like he was something vile, something contagious.

"Why don't you go look at the shoes, Rhonda?" the girl's mother said. "Why don't you pick out something to try on?"

"Take a seat," Darby said. "Have a seat. The salesman's coming right back."

The girl's mother looked up at him, the rigid smile still fixed on her face.

"Thank you, no. She doesn't want to sit."

"Makes more sense to sit and wait," Darby said. "He'll come to you."

"Really," the mother said. "No. Thank you."

The Kid kicked at Darby's shin with his socked foot. He wanted Darby to stop, to leave it alone, let it be. Darby coughed again, tried to clear the speck from his throat. He didn't want to let it be. He wanted this girl to sit next to his son.

"I'd like you to sit," Darby said.

"No," the woman said. "I've told you."

Darby cleared his throat, cleared it again. "Take the seat. Please."

The woman stepped in front of her daughter. Her smile was gone. "Do you want me to call security?"

The Kid kicked at Darby's shin. Darby sat, finally, reclaimed his seat. Lifted his hands to the woman, palms out in surrender. She took her daughter by the arm and steered her through the crowd, out of the store. Darby coughed, angry, embarrassed, looking at the other customers who quickly looked away when he met their eyes. The Kid was looking down at the backpack in his lap, adjusting the straps with shaking hands. The salesman returned with a couple of boxes and a big smile, knelt in front of The Kid and reached out for one of his feet.

They got dinner in the food court, a few slices of pizza, a couple of Cokes. Darby felt a little vertiginous walking with their tray through the open space, the high ceiling, the sea of occupied tables, the echo-chamber noise. He made The Kid hold onto his belt until they found a table about halfway in. He cleared off a clump of abandoned burger wrappers, carried the trash to a garbage station. Spat into the can, trying to clear the speck. Still no luck. Looked up and couldn't find their table, couldn't find The Kid. Looked back the way they'd come, looked to both sides. Maybe The Kid had moved, had found a new table. Sweat prickled his armpits, the back of his neck. He looked for The Kid's face out in the crowd, still holding someone else's garbage.

"Waitasecond." A man's voice behind Darby. "I know the name. I know it."

Darby turned. A tall, balding man in a wrinkled gray suit was staring at him, smiling, waiting for something, expecting something. He was holding a tray with an overlarge burrito and a paper plate of multicolored tortilla chips.

"Everclean? Everclean Cleaning Service?" The man nodded as he said it. "I'm right. I know I'm right." He stepped toward Darby, extended his hand. "Tim Nevin."

Darby looked at him, trying to place the face, the eager smile. A sales rep from an equipment manufacturer, maybe. One of the safety goons from Sacramento. Darby took Nevin's hand, nodding like he recognized the man, looking out into the food court for their table, for The Kid.

"How long ago was it?" Nevin said. "A year and a half? Maybe two years, now. Probably closer to two years, right?"

Darby didn't say anything. He didn't know who this man was, what he was talking about.

"That was something, wasn't it?" Nevin said. "I can't quite get that picture out of my head. You know what I mean. Walking in on something like that."

Darby tried to spot landmarks in the food court, things they'd passed on their way to the table. Nevin still had Darby's hand, was still pumping the handshake.

"You guys were great," Nevin said. "You saved my ass. The restroom looked brand new. Everyone came into work the next morning, nobody had a clue. We told everyone he died at home, right? Why tell them anything else?"

Darby said nothing, tried to pull his hand free. Bob would know this man. Bob would remember. This was Bob's job.

"You remember, right?" Nevin said. "Brokerage firm in Century City, right off Santa Monica Boulevard. Eleventh floor." He gave a loud, nervous laugh. "You couldn't have forgotten that fucking mess."

Darby said nothing. He didn't remember. Middle stall of the restroom, stall door open, car keys, wallet, receipts from a trip to Vegas on the counter next to the sinks. The force of the gunshot covering the tiled wall of the restroom, the ceiling, the stall walls, the toilet, the floor. Darby didn't remember. He said nothing, looked for The Kid.

"Yusef," Nevin said. "His name was Ahmed Yusef. Middle Eastern guy. Worked for us for about a year. He'd just blown a ton of money over that weekend. Company money. He had a gambling problem, a drinking problem. You remember."

"You've got the wrong guy," Darby said.

"You're the right guy," Nevin said, smiling wider, in on the joke. He squeezed Darby's hand, nodded at the tattoos on Darby's forearm. "I know you. Everclean Cleaning Service. You came in and cleaned up that fucking mess. Yusef in the bathroom stall."

Darby shook his head, took a step back. Nevin held on to his hand.

"You're joking, right?" Nevin said. "How could you forget that?"

"You've got the wrong guy."

"I do not have the wrong guy." Nevin's voice got louder, higher. Fat red blotches emerged on his neck. "Are you kidding?"

Darby shook his head. Nevin held on to his hand.

"How could you forget?" Nevin said. "This was a person. This was a person who worked for me."

"You've got the wrong guy," Darby said.

"I do not have the wrong guy. Why are you saying you don't remember?"

Darby looked out into the food court, searching for The Kid.

"Look at me," Nevin shouted, jerking Darby's arm. "How could you forget that? How can you tell me you forgot that?"

Darby dropped his tray, pizza slices and Cokes clattering, spilling across the floor. He shoved Nevin hard in the chest with his free hand. Nevin lost his handshake grip, stumbled and fell, landing on the seat of his pants,dumping chips and salsa across the front of his shirt.

"What the fuck is wrong with you?" Nevin said. "You were there. I remember you."

Darby backed away, stumbled over his dropped tray, looking out into the food court for The Kid, desperate now, panicked.

"I remember you," Nevin said. "You were there."

Darby pushed through the crowd, calling The Kid's name, his real name, a strange sound to hear, a lost word, until finally he saw The Kid's big head poking up above the crowd, The Kid standing on a chair, frantically waving his hands, guiding Darby back.

What had happened at the mall? The Kid wasn't entirely sure. His dad had gotten into an argument with Rhonda Sizemore's mom in the shoe store and into some kind of fight in the food court. He'd dropped their dinner on the floor. Then they'd left the mall, fast. The Kid was still shaking from what had happened. He was worried that maybe Rhonda's mom or the security guards at the mall had called the police.

It was too hot in the house, so they ate at the picnic table on the back porch, Chinese takeout they'd picked up on their way home. The Kid wondered what they'd eat when Y2K happened, when all the fast food and takeout places were closed or burned. The newscasts said they needed to start storing canned food, bottled water, powdered milk. They didn't have any of those things, and even if they did, would his dad know how to fix dinner from them? His mom would. His mom had been a good cook. He and his dad used to play a game at dinnertime that his dad organized. While they were waiting at the kitchen table, his dad would lean in to The Kid and whisper in his ear like he was telling The Kid a secret, giving him secret instructions, and then his dad would count, whispering as his mom approached the table with dinner, *One, two, three,* and then he and his dad would both say, *You're a good cook, Mom,* as loud as they could, and his mom would act completely surprised, smiling like she'd just won an award, like she'd never heard this game before, and she'd put the pork chops or spaghetti on the table and raise her arms in victory and hug The Kid and kiss The Kid's dad lightly, just behind the ear.

After they were finished eating, The Kid got his new backpack and made the transfer of materials from the brown paper grocery bag, careful to make sure his dad didn't see the goggles and facemask he'd borrowed from the toolbox. He pulled out the construction paper and magic markers, spread the paper across the picnic table. He folded each sheet of paper in half, addressed each to a different student in his class and the last one to Miss Ramirez. Twenty-three cards. He pulled Matthew's *Captain America* comics out of the backpack, looked for good drawings to copy, superheroes in action, running, flying, smashing faces and brick walls.

Some of the time he drew his own characters alongside the copied characters. He drew Smooshie Smith interviewing aliens on the set of his time-machine talk show. He thought of nice things for Smooshie and his guests to say to the card's recipients, words of encouragement, *You're very good at sports*, or, *You always have the right math answer*. He could picture Razz reading his *You tell some funny jokes* card and maybe thinking differently about The Kid, thinking that maybe The Kid wasn't so bad after all. In Rhonda Sizemore's card he drew Smooshie Smith trying on sneakers in a shoe store, a little joke that only she would get, something that would maybe make what had happened in the mall seem not so bad, make it seem kind of funny and stupid instead.

He sat looking at the blank paper he was going to use for Arizona's card. Almost afraid to start. If he started drawing and didn't like what he drew, he'd be short a piece of paper. But he didn't want to start and then draw something stupid. This was the first time she would see one of his drawings, and he wanted to get it right.

His dad was standing over his shoulder, sipping a cup of coffee he'd made in the kitchen.

"What are you up to, Kid?"

*Halloween Cards.*

"Can I take a look?"

The Kid shrugged. His dad sat down next to him, unclipped his pager from his belt, set it on the table. He opened the first card on the pile, read it, nodded. Opened the next card.

"These are really good, Kid. You're becoming a really good artist."

*I'm out of ideas.*

His dad got up from the table, took a sip of coffee, swished it in his mouth, spat into the darkness of the yard. Cleared his throat, sat back down. His dad still seemed upset about what had happened at the mall. The Kid wanted to get him out of that feeling. He looked at his dad's arms, the sleeves of tattoos.

*Can I draw some of those?*

His dad looked down at the tattoos, turned his arms back and forth, nodded. Held his arms out flat against the table. The Kid started drawing again. In one card, he drew the woodcut waves and the pirate ship and the rowboat. In another, he drew the Cadillac and the scorpion and the sand falling from the sky. He started to draw the red-haired woman with the big boobs, but his dad told him to move on to the next idea.

After a while, they had a system. The Kid would draw something from one of his dad's arms, write a message to whatever classmate the drawing was for, and start on the next card. His dad would take that last card with his free hand and add in background details with another magic marker: birds in the sky, leaves on the trees, woodcut splashes in the waves. His dad was a good artist. They were a team. The Kid worked his way up and down both of his dad's arms. He kept returning to the pirate ship, drawing different sections in different cards, cannons firing, the jolly roger flag flapping in the breeze. For Matthew's card, he drew the black crow with *X*'s for eyes. He drew a word balloon coming from the crow's open mouth that said, *I'm glad you're my friend.* Finally, in Arizona's card, he drew Smooshie Smith standing in front of his applauding studio audience, his arms open wide, a big smile on his face, a word balloon above him that said, *Welcome to Los Angeles!*

The Kid tapped his dad's knuckles. A letter in black script on each of the first three.

*What's that one mean?*

"You know what that one means."

*I forgot.*

"You forgot. You think I was born last night?"

*I forgot.*

"They're your initials, Kid. Whitley Earl Darby."

*Tell the story.*

"You've heard the story a million times."

*No I haven't.*

"A billion times."

*Tell it just once more. I forgot.*

His dad smiled, his regular lopsided smile. It seemed like maybe he was coming out of being angry from the mall. He got up from the table, stretched his arms over his head, pushed his hands into the bottom of his back. Cleared his throat, spat out into the yard. Finally sat back down next to The Kid.

"Your mom told me to get it. The night you were born."

*Start from the beginning.*

"What's the beginning?"

*She didn't like the tattoos at first.*

"She didn't like the tattoos at first. She wasn't thrilled with the tattoos. She put up with them."

*But she liked you.*

"She didn't like the tattoos, but she liked me. So she made me promise not to get any more."

*So you promised.*

"So I promised. I had enough anyway. But then one night you were born."

*In the hospital.*

"In the hospital. Sixth floor, maternity ward. You were born and we couldn't believe it. We'd never seen anything like you. A little kid who looked just like us, crying and peeing all over the place."

The Kid felt his face get red, his ears get hot. He always got embarrassed at that part of the story. His dad never left it out.

"That night we were in the hospital room. The doctor was gone, the nurses were gone. It was just your mom and you and me. I was sitting in the chair next to the bed, holding you. You were asleep on my shoulder. Your mom was looking at me in this funny way. She reached over and touched my hand, the hand that was holding your head. She touched these three knuckles, one at a time. Get one here, she said."

*You weren't supposed to get any more tattoos.*

"She changed her mind. She made an exception. She understood why they were important, what function they served."

What function do they serve?

"They keep track of time. Sometimes things happen and you feel that you need to mark them down."

*So you don't forget?*

"As a reminder. This is what happened. This is something that happened."

It was almost fully dark in the backyard. His dad turned on the porch light, sat back down at the table. The Kid could hear crickets chirping in the bushes, a cat crying off down the street.

"When she fell asleep, I drove up to the tattoo parlor," his dad said. "They were closing up. It was really late—really early, actually. I reached through the security gate, knocked on the window because the guy who'd done a lot of my work was in there, sweeping the place out for the night."

*What was his name?*

"Gilbert. *Beto*, we called him. He let me in and I told him what had happened, told him about you, about what your mom had said. He stopped sweeping and sat me down in the chair and went to work. The only two people in the shop, the only two people awake on that whole street, probably. Middle of the night, just the buzz of the needle and the neon sign in the window."

*How much did he charge you?*

"A million dollars."

*How much did he really charge you?*

"He didn't charge me a thing. He said it was on the house."

The Kid touched his dad's knuckles, one at a time. Tried to imagine the buzzing of the needle, of the neon sign.

*What did mom say when you got back to the hospital?*

"She was still asleep. You were back in the nursery, asleep too. Rows of cribs, all the babies that had been born that day. I wanted to show you the tattoo. I stood outside the window of the nursery and held up my hand so you could see the bandage. I held my hand there and waited for you to open your eyes."

*Did I?*

"You did, Kid. You opened your eyes and looked right at me."

*What did I do?*

"Wet yourself, probably."

*What did mom say when she saw the tattoo?*

"She didn't say anything. There was nothing to say. I sat next to her bed and when she woke up the next morning I took off the bandage and she held my hand. And we sat like that until the nurse came in with breakfast."

His dad got up from the picnic table, swished some coffee around in his mouth, spat out into the yard. The Kid didn't know why his dad was spitting so much. Pieces of rice stuck in his teeth, maybe. Maybe he hadn't liked the dinner.

"How's that story hold up?" his dad said.

*Pretty good. It's a pretty good story.*

His dad sat down again and they went back to work on the cards. They were almost finished with number twenty-three when his dad's pager began to buzz, vibrating loudly, turning itself in circles on the table.

Darby opened the door into the darkness of the hotel room. The crew was suited up, masked and gloved, buckets in hand. Bob held the camera at his hip. Darby felt along the wall for a light switch. No luck. He moved inside slowly, carefully, his boots making a strange noise with each step, a crinkling sound out of place in what should have been a plushly carpeted room.

He found and flipped the switch, throwing light into the small suite, two connecting rooms facing the ocean. He looked down at his boots. A layer of black plastic covered the floor, covered the floors of both rooms, garbage bags that had been sliced into long sheets and duct taped together. The plastic was covered in fluid that had leaked from the bed, collecting in pools where the bags bunched, running in syrupy streams to the outermost edges, spilling off to soak the thick carpeting beneath.

"Wonderful," Bob said. "Just fucking wonderful."

This happened a few times a year. They stepped into a job site and onto plastic or rubber or cardboard, jury-rigged surfaces whoever was about to create the mess thought would make the cleanup easier, would prevent damage to the surroundings. It never worked out that way.

Bob took the *Before* photo and they moved into the bedroom, settling their gear.

There were greeting cards on top of nearly every flat surface, the bedside table, the dresser, the coffee table by the sliding glass doors that opened onto the balcony. Maybe forty or fifty cards in all. The cards said *Get Well Soon.* The cards said *Our Thoughts Are With You.* There were small stuffed animals, teddy bears and rabbits and puppies. Helium-filled balloons hovered at the ceiling with messages similar to the cards. There were pictures everywhere, small framed photographs and blurry color computer printouts, members of a family, multiple generations, the recurring face that of a smiling, heavyset woman. The pictures followed her from her twenties to what looked like her late forties, her soft face getting bloated with sickness as the pictures became more recent, the skin around her eyes puffing and sagging, her curly brown hair disappearing, replaced by a flower-print bandana wrapped around her head.

Darby slid open the balcony doors, letting in some ocean air. The cards in the hotel room looked like the cards he and The Kid had received a year ago, the cards that had shown up in the mail or had been left on the front porch. *Our Condolences* and *Our Thoughts Are With You During This Trying Time*. Signed by other teachers from Lucy's high school, students, parents of students. The cards arrived for a week, two weeks, and then the books started arriving, paperback bereavement manuals on how to cope, how to get through. Some with religious overtones; some written for children, colorfully illustrated, intended for The Kid. Darby would find them in the morning on the front porch or in the bed of the pickup, covers damp and curling with dew. He'd had no idea who was leaving them. *When Someone You Love has Passed* and *You're Never Alone*. Two or three a week, waiting for him in the first flat light of morning.

He'd sit in the pickup at night, waiting for the pager to buzz, reading the paperbacks by the dome light. He looked through them all, even the children's books. He looked for a sentence, a combination of words that would make sense, a line that would shake him with the force of understanding. Some clue, some secret. What to do now. He found nothing. In all the books, nothing. He boxed them up, put them away in the garage.

Lucy's friend Amanda came with dinner in Tupperware containers. She'd ask how Darby was doing, how The Kid was doing. He could see her struggling to find the words, to ask the right questions, but there was nothing to say. He knew this. He'd read every one of those books. The Kid was right. His silence was the correct response. But Amanda talked and Darby listened and nodded and told her that he and The Kid were doing okay. She'd touch him on the shoulder sometimes, as she was leaving. She'd put a hand on his shoulder and stand like that for a minute, unsure what to do next. She was Lucy's friend. She didn't know what to do, how to act now that Lucy was gone.

New bereavement books kept arriving, delivered in the hour or two when he slept. One night, long after The Kid was in bed, he sat out on the dark porch, waiting. After a couple of hours, a familiar black sedan crept down the street, headlights slowly approaching. The car stopped in front of the house. Darby could see Amanda's face by the dashboard light. She left the car idling in the street and jogged to the front gate of the yard, sandals slapping against the balls of her feet. She was holding a paperback book. She opened the gate, took a few slower steps toward the pickup. She gasped when she saw Darby sitting in the dark, put a hand to her chest, startled. When he spoke, his voice sounded strange in the night, blunt and loud. It sounded like someone else's voice. It drove her from the yard, still holding the book, back to her car, away down the street.

We don't need any more books, he'd said. That strange voice. Stop leaving them here. We don't need any more books.

She didn't come back. The books stopped arriving, the Tupperware containers stopped arriving. From then on, Darby and The Kid spent every night at drive-thru windows, in fast food parking lots, sitting out on the back porch with pizza boxes and Chinese food cartons.

Bob turned on the TV in the hotel room, found the all-night news. The Tehachapi group's website had been discovered, excavated from deletion by state computer programmers temporarily pulled from working on the Millennium Bug. There were message board postings from the group's members over the last year discussing the rejection of their regular lives and the friends and family who refused to listen, to prepare for the coming disaster. The group's members had coordinated carpools, flight information, rides from the airport and train station, their migration to the compound, a town of their own that they would call Reality, California.

The crew went to work on the room. The fluid slid in every direction when they tried to towel it up, spilled off the sides of the plastic when they attempted to roll and remove the sheeting. Bob cursed a steady stream, kept one eye on the TV. They were showing photographs of the citizens of Reality, men and women and children, mostly white, mostly smiling, vacation photos, school photos, photos taken in their cubicles at work. The newscaster read the name and age and occupation for the person in each photo, the city they were from, the place they'd left behind to come to the Tehachapis.

They finally managed to soak up the fluid from the plastic and redbag the duct-taped sheets. Darby and Bob started on the mattress, cutting the wet padding into squares. Roistler knelt on the floor by the TV, doing the same to the soaked carpeting.

"I spoke to her yesterday morning, when she checked in."

It was a woman's voice, accented, eastern European maybe, a slight rounding and widening of the vowels. Darby turned to see a cleaning woman standing in the doorway between the two rooms of the suite, watching them work. She looked to be about thirty, compact, pale-skinned. A broad face and deep set eyes. She wore a starched blue dress and a white apron, the uniform of the hotel. Her nametag said *Stella*.

"I was still cleaning the room from the last guest when she came in with her suitcase," Stella said. "She told me to take my time, that she didn't mind the company. She placed those pictures around the room while I changed the sheets on the bed."

"You should really go back outside," Bob said.

Stella didn't reply, remained standing in the doorway, hands together at the tie of her apron, looking at the pictures arranged around the room.

For some reason, Bob didn't press the issue, just went back to cutting the mattress. Maybe it was because Stella seemed unfazed by the cleaning, by the things they cleaned. Maybe it was because of the sound in the hotel room, a woman's voice, a calm voice, an unusual thing at a job site.

"She asked me if I was married and I told her that I was not," Stella said. "She said it was nice to be married. She said she missed how nice it was."

Bob stood from the side of the mattress. Darby thought he was going to lead Stella out of the suite, but instead he walked to the TV, turned down the volume, knelt back by the bed and resumed cutting. When Roistler saw that Bob was going to let her stay, he pulled a pair of foam earplugs out of the pocket of his moonman suit, wedged them into his ears.

"I saw her again yesterday afternoon," Stella said. "I was having a cigarette in back of the hotel. She was walking across the parking lot, carrying shopping bags. She had been to the grocery down the street. She had bought boxes of garbage bags. I thought that was a strange thing to buy. She smiled when she saw me, smiled at my cigarette. She made the motion of smoking one herself, then she disappeared into the back doors of the hotel."

The effort it took to cut and tape and lay the plastic sheeting. Darby tried not to think of this, tried to shake the image out of his head, but he kept returning to it, the woman from the photos on her hands and knees, sick and tired from illness and treatment, spreading garbage bags across the hotel room floor.

He could feel the speck in the back of his throat. When the feeling got to be too much, he walked out onto the balcony, pulled off his mask and spat into the salt air.

The TV showed more photos of the people in the compound, one picture fading into the next, an unbroken stream of smiling faces.

Stella looked to the corner of the room, the redbags filled with black plastic. "I will stay until you are finished working," she said. "I feel that possibly some of this was done for me."

Darby stood alone in the room, holding the camera. The bed and carpeting had been removed, the walls scrubbed clean. Bob was down in the manager's office completing the paperwork. Roistler was out packing the vans. Stella had disappeared sometime before, after they'd finished the job and hauled out the last of the redbags.

He looked through the camera's viewfinder. The TV played in a corner of the frame, another helicopter shot of the compound. He lowered the camera and walked to the TV, switched off the set, stood back in the doorway between the rooms. Looked through the viewfinder again. The silence of the unfinished room roared in his ears. He thought of the sick woman buying garbage bags at the grocery store, placing photographs and cards on the dresser and tables. He thought of the woman kneeling on the floor, cutting and spreading the black plastic.

There was something on the bedside table he hadn't noticed before, lost among all the cards and photographs. He lowered the camera. It was a small plastic snow globe, a winter mountain scene. A pair of tiny lawn chairs sat at the base of a steep mountain. Two pairs of skis were stuck upright in the snow between the chairs. A bucket of frosted beer bottles rested beside the skis. Darby picked up the globe, shook it. The snow lifted and swirled in the water, drifted back down onto the lawn chairs, the bucket of beer. There was a message printed in raised white type across the base of the globe. *Wish You Were Here.*

He thought of the woman lying on the bed, exhausted, head turned to the side, watching the snow in the globe gathering at the base of the mountain.

He put the globe into the bottom of his bucket, covered it with the last half roll of unused paper towels. Felt the feeling lift from his body, the noise in his head going still. The room finished, the room complete. He stepped back into the doorway, raised the camera to his eye, took the picture.

He turned to leave and Stella was standing in the outer room of the suite, looking past him into the clean bedroom.

"I have not been able to work well today," she said. "They told me I should go home but I did not want to go home, I wanted to keep working."

Darby pulled the developing photo from the front of the camera.

"I am afraid to open doors," she said. "I have not been able to open a door since I opened this one."

Darby stayed silent. Looked at her hands, her wrists.

"Something like this," she said, "so close to you, to your body, your face. You breathe it in. How can you not? The room is sealed and then you open the door and you breathe it in, whatever was left. I cannot stop thinking about it. How do you stop thinking about it?"

Darby stayed silent, gripped the handle of his bucket.

"It is incredible, what you have done," she said. "Someone will stay in this room, tomorrow maybe. I will clean this room how many more times? You would never know." She looked at the bed, the dresser. "May I?"

She wanted to enter the room. Darby took a step back, allowing her to pass. She walked slowly, looking at the floor, the walls, the furniture. She didn't touch anything, kept her hands pressed to her apron, as if she didn't really believe in what they'd done, as if she still saw the room the way it was when she'd first opened the door.

There was a cardboard box on the floor of the bedroom, filled with the family photos, stuffed animals, the cards they'd taken from the room. The box would sit with the hotel manager until someone claimed them or he threw them away. Stella crouched beside the box. She lifted them carefully, one picture to the next, until she finally settled on the most recent, the woman she remembered, smiling bravely in a hospital bed, surrounded by many of the same cards and flowers and stuffed animals in the box. She turned back to Darby.

"If you will not tell anyone," she said. "I would like to have one of these pictures."

She looked at Darby, then down at his bucket, the roll of paper towels he'd set on top of the snow globe. She stood with the photo in her hand, smoothed the front of her apron.

"No one notices such things," she said. "But I would like to take it with me."

The Kid waited in bed, listened to the pickup pull away down the street. When he was reasonably sure his dad wasn't coming back, he got dressed, double-checked that the mask and goggles were still in his new backpack, pulled his flashlight from under the bed and went down through the dark house, out the security door to the front porch.

Night on the street. Half moon high overhead, lighting the black sky to gray. He knew that he shouldn't be out there. What would his dad do if he knew The Kid was out of the house, ready to go out into the city at night? Blow his stack, probably. The Kid would see his dad in full anger mode, in red-face, jaw-clenching mode. He knew he should be back in bed, waiting for his mom to come home, but he was afraid that they were going to tear down the burned house. He was afraid that he'd never find out more about that wing drawing, about the giant chalk bird's wing or whatever it was, floating out of the front door.

He headed up the street, past the apartment building and the vacant lot, up the hill to the intersection. There was some traffic on Sunset, adults going to restaurants or bars while the kids of the city slept. Traffic lights changing, a few horn honks. The mysterious world of night. The Kid was a little afraid, a little thrilled. He kept his head down, worried that an adult he knew would drive by, that Amanda or Bob would pass on their way somewhere and recognize The Kid standing at the corner waiting for the stoplight. He kept an eye out for his mom, like he always did. He looked into cars stopped at the intersection, searching for the familiar face.

Where had she gone? Was she in Chicago with The Kid's grandmother? Was she living in that upstairs bedroom, where he and his mom had stayed the time they went out to visit? That sad blue room?

The Kid didn't know. For a while after she was gone, The Kid's grand-mother would call the house. When The Kid picked up the phone and heard his grandmother's voice, he'd wanted to ask if his mom was there, if she was staying up in that room. But he had already made the Covenant, so instead of asking anything he just listened to his grandmother saying, *Hello? Hello?* on the other end of the line until one of them hung up.

There had been a memorial service. The Kid and his parents didn't have a church, so Amanda organized it at her church in Burbank. It wasn't a funeral like The Kid saw on TV shows, because there wasn't any coffin. This confirmed The Kid's suspicions. He asked his dad why there wasn't any coffin and his dad said it was because his mom hadn't wanted a coffin. She'd wanted to be cremated. His dad asked him if he knew what this meant. The Kid knew what it meant. He couldn't remember where he knew it from, but he knew it. It meant that they burned the body until it was ashes.

There were a lot of people at the service. Bob and his dad's boss Mr. Molina and his family, Amanda and her husband, teachers and students from his mom's school. People got up and said nice things about his mom, read poems they said reminded them of his mom. It seemed like a lot of work. All those people fooled by The Kid's dad. The Kid kept his mouth shut, didn't say anything, didn't tell anyone that they were being fooled. During the service, The Kid kept look-ing over at the group of his mom's students. It would have been so easy to find out for sure if his dad was lying. Just go over to the stu-dents and ask if his dad's story was true. Ask if they'd really seen his mom fall on the floor. Ask which one of them had carried her down to the nurse's office. It would have been so easy. But The Kid kept his mouth shut, sat in his new black suit, didn't say anything. He was sad and embarrassed, just like his dad. Sad and embarrassed that his mom had been so fed up she'd had to leave.

The Kid's grandmother didn't come out from Chicago for the memorial service. This also confirmed The Kid's suspicions. Why waste money on a plane ticket for something fake? Why come to a memorial service if the person the service was for was maybe really staying in that upstairs bedroom?

He crossed Sunset, then down the sloping sidewalk alongside the strip mall. He passed the red-lit *Gift 2000* sign on the side of the building. He passed the big cardboard box, heard rustling, snoring inside. The streets grew quieter the further he got from the intersection. No movement, no cars except those sleeping at the curb, a few dogs barking from backyards, blue TV glows in living room windows. The burned house was still there, sitting silent and dark. A streetlight gave off just enough light to see shapes, outlines, the figure of the house, the roof, the porch. The blown-out windows were even darker than the night around the house, bottomless black, neverending pits.

The Kid stood in the front yard and thought about going home, going back to bed. He thought about getting into trouble with his dad, about missing his mom when she finally came home. But then he saw the eagle's wing, or whatever it was, the chalk drawing on the front wall of the house, and he stepped up into the dull heat of the front porch, put his hand on the steel security door and pulled.

The smell from inside was still strong, but The Kid was ready. He put on the safety goggles, the paper facemask. He took a deep breath and stepped into the house.

So dark inside that the darkness looked purple. The Kid switched on the flashlight. The beam played wildly across the front room. There was no paint on the walls. There were no walls on the walls. The walls had been burned of plaster, burned down to the wooden skeletons of walls. There were small clumps of metal on the floor. The Kid knelt beside one, shone the flashlight on it. Forks, knives, spoons, all fused together. They looked like little meteors. This must have been the dining room. The Kid took careful steps, glass crunching under his feet. What was left of the windows, maybe, picture frames and flower vases. The Kid could still smell the awful smell, but not as much, not as bad. The goggles and the mask were working.

A doorway led into a small kitchen. The flashlight made shadows jump, made things move, grow, shrink. The blown-out window above the sink let in some moonlight. Pinprick holes in the ceiling let more moonlight through in thin white columns. There was shattered glass all over the countertop, over the broken tile floor. The cabinets on the wall sagged where they hung. They looked like diseased lungs. They looked like cigarette smokers' lungs The Kid had seen in science books, scorched and heavy.

He went down a short hallway. Two more doors at the end. There was a small pile of rubble in the doorway on the right. He shone the flashlight into the room. One blown-out window and a bed frame, the mattress charred, the sear stain spreading up the walls, reaching across the ceiling back to the doorway. This room felt hotter than the others. This was where the fire had started. The person had been trapped in here. The Kid knew this. He didn't know how, but he knew this. The person who lived in the house had burned in this room.

He crossed the hallway into the second room, the biggest in the house. More tiny holes in the ceiling letting in little shafts of moonlight. This looked like it had been the living room. There was a couch against the back wall, blackened and gutted. Big piles of ash and scraps, burned bookshelves and books and rugs. There was an exploded TV lying on its side on the floor. More crunching under The Kid's sneakers. Glass and something harder, maybe another fork-and-spoon meteor. The Kid knelt, shone his flashlight at the floor. Thick pieces of colored chalk, white and yellow and red.

He shone the flashlight across the room, corner to corner to corner, the beam finally stopping on the opposite side of the room and the image that nearly covered the far wall. It was a chalk drawing of a red haired woman in a daisy-yellow dress. Her eyes were closed, her arms were at her sides and her small body stretched up, lifting toward the ceiling. Her bare feet were a few inches out of a pair of brown and black cowboy boots. Angel wings unfolded from behind her shoulders.

This was the person who died, the woman who burned in the bedroom. The Kid knew this.

The drawing was sort of cartoony. The woman was short, but her features were oversized—her round eyes, her long eyelashes, her big hands and feet. The woman's head was tilted up as she rose, her eyes closed, a peaceful little smile on her face. The drawing was taller than

The Kid. The top of his head only reached the bottom of the woman's chin. He looked up. The roof had a hole in it, right above where the woman was drawn. Black sky above, hint of moonlight. The hole she would pass through on her way up, he guessed. He wasn't sure if the hole had been there before the drawing, or if whoever had drawn the woman had knocked out the hole to let her through.

He wondered when someone had drawn this. If they'd done it in broad daylight, the middle of the night, what. If they'd gotten someone's permission. He wondered whose permission they'd have to get. The city? The police? The Kid wasn't sure. He had a feeling whoever had done it hadn't gotten permission. It seemed like something done secretly, like the tags on the walls of buildings. Someone draws or paints and then runs the other way. Like the tags but really not like the tags. This was something else. This was more like the murals disappearing underneath the tags.

The woman was missing a hand. Her left arm ended at the wrist. The Kid didn't think this was intentional. Whoever had drawn the angel had run out of time, gotten caught, something. The hand wasn't missing; it was unfinished. Maybe the artist would come back and finish it. Maybe they would come back tonight; maybe they were on their way over right now. Maybe the artist would find The Kid in the house and be angry that The Kid had gotten inside, that The Kid was looking at the unfinished drawing.

The Kid was getting nervous. He didn't want to get caught. He backed out of the room, down the hallway, through the living room. Opened the security door, peering outside to make sure no one was on the porch waiting for him. The yard and street were quiet. He stepped out onto the porch, took off the goggles, the facemask, put them back in his backpack. He closed the security door tight behind him. There was no way of locking the door. Anyone could get in there, the chalk artist, the homeless person who slept in that big cardboard box, anyone. Next time he went inside the house, someone could be hiding inside, waiting to pounce. How would he know if someone was in the house?

Of course. Scotch tape. He had seen this tactic before in a detective comic. The Kid rummaged through his backpack, found the end of the roll they'd used while making the Halloween cards. Tore off a small piece, stuck half on the edge of the security door, half on the door jamb. Nearly invisible. If anyone opened the door, the tape would break and The Kid would see it before going inside next time. Sometimes The Kid was amazed at all the things he knew.

He ran home as fast as he could, back up the hill, across Sunset, down his street, afraid that he'd see the pickup parked in the driveway, his dad sitting on the porch, angry and waiting.

The house was dark when he got home. The pickup wasn't in the driveway. The front doors were still closed and locked. He got back into his pajamas, back into bed. Really tired, suddenly, his heart and his breathing finally slowing. At least he hadn't missed his mom coming home. He was disappointed that she wasn't there but he was also glad that he hadn't missed it. He tried to keep awake, tried to keep his eyes open so he'd hear it when she came through the door, but it was no use, he was so tired. Mad at himself as he crashed into sleep, dreaming of fires and ashes, feathers floating on walls, a glowing chalk angel trapped in a room while her house burned down around her.

three

There was a fire truck on the street in front of the house when Darby got home mid-morning. A small group of onlookers had gathered at the corner, older people from the neighborhood, grandparents, great-grandparents, a few children too young for school.

The fire truck was blocking his view of the house. Darby's first thought was the lights. The Kid had left the lights on in the house and one of them had caught fire, old wiring, a bad bulb, a bad fuse. He stopped the pickup on the other side of the street, ran across to the fire truck.

The Kid. Had The Kid already left for school, or was he still inside when the fire started? The security bars, the security door. The Kid trapped inside while the house burned.

Darby came around the fire truck, up onto the curb. The house looked just like it always looked. Nothing was burning, there wasn't any smoke. He caught the toe of his boot on something lying on the sidewalk. The manhole cover, pried up, lying flat on the cement. He turned just in time to see a firefighter lower himself into the open manhole and disappear.

Another firefighter stood over the hole holding a large beach blanket, her arms spread wide as if waiting for something to leap out, as if she was going to catch it in the blanket when it did. The blanket was red and white and green, had a large Mexican beer logo splashed across its front.

"Please keep back, sir," she said. "We don't know what's in there."

Some kind of inhuman noise issued from the manhole, a ragged, fearful growl. The crowd at the corner moved back a few steps.

The firefighter inched closer to the hole, adjusted the towel. "Everything all right down there?"

The first firefighter's voice came up through the hole. "It's a big one. Be ready, Pat. I'm going to lift it out."

Pat moved into position, bent her knees, nodded at Darby to move away. "Take a few steps back, sir. Keep a safe distance from the hole."

The first firefighter's voice came up through the hole, talking to someone, something down there. "It's okay, big fella, I'm not going to hurt you."

The growl again, lower this time, a warning, and then the sounds of a struggle down in the hole, some splashing, cursing from the first firefighter, and then a head appeared, a big black dog, wet and wild-eyed, up through the open manhole. The body followed and Pat embraced it in the towel, pulling as the first firefighter pushed. The thing kept coming, an enormous animal, soaking wet and half-starved; a hairy, trembling bag of bones. Finally it was up and out, wrapped in the towel, shivering. The first firefighter lifted himself out of the hole, his uniform wet, his wading boots covered in sludge. He coughed and spat into Darby's yard.

"That fucker's gigantic," he said.

He held the dog down while Pat pulled a length of rope from the fire truck and tied a loop at one end. The animal thrashed under the towel. The crowd at the corner moved a little closer, whispering in Spanish and English. The first firefighter pulled the towel down to expose the dog's head and Pat slipped the loop over, tied the other end around a link in Darby's front fence. The dog bucked at the constraint, flashing its teeth, and the firefighters backed away, letting the animal claim the towel, shake the water off its patchy fur.

It was a pathetic sight. Open sores covered its tail and hind end. Its eyes were bloodshot, rimmed with a greenish discharge. Its legs were so weak that it could barely stand. Whenever it gained its footing it would topple again, falling flat on its face to a wounded cry from the crowd at the corner. The firefighters shared a plastic bottle of hand sanitizer at the truck, radioed for animal control.

A skinny kid with an uneven buzz cut broke from the crowd, ran back to his house. A minute later he returned with a plastic dish of what looked like wet cat food. He handed it to Pat. She set it down on the sidewalk, nudged it toward the dog with the toe of her rubber boot. The dog sniffed, hoisted itself up onto its toothpick legs and fell face first into the food. Another cry from the crowd. Pat turned her head, winced.

The boy asked the first firefighter how long the dog had been down there, where it came from.

"Probably a week," the firefighter said. "Maybe more. Could have come from anywhere in the area, wandering around down in the sewer. Reached a dead end under this manhole cover and couldn't turn around. Got stuck."

"How'd he get down in there?"

"Crawled in through a curb inlet. Chased something down. Got pushed in, shoved in. Who knows?"

"Who does he belong to?"

"Nobody," the firefighter said. "Everybody. He's now a ward of the City of Los Angeles."

The animal control van came. A pair of uniformed officers muzzled the dog, lifted it up into a cage in the back of the van. The firefighters replaced the manhole cover, climbed up into the fire truck and drove away with a quick burst of their siren, waving to the thinning crowd.

Darby knelt on the sidewalk, untied the rope from the fence. He thought of the dog under the manhole cover for a week, maybe more. The dog under there while Darby sat through the night in the pickup, while he tried to sleep during the day. The dog under there while The Kid stayed alone, while the sidewalk graffiti was sprayed. The dog under there while Darby was at job sites, while he was cleaning the hotel room by the beach.

The ring and the snow globe were in the glove compartment of the pickup. He went back to work in the garage, pulling boxes, clearing a path to the workbench and the drawer at the back.

The pager buzzed on his hip. He ignored it, continued to pull boxes. The pager buzzed again. He unhooked the new cell phone from its holster, called the dispatch office.

"Everclean Industrials." It was Bob's voice that answered the phone. Darby said nothing, confused, wondering if he'd somehow dialed the wrong number.

"Everclean Industrials," Bob said.

"Bob, it's me."

"I just paged you. Took me twenty minutes to figure out how to do it."

"Where's Mrs. Fowler?"

"Home sick. Are you en route?"

"Not yet. The Kid's sick." The lie came quickly, easily. Standing in the driveway surrounded by boxes.

"What's he got?" Bob said.

"I don't know. I've got to pick him up at school. Something with his stomach, throwing up, the whole business." The lie came quickly, easily, but he couldn't leave the ring and the globe in the pickup. He had to get them into the workbench.

"Hang on a second," Bob said. He coughed loudly away from the receiver, came back. "This is a small job, David. Don't bother. Stay with The Kid."

"Is Roistler there?"

"Roistler took a personal day." Bob coughed again, cleared his throat. "Don't worry about it. It's a one-man job."

"What's the address?"

"Eucalyptus and Manchester. Down in Inglewood."

"I'll come once The Kid's home and settled. An hour, tops."

"Don't sweat it. It's a one-man job. Stay with The Kid. He needs you more than I do."

Darby clipped the phone back into its holster. There were no one-man jobs. He knew this. It had been Everclean policy from the beginning. Every job was a team job. But he couldn't leave the garage now. He pulled boxes for he didn't know how long, until he was soaked in sweat again, until he had finally reached the workbench at the back. A couple of hours, maybe. The top drawer of the work-bench, nothing but an envelope inside. Darby put the ring inside the drawer. He put the globe inside the drawer. He felt that same settling sensation from the storage facility, something completed, something done.

He had closed the drawer, was hauling the boxes back into the garage when the pager buzzed again.

The Kid was trying to draw women's hands in his notebook. He wasn't very good at it. His drawing was too blocky, the lines were too thick. He tried to draw like the chalk drawing in the burned house, the lines smooth and flowing, delicate. He kept crossing out, starting over, crossing out. Two pages full of mutant-looking hands already. He couldn't get his pencil to do what he wanted it to do.

Matthew sat across the lunch table. He dipped his French fries into a small blob of ketchup, one at a time, bit the ends off slowly, chewed, placed the uneaten halves into a pile beside his plate.

Michelle set her tray down on their table. A thick slab of greasy cheese pizza, a small pile of cupcakes and Twinkies, a half-pint of chocolate milk. She sat down next to The Kid, tore the cellophane off the first cupcake with her teeth.

"Did you hear about Rey Lugo?" she said. "He had to get his stomach pumped. And it turns out that he's a hemophiliac, which means he could get AIDS and die."

"Where'd you hear that?" Matthew said.

"Don't worry about where I heard it. I heard it from people."

"What people?"

"Don't worry where the fuck I heard it. It's the truth. It's real."

Matthew made a sour face, looked down at his French fries. He didn't like Michelle, didn't like her curse words or her taking of the Lord's name in vain, what he called her blasphemies.

The Kid tried to draw Michelle's hands while she ate, but her hands were bigger than the chalk drawing's hands, fat and stubby, with little half-moons of dirt under the chewed fingernails.

"I saw you guys talking to that new girl," Michelle said, mouth full, black chocolate mush between her teeth. "I saw her sitting with you at recess."

"So what?" Matthew said.

"Is she your friend?"

"Maybe."

Michelle looked over to the other side of the courtyard, all the tables filled with kids. "Looks like she has some new friends."

The Kid turned. Arizona was sitting at the end of a table across from Rhonda Sizemore. Brian Bromwell stood at the head of the table. They were all smiling and laughing about something. The Kid felt that familiar cold flush in his stomach. Maybe they were telling her about him, about his B.O. and bad breath. Maybe they were telling her not to stand too close, not to catch anything contagious.

"She can talk to whoever she wants," Matthew said. "It's a free country."

"They're probably talking about their periods," Michelle said. "Rhonda Sizemore already has her period, I'll bet you ten bucks. She's that kind of person."

"I don't even know what you're talking about," Matthew said.

"Yes you do."

"No I don't."

"You know what I'm talking about," Michelle said. "Blood and babies."

They sat on opposite sides of the desk in Molina's office, looking out the open window into the garage. The TV in the waiting area showed a makeshift command center that had been set up a few hundred yards from the gates of Reality, California. A couple of tents, a podium and microphone, tall stands of TV lights. A BATF spokesman in a blue polo shirt stood at the podium fielding questions.

Molina loosened his tie, closed his eyes, fighting a headache. He pressed his fingertips to his eyelids.

"The story's not really clear," Molina said, "It wasn't really clear to the cops. All I know is what Bob wrote in the log before he left for the job. The call came in, a woman in a closet, a hanging. The police had come and gone, the coroner's people had come and gone."

Mrs. Fowler came into the office and set two Styrofoam cups of coffee on the desk. She left without saying a word, back through the door into the dispatch office.

"Who called in the job?" Darby said.

"The guy who owned the house. The police found one of his tenants in a closet and he wanted it cleaned."

Darby looked at the framed photos on Molina's desk. Molina's wife and daughters at a motel pool in Vegas. A photo of Molina's mother standing in a faded housedress, her dark face set, looking directly into the lens.

Darby thought of the photos from the hotel room, Stella lifting a picture from the box, holding it to her chest.

"The police came and did their thing," Molina said. "The coroner's people did their thing. Everybody left. Bob showed up and started the job. A couple hours later, the neighbors hear something and call the police again. The police enter the house, guns drawn. They find Bob standing in the bedroom closet, screaming."

Molina stuck a finger in his coffee, stirred the cream into a brown swirl. "He had already completed the job. The place was clean, the van was packed. He was just standing in the closet screaming."

Darby looked out the window at the TV. The BATF spokesman was telling the reporters that they had lost communication with the Realists, but that they were hoping this was only a temporary situation, that they'd soon reestablish contact.

"Where were you?" Molina said.

"The Kid was sick."

"You should have called. You could have brought him over to our place. The girls would have looked after him."

"Bob told me it was a one-man job."

"There's no such thing."

"I know."

"How long have we been doing this, David?" Molina stood, walked to the window. "No matter what Sacramento says. No matter what the safety reps say."

"I told him I'd meet him down there once The Kid was asleep."

"So what happened?"

Darby shook his head. "I don't know."

The BATF spokesman was saying that they weren't sure if children were present in the compound, but that it was certainly something they were looking into, it was certainly something that would change the dynamic of the situation if it were true.

"Where is he now?" Darby said.

"Home. I told him to stay home a while. A week or so, however long. He said he was going to get a case of beer, watch TV, get drunk. I said that sounded like a good idea."

Molina picked the cups off the desk, poured the coffee into the garbage can. "There's no such thing as a one-man job, David. You know this. There's no such thing."

On the day after the doorbell had rung and the cops had stood on the porch and told him she was gone, the day after he'd told The Kid, after he'd called Bob, after he'd slept that first night in the cab of the pickup, he stood at a pay phone on Alvarado Street and dialed the number from the slip of paper in his wallet, waited through the long-distance clicks, listened to the phone ringing in Chicago.

He'd kept the paper in his wallet for years, since the time Lucy took The Kid to visit her parents over a summer break and it seemed like maybe they weren't coming back. The Kid was three at the time; they had just celebrated his birthday. Lucy had left the phone number on the kitchen table, taken The Kid's hand, lifted her suitcase and walked out of the house to the taxi waiting at the curb. Darby stood on the porch and watched them go. It was a planned vacation. Twelve days with her parents, then a return flight home. But it had become something else in the weeks leading up to the flight. The trip to Chicago was an unanswered question. Neither of them had said it explicitly, but the return ticket home no longer seemed guaranteed.

He'd called the number every night to talk to The Kid before he went to bed, to talk to Lucy for a while, soft night voices on the phone, Midwest to west coast, back and forth, a delicate negotiation, neither sure exactly what they wanted the outcome to be. Every night, twenty minutes, an hour, talking like they were discussing something that had already happened, something that had come and gone. Darby listless those twelve days, watching TV in the empty house, going out on jobs, drinking with Bob, aching for a cigarette. Thinking that maybe this should be the end, that it would be easier this way, it would be better for all of them. The Kid would adjust, The Kid would adapt. Kids did that, they survived. But he still found himself counting the days until their planned return, and then counting the days after, the postponement of the return, the no man's land after the plane tickets expired. At night he'd call the number and Earl would answer the phone, always Earl, his daughter's sudden guardian. Darby would ask to speak to Lucy or The Kid and Earl would put him through a whole rigmarole of bullshit, *Let me see if they're awake, Let me see if she's taking calls,* his voice leaking acid. On the fifteenth night, something in Darby's voice set Earl off, something in the way he asked to speak to Lucy, and Earl finally burst, barking at Darby in a hoarse whisper, *I swear I can make it so you'll never see either of them again*, this then triggering Darby, an explosion on his end of the line, a release, Darby raging in the living room, phone to his mouth. *You faker. You fraud. Suddenly you're a father again? Fuck you, you phony. Fuck you, you fraud.*

End of conversation, obviously. The line going dead out in Chicago. Darby left standing in the dark living room, holding the dial tone. He heard nothing for two days. He didn't know what to think, whether this was it, whether it was really over. And then, early on the morning of the third day, he heard an unmistakable sound, the popping of a taxicab's trunk. He went to the living room window, watched Lucy and The Kid get out of the cab and stand on the curb while the driver lifted out their suitcase. He'd never been so relieved in his life. The sound of a taxicab's trunk popping. He hadn't known what he wanted, but now he knew. He'd kept the slip of paper in his wallet to remind himself of that sound, of what was possible, what he always thought would be the worst-case scenario.

He stood at the pay phone on Alvarado the day after they'd told him she was gone, listening to the ring on the other end of the line. He half expected Earl to answer the phone, Earl's booming salesman's voice, until he remembered that Earl was gone, that Earl had been gone for almost a year.

The line clicked again and Darby heard her voice, Lucy's mother, sounding so old, so tired. *Hello?* Less a greeting than a resigned invitation to speak. A voice long-used to receiving bad news on the phone.

*Hello?* Dolores said again. That same weary tone to her voice. Hello? Hello?

He just started talking. He knew that if he didn't, he wouldn't have the courage to say anything, so he just started talking, telling the story of Lucy teaching a lesson and then falling in her classroom, Lucy lifted and carried down the hall by a student in her class, a star football player, followed to the nurse's office by a trail of concerned students, and then the cops standing on the front porch of their house, hats in hands, informing Darby as Lucy's next of kin. He told Dolores the whole story in what seemed like a single, unbroken breath. It was the most he'd ever spoken to her at one time.

Dolores said nothing. Darby listened to her breathing for a while, pictured her sitting in the dining room of the house in Chicago, late afternoon, fading light in the windows, autumn in the Midwest. She said nothing, and then she said, *Thank you for calling*, and the line clicked back to the dial tone.

She didn't come to the memorial service. Darby wasn't surprised. He understood, it made sense why she hadn't come. She was alone now and she'd had too much of this, too many phone calls taking pieces of her away.

He stood outside the Everclean garage, called Bob's aunt's house from the new cell phone. On the third ring, Bob answered the phone, his voice boozy and thick.

"If you're calling to apologize, I don't want to hear it. Wasn't your fault."

"I should have been down there."

"It was a stupid thing. Wasn't your fault." Bob coughed away from the receiver. "Molina tell you about my forced leave of absence?"

"He said he told you to take some time off."

"He told me to take a week, then we'd discuss if I was ready to come back. I said I was embarrassed enough, I don't need a week. Give me a night, two nights."

"Take the week."

"I don't need a week. How's The Kid feeling?"

"He's fine."

"What was it? The flu?"

"Something like that."

"Flu-like symptoms?"

"Just something he picked up. Nothing serious."

"Bring him by when he's feeling better. I haven't seen him in a month of Sundays."

"I was on my way down, Bob. I was just about to leave the house."

"I don't want to hear it. Wasn't your fault. It was a one-man job."

"There's no such thing."

"Tell Molina two days," Bob said. "Forty-eight hours and I'll be back. Tell him to take his leave of absence and shove it up his ass."

Miss Ramirez was frazzled, running out of patience. It was near the end of the day, the class restless, kids hanging over the sides of their chairs, pushing their seats back on two legs, one leg, whispering, passing notes, popping up, sitting down, bouncing like crickets. Every ten seconds she had to tell another student to sit down, pay attention, put their hands where she could see them.

She cleared her throat and said that she had an important announcement. There was a serious situation in the schools right now. There was something very dangerous circulating among older kids at the high schools, something they had to look out for. She held up a sheet of paper. In the center of the page was a stencil of a large blue star. The kids looked at the star. A few whispered to each other. They'd heard about this from their older brothers and sisters, from their older cousins. Miss Ramirez shushed the room. She said that some older kids had gotten hold of these blue stars, and that these blue stars were actually illegal drugs. She said the real stars were much smaller, about the size of a dime, and they were printed on little pieces of paper. They worked like tattoos. A person who used illegal drugs would lick a spot on their hand or arm and then press the blue star to their skin. She said that they all needed to look out for the blue stars, and if they saw them, to run away. If an older kid had a blue star, if an older kid tried to lick their arms or hands and press a blue star to their skin they were to yell and run away, they were to tell an adult immediately.

Agitation in the classroom. The end-of-day excitement had turned to something else, nervousness and fear. No one wanted their arms or hands licked. No one wanted a blue star pressed to their skin.

Miss Ramirez said that they'd all seen the police car and ambulance at the school. She said that she wasn't trying to scare them, but Rey Lugo had gotten very sick because of one of the blue stars. Someone had pressed a star to his arm before he got to school that day. Rey was still in the hospital, recovering. He would be okay, but it was a very serious situation. She repeated her earlier warning, that if anyone approached them with a blue star they were to run away and find an adult.

The agitation in the classroom grew. No one wanted to be like Rey Lugo, walking down the hallway in a scary daze, throwing up into their hands.

Miss Ramirez passed copies of the paper down the rows. It was a letter to parents, with the stencil reproduction of the star in the middle of the page. The kids read the letter to themselves, mouths working, trying to find any information Miss Ramirez had withheld for their parents' eyes only, anything they weren't supposed to see.

The Kid looked at the star, touched its points with his fingertips. He imagined being zombie-fied by the star like Rey Lugo, emptied out by the illegal drug it held. The thought was scary, but he couldn't stop thinking it. He imagined staring off down to the end of the hallway in disbelief, seeing things that weren't there. What had Rey seen? What would The Kid see? He wondered this as the bell rang, as the classroom emptied. He touched a point of the star. What would he see that he couldn't believe?

They ate dinner in the parking lot of a burger place on Temple Street, listening to a Country station on the radio, Darby trying to forget his conversation with Molina, the thought of Bob alone at the job site, Bob screaming in a closet.

"What do you want to go as?" Darby said.

The Kid chewed the last of their fries. *Go as what?*

"To your Halloween party. If you could go as anything. If you could dress up as anything."

*We could just go to the drug store and see what they have.*

"We can't buy a costume," Darby said. "We've never bought a costume."

*It's easier just to buy one.*

Lucy had always made The Kid's Halloween costumes. She couldn't sew, but she cobbled things together, old clothes and accessories, props made from household items. The Kid as a pirate one year; the President of the U.S. the next. A bag of groceries in fourth grade, her best work in Darby's opinion, The Kid wrapped in a giant brown paper bag she'd made out of a month's worth of supermarket bags, empty cereal boxes and milk cartons and soup cans poking out of the top, an itemized receipt taped to his front. The Kid won second place in the school's costume contest that year, brought home a gift certificate for a children's bookstore that he was so proud of he refused to redeem, keeping it displayed on a shelf in his bedroom instead.

Darby turned in his seat, looked at The Kid. "You're going to go to school with those cards, those great cards we made, and you're going to show up in a cheapo costume?"

The Kid shrugged, took a pull on his root beer.

"No way," Darby said. "We need a costume worthy of those cards."

They went to the thrift store on Vermont Avenue, looked through the overburdened racks of second- and third-hand clothes, shirts and pants and three-piece suits. The Kid started to brighten a little, started to warm to the idea. He decided that he'd dress as a character from his comic: Smooshie Smith, Talk Show Host of the Future. They couldn't find anything in the boys' section, but over on the mens' rack Darby found the perfect Smooshie Smith blazer, yellow and green checked, loud as a police siren, small enough that it would only look slightly absurd hanging off The Kid's slim shoulders. The Kid came over with a clip-on tie he'd pulled from a display, stripes that clashed beautifully with the blazer's checks, a knot as big as Darby's fist. Darby navigated The Kid into the blazer, clipped the tie to the front of The Kid's school shirt. The Kid looked ridiculous. The Kid looked great. They could roll the blazer's sleeves under, pin the extra fabric at the back. He steered The Kid to a full-length mirror by the restrooms. The Kid grinned at his reflection. They bought the blazer and tie, a mustard yellow dress shirt, a pair of lime green golf slacks. The whole outfit came to five bucks. The Kid insisted on paying with money he'd saved from his allowance. He still felt bad about the ruined clothes from his gym locker. Darby let him pay, hoped it would put the issue to rest.

Back at the house, Darby pulled a kitchen chair out onto the front porch, plugged the electric clippers into an outlet in the living room, ran the cord out through the window, between the security bars. Turned on the living room lights, the porch light, so he could see what he was doing. The Kid sat in the chair with a bath towel draped over his shoulders, while Darby cut his hair. The buzz of the clippers in the quiet of the evening, the sound of the radio through the open windows of the pickup, the same Country station, a Merle Travis song, *Sixteen Tons*. Darby turned The Kid's head gently, careful to get the cut symmetrical, not to go too short, not to nick The Kid's scalp. The Kid used to sing while Darby did this, that overloud voice belting TV commercial jingles and sitcom theme songs, Lucy back at her desk in the darkening house, grading papers, singing right along, Darby trying to keep The Kid's head still while he sang, while he kicked his feet to the rhythm and turned to warble a line back to his mother. Darby kidding The Kid every couple of minutes, a little strangled noise to imply that he'd screwed the cut up horribly, an old joke, The Kid rolling his eyes, not too concerned. The idea that his father could make a mistake was so ridiculous that it didn't warrant a serious response.

The Kid sat still now, looking out across the front yard at a skinny stray cat crossing under the streetlight. Darby held The Kid's head in his hands, hummed along with Merle Travis, trying not to think of Bob in a small closet, screaming.

When he was done, he patted The Kid on the shoulder, the all-clear sign. The Kid hopped down from the chair and shook out his towel, went inside to get the broom and dustpan.

Darby didn't want the night to begin yet, didn't want The Kid to go up to bed. The looming silence of the house pressed behind him, a ferocious thing, something Darby had to push back against, something he had to keep at bay. He didn't want to be alone in the house, in the pickup, waiting for a call on the pager.

He pulled an empty cardboard box from the garage, some glue, some tape, a halfway-sharp scoring razor. He found a nearly fuzzless tennis ball in a back corner near the drawer where the ring slept, where the snow globe slept. He opened another drawer where he kept odds and ends he'd collected over the years, things he thought might be useful someday in the house, knobs from the original kitchen cabinet doors, snips of multicolored electrical wire, an unused light switch. He carried everything back onto the porch. He cut the box into flat slabs, drew an outline on the cardboard, erased when he screwed up, drew again. The Kid came out with the broom but never started sweeping, more interested in watching what Darby was doing. Darby finally got the outline right, cut out the shape with the razor. Rolled the cardboard into a tube and glued the ends together. Held the ends, waiting for the glue to take. The Kid stood over Darby's shoulder, trying to figure out what he was making. Darby didn't say anything. He liked watching The Kid trying to guess, the look of serious concentration on his face. He cut a hole in the bottom of the tennis ball, the same diameter as the cardboard tube, fixed the tube into the hole. Screwed a couple of cabinet knobs into the sides, looped some of the colored wire around the tube's base, cut another small opening in the side and fixed the light switch into place. He held up the finished creation, tapped the tennis ball a couple of times with his finger, blew into the tennis ball, spoke into the microphone.

"Check, check, one-two."

The Kid's face split into a full-toothed smile, a look of genuine, delighted amazement, something Darby hadn't seen in a over a year.

Darby swept the porch while The Kid tried on the full costume up in his room. After a few minutes he came down the stairs, attempting to hold the microphone and write in his notebook at the same time.

*How do I look?* He stood on the bottom step, lifted the microphone up to Darby for an answer.

"You look great, Kid. You look like a million bucks."

The Kid smiled again, hopped off the bottom stair and did his old trademark move, the soft shoe *ta-da!* sidestep Lucy had taught him, landing with his legs stretched to their limits, his arms extended, hands shaking for emphasis. It was the way he'd once ended every episode of *It's That Kid!*, the exclamation point of the show, his final goodbye to the audience before leaving the stage. The Showbiz Shuffle, Lucy had called it. Darby clapped for the Shuffle. He and Lucy had always clapped for the Shuffle. The Kid smiled and nodded at the applause, lifted the microphone to his mouth. Darby realized that he was holding his breath, hoping that The Kid would be overcome by the moment and say what he'd always said in response to applause, Thank you, *Thank you very much.* That The Kid would speak into the microphone. But The Kid just smiled and nodded, bowing once, twice, acknowledging the applause, backing up the stairs to his bedroom, making his silent exit.

The Kid woke before his alarm with a different feeling in his stomach. A fluttering in his belly, not entirely bad. Nervous butterflies. He got washed up in the bathroom, rolled deodorant under his arms, brushed his teeth, gargled, zipped up his costume pants, buttoned his costume shirt, wrestled into his blazer, clipped on his tie. Stood in front of the bathroom mirror, practicing his Smooshie Smith smile.

His dad came in from the pickup. They sat at the kitchen table and his dad drank coffee while The Kid picked at his cereal, too nervous to eat. His dad drove him to school so nothing would happen to his costume along the way. The Kid checked his new backpack for the millionth time, making sure the cards were still there, all twenty-three, that none had gotten bent or ripped, that they were lying safe and flat between his math and reading anthology books.

They pulled up outside the front gate. The Kid tapped the tennis ball on his microphone with his finger, moved the mic from one hand to the other, practicing his technique, the smooth exchange from left to right.

*Where's Mom?* He wanted to ask that question and hold the microphone out to his dad. He wanted his dad to know that he knew the truth, that it was okay, he understood, but he just wanted to know where she was, if she was safe. He just wanted to know if maybe she was coming back. The Kid wanted this moment to be an exception from the Covenant so he could ask that one question. That would be it, two words: *Where's Mom?* It wouldn't even be him asking, it would be Smooshie Smith. But he knew he couldn't risk it. He'd kept to the Covenant for this long, he couldn't go back on it now. He nodded to his dad and got down out of the pickup.

Vampires, cowboys, cops, race car drivers, Lakers players, rock and roll stars. The schoolyard was filled with costumes. The Kid felt dizzy. Norma Valenzuela dressed as a firefighter. Razz wearing a t-shirt that said, *This is My Costume.* Rhonda Sizemore in a puffy blue dress, carrying a plastic scepter, wearing a golden crown on her head. Some of the kids thought she was dressed as a princess, but whenever they said that she corrected them. She was not a princess, she was the queen.

The Kid found Matthew standing by the dodgeball wall, glowering at the other kids in their getups. Whenever someone asked where his costume was, Matthew told them that it was a super-powered costume, that the costume was invisible. The other kids didn't seem to be buying it.

"Is it true about your dad?" Matthew said.

*What?*

"That he tried to fight Rhonda's mom at the mall? That she almost had to call the police?"

*Not exactly.*

"They said that maybe he's making the blue stars."

*Who's making them?*

"Your dad. Because of all his tattoos. They said he's making the blue stars and giving them to older kids to stick onto littler kids."

*That's not true.*

"I didn't say it was true," Matthew said. "I'm just telling you what I heard."

Brian was talking to Arizona on the far side of the yard. He wore yellow running shorts, a yellow tank top with a white number 1 on the back, wristbands, a headband. The Kid didn't know if he was dressed up as some famous runner that The Kid didn't know about, or if he was just dressed as himself, if that was famous enough. Arizona was dressed as a forest ranger. She wore a wide-brimmed brown hat and a green shirt and slacks, carried what looked like a fishing net on the end of a short stick, something to catch bears, maybe, coyotes in the woods.

The classroom was anxious, fidgety. They did the math lesson, social studies, language arts. They made mail pouches out of orange and black construction paper and taped them to the sides of their desks. Special delivery. The Kid made a sign, taped it next to the mail pouch. *Come be Interviewed by Smooshie Smith, Talk Show Host of the Future.*

He was nervous about how his cards would be received. He tried not to think about it. Instead, he watched Miss Ramirez's hands as she wrote vocabulary words on the dry erase board. He drew Miss Ramirez's hands in his notebook, tried to get the smooth lines right, the crooks and curves, the shading and shadows that made her fingers look like flesh and blood, like real, alive hands.

At lunch, The Kid and Matthew sat at their table, picked at their food. Michelle wasn't around. The Kid guessed that she was in Mr. Bromwell's office, talking about whatever she talked about. Her real dad in Minneapolis. The Kid asked Matthew if he wanted to be interviewed by Smooshie Smith, but Matthew shook his head. He was in a bad mood. He told The Kid that he didn't care if it meant he would go to hell, he just wanted to wear a stupid Halloween costume.

Arizona sat down beside The Kid, set her fishing net on the table.

"I want to be interviewed," she said.

The Kid looked at her.

"I want to be interviewed. I saw your sign."

Sweat started on the back of The Kid's neck. He tried to get it together, calm down, tried to think back over the talk-show tapes, all the things he'd learned and practiced. He took a sip from his juice box, hoped that his bad breath would go away, even if just for the length of the interview.

He flipped the switch on the microphone, adjusted the volume knob. Turned to a blank page in his notebook. Matthew looked up from his lunch, the only member of the audience.

*How do you like it in California so far?*

Arizona smiled, self-conscious. She leaned forward and spoke into the microphone.

"I think it's great. I like it here a lot."

*What's better about this place than the place you used to live?*

"The people are nicer."

*Really?*

"The people are much nicer."

*Have you made any friends?*

"Lots."

*Name three.*

"Rhonda S., you, Matthew."

The Kid felt his ears burning. He looked across the table. Matthew was looking down at his lunch again, but his ears were red, too.

*Let's take a question from the audience.*

The Kid and Arizona looked at Matthew. The Kid held the microphone across the table.

Matthew swallowed the mouthful of sandwich he'd been chewing. "Is Brian Bromwell your friend?" he said. "And if so, why?"

*One question at a time.*

"It's a question and a follow up question," Matthew said. "I know my rights."

The Kid turned the microphone back to Arizona.

"He is my friend," she said, "because he's very sweet and very funny."

Matthew rolled his eyes, looked back down at his lunch.

Just hearing the name made The Kid turn to find Brian in the yard, make sure he was a safe distance away. He was over on the other side of the pavilion, standing at the head of Rhonda's crowded table, next to Arizona's empty seat, watching the interview at The Kid's table. His eyes were narrowed, trying to figure out what was going on. He was too far away to hear, but The Kid still felt that flush of cold fear in his belly.

*How is he funny?* The Kid wrote, turning back to Arizona. *Funny looking?*

"No," she said, giving The Kid a disapproving look.

*Funny smelling?*

"No," she said, laughing a little. The Kid felt tingly, felt electric writing this about Brian while he was standing within sight, when he could come over at any minute. He felt brave for some reason, saying these things, brave, or stupid, or both, that little laugh from Arizona egging him on, making him braver, stupider.

Matthew read what The Kid was writing, looked across the tables at Brian, fear on his face, too, but something else as well. Excitement.

*Funny how?* The Kid wrote. He waited a few seconds for the anticipation of his guest to build, for the anticipation of his audience, patient, patient, waiting like he'd seen and rehearsed all those times with his mom the mornings.

*Funny in the head?*

And at this Arizona laughed out loud, a musical jingle, and Matthew laughed along, too, and The Kid could hear the applause from the studio audience, a delighted roar rising, cheers and clapping and guffaws.

Arizona's hand was holding his arm. She was laughing so hard that she was holding The Kid's arm without even knowing it.

*Thank you,* The Kid wrote when the applause had died down a little. *Thank you very much.*

It was time, finally. They opened their folders and bags, reached into the furthest corners of their desks, digging for their Halloween cards. The Kid opened his backpack, carefully slid out his cards. Counted them again quickly, one last time. Gave them the final once-over. He thought that they looked good. He was proud of the cards, the combination of his drawings and his dad's backgrounds and added details. They'd made a good team.

The kids lined up in front of the board, boy-girl, boy-girl, all clutching their cards to their chests. Rhonda Sizemore went first, threading her way through the desks, dropping cards into the corresponding mail pouches. The other kids followed one at a time. When it was The Kid's turn, he started down the first row, placing the right card into each pouch. He tried to ignore the kids still standing at the board, holding their noses whenever he passed.

When they returned to their desks and started digging through their mail, they found that Miss Ramirez had placed a card and a few pieces of candy in each pouch, foil-wrapped chocolate pumpkins and bright orange suckers. The kids tore open their candy, reading their cards and chattering while Miss Ramirez sat behind her desk and wrote in her grade book. The Kid didn't need to count his cards to know that there were far fewer in his pouch than there should have been. Twenty-three kids in the class minus himself plus Miss Ramirez should have made for twenty-three cards. He looked back at Michelle's desk, thinking that she'd probably received even less cards than he had, but her desk was still empty. She was still at Mr. Bromwell's office or had gone home or something. He looked over at Matthew's desk, but Matthew seemed to have quite a few cards. Not twenty-three, but quite a few.

Six cards. The Kid had received six cards out of twenty-three. One from Miss Ramirez that said, *Whitley, I appreciate your spirit and sense of determination.* One from Matthew that said, *Kid, I'm glad you come over for dinner and don't forget our deal about the comic books.* One from Arizona, a handmade card, a drawing of a buttercup under a bright blue sky that said, *I hope we're friends long enough for you to tell me the secret.*

Six cards. The Kid knew that he shouldn't feel bad, knew what his mom would have told him, that he should be happy for the cards he got, that he should appreciate those cards and not worry about the ones he didn't get. He knew he shouldn't feel bad, but he did anyway.

One of the cards was from Rhonda Sizemore, a store-bought card with a painting of a jack-o-lantern on the front. Inside, she'd written, *Whitley Darby, I appreciate your perfect attendance.* It didn't make any sense. It didn't mean anything. The Kid didn't have perfect attendance. He had terrible attendance. He could picture Rhonda and her mother reading the list of students in the class, writing out a card for each one, saying something nice and meaningless rather than saying nothing. *I appreciate your perfect attendance.* It made The Kid feel worse than if he hadn't gotten a card from her at all.

Miss Ramirez told them to finish up with their cards and candy. A procession began to the trashcan at the front of the room, kids throwing out candy wrappers and foil and envelopes. The Kid popped his chocolate pumpkin into his mouth, crumpled the wrapper, made his way up to the trashcan. Backpacks were zipped, chairs squeaked and settled as the kids got ready to switch classes for science. The Kid opened his fist and let the wrapper fall into the garbage, on top of the other wrappers and empty envelopes and old test papers.

There was something else in there, piled with the trash. Something with the wrappers and envelopes and banana peels and wads of bubble gum. The Kid's heart was pounding. He moved a chocolate-stained envelope out of the way. His cards were in there. What seemed like the entire class's worth, crumpled and thrown away. He recognized them all. The pirate ship cards, the tall city building cards, the Smooshie Smith cards, all the drawings of his characters and his dad's tattoos. Some of the cards torn, some of the cards balled up, some smeared with chocolate fingerprints, wrapped around half-chewed suckers. His cards were in there. All of the time he and his dad had spent working at the picnic table, all wasted now. He heard giggling, Razz and a couple of boys from the back of the class. The Kid turned, looked out into the room, blurry-eyed. Some of the girls stopped whispering and looked away when he looked at them. Other kids were holding their noses and smiling and they didn't look away, they pinched their noses tighter and smiled wider when he looked at them. They didn't care if he saw them or not. Why should they care? The Kid was garbage, just like his cards.

He looked over at Matthew but Matthew looked down at his science book. Where was his card, the card The Kid had made with the black crow with *X*'s for eyes? *I'm glad that you're my friend.* Was that card in the garbage, too?

The Kid walked back down the aisle toward his desk, past the sniggering and pinched noses, past Razz gagging. When he got to Rhonda Sizemore's seat, she looked up at him, her nose wrinkled in disgust. He felt the same way he'd felt at the mall, ashamed and embarrassed that his dad had seen Rhonda not wanting to sit next to him, angry that she looked at him like he was a piece of garbage. He forced himself to look at her, look her in the eye, and when her expression didn't change, he took a quick, backhanded swing and knocked the crown off her head, just like that, and then he had a handful of her hair and was pulling, hard, Rhonda screaming, the kids around her screaming, The Kid yanking Rhonda out of her seat, some of her hair coming out into The Kid's hand, and then Miss Ramirez was there, grabbing The Kid roughly by the arm, prying his fist open, dragging him out of the classroom into the hall. Miss Ramirez's face was bright red. She shouted at him in a raspy whisper. She didn't know what the hell had gotten into him. He was to stand out in the hall until she checked on Rhonda, and then they were going directly to the vice-principal's office.

Miss Ramirez went back into the classroom. The Kid could hear Rhonda sobbing, other kids yelling, the room in an uproar. His whole body was shaking. Loose strands of Rhonda's hair were stuck between his fingers. His face was wet. He must have been crying, but it didn't feel like he was crying, he was too angry and upset. He was worried what Arizona thought of him now, if she thought all the other kids had been right, if she thought he was an untouchable. He wanted to go to Mr. Bromwell's office, use the phone, type in the Morse Code *S.O.S.*, have his dad come and pick him up. He wanted to go to the drive-thru, sit in the parking lot with their burgers and fries, listen to a game on the radio. He wanted it to be baseball season. He wanted everything to be different.

He stood in the hallway, really crying now, fists balled at his sides, what sounded like screaming in his head, so it took him a second to hear it, a high-pitched whine coming down the hall, the grinding and groaning of shifting wood, and then the sound turned the corner and they were upon him, passing in front of him in a rush, blue and green woodcut waves sliding down the hallway, rising and falling, shifting back and forth, the little woodcut rowboat coming his way, tossed by the waves, the woodcut men paddling, their arm hinges squealing with the strain, and then an even louder noise, an incredible grinding racket as it appeared around the corner, the massive pirate ship filling the hallway, skull and bones on its wooden flag flying, the ship bearing down on the doomed rowboat, splinters spraying as its prow crashed through the waves, the cacophony filling the hall, the school, The Kid's head, and he turned just in time to see

another wave coming right toward him, hard wood, the wave coming down the hall with terrific speed, twice as tall as The Kid, almost
upon him, ready to crush him or sweep him away if he didn't move,
if he didn't run and get out of the way.

The Kid blinked away tears, stood and watched the wave lifting
above him, reaching the top of its height and then curling over, its
shadow covering him, the wave ready to crash back down.

The Kid plugged his nose, closed his eyes. Didn't move.

She was sitting on the steps outside a Pico Boulevard apartment complex when Darby first saw her. A Saturday afternoon in early fall. He was working floral delivery at the time, a job he'd held for the better part of a year, driving a purple van with a painting of a group of smiley-faced, slightly unhinged-looking flowers waving on the side. He drove slowly, twisting his head under the windshield, searching in vain for house numbers, something resembling an address, and then there she was, sitting on the steps, reading a newsmagazine, smoking a cigarette. Jeans, white t-shirt, glasses, blond hair tucked back behind her ears. Barefoot. The magazine in one hand, cover folded back, the cigarette in the fingers of her other hand. Legs crossed, foot dangling. Looking bored, annoyed, a little put off. He knew the flowers were for her even before he saw the number on the wall above her head. He double-parked the van, climbed into the back, checked the name on the card. *Lucille*. Made sense, somehow. She looked like a Lucille. He opened the box. Six roses, the industry-standard peace offering. He opened the card. An apology from someone named Roger. He hopped out onto the street, headed up the sidewalk. Took another glance at how she held the cigarette, how her foot dangled, that formidable look on her face as she read the magazine, the cigarette in the corner of her mouth as she turned the page, squint-eyed in the smoke. Lucille. Darby crumpled, then pocketed, the card.

She lifted her head when he got closer, looked him over, the long white box in his hand, the tattoos, the purple polo shirt with the smiling flowers on the chest. He was suddenly, abnormally self-conscious, wishing he had something else to wear in the van, a jacket, something to cover up that ridiculous shirt.

She took a drag on the cigarette as she watched him approach.

"Hey, look," he said. "I'm at the end of my shift and I've got this unclaimed delivery."

She lifted her eyebrows over the rims of her glasses, nodded, not particularly interested.

"They're just going to sit in the van, die on the way back to the shop."

"Are you offering them to me?"

"I'll trade you. You got another cigarette?"

"What are they?"

"Roses."

"What color?"

"Red."

She thought about this, took another drag on the cigarette. Reached for her pack on the step behind her, shook one out, handed it to Darby.

"That happen a lot?" she said. "Unclaimed delivery?"

"You don't believe me?"

She passed him a lighter. "I just don't want to take somebody else's flowers."

"Unclaimed delivery," he said. "Happens more than you'd think."

He blew off the rest of his shift. They sat and talked for the better part of an hour, and as he left they made a date for later in the week. The next day, he came up with maybe the first-ever mental catalogue of the all the clothes he owned, everything crammed into his closet or heaped on the floor of his apartment. T-shirts, jeans, work pants, boots. He couldn't think of anything he wouldn't be embarrassed for her to see him in. He went to the Sears on Santa Monica Boulevard, made his way through the tight paths between clothing racks, looking for he wasn't quite sure what. Something suitable. Finally found a sale shelf with a yellow, short-sleeved button down. It fit, it looked sharp. He wore it the night of the date, feeling that maybe it was good luck.

They went to dinner, went to a movie. They sat in a diner in Echo Park, drinking beer and then coffee until three or four in the morning. She talked nonstop. She told him about her school and her students. She told him about her love of the Dodgers, which was passed down from her estranged father, some kind of con man in Chicago from what Darby could gather. She told him what she liked to cook. He sat and listened mostly, amazed at her level of investment, how deeply she cared about each thing she told him. He sat and listened and watched, happy to do so, the sound of her voice blanketing everything.

Darby considered it a perfect thing, that night, one of the two perfect nights of his life. Sitting in that diner listening to her talk.

He'd just come back from the restroom, right after the waitress dropped off the check, right before they drove back to Darby's apartment, and Lucy leaned over on her side of the booth and pulled a camera out of her overstuffed purse. She fired a shot across the table, the flash blinding Darby, popping white and gray spots in front of his eyes. He would forget all about it until years later, until one day it was there on the bulletin board above her desk in their house, an image of that night, Darby in his lucky yellow shirt on the other side of the booth, eyes wide in the flash, looking stunned and happy.

The animal shelter was a half-mile south of downtown, a concrete building with a bronze plaque out front listing the dogs and cats that had been adopted and subsequently starred in movies and TV shows. Famous rescues. Darby walked down a long fluorescent-lit corridor. The corridor smelled like a restroom, wet fur, some kind of pine-scented disinfectant. There were pens on either side of the corridor, dogs behind the cage doors lunging, snapping, whining, cowering. Chows and terriers and Chihuahuas, pit bull, pit bull, pit bull, every other dog a pit, seemed like, slant eyed and broad shouldered, pink-nosed faces like raw steaks.

Every pen had a clipboard hanging from the bars, a dossier on the dog inside with a list of ailments, vaccinations, warnings if the dog was hostile or unpredictable or both. The staff had given every dog a name, all at great odds with their physical realities, dignified names of childhood pets in good homes: Charmer, Caesar, Ranger, Scout.

The sewer dog was at the end of the corridor, last pen on the right, laying on his side against the rear wall. He opened his eyes when Darby stopped at the bars. His fur was still patchy and matted, but the sores along his backside had begun to scab over. A bowl of dry food sat untouched a few feet from his head. Darby looked at the clipboard hanging from the bars. Diagnosis of his skin condition, malnutrition. He weighed fifty-two pounds, and there was a seventy-five in brackets next to that, probably his ideal weight. Someone had drawn a question mark next to *Breed*. The space next to *Name* had been left blank.

Darby crouched by the bars. The dog lifted his head.

"They found him in the sewer." A short, husky woman was standing behind Darby. An animal control officer. She adjusted the waist of her slacks, jangling a brace of keys clipped to her belt. Her uniform was too small. It had shrunk in the wash or she had put on some weight since its original issue.

"They found him near my house," Darby said.

"Our officer said he'd been living down there for days. A week, maybe. Could have gone down at almost any point in the city, maneuvered his way around. Chasing rats or whatever for food."

"Do they know how he got down there?"

"The odds of a dog willfully crawling down into the sewer are slim to none," she said. "Which means he was pushed in there, shoved down into one of those openings in the curb."

"Inlet."

"Pushed down through an inlet. Big dog like that, had to be somebody bigger who shoved him through. Imagine that, wandering around there in the dark. Who knows what else is down there. Rats would be the least of my worries."

The dog watched them warily, his eyes moving from Darby to the officer and back again.

"Is he going to make it?" Darby said.

"He'll make it. He didn't pick up anything particularly nasty down there, except for the skin condition, which we're treating. He's been given his shots. Just needs to eat, rest."

"What happens to him now?"

"If no one takes him home, we put him down. Four days from date of entry." She looked at the clipboard. "Meaning two days from today. Business days."

"Anyone come to look at him?"

"People come to look. We tell the story of how he was found and people come down to look."

"What are the chances of somebody taking him home?"

"About the same as his chances of crawling into the sewer unassisted. Dog that size will eat you out of house and home if he ever starts eating again."

The dog lifted his head higher, slowly, then got to his feet, tall and unsteady, wobbling on his toothpick legs but standing nonetheless, upright under his own power.

"Is he friendly?" Darby said. "I didn't see any warnings on his sheet."

"He's a sweetheart. He's a little scared, a little testy, but he's a sweetheart."

The dog took a tentative step toward the bars, issued a low growl.

"Don't worry about the growling," the officer said. "He's friendly. Has to be. He's got nothing left in the tank."

The officer walked back up the corridor, her jangling keys setting off another wave of barking and howling. The sewer dog adjusted his stance, found solid footing. He looked at Darby and curled a corner of his mouth, just a little, showing a yellowed fang. Darby stayed in his crouch, holding the dog's stare, admiring the sharp little warning. The dog motivated by the insult, maybe, the whole insult from sewer inlet to animal control van to pen at the pound. The dog showing teeth, making things clear, protecting the only thing he had left.

He'd been taken to the vice-principal and the vice-principal had sent him to Mr. Bromwell. Mr. Bromwell asked him why he'd done what he'd done. The Kid didn't explain about the Halloween cards. He just shrugged by way of an answer and asked if Mr. Bromwell was going to call his dad. Mr. Bromwell raised his eyebrows and asked The Kid if he thought his dad should be called. The Kid didn't know exactly where all this was going, if he was in trouble or not, but apparently no one called because when he got home at the end of the day his dad didn't mention it, didn't sit him down and give him one of those quiet talks The Kid used to get when he was in trouble, the talks where his dad told him that his behavior needed to change, and fast. Instead, his dad asked how the party went, how the cards and costume had gone over. The Kid wrote that it had been fine, it had been great. The cards and costume had been a big hit. His dad asked him if he wanted to go trick-or-treating that night, but The Kid said that he didn't think so. The party at school had been enough.

His dad had bought a bag of small-sized Hershey bars and whenever some kids in Halloween costumes came up on the porch and rang the doorbell, he answered the door and dropped a couple of bars into their bags. The Kid sat by the living room window watching the trick-or-treaters come by, or he went up to his bedroom and watched out that window if he suspected he knew the kids in the costumes. He was worried that one of the kids would tell his dad about the ruined Halloween cards or what The Kid had done to Rhonda Sizemore. He was worried that a parent would see all his dad's tattoos and start shouting that his dad was responsible for what had happened to Rey Lugo, that his dad was creating the blue stars out of illegal drugs.

He wondered if Arizona would come by, imagined her dad the military man taking her around the neighborhood, maybe carrying his machine gun for protection. If he had a machine gun. The Kid imagined her seeing his shabby house, imagined her dad and his dad getting into a fight like the fight his dad had gotten into at the mall. He kind of hoped she wouldn't come by, but he also kind of hoped she would. He didn't know which would be better or worse.

By nine o'clock or so, the trick-or-treating seemed to be over. Arizona hadn't come by. Out on the street it was just older kids, most without costumes, some just with rubber monster masks or black ski masks, running around, roughhousing, shouting and swearing at each other, climbing fences, kicking empty beer cans down the sidewalk. The Kid went into the bathroom to get ready for bed. He held his toothbrush, looked in the mirror. He had a new haircut, but it was the same Kid, the same face everybody hated, the same B.O. and bad breath. He put his toothbrush down. Why even bother?

He got into his pajamas, got into bed. Before too long he heard his dad's pager buzz. The Kid played dead while he listened to his dad getting his stuff together, felt him standing in the bedroom doorway, heard the front door locking, the pickup's engine fading down the street. The Kid got dressed again, grabbed his backpack and went back downstairs.

He stood out on the front porch. It felt darker than usual, wilder, a strange night, a dangerous night.  It was still Halloween, even though the trick-or-treaters were all home in bed. He couldn't even imagine how mad his dad would be if he knew The Kid was outside.

He locked the front door behind him and walked up the street toward Sunset. It was colder than it had been in some time. There were shadows leaping everywhere, in the alleys between apartment buildings, in the yards behind houses. Big kids, high school kids with flashlights chasing each other, jumping fences and walls, running from yard to yard, vanishing behind buildings and then reappearing in the spaces between. Sometimes a few of them got caught in the flashlight beams, and The Kid could see rubber monster masks, fright wigs, white skeleton face-paint.

He tried not to be scared. He was on a mission. He tried to think of the burned house, the angel without her hand, the pages of hands he'd drawn in his notebook. He kept walking, heading across Sunset, past the strip mall, past the cardboard box and the raggedy feet.

He stood at the bottom of the hill, across the street from the burned house. It was still standing. They hadn't torn it down yet. The question was, Was the scotch tape in place on the door? The question was, Had anyone else been inside and seen the angel? The Kid looked around, making sure there were no faces in the neighboring windows, then he ran across to the burned house's yard, up onto the soft wood of the porch.

He crouched in the shadows, catching his breath. There was something attached to the front door of the house. He crawled closer. Four glossy photographs were wedged behind the metal slats of the security door. He looked at the photos in the glow from the streetlight. The red-haired woman was in each of them. In one photo she was standing beside a bald man. They were both holding up beer cans in a salute, smiling at the camera. In another she was sitting on a woman's lap on a yellow couch. The red-haired woman was wearing the yellow dress and cowboy boots from the chalk drawing. Both the red-haired woman and the woman with the lap were laughing, heads back, mouths open, the white blast of the camera's flash reflected in the window behind their heads. In another picture she was standing beside an older lady, gray-haired, stoop-shouldered. The red-haired woman was smiling and the gray-haired woman was trying to manage half a smile. They looked alike. They had the same eyes, those big green eyes with long dark lashes. Her mom, maybe. In the last picture the red-haired woman was standing alone at a gas pump. She was wearing the yellow dress and the cowboy boots again. She wasn't smiling so much as smirking. Head cocked, hand on her hip, looking at the camera like, What are you going to do about it? That sort of look. Real tough.

The Kid couldn't say that he thought the red-haired woman was beautiful, like he thought Arizona was beautiful, or even like he thought Rhonda Sizemore was beautiful. Perfect in the face. The

198          SCOTT O'CONNOR

red-haired woman's head was too small, her nose was too big. He couldn't say she was beautiful, but something about her was nice to look at. It seemed like she was the kind of person his mom would call A Good Egg. It seemed like she probably told pretty good jokes.

There were a couple of red roses on the porch by the door, petals dry and dark, stems brittle. The Kid picked them up, looked them over, careful not to poke himself on the thorns. Who had been there? Friends? Relatives? The people in the pictures, maybe. Maybe they'd had a memorial service and come back here after, like some people had gone back to Amanda's house after his mom's fake memorial service. Maybe they'd gone inside to scoop some of the cremated ashes out of the bedroom.

The Kid ran his hand up the doorjamb, feeling for the tape. It was still there, one-half affixed to the door, one-half to the jamb. No one had gone inside. The smell of the house was still strong. He dug into his backpack, pulled on the goggles and facemask. He peeled the tape off and opened the door, trying not to disturb any of the photographs. Then he stepped inside and turned on the flashlight.

The front room looked the same. The Kid didn't know what he was expecting. That someone had snuck in and cleaned it all up? There was still glass all over the dining room floor, crunching under his sneakers. There were the little silverware meteorites, the sagging cabinets back in the kitchen. He stopped at the door to the bedroom. Everything was like he remembered, the skeleton of the bed frame, the burned mattress, the charred wall above the bed. He walked down to the living room, set the flashlight on the floor so he could see as much of the far wall as possible.

She was still there, the red-haired woman and her wings, lifting off the ground toward that hole in the ceiling, still missing a hand.

The Kid looked in his notebook at the drawings of women's hands. He'd wanted to finish the drawing, but the hands he'd drawn just didn't work, they just didn't match. He knew that he'd make a mess of the angel if he tried drawing a hand. He needed more practice.

He wondered if the angel was scared or lonely. He knew it was a stupid thing to think of a drawing being scared, but he couldn't help it. He thought of his mom in a place like this, hiding and waiting, and he knew that she would be scared, that she would wish there was something else to keep her company.

The Kid started to draw. He picked up one of the pieces of white chalk from the floor and started on the wall to his left, far away from the angel. He didn't want to infringe on that drawing. He started drawing woodcut waves. He tried to picture what they'd looked like when they'd flooded the hallway at school, tried to draw the grain and the knotholes correctly, the depth to the sheets of wood, one wave in front of the other, some higher, some lower, rising and falling. He looked around on the floor for more chalk. Found a blue piece and a green piece, started to color the waves, swirls of both colors mixing, darker at the bottom where the wooden water looked deeper, lighter at the top where it was really just splinters of foam. He climbed up on what was left of an armchair and drew a wooden seagull in the sky, flying out from behind a woodcut cloud. There were holes in the wall, big spots where chunks of plaster had fallen or burned away, exposing the house's wooden frame. He drew the waves crashing up and over the holes, treated those holes as giant rocks, even drew a seagull perched on top of one.

He worked from memory, what he had seen in the hall, what he'd seen on his dad's arm a million times. He drew the pirate ship, the curving sides of the great hull, the canons poking through, the Jolly Roger flapping up top. He drew the tiny rowboat tossing in the waves, trying to outrun the pirate ship. The two desperate men bailing water, the disbelieving exclamation points floating over their heads.

He drew until he was sweating pretty badly in the muggy room, until the goggles were foggy and the facemask was wet. He stepped down from the armchair, looked at what he'd drawn. It filled almost half of one wall, the whole picture of what he'd seen in the school hallway, what he'd seen on his dad's arm. Some company for the angel. He shone the flashlight across the drawing, feeling not too bad about what he'd done.

They took the sharp, quick curves of the freeway south, through the tunnels under the hills, the lanes gradually straightening, widening, the lit skyscrapers of downtown appearing on the other side of the last rise, the van finally drifting down the long slope of the off ramp into the streets of Chinatown. Red and green neon reflected in the windshield, across the broad hood of the van, Chinese characters, signs for shops and restaurants, the businesses all closed and gated, dark-windowed, their parking lots empty.

"What do you think?" Roistler said. "I want to know what you think."

"I don't think anything," Darby said.

"About Bob. About what happened to Bob."

"I don't think anything."

Roistler sat in the passenger seat, his flushed face lit by the orange glow of the dashboard radio, his knees jumping, over-amped and anxious.

"I'm trying to get this straight," he said. "What I'm supposed to do and what you're supposed to do."

"It's like any two-man job. Nothing's different."

"That's not true. We've never done a two-man before. I've worked with Bob and you've worked with Bob. But without Bob, we shift a spot. You do his things, I do yours."

The address on the work order was a seafood restaurant, the bottom floor of a three-story brick building. Darby parked the van at the curb. The neon sign in the front window was unlit, but a young man was standing outside the door, smoking a cigarette. He wore black slacks and a white dress shirt, a stained white apron folded down at his waist.

"Just give me a second," Roistler said, "to get this all straight."

"Nothing's different," Darby said. He opened the door, stepped out onto the street.

"Everything's different," Roistler said. "I'm you. I'm you and you're Bob."

They suited up at the back of the van. Darby approached the waiter, started to talk through the work order, but the waiter shook his head. He wasn't the one Darby was supposed to talk to. He led them into the restaurant, through the main dining room. The chairs were turned up on the tables; the low-hanging chandeliers were dark. The only light in the room came from fluorescents in the fish tanks that lined the walls. There was movement in the water, eel and lobster and crab. In the center of the room was a host's station, a wooden podium piled with menus. The waiter opened a door behind the podium, nodded Darby through.

It took a few seconds for his eyes to adjust to the darkness. An enclosed stairwell, steep and narrow, two flights up. At the top was an open door. In the light from the room beyond he could see the silhouette of a man sitting on the high landing.

Darby started up, the stairs creaking with his weight. Roistler stayed down at the bottom, holding his bucket of brushes and sprays. The waiter was gone. He'd left for the night, maybe, or stepped back outside to smoke. As he climbed, Darby could see more of the man at the top of the steps. He was thin, Asian, middle-aged. His hair was slicked back from his high forehead. He was wearing a dark suit. He sat with his head down and his wrists resting on his knees, his hands held up at a strange angle, as if he were protecting them, as if he were keeping them away from the rest of his body.

The work order said that the father would be present at the job site. The father of the girl the coroner's people had taken from the room.

The moonman suit crinkled as Darby climbed the stairs. He realized too late that he shouldn't have suited up, that Bob never suited up until after he'd talked to whoever was waiting when they arrived.

He stopped a few stairs below the man. He waited for the man to lift his head, to say something. Waited for the man to do one of the things Darby had seen Bob absorb at other job sites. Waited for the man to scream or wail, to spit curses, to throw a punch. The man did nothing. Darby could see the pale, hairless skin between the bottom of the man's pant cuffs and the tops of his dress socks, could smell the last, faint traces of his morning aftershave, clean and sweet. Roistler shifted impatiently down on the bottom step. Darby let another full minute pass before he finally spoke, before he used Bob's voice, Bob's words in the quiet stairwell.

"I'm sorry for your loss," he said.

The man didn't move. Darby didn't know if maybe he didn't speak English. The work order didn't say who had placed the call, only that the father would still be at the site. He wasn't sure what he would do if the man couldn't understand him.

The man lifted his head. He had soft, round features, but his skin was strained tight. He looked at Darby, looked at the moonman suit. His eyes were red-rimmed and swollen.

"What is your name?" he said. Perfect English. The son of immigrants. The son of the son of immigrants. "My name is Peter. This was my apartment, my family's apartment."

Darby knew that an answer was necessary, that an answer was required to pass, to start the job. He cleared his throat. The speck was still there.

"My name is Bob," Darby said. "My name is Bob Lewis."

Peter looked at Darby's gloves, the paper mask hanging around his neck. "I thought I could take care of this, but I could not," he said.

Darby nodded like he had seen Bob nod many times before, and he wondered if Bob felt the same thing he felt as he nodded, that this movement kept things away, this man and his grief, the nodding discouraged anything from attaching, anything from sticking.

Peter shifted to the side of the step, letting Darby pass into the open doorway.

"Thank you, Mr. Lewis," Peter said. "I thought I could do this, but I cannot."

Roistler knelt on the floor, scrubbing the bathtub. Darby stood beside him, spraying the walls, wiping red handprints from the tile. The handprints were half the size of Darby's hands. He scrubbed the sink, the toilet, went to work on the floor. The floor tile was red, nearly the same color as the fluid. He sprayed hydrogen chloride across suspicious areas, waited to see if it bubbled, indicating fluid rather than water spilled from the tub.

They'd left Peter down at a table in the restaurant with the paperwork. Darby had marked the time, told Peter the hourly rate, how long he estimated the job would take. Peter watched Darby intently as he explained all of this, nodded at the end, sat down with the forms.

Darby crossed from the bathroom into the girl's bedroom. There were stipples of fluid on the cream carpeting. He followed the trail over to the double bed. He lifted the comforter, the sheets, checked for more fluid. Followed the trail to a sliding glass door on the other side of the room. There was a small covered landing outside, crammed with boxes and potted plants and a pair of bicycles. Another enclosed stairwell lead down from the landing, attached to the back of the building. There was a red handprint on the wall beside the glass doors. Darby sprayed the print, let the fluid run into a dustpan.

She had come back in here after she'd done it. He knew this, it was clear to him. She'd filled the tub and slipped into the hot water and lifted whatever she'd used, a razor blade stolen from a drug store, stolen from the other bathroom in the apartment, lifted it up to the overhead light, the metal shining, and then she'd slid the blade down each forearm, wrist to elbow. Shocked by the pain, by how much it hurt, then shocked by the fluid, so much so soon. She'd quickly become dizzy with it, submerging her arms to dull the feeling, the steaming bathwater swirling pink.

He knew all of this, standing at the glass door, the red handprint sliding down the wall into his dustpan. He tried not to think of it, but he knew all of this, it was so clear to him.

She'd gotten out of the tub because she was going to be sick. She was overcome, suddenly nauseous, and the idea of being sick in the tub in addition to what she had already done shamed her to stand. She braced herself with a hand on the wall, stepped uneasily out onto the tile to throw up in the toilet. She saw the bathroom then, the mirror over the sink reflecting the room wet with bathwater and lost fluid. The sight chased her into the bedroom, stepping carefully, still dizzy, her skin prickling, strangely electric in the open air.

She stood at the sliding glass door, dripping onto the carpet, a hand on the wall to steady herself. She looked out onto the parking lot below, the blue and green dumpsters, the backs of the brick buildings that faced the street beyond. The familiar view. Everything clear and crisp, everything strange and new. The wild afternoon.

Her hand felt hot against the wall. Everything else was cold but her hand burned, her hand left a mark when she lifted it away, a slick red brand on the clean white paint.

She crossed the room, dripping, shivering, stopping again to stand at her dresser. She touched the framed photos that sat there, a picture of her and her mother standing on the Golden Gate Bridge; a picture of her sweet-faced grandmother; a prom photo of her and group of friends in gowns and tuxes, mugging and laughing in a parking lot at Disneyland. Her fingers left little red drops where they touched the frames, the top of the unfinished dresser.

She lifted her head to her reflection in the mirror that hung above the dresser. The truth of the thing, the sight of the thing, standing in her bedroom with her ruined arms open and leaking. She stood and watched, the fear setting in, the finality of what she'd done. She stood and watched herself, a bright red puddle forming on the carpeting that always felt so soft between her toes.

Her vision was failing. This was the scariest thing, losing her sight, the room growing dark and dull.

There were other things here, familiar things, hairbrushes and makeup bottles, perfume, a small box of jewelry, silver rings and bracelets. There were carved wooden figurines here, small brown animals, a duck, a pig, a horse, a rabbit. She lifted the rabbit from the dresser, held it in her slick hand, and this kept her steady, the familiar touch of the smooth wood, the familiar shape between her fingers. This kept her steady until the room grew almost too dark to see. Then she replaced the rabbit and made her way back into the bathroom, slid back into the tub, the warm water embracing, her vision going, her vision gone, her body slipping beneath the surface and fading.

Darby stood at the dresser, his ears rushing, the carved rabbit in his gloved hand. The wood of the other figurines was rough, but the rabbit was worried smooth. There was a small chip of dried fluid on its belly. He pried it away with his thumbnail. All of the air in the room rushed in his ears. He pictured the rabbit safe in the drawer in the garage, with the ring, with the snow globe.

There was a loud banging coming from the stairwell. Darby set the rabbit back in its place on the dresser, went to the outer room. Peter was standing on the top step, banging his elbows against the walls of the stairwell. Darby stood in the doorway. This was what it looked like, this kind of sorrow. Peter banged twice more, three times more, then he slumped a little, let his arms fall to his sides. He took air in short, wheezy gasps.

"I came back for a change of clothes," he said. He didn't look at Darby, but into the stairwell as he spoke. "I've been sleeping somewhere else. I came back because I thought that no one would be here. She would be out with friends. Her mother at work." He took air. "Her bathroom door was closed, and I could see the light under the door, I could hear the fan. I knew before I opened the door, somehow. It had never occurred to me, I had never imagined, but somehow I knew without opening the door."

Darby listened and nodded, nodded like he'd seen Bob nod so many times. This was the correct response, to stand and nod. This kept things away.

"I opened the door, though," Peter said. "For some reason I opened it. To confirm what I already knew."

Peter didn't look at Darby as he spoke. He stared at the wall of the stairwell. This was what it looked like, this kind of sorrow.

Peter turned back down the stairs to the restaurant. He would leave Darby to his work. He took the first step and something happened, he tripped or he missed a step or his legs gave out. Something. He went down hard on the steps, crashing down on his knees, tumbling over onto his side, sliding headfirst. He ended down near the door to the restaurant. He lay there, motionless. He'd held his hands up the entire time he fell, pale white skin past the sleeves of his suit coat. He held them up now as he lay at the bottom the stairs, delicate things he'd needed to save from the fall.

Darby stopped himself from nodding. He went down the stairs, looked at Peter's hands held in the air. He did not want to touch this man. This man was contagious. His sorrow, his grief was something that could spread. Peter's body shook. He was sobbing against the hard wood of the stairs. He was injured, possibly; he had hurt himself in the fall. Darby didn't want to touch this man. This man was contagious. Darby pulled off his gloves and stuffed them into the pocket of his suit. He did not want to touch this man, but he took Peter's hands and lifted him from the stairs, righted him on the steps. Peter's head hung. He didn't look at Darby. He began to speak in a whisper, apologizing, over and over, nodding his head with each apology. Darby could feel the shame on Peter's skin, warm and slick with sweat. He let go of Peter's hands and took a step back, into the restaurant, to let Peter pass. He waited until Peter was seated again in the dining room before pulling on a new pair of gloves, clearing his throat and spitting into the darkness as he climbed back up the stairwell.

He stood in the bedroom with the camera. He lifted the camera to his eye, looked at the room in the frame. The walls were clean, the carpet was clean. The rushing in his ears felt like it would split his head in two. He could see the figurines on the dresser, the wooden rabbit. He could almost feel it in his hand. If he were to take it, he could keep it safe. If he were to take it and slide it into his pocket, the sound in the room, the sound in his head would cease.

"That's my job now," Roistler said. He stood just inside the bathroom door, his bucket packed, his paper mask hanging from his neck.

"I can do it," Darby said. He could almost feel the figurine in his hand, the smooth wood between his fingers. "Just give me a minute alone in here and I can do it."

Roistler came into the room, stood in front of Darby, filling the camera's frame. "We have to get this right. Who does what."

"This is my job," Darby said.

"Not anymore. It's my job now."

Roistler held his hand out for the camera. He said something else, but Darby couldn't hear, the rushing had grown so loud. He could only see the rabbit and then Roistler's face close in the view-finder, Roistler's lips moving. He lowered the camera, handed it to Roistler. He walked across the room, past the dresser, leaving the rabbit. Stepped into the mouth of the stairwell. He kept a hand on the wall to steady himself, to keep from falling as he took each step back down.

The Mexican restaurant was wedged between two larger stores, a pet store and a store where people brought big plastic water jugs to get refilled. *Agua fresca*. Michelle had asked The Kid to wait for her outside the restaurant while she bought a gordita. She said that she was fucking starving, and that she'd rather get a gordita there than get one at a roach coach and get sick and die. Michelle always seemed to have money for snacks, extra food, even though all the other kids joked about how poor she was. The Kid wondered where she got the money, if she stole it or something. He figured that it was none of his business, but he wondered anyway.

He didn't know why she'd asked him to wait. He'd planned on taking an alternate route from school to the burned house to work on his mural, but then suddenly Michelle was alongside him, snapping her gum, talking about something she'd seen on TV the night before about the reason for *Y2K*, the microchip in all the computers that was going to fail at midnight on New Year's Eve. Apparently, whoever had invented and programmed the chips hadn't thought there would ever be a year 2000, and so the chips didn't know what to do when it actually became that year. The people on TV said that the chips were going to fritz out and that was what would screw everything up, banks and cars and the stock market and tons of stuff with the army, tanks and fighter jets and nuclear missiles. The people on TV said that the trick was to figure out a way to convince the computers that the guy who'd invented the chips was wrong, that the year 2000 could actually exist. The Kid asked Michelle if the people on TV had figured out how to do that, but Michelle said she didn't know, she'd fallen asleep on the couch before the end of the show.

Michelle came out of the restaurant, her gordita already half eaten, shreds of cabbage poking from of the corners of her mouth.

The Kid tried to remember if she'd spit out her gum before she'd gone inside. He thought that maybe she hadn't, maybe the gum was still in her mouth mixed with the cabbage and chicken.

They walked back toward the school, even though this was the exact opposite way The Kid wanted to go. Brian and Arizona were standing together in front of the school's big sign. Brian was wearing his track and field uniform, the same thing he'd worn on Halloween, stretching his legs up behind his back like his dad did during The Kid's sessions. Brian saw The Kid and Michelle and leaned over to Arizona, whispered something in her ear. The Kid remembered how Arizona smelled when she'd leaned over to see the drawings in his notebook. Soap and strawberry shampoo.

He could imagine what Brian was saying. *Don't look now but here come those monsters, here come those pigs.* The Kid hated this, suddenly and fiercely, hated whatever Brian was saying and hated walking with Michelle, hated Arizona seeing them together. He thought that they probably did look like pigs, Michelle stuffing her face, talking about how much she hated her mom's boyfriend, using all sorts of curse words, little bits of chicken spraying from her mouth. The Kid guilty just by association. Arizona laughed at whatever Brian said, put her hand on his arm to keep steady, he was that funny. Her hand on Brian's arm like she'd put her hand on The Kid's arm. Brian didn't stop stretching the whole time, pulling one leg up behind his back.

"I bet they're going to start doing it soon," Michelle said, mouth still full.

*Doing what?*

"You know what. It."

*You don't know what you're talking about."*

"She's his girlfriend. That's what happens."

*She's not his girlfriend.*

"How do you know?"

*I know.*

"How? Is she your girlfriend?"

Michelle said this with a real mean twist at the end, like she already knew the answer. Like of course Arizona wasn't The Kid's girlfriend, like she couldn't think of a crazier idea.

The Kid closed his notebook, watched Brian and Arizona while he walked, wondering what Brian had told her, what secrets he gave out. Things Mr. Bromwell had told his family at dinner, probably, secrets about The Kid from his thick file, from his test scores and paperwork. He imagined the Bromwell family laughing at their dinner table, heads back, holding onto the sides of their chairs because they were laughing so hard. The Kid thought of Mrs. Bromwell, Brian's mom, laughing hardest of all, and The Kid thought about how unfair it was, somebody's mother laughing at him when things were so different at The Kid's house.

"Anyway," Michelle said, "I'm going to ask Miss Ramirez if I can take apart that computer in the back of the classroom. I bet I can probably fix it. You want to bet?"

Brian leaned into Arizona again, said something that made her scowl and punch him playfully in the arm.

"Five bucks says I can teach the computers that next year is going to exist." Michelle took the last bite of her gordita, dropped the paper wrapping onto the sidewalk. "You want to bet five bucks, Kid? I've got five bucks at home if you want to bet."

Michelle's apartment was in a large, whitewashed brick building a few streets from the school. Makeshift curtains of blankets and sheets hung out of some of the open windows on the upper floors. Other windows were stuffed with plants, with newspapers. Other windows were so grimy that The Kid couldn't see what they were stuffed with. There were spiked metal bars on the top of the gate behind the building, and twists of barbed wire connecting the spikes. Michelle pulled open the gate and they climbed a few cement steps to a heavy steel security door. The door was maybe twice the size of The Kid's front door, a serious piece of work.

Michelle shoved her hand down into the front pocket of her jeans. Her jeans were too tight, and she struggled to get her hand in and out again with a keychain. She unlocked the door, pulled it open. They walked in through the back hall, down a long cool corridor, past closed doors on both sides, TV noises coming from behind the doors, game shows in Spanish, talk shows in Spanish, cooking smells coming, chicken and onions, cigarette smells, and another smell, close to cigarettes but not quite, a sharp, strong tang.

"Smell that?" Michelle said. She took a deep sniff. "Somebody's smoking bud. Somebody's blazing."

They climbed the carpeted stairs at the end of the hall. Michelle was out of breath when they reached the top. She coughed a few times, pounded her chest with her fist.

"Too much smoking," she said. "What do you think, Kid? You think I smoke too much weed?"

The Kid didn't know what to think. He never knew if what Michelle talked about was true or if she was just bragging, trying to seem even tougher than she was.

"If my mom's boyfriend is home, just ignore him," she said, "If he's drunk, he might try to talk to you, ask you all kinds of stupid questions. You're better off not even answering. If he sees you answer in your notebook, he'll just start goofing on you."

They stopped at a door halfway down the hall. Michelle singled out another key on her ring, unlocked both locks, pushed into the apartment.

The room was hot and stuffy. A yellow sheet covered the windows, filtering the sunlight, giving the room a feverish feel. There was a couch against the far wall, made up as a messy bed with a sweat-stained pillow and another yellow sheet. A tin ashtray sat on the arm, a half-smoked cigarette still burning inside. Michelle's mom's boyfriend was nowhere to be seen. The TV was on loud, a soccer game with excited announcers yelling in Spanish.

"My mom's boyfriend sleeps out here most nights," Michelle said. "My mom doesn't want him in her bed because he smells like booze. So he sleeps out here most nights unless they're fucking."

She looked at The Kid, the shocked expression on his face.

"Don't even think about it, Kid. It's gross. Don't even picture it."

Michelle turned to the TV, the sprinting soccer players, didn't bother to turn down the volume.

"My sisters sleep in with my mom, unless her boyfriend's in there, and then they sleep in my room," she said. "They're real little

princesses, real girly, not like me at all. That's because my mom's boyfriend is their real dad and he treats them like princesses. He treats
me like shit because he's jealous of my real dad. He's jealous that my
dad doesn't have to put up with my mom's bitching anymore now
that he lives in the Twin Cities. I'll be out there with him as soon as
I get enough money for the bus. I'm pretty close. I could save that
much pretty quickly. You know how much a bus ticket costs, Kid?"

The Kid shook his head.

"A fucking lot of money."

A toilet flushed from behind a door at the other end of the hallway. The Kid could hear a man's groan from behind the door, the
sound of gagging, the man throwing up into the toilet.

"He's drunk," Michelle said. "That's the sound of him being
drunk."

They walked down the hall toward the bedrooms. On the wall
across from the bathroom was a framed painting of the Virgin of
Guadalupe. The Kid knew about the Virgin because she was all
around the neighborhood, painted on the side walls of banks, convenience stores, gas stations. His mom had once explained that she
was Jesus' mother, and people who believed in her believed that she'd
appeared in Mexico many years ago and performed miracles. In the
painting on Michelle's wall, the Virgin was wearing a blue shawl that
covered her head and ran down past her feet. The shawl was full of
stars. There was a shining golden crown on her head. Her hands were
pressed together in prayer, and she was looking down and smiling a
little. A small brown boy was emerging from under the bottom of
her robe. The Kid couldn't tell if he was hiding under the robe or
holding the Virgin up or what. Multicolored rays of light flowed out
from behind her toward the edges of the painting. There was a light
bulb attached to the bottom of the frame, an electric cord stretching
down to an outlet at the bottom of the wall. Michelle clicked on the
light as they passed. The shining bulb began to turn in its socket and
the painting caught the light in such a way that the rays flowing out
from behind the Virgin seemed to move, shimmering and pulsating,
turning and reaching outside the painting and the frame, across the
walls and the ceiling of the hallway.

They passed the bathroom door and the gagging noises, into a darkened bedroom. Michelle's mother's bedroom, The Kid guessed, a messy room with a big unmade bed and two smaller unmade beds, the sisters' beds, the twin princesses.

Michelle told The Kid to stand watch at the door. She told him that if her mom's boyfriend came out of the bathroom, he should make some kind of loud noise to warn her, he should knock on the wall or stomp his feet or something. The Kid stood in the doorway, listening to the loud gagging and throw-up sounds from the bathroom. It reminded him of Rey Lugo walking down the school hallway with that faraway look on his face. Rey Lugo looking at The Kid and throwing up in his tiny hands.

The Kid heard Michelle behind him, rummaging through some clothes on the floor, cursing under her breath. The Kid looked over his shoulder and saw her digging in the pockets of pairs of jeans, in the pockets of what looked like the baggy green pants that nurses wore. She flattened herself out as much as she could on the stained carpeting and reached her arm underneath the bed, pulling out old tissues and balled-up socks.

He looked back up at the painting of the Virgin. The colored light radiated out from behind her, reflecting on the opposite wall, yellow and red and purple. He wondered if the Virgin knew about the Covenant. He walked over to the painting, stood underneath. He could feel the colored light shining warm on his face. He wasn't sure how to ask, so he recited the Covenant in his head again, reminded the Virgin what he was asking for, what he had given up. Reminded her that he had stuck to his end of the deal. He recited the Covenant and waited for something, some kind of sign that she'd heard, a change in the type of light, or more light, maybe, a different glow, something. He watched the painting, watched the light, but he'd been staring at it for so long that it was hard to tell if anything was different. He lifted his hand, slowly, the light covering his fingers, his forearm, his elbow.

"Got it," Michelle whispered from back in the bedroom. "Fucking A."

The Kid looked over his shoulder. Michelle was on the other side of the bed, holding something she'd pulled out of a drawer in the bedside table.

"Let's go, let's go, let's go." She rushed around the bed and banged her elbow on the corner of a dresser. "Fucking A," she yelled, holding her arm, and then the toilet flushed again and the bathroom door opened and Michelle's mom's boyfriend lurched out into the hallway. He stopped short when he saw The Kid, squinting down with red, puffy eyes.

The Kid couldn't tell if he was white-looking or Mexican-looking or both. Kind of both. He was tall and chunky, with shaggy brown hair and a thin brown mustache. His lips and the hairs of his mustache were wet, and the hair on his head was sticking straight up, like he'd just gotten out of bed. There was a bad smell coming out from the bathroom.

"Who's this?" the boyfriend said. His voice was slow and thick. It sounded almost like he was talking more to himself than to anybody else in the apartment.

The Kid waited for Michelle to come out from the bedroom and explain what was going on. The Kid looked up at the boyfriend, waited. Finally, he looked back over his shoulder. Michelle wasn't there. She was hiding someplace, behind the dresser or back behind the bed.

"Who the hell is this?" the boyfriend said. He was definitely talking to The Kid now.

The Kid opened his notebook. He remembered what Michelle had said about not answering the boyfriend, but there didn't seem to be any other way around it.

The Kid wrote in his notebook, held it up for the boyfriend to see.

*It's The Kid.*

The boyfriend read the line, read it again, looked at The Kid. He was unsteady on his feet, weaving a little in the hallway. He put a hand against the wall to brace himself. His breath was terrible.

"Are you some friend of Michelle's?"

The Kid thought about this, about Michelle hiding back in the bedroom, about the ashtray in the living room, the burns on her stomach.

*Michelle doesn't have any friends.*

The boyfriend let out a deep, wet belch, the kind that signaled something else coming soon.

"Then what the fuck are you doing in here?"

The Kid pointed up to the painting of the Virgin, to the turning lights. The man looked at the painting and the lights for quite a while, rocking woozily on his feet, then he looked back at The Kid.

*I'm here to see her,* The Kid wrote. *I'm here because I have a deal with someone she knows.*

The boyfriend belched again, closed his mouth quickly. He shut his eyes tight and opened them again. He looked surprised to see The Kid still standing there. Then his face blanched and he turned and rushed back into the bathroom, fell to his knees, vomiting violently into the toilet.

There was a rough hand on the back of The Kid's neck, pushing him into the hallway, through the front room and out the door into the corridor of the building. They ran as fast as they could, down the stairs, out the back security door, through the iron gate and onto the sidewalk. When The Kid finally stopped and turned around, he saw Michelle about a hundred feet behind, sitting on the sidewalk, out of breath, holding her stomach. The Kid walked back, squatted down beside her.

"That fucking asshole," she said. It seemed like she was going to cry. The Kid had never seen her like this before. Scared. She held her fist out to The Kid, opened it. Inside was a wad of dollar bills.

"You hold on to this," she said. "We made a bet, and to keep it fair you hold the money on retainer. That's how you make bets. If I can't fix the computer, then you get to keep the money. If I can fix it, then you have to give the money back, plus five more bucks of your own."

The Kid didn't want to hold the money, but Michelle pushed the bills into his hand and closed it into a fist.

"That fucking asshole," she said. She punched the sidewalk, reopening the scrapes on her knuckles. "I hope he chokes on his puke and dies."

In the warm light of early morning he saw her standing naked at the kitchen window, her back to him, the phone receiver pressed to her ear. One arm was crossed under her breasts, her hand holding her ribs. A Saturday morning, almost two years before. Still a while before The Kid would be up, before Darby should be up. A job the night before at a nursing home in Whittier, a bathroom in the nursing home, a long job, six hours in a small room. He could still smell the disinfectant in his nostrils, the latex on his fingers, the rubber of the gloves.

It was strange to see her naked outside of the bedroom, outside of the bathroom. Just standing in the kitchen with the phone to her ear. He didn't know how long she'd been out there. It was cold in the kitchen; the linoleum must have been cold beneath her feet. He could see the goosebumps along the backs of her arms, the backs of her thighs.

He stood in the doorway, afraid to make a sound, afraid to move. He was afraid he would upset the delicate balance he had stumbled into, that he would tip things one way or the other. She held her ribs with one hand, her bitten nails pressed into her skin like she was holding something in, like she was worried something would come spilling out.

He could hear the howler tone from the phone, the rapid-fire stop-start bursts. No one was on the line. He wondered how long it had been since someone was on the line, how long she'd been listening to the loop of permanent signal.

He was trying not to move. He didn't want to upset the balance in the room, even though he knew now which way it was going to go. He didn't want to tip it too far too fast.

She set the phone down on the counter, opened the refrigerator, took out a beer. Popped the tab, took a long pull. Another. She turned to him like she knew he'd been there all along.

"Earl's dead," she said. "They found him in his car about a mile from his office. One of his guns in the front seat." She was staring hard at Darby while she said this. She was not wearing her glasses and her eyes were dull, unfocused. He had not moved from the door-way, even though the room had tipped, the room was capsizing.

"Dolores said it's all over the news there. It happened yesterday morning and by noon it was all over the news. She said the report-ers can barely contain themselves." She took another long pull from the can. "She doesn't want us to come out. She made that very clear. There won't be a funeral. There won't be anything to come out for."

The phone was still howling. She picked up the receiver and searched for the right button. Nearly blind without her glasses. She did this slowly, precisely, an exaggeration of a normal action. She found the button, silenced the phone, placed the receiver back down on the counter.

"It happened yesterday morning and she's just calling now. I asked her why it took her so long to call and she said, *This is a disgrace.* That was her answer. That tone in her voice that she's per-fected, that she owns so completely."

Lucy's face was tight. Her whole body was tight, motionless. It didn't look like she was breathing. Darby was breathing so hard that the sound seemed to fill the room. He watched her ribs, her breasts for a sign that she was breathing, but nothing moved until she spoke again.

Darby took a step into the kitchen, the slightest movement.

"Don't," she said. She lifted the hand quickly from her ribs, held it palm out, keeping him away. "Just don't. Please."

He stepped back, his hands hanging at his sides. The room lurched, tumbled around him.

"Don't you know, David?" She lowered her arm, clasped her hand around her ribs again, fingers pushing hard into her skin. "This is a disgrace. You shouldn't get too close."

The morning was raw, gray-blue and clear after the night's rain. Darby stood alone in the motel parking lot, facing the long row of numbered doors, one hand pressed to the side of the van, the cold metal against his palm, his fingertips. He checked the pager again, the ninth time, the tenth time, but there was no record of a call.

He had spoken to the night manager in the motel office, an older black woman at the end of her shift. She didn't know why he had come. She hadn't called for any cleaning service, hadn't spoken to anyone on the phone for hours. She eyed Darby warily, watched his hands, waiting for him to pull something, a trick, a sales brochure, a gun. She watched his hands, watched his eyes, kept a safe distance back from the counter, close to the phone.

He stood out by the van, trying to remember the order of events, why he'd driven there alone from the Everclean garage as if this were a one-man job, which he knew to be impossible. There was no such thing.

He was holding the old cell phone, the phone he thought he'd lost. It had been lying in a corner of the motel parking lot, half-covered by a stray newspaper. He picked it up and had no idea how it had gotten there, when he had been there before to drop it.

The sign in the parking lot showed the nightly rates, advertised color TV, air conditioning, free local calls. The rooms' numbered doors were all painted Halloween orange. The paint was chipping, peeling.

He'd cleaned countless motel rooms. Many of their jobs were in places like this, anonymous spaces near used car lots and liquor stores, freeway entrances. A night clerk in the office who stood a safe distance back from the counter. He didn't recognize this particular place. He didn't think he'd ever been to this place before, but he really didn't know for sure.

He tried not to think of Bob in the closet in Inglewood. He tried not to think of the apartment in Chinatown, the rabbit on the dresser, the pull of the unfinished room.

There was a newer pickup parked in front of one of the rooms, Texas plates. A plastic shopping bag filled with empty beer cans sat outside the room's orange door. The door opened and a man stepped outside, long-haired, barefoot, ten or fifteen years younger than

Darby. He wore jeans and a white undershirt. He squinted in the light and stepped out onto the walkway, carrying a plastic ice bucket. He left the door open as he disappeared around the corner of the motel. The room was dark except for a bedside lamp. A woman sat up in the bed, the same age as the man, blond, shirtless, lighting a cigarette, shaking out the match. She lifted her arms above her head, stretched. Her breasts lifted with her arms. A pink woman in a dark room. The man padded back around the corner, yawning, carrying a bucket full of ice. He took one last look around, scanning the few cars in the lot, the white van, the street beyond. He didn't register Darby or Darby didn't concern him or Darby wasn't there. He stepped back into the room. The orange door closed, locked.

Darby checked his pager again, the eleventh time, the twelfth time. No record of a call. He lifted his hand from the side of the van, his fingers numb, tingly at the tips, the rushing loud in his head. He thought of the Chinatown apartment, tried to shake the thought. He shook his tingling hand and tried to shake the thought. He opened the door of the van, climbed inside. His head loud enough to break open. He put the old cell phone in the glove compartment, covered it with the van's repair manuals. He focused on what was in front of him, he focused on his hands, got his hands to work somehow, turning the key and starting the engine, pulling to the parking lot exit, out onto the street beyond.

He waited for Arizona in the courtyard before school, standing by the front gate so he could catch her before Brian did, before Rhonda did. He decided it was worth the risk. He wanted her to know that he wasn't a bad guy, despite what had happened with Rhonda. He didn't want her to think that this was how he normally was.

He held an issue of *Extraordinary Adventures* close to his chest, the last one he'd been able to find under his bed. It was from a year or so back, and in it Smooshie Smith went forward in time to interview The Kid's parents. The Kid's mom was an old lady in the future, her glasses slipping down the bridge of her nose, her gray hair pulled back in a bun. The Kid's dad stood stooped beside her, smiling contentedly, bald except for tufts of white hair sticking out above his ears. They answered all sorts of questions about their life, about the adventures they'd had, the things they'd done and seen. Working on the house, watching ballgames. Then there was a part where Smooshie asked The Kid's mom about The Kid, about how he'd grown up, and The Kid's mom answered that The Kid had grown up just fine, that he was a great guy, a famous talk-show host in his own right. The Kid thought that maybe Arizona would read this and be convinced, see that The Kid might turn out okay.

She came in through the gate and The Kid hustled over, walking alongside until she turned and noticed him.

"Oh," she said, "Hello, Whitley." She didn't look thrilled to see him. She looked like she wasn't entirely comfortable with him walking so close.

He juggled the comic and his pencil and his notebook, getting to a blank page, keeping an eye on Brian, now approaching from the other side of the courtyard.

*I brought you something. I thought you might like to see this.*

It sounded stupid as soon as he wrote it, but it was out there now, she was reading it, he couldn't really cross it out and start over. He tried to smile with his mouth closed so his bad breath wouldn't be quite so bad.

"Thank you," she said, still hesitant, but smiling a little.

He kept up alongside her, holding his notebook and pencil and trying to find the page in the comic where his mom explained how The Kid had turned out, where his mom went to bat for him.

Brian about halfway across the courtyard now, coming fast.

*You should read,* The Kid wrote, running out of time to explain. *You should look at—*

But then Brian was there, just steps away, so The Kid just shoved the comic at Arizona, pushing it into her hands and turning to walk the other way, fast, as Brian intercepted her, as Brian walked her the rest of the way into school.

The pickup was in the driveway when The Kid got home, but there was no sign of his dad. He stepped up onto the porch, unhooked his backpack from his shoulders. Heard something from around the side of the house. A weird noise. Kind of like a moan, but kind of like a growl. He put his backpack down and took a few steps toward the corner of the house. Heard the noise again. Definitely a growl. He didn't go any further. He'd have to find his dad, get his dad to come out and look around the side of the house. That sound didn't sound good.

The Kid moved back toward the door and heard the growl again, and then another noise, sounded like something running, something coming from around the corner of the house, fast, so he picked up his backpack and grabbed the handle of the security door and heard the sound turn the corner and so he turned and then he was face to face with it, a growling, wheezing thing, a giant hairy mass of teeth and claws and wild eyes.

A dog. Almost as tall as The Kid. The biggest dog The Kid had ever seen.

The Kid jumped back, stumbling on the porch, and the dog jumped back, too, startled, shooting his legs forward like a stubborn donkey. The Kid scrambled to get to his feet before the dog could regroup, before the dog could lunge again, but then his dad was there, out from the house with his hands under The Kid's arms, lifting The Kid to his feet, holding him steady.

"It's okay, Kid," his dad said, his voice low in The Kid's ear. "He's not going to hurt you."

Was his dad crazy? How did he know this dog? How did he know this dog wasn't going to hurt them?

The dog was trembling now, swinging his great head around, looking for a way to escape. He was wearing a new blue collar, was attached to a long blue leash. The Kid tried to catch his breath, get his hands to stop shaking. He wanted to ask his dad who the dog belonged to, why he was tied to their porch.

His dad extended a hand toward the dog, palm down, letting it dangle a few inches from the thing's wet mouth. The Kid imagined the dog lunging again, attacking his dad, mauling and disfiguring his dad, leaving his dad for dead, then turning on The Kid. The dog was shaking like a leaf. He looked at The Kid, looked at The Kid's dad. The Kid knew that look. He was familiar with that look. He'd seen it in the bathroom mirror at home, the bathroom mirror at school. The look when he was so scared he didn't know what to do.

The dog didn't sniff his dad's outstretched hand, didn't lick his dad's hand, but he didn't bite it either. He just stood with his snout a few inches from the hand, legs locked, eyes wide, shaking so hard The Kid thought he might rattle apart.

The Kid fumbled in his backpack, pulled out his notebook, wrote with one eye on the page, the other on the dog.

*Where did he come from?*

"They found him in the sewer under the manhole cover," his dad said. "Right outside the house."

*Who does he belong to?*

His dad crouched down next to The Kid, kept a hand on The Kid's shoulder. "He needs some help," his dad said. "He needs a place to live."

The Kid didn't move, just stared at the dog. His dad wanted to keep this dog? He wanted this dog to live with them?

"We'll train him," his dad said. "We'll feed him and train him and pretty soon he'll forget all this, he'll forget any of this ever happened."

The dog was still shaking, looking at The Kid and The Kid's dad and back again. The Kid was pretty afraid of this dog, but he also knew that look. He knew what that look felt like.

"He needs some help," his dad said. "What do you think, Kid?"

They sat in the driveway, eating drive-thru hamburgers and fries. The dog sat on the porch, on the end of its leash, watching them. The dog hadn't touched the food or the bone his dad had bought for him. Hadn't picked up the new green rubber ball with the little bell inside.

His dad said the dog would live out on the porch for now, until they got him cleaned up and housetrained. The leash was long enough that he had plenty of room to move around, stretch his legs, could get down the steps onto the front lawn to do his business.

The Kid wasn't sure he liked the idea of that big rambling thing sitting on the porch all the time, but his dad said that the dog would get friendlier as time went on, as the dog got healthier and learned to trust them, as the dog forgot about the sewer, what had happened to him down there.

*What happened to him down there?* The Kid wrote.

"Nothing good," his dad said.

The Kid's mom had never let them have a dog. She'd been bitten by a dog when she was a girl, she had little tooth-mark scars across her left cheek and so she was afraid of dogs, didn't like them anywhere near her. The Kid had always thought that his mom overreacted around dogs, but now he wasn't so sure, not with that big thing sitting on the porch, watching them.

His dad was looking at him, waiting for the answer to a question. The Kid cupped his ear so his dad would repeat it.

"What do you think we should call him?" his dad said. "They didn't give him a name at the pound."

The Kid looked at the dog sitting at the top of the steps, staring out at the pickup, still unsure, still afraid. The Kid figured this dog needed a good name, a strong name that would make him less afraid, that might even make him brave, might get rid of his scared look. The Kid thought that maybe this dog needed a secret identity like The Kid had. A name where he could be scared sometimes and another name where he didn't have to be so scared.

*Steve Rogers*, The Kid wrote.

"Steve Rogers?"

The Kid nodded.

"Dogs don't have last names."

*This one should.*

"Who's Steve Rogers?"

*Captain America's secret identity.*

"Why don't we just name him Captain?"

*You don't have to use his last name if you don't want to.*

His dad looked unconvinced. He stuck his head out the window, called to the dog.

"Steve. Steve Rogers."

The dog didn't move, didn't change expression.

"He's not into it, Kid."

*Give him time*, The Kid wrote. *Give him time to get used to it.*

His dad got out of the pickup, walked up to the porch, held his hand out, half a foot from the dog's nose.

"Steve?" his dad said. "Steve Rogers?"

The dog didn't move. The Kid imagined the dog grabbing his dad's hand, biting down, taking two or three fingers off into his mouth. The Kid imagined the dog lunging, straining to the end of the leash, grabbing his dad's throat, tearing the skin in a fast red spray.

The dog didn't move. He looked at The Kid's dad, looked at his dad's hand. His dad turned back to The Kid, shrugged.

"Maybe he's the kind of dog that needs to get used to having a last name."

In his dream he's standing at the pay phone on Alvarado Street, talking to Lucy. He can see her in her parent's dining room, the phone cord wrapped around her fingers. In her other hand she's holding the picture she'd taken on their first date, Darby in his lucky banana yellow shirt, tired-eyed, a little drunk, smiling because he'd made her smile, because he'd heard the sound of her laughter fifteen or twenty times by then and was getting used to it, it was becoming a sound he knew.

In his dream he's trying to talk to her on the pay phone but she won't listen. She's looking at the picture in her hand and shaking her head and not listening. The picture scares him, the fact that she's holding the picture, because it means she took it with her when she left and he doesn't know what else she might have taken, what else might be missing from the house.

She's not listening and then the football player is there, the student who carried Lucy from her classroom. He's lifting her up, effortlessly, and she drops the phone and the picture and turns her head to his chest, his crisp white shirt. Darby strains to hear if she says something to him, if she confides something, he strains to see the student's face, but it's a blur, the dining room is going dark, and then Darby bolts awake in the pickup, wet with sweat, the late morning heat pressing against the windows, a man on a radio call-in show saying, *The Feds should just nuke it. The whole compound. They should just nuke it and be done with it.*

The dog sat on the porch, watching Darby, looking out into the street. He had been in that same spot the night before when Darby put The Kid to bed; had been there in the morning when Darby woke in the pickup. He didn't seem to have slept,. At some point he had eaten the food in his dish. Darby had given the dish to The

Kid to fill and The Kid had come back out onto the porch with an enormous mound of food, *Steve Rogers* written along the side of the dish in black magic marker.

The dog was a good idea. The dog would forget the sewer, forget the pound, and then the dog would be fine, friendly and fine. Trainable. The dog would gain some weight, get healthier, learn to trust them. The dog would protect The Kid when Darby was out at a job. Darby wouldn't have to worry so much about the locks, the doors, the windows, the graffiti creeping down the street, shadows approaching the house in the night. This immense thing, loyal to him and The Kid. The dog. The dog was a good idea.

He'd called Bob from the cell phone, but Aunt Rhoda said Bob was watching the news on TV, didn't want to be disturbed. He tried not to think about Bob in the closet in Inglewood. He tried not to think about the apartment in Chinatown, the carved wooden rabbit, the unfinished room.

He sat on the steps, held out one of the giant dog biscuits he'd bought at the pet store. Steve Rogers sniffed at the air, but didn't leave his corner. Darby broke the biscuit in half, set one half on the step beside him, slid the other half toward Steve Rogers. Turned back out to watch the street. Heard nothing but sniffing for a while. Then, finally, the sound of the dog rising to his feet, nails clacking on the porch as he walked slowly toward the first half-biscuit. More sniffing, then a loud crunching as the dog devoured the biscuit, grinding it between his teeth. Darby wondered if he should turn, face the dog. He could feel its great size just a few feet behind him. He wasn't so keen on sitting with his back to the thing, but he decided not to move. He just sat still, looking out at the street. He heard the dog licking its chops, then the clacking nails again, slowly, unsteadily, one heavy paw at a time, getting closer. That loud sniffing. He could see the dog's massive black snout in his periphery, darting in and out toward the half-biscuit by Darby's thigh, the snout moving warily, getting closer each time but ready to retreat at any sudden movement on Darby's part. Darby kept still, watched the street. There was silence for a few seconds, half a minute, no sign of the dog's snout.

He could feel Steve Rogers standing a step behind, a step to his right. Then the nose darted in, grabbed the biscuit and scrambled backwards on the porch, nails clacking, the sound of the dog stumbling in his haste, legs flailing, then righting himself and settling back to his corner. The crunch of those jaws grinding the biscuit to dust. Darby turned, looked at the dog. Steve Rogers swallowed the rest of his biscuit, licked his chops.

"Good boy," Darby said.

There was a small corner of paper poking up between the boards of the porch beside him. He tugged until it came up and out. Two newspaper clippings, each a quarter page or so, curled at the edges. Both dated from the previous September. The first was a student receiving a citizenship award from a business group, the girl beaming at the camera, holding a framed certificate. The second was from an interior page of the Sports section, football scores from the local high schools. A headline halfway down read, *Greene Goes the Distance.* Underneath was a black and white photo of a player in motion, running along the sideline toward the end zone, blurred by his own speed, an opposing player close behind but reaching futilely, grasping at air. The name emblazoned across the chest of Greene's uniform was the high school where Lucy taught, the familiar soaring eagle mascot on the side of his helmet. There was no article, just the photo and four word caption.

Lucy had kept a wall of fame at the front of her classroom, newspaper clippings and items from the school announcements, public recognition of her students' accomplishments. She must have intended these clippings for the board, but had lost them somehow. Darby could picture her sitting in the living room after an episode of *It's That Kid!*, after The Kid had gone to bed, carefully cutting the photos from the paper. He could picture them in her hand as she sat on the steps of the porch and drank her tea, hoping the herbs would do the trick that night, allow her a good night's sleep, even half of a good night's sleep. Could picture her setting them down on the porch to take a sip, the clippings sliding into the narrow space between the boards.

*Greene Goes the Distance.*

He turned on the light above Lucy's desk, looked at the bulletin board. He read through her class lists from that last year. Fourth period, *Greene, D.* Last seat in the middle row. The time of the fourth period class was right. Late morning, the time the two cops on the porch had told him it had happened.

Darby looked at the newspaper photo, the blurred figure running. Greene, D. He tried to imagine her in his arms, tried to picture the player without the helmet, tried to see a face, to see him in street clothes, the white game-day dress shirt, carrying Lucy down the hallway to the nurse's office.

The dog's barking cracked like a gunfight, six loud, quick shots turning Darby around, pulling him out onto the porch. The mail was there, a small rubber-banded bundle. The mailman's straw hat hustled by on the other side of the hedges, spooked by the dog. Darby picked up the mail. Bills, sale circulars, wrong names and addresses. Another envelope with Mrs. Fowler's handwriting. Inside was a smaller envelope addressed to *The Shave Head Technician With Blue Eyes.* The return address was that of the beach hotel they had just worked.

Steve Rogers sat on the other side of the porch, watched Darby open the envelope. A notecard with the hotel's crest on the front. Darby thought of the room covered in plastic garbage bags, thought of the pictures set all around the room. He thought of the cleaning woman, Stella, taking a picture from the box, lifting it carefully and holding it to her breast. He thought of the snow globe hidden away in his bucket while he watched her, thought of the snow globe hidden away in the drawer in the garage.

Inside the card was a single line of looping handwriting, dark purple ink.

*Do not worry*, it said. *No one ever notices such things.*

The Kid remembered.

He thought of weekend series at Dodger Stadium, Friday night, Saturday afternoon, Sunday afternoon, games against the St. Louis Cardinals, against the Houston Astros, the whole three days just a sweet blur of baseball. The drive from their house to the ballpark after school on Friday, the slow line of traffic on Sunset, he and his mom and dad sitting in the left field bleachers until his dad said he'd had enough of all the knuckleheads out there and they moved to seats up on the loge level, back behind third base. His mom keeping score, watching the game out on the field and then watching the game in her blue binder. The night getting cold as the game settled into the seventh inning, the eighth inning, his mom breaking out the sweatshirts from her canvas shopping bag, both The Kid and his dad glad she hadn't listened when they'd said they wouldn't need them. Dodgers win, Dodgers lose, the Pittsburgh Pirates, the Atlanta Braves, the drive back through the dark streets, home to bed and then awake to pile into the pickup again and head back down Sunset to the stadium. His mom slathering sunscreen on his arms and legs and cheeks, slathering the back of his dad's neck as he drove, waiting in the line of cars crawling up the hill into the parking lot. The second game, more cheering and yelling, another meal of hot dogs and nachos and soft pretzels and Cokes, his mom and dad with big plastic cups of yellow beer, The Kid sticking his finger into the foam heads when they weren't looking, licking his finger while his dad yelled out to the umpire a mile away, *Come on, Blue, open your eyes,* licking his finger while his mom filled a frame in her scorecard. Dodgers win, Dodgers lose, the Florida Marlins, the Philadelphia Phillies. The drive home in the dusk, knees and cheeks burned red, the sunscreen not 100% effective, the pickup inching back up Sunset in the post-game traffic, The Kid falling asleep with his head on his mom's lap, her thighs still hot from the sun. The pickup quiet except for the radio, a Country music station. His dad singing along softly with the old warblers, knowing all the words somehow, The Kid amazed at all the things his dad knew. His mom gently pulling away his ball cap, stroking The Kid's hat-matted hair. Drifting into sleep, waking back in his own bed, the cool sheets, the night air through his window, his dad's snoring from the bedroom downstairs, his mom in her pajamas standing in The Kid's doorway watching The Kid dreaming, maybe, or half-dreaming. His mom's sad smile in the dark, her whisper. Go back to sleep, baby. Get some sleep, get some rest, and tomorrow we'll do it all again.

He drew along the walls of the living room in the burned house, the last light of the day coming through the window holes, the hole in the ceiling. He'd have to get home soon, make up a story for his dad about how he'd been over at Matthew's working on the comic book, but for now he drew, using the rest of the chalk from the floor and then chalk from boxes he'd bought at *Gift 2000* on his way over, finishing the woodcut waves around the pirate ship and rowboat, then starting a new drawing on the opposite wall, copying pictures from his notebook, drawings of the streets on the way to school, the city mural from under the bridge, crooked light poles, telephone wires hanging over saggy buildings, gang tags on the bus stop shelter, birds in the sky. He drew the hill sloping down from Sunset, the strip mall, the new *Gift 2000* sign. He was bringing the red-haired woman news from the outside world. He thought that maybe she'd like to see the rest of the neighborhood again, thought she'd like to see all the familiar things she was missing, all the new developments, the cardboard box with the sleeping feet sticking out, The Kid's own house with the security bars, the big black dog sitting on the front porch.

These were things his mom was missing as well. The Kid knew this, knew he was drawing for the red-haired woman but also that he was drawing for his mom, hoping maybe she could see this somehow. He was keeping them both up-to-date, helping them to feel less alone.

He finished the dog's snout, the food dish that said *Steve Rogers* along its side. He stood back from the wall, looked at what he'd done, feeling pretty good about it, feeling pretty proud. He looked at the red-haired woman, her wings spread, her body stretching up toward the hole in the ceiling. He thought that maybe she'd be less lonely now, but he wondered if maybe she'd like some other company, if maybe she'd like to have somebody new in the house, somebody other than The Kid.

He hitched his backpack up across his shoulders, looked at the whole thing, the angel, his mural, and thought that maybe he'd like that, too. Maybe he'd like somebody else to see what he had made.

four

They took the dog out to the backyard and filled a metal tub with water from the hose. The Kid brought out a bottle of shampoo from the bathroom. He was worried that it wouldn't work because it was people shampoo, not dog shampoo, but Darby told him it would be fine. The dog wouldn't know the difference.

Steve Rogers stood watching them from a far corner of the yard. Darby shut off the hose and squatted in the dirt.

"Steve. Come here, boy."

The dog looked at him, looked at The Kid. Stayed put in the corner.

"Come here, boy. Come here, Steve."

Darby stood, walked slowly toward the dog, talking softly, repeating the dog's name. The hair along the dog's spine rose as Darby approached. The dog bared a fang, issued a low growl.

Darby crouched again, pulled a biscuit out of his back pocket, broke it in half. The dog squinted at Darby's hand, kept growling. Darby moved in closer, held out the biscuit. The dog stopped growling, sniffed the air.

"Come here, Steve. Come here, boy."

The dog shuffled forward a step, sniffed, darted his head forward and back like he had on the porch, moving his snout closer to the biscuit with each move. He finally made a lunge, grabbing the biscuit with his front teeth, but Darby held on, the dog pulling for a second and then giving up, letting go, standing and squinting at Darby. Darby held out the biscuit again. The dog darted his nose, grabbed the biscuit, and this time Darby let the biscuit go. The dog stood crunching. Darby reached out, slowly, and put his hand on the back of the dog's neck. Ran his hand along the dog's back, flattening some of the standing hair. The dog crunched the biscuit, watching Darby's free hand with one wary eye. Darby moved his hand up to the dog's head, scratched behind a half-bitten ear. With his free hand he held out the other end of the biscuit. The dog took it, crunched some more. Darby placed his hand on the dog's side, moving both hands along his ribs, his flanks, careful not to touch the sore spots. The dog finished the biscuit but stayed where he was, getting scratched.

"Kid," Darby called back. "Come on over."

He could hear The Kid's slow approach, his sneakers shuffling in the dirt. The Kid stopped just behind Darby, clutching his notebook, watching the dog, watching Darby's hands, scared.

"It's okay, Kid. Give me one of your hands."

The Kid shook his head.

"This is how he'll know," Darby said. "This is how he'll know we're his friends."

The Kid took one hand off his notebook, held it out to Darby. Darby took a hand off the dog, took The Kid's hand in his own, moved it gently toward the dog. The Kid's hand was shaking, so Darby added The Kid's name when he spoke to reassure the dog.

"It's okay, Kid. It's okay, Steve."

Darby kept his other hand at the dog's neck, ready to grab and pull if need be. The dog looked at The Kid, looked at The Kid's hand inside of Darby's. Moved his snout closer. The Kid's hand shook even more.

"It's okay, Kid. It's okay, Steve."

The dog's nose was right at their fingers. Darby tightened his hand on the back of the dog's neck, squeezing the scruff, just a little pressure, just enough so the dog would know. The dog's cold nose touched Darby's fingertips, touched The Kid's.

"Go ahead and get that other biscuit out of my back pocket," Darby said.

The Kid moved and the dog tried to lurch back, spooked, but Darby held his scruff, kept him in place. The Kid pulled the biscuit from the pocket of Darby's jeans, broke it in half.

"Hold it out for him, Kid. Go slow."

The Kid held the half biscuit in his palm, lowered his hand. Slowly, slowly, his hand shaking.

"It's okay, Steve. It's okay, Kid. Nice and easy."

The dog sniffed, squinted up at The Kid. The Kid held his hand out further, toward Steve's snout. Darby tightened his grip on the dog's scruff. The dog did his nose-dart, sniffing at the biscuit, moving his head in and out. The Kid held his hand as steady as he could. The dog opened his mouth, waiting for Darby's response at the back of his neck, then moved his head in, taking the biscuit in his teeth.

"Go ahead," Darby said. "You can pet him now."

The dog crunched the biscuit, watched The Kid's hand move over the top of his head. Darby squeezed Steve's scruff, the skin tight between his fingers. He talked low to the dog and The Kid. The Kid set his hand down on top of the dog's head. Patted the dog's head once, twice, then moved his hand over the dog's ears, down to Darby's hand at the back of the dog's neck. Darby took The Kid's hand, squeezed it over the dog's scruff, moved his own hands away. The dog finished the biscuit, The Kid holding him by the scruff. Darby stood, knees popping, took a slow step back. The Kid put his free hand on the dog's back, patted down the hair that was still standing on end.

They ordered pizza and sat in the pickup listening to the news. The day getting soft, the sky going pink. Steve Rogers lay on the front porch, droopy-eyed, drying in the evening air. Darby couldn't stop thinking about the apartment in Chinatown. The unfinished room, the rabbit on the dresser. The speck, the fleck in his throat; he coughed to try to jar it loose, spat out the window onto the lawn.

The Kid was pulling the sleeve of his undershirt, asking him something in the notebook.

*What was it like?*

"What was what like?" Darby said.

The Kid turned a page, clicked on the dome light so it was easier for Darby to read.

*Where you grew up.*

Darby pushed back at the thought of the unfinished apartment. He focused on The Kid, on The Kid's question.

"It was quiet," Darby said. "That was the main thing. How quiet it was."

*How quiet was it?*

Darby turned the radio down. "What do you hear?"

The Kid tilted his head toward the window, listened. Wrote slowly, as each thing came to him.

*Fire sirens. Helicopter. Cars on Vermont.*

"There was none of that," Darby said. "There was still some noise. Cars that came through on the highway, big rigs, air conditioners in some of the trailers, generators humming. But not like this. And there was nothing at night. Everything was still. No noise except coyotes howling out in the dark, past where the last lights reached."

*What did that sound like?*

"Sounded like coyotes howling."

The Kid shook his head. He didn't know that sound.

Darby took in a deep breath and let out a loud coyote howl, held it until his lungs had emptied. The sound trailed away out of the pickup, through the yard, up and over the house.

The Kid smiled.

"Sounded like that," Darby said.

It was the stillness that he missed, that came back to him in dreams. The flat, deadened days, heavy with sun and heat, the air unmoving, Darby floating on his back, watching the tops of palm trees against the purple sky as he drifted slowly, one end of the pool to the other.

A retirement community was being built at the foot of the mountains, about a mile from the trailer park. A walled neighborhood of flamingo pink bungalows arranged around the curving greens of a private golf course. Construction would take most of the summer, trucks moving sand, moving earth, a large crew of white guys and Mexicans and a couple Cahuilla Indians building the bungalows, importing great loads of sod, palm trees, shrubs, rose bushes. Seeding grass, digging ponds, installing fountains, paving streets, laying the high cement perimeter wall, painting it all pink. Darby was fifteen years old and he and some friends biked down there almost every day after school, during school if they ditched, and asked for work, unloading trees from trucks or seeding the grass or hauling tools from one end of the site to the other. Chickenshit, buck-an-hour jobs, but some cash for beer or cigarettes, for a bag of weed or a packet of ephedrine tablets from the truck stop by the highway. It was like some kind of saccharine fever dream, the place taking shape around them, pastel stucco and sculpted hedges, grass so green it seemed fake. The workers rode golf carts around the thin, twisting streets, gunning the carts as fast as their electric engines would go, taking the corners on two wheels, tipping over more often than not, disgorging tools and sod and mulch across the rich new asphalt in a torrent of belly-laughs and curses, calling for Darby and his friends, whoever had shown up that day, because this was one of their jobs, cleaning up after the workers had flipped a cart.

As the months went on, fewer of Darby's friends went with him to the site. They didn't understand his fascination with the place. It was hot, repetitive work, no money, all to build houses where rich old people would come to die. But Darby was entranced by the place, by the process, the progression of its construction and the accumulating end result. The strangeness of what was being built. He went down to the site almost every day. The foreman grew to expect him, had a list of things for him to do when he arrived, chewed him out if he didn't show.

At five o'clock they'd call it a day and sit out on the newly poured cement patio behind the first tee, or by one of the pools they'd filled prematurely, soaking their feet, drinking beers, passing bottles of tequila. When it got dark, someone would give him a ride home in the back of a pickup, drop him off at the entrance to the trailer park, muscles aching, woozy with booze and sun. He'd sit in the front room of the trailer and have a beer with Eustice and tell her all the things he'd learned at school that day. She'd listen and smile, Darby never quite sure if she believed his stories or just liked to hear him tell them.

There were days when it was too hot to work, and Darby would find the front gate locked, no sign of activity within. He'd climb the wall and walk the streets, the golf course, careful to stay off the seeded areas, giving the grass a chance to grow. He felt protective of the place. He'd helped build this, helped bring this remarkable thing to the desert. He relished those days alone, knowing it would all be over soon, that the crew would go on to the next job, leaving him behind, and the place would be filled by a colony of the aged, retirees and blue hairs, leather-skinned sunbathers by the pool, visiting grandchildren, the cautious carts of morning golfers, afternoon naps and cocktail hour, a massive Lincoln or Buick in every garage.

He would find a filled pool and strip down to his underpants, lie on his back and float. Watching the tops of palm trees moving against the purple sky, feeling the warmth of the water, his skin taking on sun. When his ears bobbed under there was a rushing sound, a seashell roar, and when they came back above there was nothing, just the silence of the desert. He'd float until the day faded, and then he'd gather his clothes and walk back along the coiled streets, evening coming slowly, the stillness around him becoming more complete.

In his bed in the back room of the trailer he slept soundly those nights, despite the heat, and on the rare occasion that he slept soundly now out in the pickup it was because he had dreams of that place, the last weeks before the colony arrived, the floating stillness, an entire day like a held breath.

He told The Kid all of this, minus the drinking and drugs. The Kid listened, looked out the windshield of the pickup at the dog dozing on the porch steps. Darby sat back in the seat, looked out at the house, the graying sky beyond. The night around them had paused, the silence had paused, so Darby kept talking.

One night toward the end of construction, after a couple of hours sitting and drinking at the first tee, some of the crew drove to a tattoo parlor in Palm Springs. Darby tagged along. He wanted to be part of this. A rite of manhood. Ink on your arm. He sat in the neon-lit shop, listening to the needle buzz, sketching an idea on the back of a hot rod magazine while the other guys got their tattoos.

The artist was a Cahuilla with a Fu-Manchu mustache named Gil, and when it was finally Darby's turn, he showed the sketch to Gil, to the other guys, who all thought it was some kind of headless snake. A long, elaborate curve that would start at the top of Darby's right shoulder, twisting and turning in on itself, branching off into other curves that circled his bicep before meeting again down at his elbow. Darby let them believe it was a snake. He knew that the truth would bring a shower of ragging and name-calling. The curves were actually the streets that moved through the retirement community, the white stone paths that hugged the bungalows and the greens of the golf course. He had walked them countless times, was able to draw them accurately from memory. It was a map of what they had built, but he let them believe it was a snake. Darby pulled off his t-shirt and Gil swabbed his arm and got to work. He didn't object when Gil added a snake's head to the end of the curves where all the streets met, what would be the community's front gate, didn't object when Gil inked yellow eyes and a flicking tongue, an inscription below the open mouth: *Don't Tread*. The map was the important thing, getting it down so he'd never forget what they'd built.

Within a week they were finished, the last bungalow up, the last fairway seeded. They took a final, celebratory drink at the eighteenth hole, packed the equipment and locked the gate behind them. The crew split and moved on to other jobs, some going back to Los Angeles, some going north or east where more golf courses were being conjured from the desert. Only Darby remained, back to school, back to his friends, who were all impressed with the badass snake twisting down his right arm. His skin was still tender and pink when he saw the first cars pull off the highway, air-conditioned Lincolns and Buicks, windows rolled up against the heat, the first gray settlers heading up toward the pink stucco walls.

He never went back. He was tempted, he thought about hopping the wall late some night, sneaking past the dozing security guards, stripping down and sliding into the cool water of one of the pools. But he resisted the urge. He knew it wouldn't be the same, knew that the place no longer belonged to him. In another year, he would buy a battered GTO with the money he'd saved from the job, and six months later he would leave that place for good, leave school and Eustice and the trailer, heading west into the sprawling city.

The Kid had his head cocked toward the open pickup window, listening. He'd continued his list of night sounds in his notebook. *Dog barking, woman yelling, back gate swinging open and shut.* Darby watched the curve of The Kid's ear. It was her ear, Lucy's; it was the same gentle slope. The Kid was growing to look more like her, had her ears and her eyes, her unruly thatch of straw-blond hair. Darby didn't know where it would end, if it would end. Didn't know if soon he would look over at The Kid and see more of her face than he could bear.

*I want to go,* The Kid wrote. *I want to see the place where you grew up.*

Darby looked back at the house, turned the radio up. A survivalist expert and a talk show host were debating the Tehachapi situation, what should or shouldn't be done if it was discovered that children were in the compound.

"We'll go," Darby said. "Someday we'll drive out and I'll show you where I'm from."

*I* f you want to see a secret, meet at midnight at the bus stop outside the library. The city library, not the school library. You can't tell anyone else what we're doing. You'll have to sneak out of your house without getting caught. Bring a flashlight. Write I WILL BE THERE on the back of this note if you want to come. If you don't want to come, flush this note down the toilet. TELL NO ONE ELSE.

The Kid made two of these notes while the class was waiting in line for lunch, careful to make sure no one else saw. He folded the first note into the palm of his hand and then offered his hand to Matthew to shake. Matthew looked at him like he was crazy. They'd never shaken hands before. But The Kid kept thrusting out his hand until Matthew took it and felt the note hidden there. Matthew looked at the folded paper. The Kid gave him a secretive, under-the-eyebrows look, and Matthew pushed the note down into the front pocket of his pants.

The Kid knew that girls didn't really shake hands, so for the second note he walked past Michelle and dropped the folded paper at the toe of her grungy sneaker.

"Kid, you dropped something," she said, too loud, and a couple of the girls in line turned to look, their faces scrunching with disgust seeing Michelle and The Kid standing so close by.

The Kid pointed quickly at the note, looked away, tried to act like nothing was happening.

"Kid, you dropped something," Michelle said again.

The Kid shook his head, kicked the note up onto Michelle's sneaker, walked quickly to his place in line. When he looked back, Michelle was bending over, picking up the note, unfolding the paper, mouthing the words as she read.

The Kid laid out the plan at lunch. Michelle didn't have a problem with the plan, but Matthew complained that there was no way he could get out of his house without his father knowing. The Kid told him he would have to find a way if he wanted to come. Matthew said that this was no problem for The Kid because The Kid's dad wasn't always around at night. The Kid told Matthew that he understood there were risks involved, but that what he was going to show them would be worth the risks.

Michelle pulled her note out of the pocket of her jeans, turned it over, wrote *I WILL BE THERE* on the back. Slid it across the table to The Kid. Matthew looked at his note. He couldn't decide. He seemed even smaller than usual. He looked like he was going to cry with the weight of the decision.

"Stop being such a pussy," Michelle said. "Stop being such a whiny bitch."

"You don't understand," Matthew said.

"What don't I understand? You're either a whiny bitch or you're not."

Matthew grabbed The Kid's pencil, scribbled *I WILL BE THERE* on the back of his note, pushed it across the table to The Kid. Sat back with his arms folded. He still looked like he was going to cry.

*Then it's settled,* The Kid wrote. *We'll meet tonight.*

The Kid took the fastest route home, even though it was a route he didn't particularly like, the least safe of all his routes. He wanted to get home and start planning the midnight excursion. He'd need to go back into his dad's toolbox and borrow a couple more masks and goggles for Matthew and Michelle. He might need to draw maps in case they got separated on the way to the burned house. There was a lot to do.

The real shortcut part of the route was a long, tight alleyway between two apartment buildings. The opening of the alleyway was on a side street past Sunset, and the other end dumped The Kid out just two blocks from home. It was like a galactic wormhole in an outer space comic: you went in the mouth, down the long stretch, and came out the other end at an impossible distance. The alleyway was only about two of The Kid's shoulder widths wide, so once he entered he had to either continue forward or head back. There were no other options, there was nowhere else to go. This was why he didn't really like that route. He knew that the alley was the perfect place for an ambush.

He stood in the entrance, looked all the way down its length to the daylight at the other end. That light was only two blocks from home. If he ran fast enough, if he was quick enough and lucky enough, he'd be there in no time at all.

He took a deep breath and sprinted into the alleyway, sneakers jumping, arms pumping, pushing as hard, running as fast as he could for that opening.

He wasn't quick. He wasn't lucky. They'd known somehow, or they'd guessed correctly. Halfway down the alleyway, Razz appeared at the opposite end, blocking the exit. The Kid stumbled to a halt, falling to one knee, a cold tingling in his fingers and toes. He turned back, desperate to see that the entrance was still clear. But there was something there, a familiar figure backlit by the falling sun. The figure moved in slowly, tall and lean, an exaggerated horror-movie stalk, its long arms out, fingers dragging across the red brick of the alley's walls.

Brian made pig noises as he approached, *oink oink* sounds through his nose. He called "Here piggy, piggy," in a low, soothing voice, a voice like The Kid's dad had used with Steve Rogers, a voice used to trap an animal.

Razz walked in from the other end, laughing a little, a raspy hatchet sound.

"I keep seeing you around my girlfriend, piggy," Brian said. "Why do you keep bothering my girlfriend?"

The Kid wished he had some of the courage he'd had back at school that day, when Arizona was a guest on his talk show, when he was making those jokes about Brian. The Kid wished he had the courage to open his notebook and write, *She's Not Your Girlfriend*, or, *You might think she is, but she isn't*. But The Kid's courage had fled, had found a way up and out of the alley.

"She tells me you keep bothering her, you keep following her," Brian said. "She said you smell like piss and shit. That you get so excited around her that you piss and shit yourself."

Arizona wouldn't say those things. The Kid knew she wouldn't say those things, but there was nothing he could do about it. Brian saying them out loud made them as good as true.

"*Cochino,*" Razz growled. "Here, piggy, piggy."

The Kid was breathing hard, sweating. There was no way out of the alleyway. No way past Razz, certainly no way past Brian. He looked around frantically for something he missed, something he wasn't seeing, some way out, some way around, but there was nothing. He'd made an awful mistake, taking this route home.

"I don't want you going near her," Brian said. His tone was changing, getting deeper, rougher. He bit off the ends of his words. "I don't want you talking to her, sitting next to her, touching her. I don't want you infecting her, pig. Do you understand me?"

Brian was maybe ten feet away. The Kid looked at Brian, tried to nod, to give up, but his head wouldn't move.

"I didn't hear you," Brian said.

The Kid tried to nod, but nothing worked, nothing moved. He imagined what a relief it would be to call out, to yell, *Help! Help!* What a relief it would be to let his voice loose.

Razz shoved The Kid in the back, hard. The Kid stumbled forward, stopping a few feet from Brian.

"I know you can talk," Brian said. "I want to hear you say something. If I don't hear you say something, I'm going to kill you."

Razz shoved him again from behind. The Kid flew forward, crashing into Brian, and Brian pushed him back into Razz, and then Brian was upon him. The Kid started swinging, kicking, hitting Brian in the chest, in the arms, but this only made Brian stronger, only made him furious, tight-faced and red, and then Razz was pulling The Kid to the ground and Brian was on top of him, teenager-strength almost, dad-strength almost, pinning him down, holding The Kid's wrists with his hands, trapping The Kid's legs with his legs.

Brian rolled The Kid over, face first into the broken cement, a patch of dirt. The Kid couldn't breathe, his nose and mouth pushed into the ground.

"Say something," Razz said.

The Kid couldn't breath. There was dirt in his mouth. He struggled, panicking. He couldn't breathe, but Brian wouldn't let him up. The Kid's nose was mashed into the cement, felt like it was going to break.

"Say something and we'll let you go," Brian said.

He could say something. He could force out a sound, a noise, something close to a word. Maybe that was really all they wanted. Maybe they'd let him up and leave him alone, maybe they'd never attack him again, maybe the incidents would end, the meetings with Mr. Bromwell, maybe it would all be over if he said something, if he broke the Covenant.

"Do it," Brian said, pushing The Kid's face harder into the ground. "Say something or I'll kill you."

A sound, a noise, something close to a word, and maybe they'd let him up, let him go home. Who would know if he broke the Covenant? Who would hear in this stinking alleyway?

"Make him say something," Razz said. His voice was getting fainter, drifting further away. The Kid couldn't see anything but black. "Make him say something or he'll die in the dirt."

But The Kid thought of his mom, alone out there somewhere. He thought of breaking the Covenant and the awfulness of knowing that his mom would never come back, that he'd never hear her open the front door of the house. He felt how hopeless that would be, how unbearably sad, and he thought about his dad, sitting in the pickup at night, waiting for her to come back, thought about having to tell his dad that he had broken the Covenant and she wasn't coming home.

"Do it," Brian whispered into The Kid's ear. A tribal chant. "Do it, do it, do it."

The Kid shut his mouth, biting a thick mouthful of dirt, blocking the last possible passage of air. He thought of his mom coming through the front door, his mom returning, that sound he had waited for, and he knew this was still possible, knew he had preserved this chance, so he shut his mouth, clenched his jaw. He heard a voice far off, back off and away, Razz or Brian, someone saying something, and then he felt a final push into the dirt and the darkness overtook him completely.

The Kid and his dad were on the road. They were going from town to town in the pickup, days and days of road and then a town, days and days of road and then a town, moving slowly across the map of the country, west to east. In the towns they asked questions of people on the streets, people working in stores, asked if anyone had seen The Kid's mom, if she'd passed this way. They had a picture that they showed around, a snapshot from a couple of years back of The Kid's mom sitting at the kitchen table, eyes closed, chest inflated, just about to blow out the candles on her birthday cake. The Kid was standing beside her, hands clasped over his heart, smiling, watching his mom do something he thought only kids were supposed to do. His dad wasn't in the picture because his dad was taking the picture. They showed it around everywhere they went, asking people to look at the woman blowing out the candles. *Take a good look. Are you sure you don't recognize her? Take a good look. Don't be so quick to say no.*

At the beginning of the trip, The Kid's dad had admitted that he'd lied to The Kid, that he'd lied to everybody. That The Kid's mom hadn't fallen in her classroom, hadn't been carried by one of her students. He told The Kid that he was sorry. The Kid listened to his dad's explanation, and then he wrote, *It's OK, I understand.* The Kid did understand. The Kid thought that if he had a kid and something like this had happened, he probably would have done the same thing.

Every night, he and his dad parked on the outskirts of what-ever town they'd been through and lay in the truck, under the stars, head to feet on the bench seat, and The Kid hosted his talk show, a series of special episodes, *It's That Kid Across America!* His guests were people they'd met earlier in the day, people they'd asked for information about his mom, bus drivers, bank tellers, supermarket checkers. But on the show The Kid didn't ask about his mom, he asked questions about his guests' lives, where they'd grown up, what their interests were, if they had any special talents or hobbies. He wrote their answers in his notebook, what he imagined their answers would be.

His dad watched the show, drank beers, smiled at the jokes. It was hard to sleep in the truck. The Kid didn't know how his dad had done it for so long out in the driveway. Maybe he hadn't, maybe he'd just laid out there awake, thinking, sad that he'd had to lie to everybody, had to lie to The Kid, waiting for The Kid's mom to come home.

They weren't traveling in a straight line. A straight line would have been the fastest route between Los Angeles and wherever they were going, but The Kid's dad didn't want to leave any stone unturned, so they zig-zagged across the map, slowly, dipping down, dipping up, but always moving further away from home. It got colder as they drove. The days got shorter. At night, they began to roll up the pickup's windows when they slept. When they woke in the morning, after dozing for an hour or two, they found frost on the windshield, little crystallized paw prints on the hood of the truck.

In a town somewhere deep in the mountains, they stopped so his dad could get a cup of coffee at a gas station. The Kid stood outside, breathed hard on the gas station window, wrote his name in the foggy breath with a gloved finger. His real name, *Whitley Darby*. It seemed strange to see it, like a secret someone had just told. He breathed along the window some more and drew the angel from the burned house, drew her wings and dress and cowboy boots. He tried to draw the missing hand, but he still couldn't get it right. His dad came out of the gas station, blowing on his cup of coffee. The Kid kept drawing. He needed to finish the angel because the angel was a signal. He knew that now. When he finished the angel, she would fly up through the hole in the burned house's roof and find The Kid's mom out in the country somewhere, tell her it was okay to come home. His dad started the pickup, tapped the horn, ready to leave.

The Kid couldn't get the drawing right, finally pulled himself away from the window, the unfinished hand.

That night, head to toe in the pickup in a grocery store parking lot, The Kid explained the Covenant to his dad. He filled two pages in his notebook. He wrote fast, surprised at how much he wanted to tell, how relieved he felt writing it all down. His dad read the explanation. The Kid wasn't sure how his dad felt about it. If he was mad or sad or what. His dad had The Kid's socked foot in his hand, and he squeezed it while he reread the story. The Kid didn't know if he should keep to the Covenant or not, but he decided that he would do whatever his dad said, whatever his dad thought was right. His dad usually knew what was right, even if sometimes it meant he had to lie.

Finally, his dad let out a long breath and said that The Kid should keep to the Covenant. He said that he knew what The Kid was doing was hard, but he had to be strong, he had to stick to his word. He said The Kid was their only hope.

The Kid was disappointed and relieved to hear this all at the same time. He'd thought that maybe the whole thing could be over, maybe they could just go home and try to forget about everything that had happened, but he was relieved because he wasn't sure he remembered how to talk, he was scared to talk, and he was scared to break the Covenant. He didn't want to ruin their only hope. He didn't want to give up on finding his mom. He'd gone this far, and he couldn't turn back now.

He felt a dull pain in his chest, a hurting pressure. This was normal. This happened sometimes. Sometimes he missed his mom so much that he had trouble breathing. Sometimes he missed her so much that his chest hurt.

The Kid woke in the alleyway. It was darker, later, getting on into evening. He pushed himself up to his knees. His nose was sore, his chest was sore. There was dirt and grass in his mouth. He couldn't remember what had happened, and then he remembered. Brian and Razz had ambushed him, beaten him up. They were gone now, they'd left him to die in the dirt.

She was there, of course, walking down the alley, fast, face concerned, glasses slipping down her nose. She'd come looking for him when he hadn't come home on time. She'd checked all his routes, she'd known all his routes somehow and found him here. She was coming down the alleyway, concerned but relieved to have found him.

"You had me scared, Whitley," she said, a little anger mixed in with her relief, more than a little, but The Kid didn't mind, that was okay, that was fine as long as she was back, as long as the awful dream was over. He wanted to hug her, throw his arms around her, he was so relieved she was here. But he didn't, that would be silly. His mom didn't know about his dream, the terrible thing he'd dreamed had happened.

"What are you doing here?" she said, and then she got close enough to see his face, the dirt on his cheeks, in his mouth. She knelt on the ground next to him, put her hand to his face. "What happened?" she said, and he opened his mouth to tell her.

The Kid woke in the alleyway. It was darker, later, getting on into evening. He made his way down to the end of the alley, out onto the sidewalk. He walked in the dusk, lighted store signs flickering on above him, streetlights switching on.

The world was the same, everything was the same. The Covenant was still the Covenant. His mom was still gone. He'd been beaten up and knocked out and now he was awake. That was all, nothing else.

The driveway was empty when he got home. Steve Rogers was sleeping on the steps of the front porch. When The Kid came into the yard, Steve stretched, got to his feet, and moved to the other end of the porch, like maybe he knew The Kid wouldn't step over him if he was lying on the steps. The Kid climbed onto the porch, unlocked the security screen, the front door. He still had his backpack, his notebook. All was not lost. They were still meeting at midnight to go to the burned house. He would still show them the mural, he would still show them the angel. He went inside the empty house and started turning on lights.

They've got loudspeakers set up by the command post, blaring messages from the survivalists' families," Bob said. "They've stepped up their efforts, now that they know there are kids inside. Sometimes on the overnight broadcast, the newscasters shut up for a few minutes and you can hear these mothers' and fathers' and little kids' voices, pleading with the Realists to come out."

Bob had called and Darby met him at the fish fry. Darby found him in their usual booth, an untouched plate of fish sticks in front of him, a new pack of cigarettes on the table next to a six-pack in a brown paper bag. Only two cans were left when Darby arrived, one set in front of Bob, the other waiting for Darby.

"That's what they're calling them on the news now," Bob said. "The Realists."

There was a helicopter shot on the TV behind the counter, searchlights raking the roof of the compound, the surrounding scrub brush and dust.

"What have I missed?" Bob said. "How many jobs?"

"Just one."

Bob shook his head, sucked his teeth. This was unacceptable, this dereliction of duty. "What was it?"

"Nothing much. The usual."

"What's the usual?"

Darby tried not to think of the unfinished room, the wooden rabbit. "An apartment in Chinatown," he said. "Couple of rooms, couple of hours."

"Just you and Roistler?"

Darby nodded.

"You do the talking?"

"There wasn't much to say."

"To who?"

Darby turned his beer can, waited for Bob to correct his mistake. They never discussed details of a job after the job was complete. They never asked these kinds of questions.

"Who was there?" Bob said.

"The father of the girl they found."

Bob took a breath, looked at his plate like he was imagining the scene. A father in a doorway. What the father would have said, what Bob would have said.

"What did you say?"

Darby opened his beer. "I'm sorry for your loss."

The woman at the cash register sprayed the top of the counter with a bottle of cleanser, wiped it down with a gray rag.

"What did Molina tell you about the Inglewood job?" Bob said.

"He said there wasn't much to tell."

Bob looked at the TV, nodded like maybe this was correct. "It wasn't much of a mess. Some fluid on the carpet in the closet, some spray on the walls. No different than any other job." Bob picked at the batter of a fish stick with a split fingernail. "It was hot as an oven in that closet, though. I was sweating like a pig in the suit, and that made it harder than it should have been. The goggles and the mask. Everything wet, slippery."

Bob took a drink. The receipt for the beer and cigarettes was stuck to the bottom of his can.

"How many of those have we done?" he said. "A hundred? A hundred closets?"

Bob pulled a clean cigarette from the pack, tapped it on the table, turned it in his fingers. The golden stains on his fingers matched the stains in his mustache. Darby could smell him from across the table, stale beer and sweat and menthol.

"I sprayed the walls, tore out the carpet," Bob said. "This is maybe eight feet square of carpet, that's the size of the closet. An overhead light bulb with a chain. She'd taken most of the clothes out to make room, laid them out across the bed."

The volume was up on the TV and the feds' loudspeaker could be heard, recorded voices of the families pleading with those inside.

"Before that job, I never thought about it," Bob said. "You know what I mean. I never let myself think about it."

*Come out, please*, they said. Women's voices in the night, men's voices, children. *Come out, please. Come home.*

"And then I did," Bob said. "Just for a second, in that closet. And now I can't stop thinking about it."

A woman in a closet; a girl in her bedroom with a wooden rabbit in her hand. Darby had to make a conscious effort not to squeeze his beer can too tightly, to keep his fingers from pressing dents into the aluminum. He tried to focus on anything other than what Bob was saying, but the only other noises were the voices on TV.

*Please come out. Honey, please. We just want you to come home.*

"I can imagine the fear," Bob said. "This woman in her closet tying this cord around her neck. To make that decision and go through with it. I can imagine it now. I can't stop imagining it."

The woman behind the counter sprayed the tile walls, wiped them with the gray rag. The rushing in Darby's ears was hard, insistent. He gripped the beer can. He needed something in his hands. The thought of the room in Chinatown pulled at his legs, at his arms, so he squeezed the beer can to stay rooted in his seat.

"I know we don't talk about this," Bob said. "I know the rules. I made the rules. But I can't stop thinking about it now."

Bob shifted his weight in the booth, took the last drink of his beer. He noticed the receipt stuck to the bottom of the can and pulled it loose. He read through the receipt, eyebrows raised, like this was an interesting thing he'd found, like this was an important thing.

"I got into the car that night," he said. "What you're talking about. The job in Chinatown. The pager buzzed and I got dressed and got into the car. But I never made it onto the freeway. I drove around the block a few times, went back home."

Bob folded the receipt carefully, slid it into the pocket of his shirt. He looked at his hands, the cigarette in his fingers. Darby closed his eyes, held tight to his beer can. He felt the booth, the restaurant falling away. The rushing in his ears was almost unbearable, the relentless white roar.

"I don't know if I'll be back, David," he said. "The next time the pager buzzes I'll get in my car, but I don't know if I'll be back."

The Kid washed the dirt and grass out of his mouth, dabbed his bloody lip with a wad of toilet paper. Looked at himself in the bathroom mirror. There was nothing noticeable from the attack in the alleyway. No bruises, no scars.

He borrowed two more facemasks and pairs of goggles from his dad's toolbox. He packed his backpack with the supplies, the flashlight and extra batteries. His dad still wasn't home. He sat on the edge of his bed and watched his clock go from 11:00 p.m. to 11:30 to 11:45.

They were at the library bus stop when he arrived. Michelle sat large and impassive at one end of the bench. Matthew sat at the other, his hands and feet crossed in nervous knots. Michelle was blabbing about something, but Matthew wasn't listening. He rocked back and forth on the bench, having second, third, fourth thoughts about this whole thing.

The street was quiet. There was a low electric hum from the traffic light hanging above, a sharp click when it changed colors, but there weren't any cars, wasn't any traffic. The Kid stood in front of the bench. Michelle and Matthew looked at him, their faces shining red, then green in the traffic light glow. The Kid felt that he should announce something. His troops had gathered, improbably, in the middle of the night, by his orders. Something should be announced. He pulled out his notebook and pencil.

*I'm glad to see you all made it.*

This seemed less than inspiring. Michelle yawned. Matthew shivered a little in the chilly air.

The Kid led them across Sunset, down the hill, past the school. He had to keep reassuring Matthew that it wasn't much farther, that he wasn't taking them all the way across the city. Matthew jumped at every noise, shining his flashlight anxiously, afraid of every shadow. Michelle shlumped along a few steps behind. She had her own overstuffed backpack strapped across her shoulders. The Kid didn't know what was inside. He hadn't asked them to bring anything but flashlights.

They walked alongside the long wall of the strip mall. They passed the bare feet sleeping in the cardboard box. They crossed the uneven sidewalk down into the next neighborhood, until finally they stood in front of the burned house.

"What's that smell?" Matthew said. He covered his nose with the sleeve of his jacket.

"It smells like a dead person," Michelle said. Their voices sounded so loud in the night. The Kid jabbed a finger to his lips, calling for silence. He walked up onto the porch, motioned for them to follow. At the front door he turned. Matthew and Michelle were still standing on the sidewalk, looking up at the house, the dark eyes of the burst windows. The Kid waited, letting them take it in. Then he motioned again and Michelle came up onto the porch.

"I'm going to stay out here," Matthew whispered.

"You can't," Michelle said. "You'll get caught. You have to come inside."

"I won't get caught. I swear. I'll stay out here."

"I'll come down there and carry you in."

"I'm not joking."

"Me either."

Matthew looked at Michelle, looked back up the street the way they had come. The Kid could see him weighing his options, deciding whether or not walking back home alone was worse than going into the burned house. Finally he shook his head, angry with himself for even going this far. He ran up and joined them on the porch.

Michelle pulled her flashlight out of her backpack, shone it around the porch. The light flickered and went dark. She clicked it on and off a few times. No luck. "Fuck," she said, whacking the flashlight against her thigh, trying to bring it back to life. "Fucking piece of shit."

The Kid crouched, motioned for them to huddle around. He shone his flashlight on the steel security door, the photographs wedged in behind the bars. He moved the light slowly across the photos, letting them see the faces, the woman with the red hair, her friends and relatives. It was important to him that they saw this before they saw what was inside. He felt they should know her a little, felt they should know what her mom had looked like, the kinds of places she'd visited.

"Who put these here?" Michelle whispered.

*Friends,* The Kid wrote. *Relatives.*

"How many of these people died here?" Matthew said.

They both looked at The Kid. He could see they were a little afraid of what the answer might be. The Kid held up one finger. Matthew looked back at the photograph of the red-haired woman alone, smiling at the camera in front of the gas pumps. He wrinkled his nose again at the smell.

"Is she still inside?" Matthew said.

They both looked at The Kid again. He wasn't trying to scare them, but he felt he had to tell the truth. He nodded.

The Kid took the paper masks and goggles out of his backpack, handed them out, demonstrated how to put them on. Then he pulled the security door open and they all squeezed inside.

The flashlight played against the walls and floor of the little front room. Someone held onto the back of The Kid's shirt. It felt strange to be the one who wasn't afraid. He moved the light around so they could see the holes in the walls, the jagged pile of wood that had been the table and chairs. The Kid could hear their hard breathing through the paper masks.

It was Michelle's hand grabbing the back of The Kid's shirt, which surprised him.

He led them through the kitchen, across the busted tile, past the charred appliances. He shone the light straight up so they could see the holes in the ceiling, the night sky beyond. They stopped at the pile of rubble at the bedroom door, stood looking at the remains of the bed. Michelle and Matthew were both holding the back of The

Kid's shirt now. He turned and pulled them slowly down the hall, into the living room at the back of the house.

He held the flashlight over his head to illuminate as much of the room as he could. The ruined drapes and furniture husks, the TV with its head blown off, the small clumps of melted picture-frame glass. Then he moved the light across the walls, gradually revealing the mural, starting at the rolling waves and the pirate ship and the rowboat, moving along the streets of their neighborhood, the houses and the school, finally bringing the light to rest at the center of the far wall, the unfinished drawing of the red-haired woman lifting off the ground.

The Kid set the flashlight on the floor, clicked on the high beam to show most of the mural at once. Michelle let go of his shirt, walked to the wall. She stood in front of the mural, held her fingers out, a few inches from the chalk. Followed the lines of the waves as the water turned to asphalt, the rolling streets of the neighborhood. She ended in front of the red-haired woman, looked down at her boots, up at her eyes, further up to the hole in the ceiling.

"You did this?" Matthew said to The Kid, his voice muffled behind the paper mask.

The Kid nodded. *Except the angel.*

"What's her name?" Michelle said, still facing the red-haired woman.

The Kid shrugged. Michelle turned to him for a response and The Kid shrugged again.

"She's not really here," Matthew said. "It's just a drawing of somebody, not the actual person." This sounded to The Kid more like a question than a statement of fact.

"How long did it take to draw this?" Michelle said. The Kid joined her at the wall. Matthew came along behind, still clutching The Kid's shirt.

*A few days.*

"You come here by yourself?" Matthew said.

The Kid nodded.

"No one else knows?" Michelle said.

The Kid shook his head.

Michelle looked back at the red-haired woman, moved her hand around the white-chalk glow of her face and arms.

"We shouldn't be here," Matthew whispered. "This isn't what you're supposed to do with dead people."

"So what?" Michelle said.

"This is a blasphemy. This is something against God."

Michelle wasn't listening. She traced the outlines of the angel's wings, followed the curves of the feathers, keeping her fingers a few inches from the wall. At the tips of the wings, she lifted her hands away, let them drift up a little toward the hole in the ceiling, the cool darkness beyond.

Matthew complained most of the way back, sure that his father had woken up by then, found him missing, called the police. Michelle was strangely quiet, preoccupied. At the corner of Sunset, she tossed her dead flashlight into a garbage can.

They parted ways at the bus stop. Matthew hustled down the sidewalk toward his street, breaking into a run when he reached the gated liquor store on the corner. The Kid nodded to Michelle by way of goodbye, started back around the library toward home.

She was still there when he looked back, sitting on the bus stop bench. He didn't know what she was doing, why she'd be waiting for the bus. The Kid walked back to the bench.

"I'm not going home for a while," she said. "I'm going to stay out here."

*Why?*

"Never mind why. None of your business why."

*How long?*

Michelle shrugged. She opened her backpack and pulled out a Twinkie. She tore open the cellophane and bit off the top half of the cake.

*Longer than an hour?*

Michelle didn't answer, took another bite of the Twinkie.

*Where are you going to sleep?*

"Here," she said, mouth full. "I'll sleep right here."

*You can't sleep here.*

"Why the fuck not?"

*You'll get mugged or killed.*

"Good," she said. "So what?" Then she changed her mind. "Nobody's going to kill me. I'll fuck up whoever tries to kill me."

You can't sleep out here.

"You don't believe I could do that? Fuck somebody up?"

*I believe you.*

"Then what's the problem?" She popped the remainder of the Twinkie into her mouth, balled the cellophane, tossed it toward the overflowing garbage can at the end of the shelter.

The Kid looked up at the library. There was a nice lawn around the building, deep and dark. There were trees against the stone wall, places to hide, to sleep.

*You can sleep up there by the library,*

Michelle swiveled on the bench, looked up at the lawn, the trees. The Kid followed her to the side of the building. She dropped her backpack in a corner by the wide stone steps.

"Good. I'm here," she said. "You happy? Go home, Kid. See you later."

The Kid pulled a couple of Matthew's *Captain America* comics out of his backpack, handed them to Michelle.

"What am I going to do with these?" she said. "I can't even see the pages."

He took out his flashlight, handed it to her.

*I need it back.*

"Fine. Good," she said. "You'll get it back."

She clicked on the light, tested it against the side of the library, shining it up into the shadowy reaches of the trees.

The Kid zipped up his pack, readjusted it on his back, walked across the lawn to the sidewalk. When he looked back he could see the yellow circle of the flashlight beam moving across the side of the library, up into the trees, out through the lawn, scanning the terrain. At the end of the block he looked back again, but this time the light was off, the library lawn was dark again.

They had been waiting for he didn't know how long, Darby and The Kid, sitting at the kitchen table, macaroni and cheese cooling on their plates. Lucy had placed the dishes on the table and then she had left quickly, up to the bathroom, closing the door behind her. A few minutes later Darby knocked and she'd said that she was fine, she was all right. She'd be down in a minute. He'd taken his seat at the table again, told The Kid they could start as soon as his mom came back down.

Darby took sips of his water. There was no alcohol in the house, not even a beer in the fridge. This was a decision they'd made, he and Lucy, a month or so before, after the phone call about Earl, after a few days of Lucy calling in sick to school, unable to leave the house. The house was completely dry. This was a decision they'd made, after she'd gone to see her doctor and he'd written her a prescription, a medication that was supposed to help.

They'd been waiting for he didn't know how long. He stood outside the bathroom, quietly saying her name, his ear to the door. He could hear something, some kind of rhythmic movement from inside the bathroom, the fabric of her clothes rubbing against themselves. He said her name but there was no answer, hadn't been an answer for ten, fifteen minutes.

He opened the door, slowly, still saying her name. He didn't want to scare her. He had scared her before, had come upon her in the kitchen or the bedroom and surprised her somehow, like she'd forgotten he was there, a stranger, an intruder in the house.

She was sitting on the floor, her back to the toilet, her hands covering her ears, eyes shut tight, rocking from side to side. Her lips were moving but she wasn't making a sound.

Lucy, he said, but she didn't open her eyes, didn't move her hands from her ears.

He stepped inside, closed the bathroom door behind him. He didn't want The Kid to follow him in. He knelt down beside her and said her name again and when she didn't respond he took her wrists in his hands and at this her eyes snapped open, wide and wild and terrified. She shifted herself away, out of his grasp, up against the wall, still rocking, still clutching her ears, looking at Darby like she had no idea who he was.

He stood across from the seafood restaurant, watched the same waiter pull the security gate closed and head up toward the bus stop, hands in his jacket pockets. The street silent, motionless this late. Darby watched the dark windows of the restaurant, the apartment above. He spat onto the sidewalk, tried to clear the speck. He'd thought he could keep himself from coming here, thought that once he was here he might be able to turn away and go back home. He'd thought he might be stronger than this.

He spat again, put his head down and crossed the street.

There was a small window at sidewalk level on the side of the building. No glass, just the side of a cardboard box stuffed into the frame. Bars, Darby thought. Steel bars, a security screen would prevent something like this. He pulled the cardboard out of the window, lay flat on the sidewalk, pulled himself inside. A basement, dark and musty, the smell of laundry detergent, mildew. The only light was from outside, neon shop signs and a streetlight through the open window. He climbed the staircase at the far end of the basement, opened the door at the top, trying to minimize the scream of the old hinges. He squeezed out into a back hallway where he found a flight of steep steps. The stairwell that gripped the back of the building, he guessed. The steps that led up to the plant-choked landing on the other side of the apartment's sliding glass door.

He took the steps, careful with his weight on the creaky boards. At the top landing, he could see the streets of Chinatown below, the towers of downtown beyond. He maneuvered carefully through the piles of boxes, the plants, the twisted knot of bicycles. Stood at the glass door. He pulled the handle and the door slid open easily.

The room smelled familiar, Everclean carpet cleanser and disinfectant. He let his eyes adjust and focus, the darkness pulling back to gray, revealing shapes, outlines. The bathroom door, the bed, the dresser. He stepped through the room, the rushing in his ears so loud he'd be unable to hear if someone was coming up the stairs after him, if someone was coming in from the front. He stopped a few feet from the dresser when another shape revealed itself, inches from his next step.

There was a body on the floor.

Darby didn't move, didn't breathe, waited for more of the darkness to recede around the shape.

There was a sheet spread out across the carpet, and a pillow, and a man curled into both, asleep. Darby could see more the longer he stood still, the longer he held his breath. The visible half of the man's face, pale white in the darkness. It was the father; it was Peter. The toe of Darby's boot was almost touching his ribcage.

He waited for Peter to wake with a start, jump to his feet, howl at the intrusion. Waited for the man to rightfully defend his home. Nothing happened. Darby watched the man, his body twisted on the floor, his hands clinging to the sheet. Holding on while he slept, still dressed, in the same clothes he'd worn during the cleanup.

Darby nodded, kept nodding his head, keeping it away. This was what it looked like, this kind of sorrow. Darby nodded, took a breath, stepped around Peter, further into the room.

The dresser was as he'd left it, the photographs, the bottles of perfume and hairspray. He picked up the wooden rabbit, held it in his hand. His hands were shaking, hadn't stopped shaking since he'd left the fish fry. He was sure that the noise of his shaking would wake Peter, that the man would rise up behind him in the mirror over the dresser, but there was nothing, no reflection but his own dark shape.

Dawn light through the grimy windows of the garage, dust swirling in tight spirals, the ragged crow of a rooster somewhere in the neighborhood. Darby set the wooden rabbit into the drawer with the ring and the snow globe. Tired, unsteady on his feet. He took the newspaper clipping from his pocket and placed it into the drawer. *Greene Goes the Distance.* He closed the drawer and stood in the garage and waited for what he hoped would come, waited for the relief, the feeling of the finished thing.

The Kid stood by the dodgeball wall before school. He saw Razz joking with some other kids in his tagging crew, saw Brian and some boys from the track team, saw Arizona talking to Rhonda Sizemore. No sign of Michelle or Matthew. He wondered how long Michelle had stayed out by the library, what time she'd finally gone home. He wondered if Matthew had gotten caught by his father, if he'd spilled the beans and told everything about the burned house, about the Covenant.

Finally, Michelle came through the gate into the courtyard, backpack slung over her shoulder, her shirt and jeans wet with dew from the library grass. She gave The Kid a warning look as she passed, like he shouldn't make a big deal, like he should stop staring at her. But he couldn't stop staring at her. She'd slept all night out next to the library. He couldn't believe it.

By lunchtime, Matthew still hadn't shown up. The Kid and Michelle sat alone at their table. She'd eaten all the food in her backpack the night before, and she didn't have any money, so The Kid let her eat his lunch. She wasn't too thrilled with the apple or the carrot sticks, but she devoured the sandwich.

*How long are you going to sleep there?*

Michelle shrugged, spoke with her mouth full of peanut butter. "As long as I want. Maybe I'll move around, sleep somewhere else every night. Plenty of places to sleep."

She seemed particularly fearless now. The Kid ate the carrot sticks she'd abandoned on the table.

"You think Matthew got caught?" she said.

*I don't know.*

"I'll bet he got caught and his dad beat the shit out of him. You ever see that? His dad beat the shit out of him?"

The Kid shook his head.

"Your dad ever beat the shit out of you?"

The Kid shook his head.

Michelle rolled her eyes.

*Why aren't you going home?* The Kid wrote.

"Is that your business?"

The Kid shrugged.

"I mean, what the fuck business is it of yours, Kid?"

*You've got my flashlight.*

Michelle bit off another large hunk of the sandwich. "I'm sick of my mom's boyfriend's bullshit, that's why I'm not going home. I'm getting pretty close to fucking killing him, so I thought I'd better leave. Is that a good enough answer for you?"

*Yes.*

"You believe I could actually do that? Kill her boyfriend?"

The Kid didn't want to answer.

"You believe I could do that?"

The Kid nodded. He believed her. She'd slept outside all night.

"You're fucking right I could do it," she said. "Who cares anyway? You think they even noticed I was gone? My mom or my sisters? They could give a shit." She popped a straw into The Kid's juice box. "Remember that money my mom keeps for me in her bedroom?"

*Yes.*

"Her boyfriend came in while I was getting the rest of it. He went completely fucking crazy. Threw me all around the room. He's lucky my sisters were there, or I would have fucking killed him. But I didn't want them to see that. Better I just get out of there." She stuffed the rest of the sandwich into her mouth, took a long drink of juice. "You happy now? That a good enough explanation for you?"

The Kid nodded. He wasn't happy, but he nodded anyway.

"How many times have you gone to that house and drawn on the walls?"

*A few.*

"You ever get scared in there?"

*Sometimes a little.*

"Well, you're sort of a pussy, Kid." She drained the juice, pulling on the straw until the box crumpled in on itself. "After school, get some food from your house, bring it to the library. Whatever you got. No carrots, no apples. Anything else. More juice. Can you do that?"

*I can do that.*

"Good. Good boy." She looked across the table at The Kid's face. "What happened to your lip? You get punched or something?"

The Kid was surprised she noticed. No one else had noticed. He thought he'd done a good job of covering it up.

"Who did it? Your dad?"

The Kid shook his head. *Brian B. and Razz.*

Michelle brushed the sandwich wrapper and the empty juice box off the table. "I'm telling you, Kid," she said. "A badass scar would keep those fuckers away. A badass scar would change everything."

The Kid crouched behind a bush in the Crump's backyard, looking up at Matthew's bedroom window, wondering how to do this. On TV, people were always throwing rocks at windows to get the attention of whoever was inside. But The Kid thought that throwing a rock would probably break the window. Then again, he didn't have a very good throwing arm, so he probably couldn't even hit the window from this distance. It was what his dad always called a moot point.

He couldn't even be sure that Matthew was home. Matthew's mother's car was in the driveway, but his father's was gone. Who knew what Matthew had told his parents? The entire Crump family could be at their church right now, praying to break The Kid's Covenant.

Shiny white pebbles were arranged around the bottoms of the bushes and trees in the backyard. The Kid scooped up a few, stayed in a crouch, ran over behind the garbage cans beneath the kitchen window. No sign of anyone inside. He leaned back and threw one of the pebbles up at Matthew's window. The pebble reached the height of the window, but stayed about three feet out from the house. It hung in the air for a second, then fell back to earth. The Kid had to duck to avoid catching it in the eye. Still in the crouch, he ran back out into the yard, about halfway between the bush and the house, then he turned and threw another of the pebbles at the window. He watched it fly, arcing too high but then dropping in a slow, smooth curve, striking the glass of the window with a loud crack. The Kid ducked back behind the bush, sat on the ground, breathing heavily. Maybe he'd broken the window. He didn't even think he could throw that high or that hard and now maybe he'd broken the window. A dog started to bark a few houses away. He waited for the sound of the back door opening, Matthew's mother coming out of the house to look for the culprit. Or the sound of sirens, even, if Matthew's mother had called the police.

The dog stopped barking. The Kid peered around the bush, looked up at the window. It wasn't broken from what he could see. But Matthew's face was there, looking out into the yard, searching for the source of the noise. The Kid stood from behind the bush, waved his arms. Matthew looked down, saw The Kid, motioned for him to duck back down. The Kid sat on the ground, waited. He heard the back door open, then the padded sound of running footsteps across the lawn. Matthew jumped the last few feet to the bush, landed in a heap beside The Kid.

"What are you doing here?"

*What happened? Why weren't you in school?*

"I'm sick. I had an asthma attack last night after I got home. My mother kept me out of school."

You got caught?

"Why do you think I got caught?"

*You weren't at school.*

"I just told you I had an asthma attack. Why would I get caught? Did you get caught?"

*Did you tell your dad anything?*

"About what?"

*About anything?*

Matthew sat against the bush, looked out into the back half of the yard.

"I'm sick of keeping these secrets," he said. "You ask me to keep too many secrets."

That wasn't an answer. The Kid wanted an answer.

*Did you tell?*

"No."

*Are you going to tell?*

"I don't know."

*You promised not to tell.*

Matthew said nothing.

*Loose lips sink ships.*

Matthew didn't smile at The Kid's joke, the familiar phrase. He was holding the pebble that The Kid had thrown. He must have picked it up on his mad dash out to the bush. The white of the rock was bright against his skin.

"I don't think we should be friends for a while," Matthew said. "I don't like having all these secrets." He put the pebble back in its spot under the bush. He didn't look at The Kid. After a few seconds, he stood and ran back inside.

The house was empty when The Kid got home. He went out to the garage, lifted the door as high as he could manage, crawled underneath. Golden light inside from the high grubby windows. The last few minutes of the day. Dust jumped and stirred from the floor as he made his way back, squeezing between boxes, crates, old bikes, long-ago chairs and tables. He saw his wooden crib in a far corner. He saw his metal rocking horse in another corner. Toward the back of the garage he found what he was looking for, a box labeled *Extraordinary* in his mom's handwriting. More unsold issues of the comic book. He thought Michelle might like these, something to read if she couldn't get to sleep outside the library.

The sunlight faded slowly through the windows. He stood between the boxes and could feel it pulling away. Day almost done. Back at his dad's old workbench he looked for extra batteries, another flashlight. He opened a drawer and found a small stack of Country & Western cassettes. He opened a drawer and found nothing but yellow blocks of sticky notes. He opened a drawer and found a snow globe, a wooden rabbit, a gold ring, an envelope that was sealed shut. A piece of newspaper with a picture of a football player.

He took the rabbit out of the drawer. It looked hand-carved, like someone had whittled the shape and features out of a small piece of dark wood. A good-luck charm of some kind, maybe. One of the rabbit's ears was higher than the other. One of its feet was chipped off. He rubbed his thumb across the smooth wood, the little dips and pits. He put the rabbit in the pocket of his slacks.

There was a cassette on the workbench. It was one of his old tapes. He recognized the brand on the unmarked label. His old tape recorder was out, too. He hadn't thought about his recorder in a long time. All of the things he used to tape, the talk show, the sounds around him on the street, voices and noises. He could barely remember all the things he'd recorded.

It was getting dark. If his dad hadn't gone to work, then he might be home soon. The Kid took the comics and the recorder and the cassette and made his way back through the garage, into the house, back upstairs into his bedroom. He hid the cassette and recorder under his bed next to the calendar, put the comic books into his backpack. He took the wooden rabbit out of his pocket and put that into his backpack, too, way down at the bottom where it wouldn't be found.

He stood in the bathroom doorway, holding her bottle of pills.

He said, What are you doing?

I don't know what you mean.

He said, You haven't been taking these.

I don't know what you're talking about.

He said, You're not taking these. His voice rising. It was early morning, after another sleepless night. She stood in the short hallway, the space between the bathroom and The Kid's room. Only halfway into her shirt, one arm through the sleeve, the other dangling across her bare belly. The Kid was down at the kitchen table, eating his cereal.

He said, Why aren't you taking these?

I'm late, she said. I'm running late for school.

Then you're going to be late. I want to know why you're not taking these.

Do you count them? She took a step toward him, her voice ringing off the tile in the small room. Do you keep track?

I do, he said. I keep track. I count. Every morning after you're gone, after The Kid's gone. I pour them out on the edge of the sink and I count.

This is your job now?

This is my job. It's my job to make sure you're okay. To make sure you do what you're supposed to do.

What am I supposed to do, David?

You're supposed to take your pills.

The pills don't work.

They don't work if you don't take them.

The pills don't work.

How long has it been? he said.

Count them.

How long?

You tell me, she said. Pour them out and count them.

Darby stood in the motel parking lot, watching the orange doors. Late afternoon, traffic tight on the street behind him, the air ripe with exhaust. He checked the pager again. The second time, the third time. There had been no call.

"Are you watching TV?" Bob had left a message on the cell phone. "Turn on your TV. There's a line of cars backed up on the access road to the Tehachapi compound. Cars, trucks, RVs. I'm looking at a line maybe a mile long. People who saw it on the news. They want in. This woman in an RV said she thinks the compound is probably the safest place on earth. The feds are turning them back, but more just keep coming."

The pickup with Texas plates was gone. There was an older station wagon in one parking spot, a rusted hatchback in another. He stood with one hand pressed to the side of the Everclean van. He cleared his throat. Taking the rabbit, saving the rabbit, putting it in the drawer with the other things where it could be safe, hadn't helped. The speck was still there. It was surfacing; it was up in his mouth now. He needed to open his mouth to spit, but he was afraid to open his mouth.

He stood in the parking lot and looked at the orange doors. He clenched his teeth, bit the insides of his lips, his tongue, afraid to open his mouth, afraid of what would come out if he did.

The Kid remembered.

A year ago, about. His dad was standing in the living room, waiting for his mom to come home from school. She was late again, and his dad was upset, looking out the front window and checking the clock on the microwave. An hour late, over an hour. The Kid was waiting to watch the end of the talk show they'd begun that morning, but his dad told him just to start watching the show and she could catch up when she got home. The Kid's dad checked out the window, checked the clock on the microwave. The Kid finished the show, started playing around with the tape recorder Bob had gotten him for his birthday. Practicing some jokes from the show, some jokes of his own. He was working on his singing, part of a song they played between innings at Dodger games when his mom came through the front door.

She walked by his dad into the kitchen, started fixing dinner. Didn't say a word. His dad wanted to know where she had been. She said that she had stopped for a drink after work and his dad asked if it was just one and then they were arguing, starting to raise their voices, so The Kid sang even louder, trying to block it out.

His mom pulled a bottle of olive oil out of the cupboard. It slipped from her hands, fell to the floor. His mom's movements a little clunky, a little inexact. The cap popped off, spilling oil across the linoleum in a shimmery pool.

"Goddamnit," his mom said.

"Lucy," his dad said, that low warning voice.

"Goddamnit." His mom just about yelling now, so The Kid had to sing even louder to block it out.

"Kid," his dad said. "Take it outside, okay?"

But The Kid didn't want to take it outside. He wanted to be even louder, to blot this out, get it to stop. He kept singing, all the parts of the song that he knew.

His mom knelt in the kitchen, wiping at the oil with a dishrag, but really just spreading the oil even further across the floor.

"Kid," his dad said, but The Kid kept singing as loud as he could and then his mom dropped the dishrag and grabbed the bottle and banged it on the floor, once, twice, three times. Trying to get it to break, it seemed like, and when it wouldn't break she started banging it even harder.

"Shut up," she said. "Whitley, goddamnit, will you please shut up."

The Kid stopped, standing between the living room and the kitchen, not sure what to look at, who to look at.

His mom banging the bottle again. "Godammnit just please shut up."

"Enough," his dad said. Grabbing her hand, grabbing the bottle. "Lucy, that's enough."

His mom stayed kneeling on the kitchen floor, staring at the microphone hanging from The Kid's hand. Shaking her head. Not crying, just shaking her head.

"Please," she said. "Please."

The phone rang and for a second The Kid didn't know where he was, what was happening. He tried to focus on the glowing hands of his alarm clock. Just after one in the morning. The phone rang again. He got out of bed, went to his window. The driveway was empty. His dad still hadn't come home. He went down into the dark kitchen, picked up the phone, waited. There was noise on the other end of the line, air-hiss. The Kid thought he could hear cars in the distance, traffic sounds.

"Kid?" It was Michelle's muffled voice. She sounded far away. "Kid?"

The Kid waited, the phone cool to his ear.

"Kid, someone took my bag." Michelle's voice sounded strange. Scared. Like when they'd run from her mom's boyfriend, maybe worse.

"They took my bag and so I just ran. I found your last name in this phone book. I remembered your last name and street and found it." There was a rush of air in the receiver as she turned her head, looking around to see if she was being followed, maybe. "I'm going to the house," she said. "I'm going to sleep at the house."

For a second The Kid thought she was coming to his house, but then he figured out what she meant. He wanted to tell her that she couldn't go there, that was one time only. He wanted to tell her that place was his, but there was nothing he could do.

"Come meet me at the house if you can," she said. "I need another flashlight, anything else you can bring." Her voice shaking like she was going to cry.

"They took my bag," she said. "I couldn't stop them. They just took it."

The Kid came up onto the porch of the burned house. He heard breathing in the darkness. Michelle sat in the corner, arms at her sides, legs splayed out in front of her. She was trying to catch her breath. She had run there from wherever she'd been. The library, wherever. There was a hole in the knee of her jeans that The Kid didn't think had been there before. He wondered why she hadn't gone inside the burned house, but then he realized that she was afraid to go in without him. She was brave but she wasn't that brave.

She didn't want to talk about her bag, what had happened to it. She was angry and scared in equal parts. The Kid was a little afraid of her in this state. It seemed like she might snap at any second, take it all out on him.

He'd brought sandwiches, the last of the juice boxes. He couldn't find another flashlight, but he'd found a book of his dad's matches in one of the kitchen cabinets. He knew that he wasn't supposed to touch matches, that it was possibly dangerous to give them to

Michelle, but then he figured, what was the worst she could do to the house? Burn it down?

"Did Matthew get caught?" she said.

The Kid shook his head.

"So nobody knows about this place still?"

The Kid shook his head. He didn't want to talk about Matthew, didn't want to talk about secrets. He opened the security door. The air inside the house didn't seem so bad anymore. The Kid didn't think they needed the goggles or masks. He led her inside, through the front room, down the hall. It was almost completely dark. Only the light from the street through the window-holes, the holes in the roof, but he knew the place well, could make his way through. Michelle held onto the back of his jacket the whole time.

Moonlight shone through the hole in the living room roof, illuminating parts of the red-haired woman, the white glints on her boots, the glow of her skin. She looked ghostly for the first time, looked like an actual ghost. The Kid needed to finish the drawing, complete the signal, but he didn't want to rush without knowing how to draw a good hand. He needed more time to practice. Better to get it right than to rush and screw it up completely.

The Kid set down his backpack, unloaded the cookies and sandwiches and juice. He took out the issues of *Extraordinary Adventures* he'd found in the garage.

"Now what?" Michelle said.

The Kid didn't know. He didn't want her to stay there, but he couldn't think of a better place. He took out the book of matches, thought for a second, motioned for Michelle to stay put. He made his way back through the house, out onto the porch. The small ring of candles was still there. Maybe he shouldn't touch the candles. Maybe taking a candle would be a real blasphemy, like knocking over a gravestone. But what was Michelle going to do, sit back there in the dark all night? He took the largest candle from the ring, a red candle in a tall glass holder. The Kid didn't like this at all, but what was one more blasphemy at this point, really?

They sat on the living room floor. Michelle ate the sandwiches, drank the juice. The candlelight flickered on the walls, making different parts of the mural jump and move.

"Sorry about your books," Michelle said. "Your *Captain America* comics. They were in my bag."

The Kid hadn't thought about that. Those comics were gone now, too. He was a little angry with her, being so careless with things that weren't hers. Those were good comics.

Michelle finished the juice and The Kid stood, brushed off the back of his pants.

"Where are you going?"

He tilted his head toward the hallway.

"You're going home?"

He nodded.

"When does your dad get home from work?"

The Kid shrugged, picked up his backpack, strapped it over his shoulders.

"If he's not going to be home for a while, you might as well stay here."

That sound was back in her voice, the shaky sound from the phone call. The Kid set his backpack on the floor, sat down beside her, took out his notebook.

*Is your mom looking for you?*

"I don't know," Michelle said. "Probably not. Who cares? I've been gone before."

*When?*

"Last year. I slept in a garage at the end of our street for a couple of days."

The Kid tried to remember when that would have been, tried to remember seeing her in class last year, noticing something different about her.

*Were they mad when you came back?*

"Who?"

*Your mom and her boyfriend.*

"Yeah, they were pretty fucking mad."

*What's going to happen this time?*

"When?"

*When you go home.*

"Nothing's going to happen. I'm not going home."

*You can't stay here forever.*

"I know that. You think I don't know that?"

*I can't bring food every day.*

"Kid, I know that, for fuck's sake. Just shut up about it already."

She picked up an issue of *Extraordinary Adventures*, flipped angrily through the pages. She wasn't careful with the comic at all. The Kid worried she was going to rip the cover.

"Those fuckers just came at me," she said. "Some drunk bums. They came out of the dark and started grabbing at me. I fought them, but I don't know how many there were. There could have been ten of them, I don't know. All those grabbing hands. If there were less of them I could have fought, but there were too many. So I ran out of there, but they had my backpack."

The Kid thought about his mom maybe sleeping outside, sleeping in a park somewhere on the way to Chicago and getting attacked by some drunk men.

Michelle said, "Is it true that you stopped talking because your mom died?"

The Kid thought about this. The answer was yes and no. The answer was more complicated than that. He made his usual decision, that it was easier just not to answer.

"What happened to her?" Michelle said.

The Kid figured it was better to tell her his dad's story. His own story was too complicated.

*Something exploded in her head.*

Michelle thought about this for a second. The Kid could see her picturing it, what she thought it meant.

"Why?"

*She was sick with something that she didn't know about.*

"Who told you that?"

*My dad.*

Michelle put one comic down, picked up another. "I wish my mom would die. I wish something would explode in her head. My mom's boyfriend, too. My sisters. I wish everybody's head would explode." She sat back. "Did you ever wish that? That your mom would have died?

*No.*

"Your dad?"

The Kid didn't answer. He looked at the mural, the cannonballs flying from the guns on the pirate ship.

"Did you ever wish that? If you could have picked one or the other?"

*Yes.*

"It's a fucking bad thing to think," Michelle said. "To wish for someone to be dead. But I think it all the time. Do you think it's possible to think about it hard enough for it to happen? It's a stupid thing to wonder, but I don't know. Maybe if you just have that thought long enough it becomes something else. It just happens, finally. Like what's going on with the computers. They don't believe that next year is going to happen, so they get all fucked up and destroy the world and then next year really doesn't happen." She finished flipping through the comic, set it on the floor by the candle. "Are you mad about the books? That I lost those comics?"

*Not really.*

She looked around the room, at the mural, the hole in the ceiling. "Are you going to go home soon?" she said.

The Kid nodded.

"You want to stay until maybe I start sleeping? I'll start sleeping and then you can leave."

The Kid knew he should go home, knew his dad would be angry if he came home and The Kid wasn't there, but he also knew he couldn't just leave Michelle alone like this.

He turned the page in his notepad. *Okay.*

She moved the comics and juice boxes away from the candle, tipped herself over onto her back. Didn't put her hands up under her head, just let her head rest on the hard wood. She looked up at the ceiling for a while, her eyes drooping closed.

"Once I start snoring or whatever, you can go," she said. "Until then, just sit here for a while, okay?"

The Kid nodded again, even though she couldn't see him. He sat there while the candle flickered, a half hour, an hour, different parts of the mural appearing and disappearing. He thought about Matthew, if maybe they would never be friends again. He thought about Arizona and if she'd read the comic, if she was still afraid of him. He thought about Michelle wishing that everyone she knew was dead. He thought about something exploding in his mom's head. A half hour, an hour, maybe longer, until Michelle's snoring filled the room.

He left the rabbit there with her, the wooden rabbit he'd found in his dad's drawer. He left it sitting on the floor between the candle and the door, a strange thing to do, a stupid thing to do, like this little wooden rabbit could protect her somehow, like this thing could guard the room. But he did it anyway, stupid or not. He didn't know why. It just seemed like the right thing to do. He left the rabbit and strapped his backpack over his shoulders and crept quietly out of the house, back up the street toward home.

He rarely went into that room. He did not sleep in the bed. It was their bed, the bed they'd bought when they moved into their first apartment, a drafty, leaky pair of rooms off Wilshire Boulevard. The bed they'd brought with them when they bought the house. The bed Darby had to be dragged out of on Saturday mornings. The bed she sat awake in many nights, drinking tea, reading magazines, waiting for sleep. The bed where they argued. The bed where they woke pressed close, with tangled limbs. The bed where they made The Kid.

On the day the cops told him she was gone, after Bob had come and gone, after The Kid had gone upstairs, Darby had tried to sleep in that room. He'd turned out the lights, gotten into bed. The room was cold and quiet. After a while, he could hear a noise from The Kid's room, a muffled whimper that grew slowly to a moan, to loud crying. He could hear dull thumps, The Kid punching his bedroom wall. He knew he should go up, hold The Kid until he was able to sleep or until morning, whichever came first. But he stayed in the bed, pressed the pillow over his ears, unable to move, ashamed at what he couldn't do. His son moaning in the house. He held himself under the pillow until the sounds of The Kid faded away, until he could hear nothing but the rush of blood in his ears. He woke hours later. The room was dark, the house was silent. He could smell her, the warm smell of Lucy asleep, her hair and sweat. He wanted to cry out with relief. He'd had some kind of terrible dream. He reached across the bed for her, her warmth in the night. He found nothing but cool sheets, empty space. A shock ran through him. The truth of the thing. He got out of bed and went outside. He climbed into the pickup and sat shaking. He had to fight the urge to drive. He knew that if he started the engine, if he pulled onto the street, he would never come back. He knew that if he started the engine he would leave his son. He threw the keys out the window to get them away. He turned on the radio. He sat on his hands so he wouldn't open the door, retrieve the keys, drive. Talk shows on the radio, diet advice, real estate advice. He thought about her smell in the bed, he held that scent with him until he couldn't hold it any longer, until it slipped from him, until it was gone. He sat on his hands and told himself the story that he had told The Kid, the story he had told Bob. He sat until he could picture her falling in her classroom, the awful scene, her cheek pressed to the cold floor. He sat until he could picture a student from her class lifting her, holding her in his arms, carrying her down the hall. He sat until he could see that she was not alone in that last moment, until he could picture her being held, even if he was not the one holding her. He sat in the pickup until the sun came up, until the story he had told The Kid became the only story he knew. He pulled his hands out from under his thighs. They were dumb and lifeless, unresponsive. He shook them, waited for some feeling to return, the first pricks of electricity in his thumbs, his fingers. He looked up and saw The Kid's face in his bedroom window, The Kid looking down at him in the truck, and he was overcome by the shame of what he couldn't do, what he had been unable to do, sitting in the pickup, desperately shaking his hands.

He rarely went into that room. He did not sleep in that bed.

The trick of the job is to forget what happened.

They ate drive-thru chicken for dinner, sitting in the pickup in the restaurant parking lot, listening to the radio news. The Kid didn't eat all of his dinner, said he wasn't that hungry, he'd take what was left to school the next day for lunch. He wrapped the leftover chicken in a napkin, wondered if his dad believed him, if it was obvious that he was lying. He knew you could tell someone was lying by the sound of their voice, like that day his dad had told him the lie about what happened to his mom. But he wondered if someone could tell you were lying just by the things you wrote, by the way your words looked in a notebook.

His dad kept clearing his throat and covering his mouth, holding his mouth closed like maybe he was going to be sick, maybe he was going to throw up. The Kid wondered if his dad had food poisoning from the chicken, or if maybe The Kid's B.O. and bad breath was making him sick. He tried to sit as far away from his dad as possible, close to the door, tried to keep his own mouth closed and breathe through his nose.

They pulled into their driveway and The Kid could see something strange happening on the front porch, some weird movement. His dad had forgotten to leave the porch light on and The Kid could only see the outline of something, hear something thrashing around. The dog. The dog moving in an unnatural way.

His dad ran up the yard to the porch. The Kid approached slowly, not sure what was happening. His dad fumbled with his keys, unlocked the security screen, the front door. Reached in and turned on the porch light. A burst of moths from the bulb, fluttering out into the night. The dog lay on his side on the porch, flopping violently, snapping his jaws, his eyes rolled up into its head.

"Steve," his dad said. "Steve Rogers."

The dog kept flopping, stiff-legged, making strangled gargling sounds from his throat. The Kid stopped at the foot of the steps, not sure what to do.

His dad maneuvered around the porch, trying to get into a good position where the dog wouldn't bite him. He finally knelt, put his hands on the dog's sides, held him down.

"He's having some kind of seizure," his dad said. "We just have to hold him steady until it passes." His dad didn't sound so sure. His dad didn't sound completely convinced by his own explanation.

"It's okay, Steve," his dad said. "This is fine, this is okay."

The dog thrashed, bucked, sputtered.

His dad looked at The Kid, saw that The Kid was scared.

"Take notes, Kid," his dad said. "That's your job during this. Take notes about how we get him through this."

The Kid pulled out his notebook, his pencil. Wrote down what his dad had said to the dog, the first step. This is fine, Steve. *This is okay.*

The dog thrashed and jerked under his dad's hands. His dad held the dog down, adjusted himself on the porch as the dog moved.

"We've got to get his tongue," his dad said. "We've got to hold onto his tongue so he doesn't swallow it."

The Kid wrote this down. He thought of that long, gray tongue wrapping in on itself, working its way down into the dog's throat, cutting off the air. He thought of his own face in the dirt in the alleyway, Brian's weight on top of him, holding him down, The Kid unable to breath. The Kid knew how the dog felt. He nodded to his dad. He hoped his dad knew what he was doing.

His dad put a knee on the dog's ribs to hold him down. He grabbed the dog's snout with one hand, his jaw with the other. Pried the dog's mouth open. Steve Rogers's teeth flashed in the porch light, snapping at his dad's fingers. His dad reached around in the dog's mouth, wrestling with his tongue. Looked like he got it and lost it a couple of times. The dog bucked again, harder this time, and his dad's knee slipped. The dog's jaws came down on his dad's hand, and his dad fell back onto the porch.

"Fuck," his dad yelled, shaking his hand. The Kid wrote this down, even though he wasn't supposed to use that word. He figured this was an extraordinary circumstance, and this was his job, to take complete notes.

His dad's hand was bleeding. He wiped it on the leg of his jeans, moved back in toward Steve Rogers. "Forget the tongue," he said. "We just have to hold him steady." He held the dog with his hands this time, one hand on the dog's ribs, one on the side of its head, careful of the snapping jaws, holding Steve Rogers steady to the floor of the porch. Dad-strength.

The dog began to shake. A new phase of the seizure. The dog stayed in place and vibrated under his dad's hands, just shook and shook. The Kid took notes. The dog started to pee, just squirted out pee onto the porch. His dad ignored the pee, talked softly to the dog.

"It's okay, Steve. It's all right. We'll wait. We'll just wait."

The shaking went on for some time. Finally it slowed; finally it stopped. Just a few random twitches. The dog was panting hard, his head against the wood, tongue spilling out of the side of his mouth, a white froth making a wet spot on the porch. His dad held the dog steady, held the dog in place, ran his hand gently along the dog's ribs. The Kid wrote this in his notebook.

"We did it, Steve," his dad said, hand bleeding, breathing almost as hard as the dog. "We did it, Kid. It's going to be all right now."

He sat at the kitchen table with his coffee and looked out the window into the backyard. Steve Rogers sniffed the perimeter, lifted his leg every few steps, marking. The dog seemed to be okay, seemed to have forgotten what had happened the night before.

She'd lain here naked one morning, her body spread out across the kitchen floor, a growing smile on her face, their new house, a house of their own, taking his hand and pulling him gently down to her.

She'd stood here late one night and called the toll-free number on one of her father's infomercials that had surfaced on TV. Darby had stood in the bedroom doorway and listened to her on the phone, saying she didn't want to order anything, she wasn't interested in buying anything, she just wanted to see who would answer when she called.

She'd sat sprawled here one evening, banging a bottle of olive oil on the linoleum, trying to get it to break, trying to get something to break.

He sat at the kitchen table drinking his coffee. He could hear that bell in his bad ear, that faraway morning ring. He stuck his finger in his good ear.

There it is, he said. Can you hear that? There it is.

He stood at Lucy's desk at the back of the house, looked at the class list, the last seat in the middle row. Thought of her in the arms of someone he didn't know. *Green, D.* It was a game day, a Friday. On game days you wear your best clothes, pressed black slacks and starched button-down shirts, perfect and white.

"Greene, D." He said the name out loud, shifting the silence in the house. He said it again, "Greene, D." It was an actual thing, a true thing. It existed. It made a noise in the quiet house. He said it again and again, the sound filling the rooms, creating something from nothing.

No one but The Kid seemed to care when Michelle didn't show up at school. Miss Ramirez marked her absent in the morning and that was it. The Kid sat and looked at Michelle's empty desk. He couldn't believe that no one else knew what he knew. He wondered if she was okay, or if something had happened, if the grabbing men from the library lawn had somehow tracked her down.

At lunch, he and Matthew sat in silence at their picnic table. It was the night that The Kid usually went to Matthew's for dinner, and The Kid wanted to ask him if that was cancelled, but whenever The Kid looked over at him, Matthew looked away. The Kid figured that he probably had his answer.

In the library, he heard excited whispering, tried to ignore it. Rhonda Sizemore and Arizona and a couple other girls were standing on the other side of the shelves in the next aisle. The Kid could see them in the spaces between the books. They were pulling books from the shelves, pretending to read the back covers while they whispered. They weren't whispering about the books, they were whispering about him. The girls telling Arizona that The Kid had gone crazy when he'd attacked Rhonda Sizemore. That The Kid's dad had gone crazy in the mall, gotten into a fight in the food court. That his dad made blue star tattoos in a bathroom laboratory. The Kid couldn't see Arizona's face clearly, couldn't see what her reaction was. He tried to ignore the whispering, concentrated instead on the titles on the spines of the books as he moved down the aisle. He was looking for information.

This was something his mom always told him when he woke up in the night with a scary thought, something he'd heard at school, on the TV news, something he didn't understand, something that had been mottled and magnified by a dream, plastered across the front of his brain. Look it up, she'd tell him, sitting on the edge of his bed or down on the living room couch, a single lamp alive in the darkness. Find out the truth, she'd say. Go to the library. It's harder to be afraid of something that you understand. And it usually worked. It usually made him feel better, finding the subject in a book or a magazine, the certainty of answers in writing, facts in print, knowing that someone else had already tackled that thing, had already felt that fear.

He was in the section of the library devoted to animals. A shelf with nothing but books about dogs. A book with nothing but diseases that afflicted dogs. His mom had been right. The Kid sat on the smelly carpet, his back to the shelves.

The pages were filled with descriptions, glossy color photographs. Page after page of canine affliction. There were blotches, blights, bumps, rashes. There were parasites, fleas and ticks, worms that lived in dogs' intestines, in their skin, in their hearts. There were broken bones, sprained joints, arthritic limbs. There were urinary tract infections, bowel disorders, heart and lung diseases. There was no end to the list of things that could go wrong.

There were diseases of the brain that lead to fits and seizures, neurological malfunctions illustrated in the book by drawings of an electrical storm over the dog's head, dark clouds with lightning bolts. There were photographs of dogs gripped by these malfunctions, dogs lying on kitchen floors, bathroom floors, legs shot out and stiff, jaws snapping, mouths frothing, eyes glassy and wild. Dogs that looked like Steve Rogers on the porch, about to bite The Kid's dad, about to pee all over himself.

*Canine Epilepsy.* A term for it, a name. Something already discovered and researched. There was no known cause, no definite reason some dogs had seizures. Maybe it was inherited from the dog's parents, maybe the dog had some trauma to its head. A blow, a beating. Maybe it had been trapped in the sewer for days, weeks, eating rats, maneuvering in the dark. There was no reason. It was just something that happened.

There was a loud whisper from the other side of the bookshelf, Rhonda Sizemore telling Arizona to *Keep away from him*. The Kid tried to ignore it, tried not to worry if Arizona would believe what she was being told, if she'd follow this advice. If she'd be scared away completely. He concentrated on the book instead.

The book said that there was no real way of predicting when a seizure was going to occur, but sometimes the dogs knew. Sometimes the dogs acted funny. This was called the aura phase. Also called the prodrome phase. During this time, a few minutes before a seizure, a dog might act frightened, spooked, might come looking for comfort, for company. The best thing to do during this phase was to get the dog to a safe, open area, away from furniture or sharp objects, away from electrical cords they might get tangled up in.

During the seizure, there wasn't too much that could be done. The dog will shake, the dog will make unnatural noises. The dog might lose control of its bowels. Its tongue might turn blue. These were all documented things, things people had seen and experienced before. There were pictures in the book. A seizure usually lasted two to three minutes. The book said that you should write down details of the seizure, keep a written record of what was happening. Keep your hands away from the dog's mouth. Don't worry about the dog swallowing its tongue. The dog won't swallow its tongue. Its tongue is too long. Be patient. Stay calm. It will only last a few minutes.

The Kid wrote these things in his notepad under the heading *Steve Rogers, Epileptic*. It was reassuring, transferring this information from the library book to his notebook. The comfort of a known thing.

After school, he took a long, roundabout route to the burned house. He didn't want to stay outside, vulnerable on the street to Brian or Razz, but he was in no hurry to get to the house. He was afraid of what he would find. He expected police cars, TV news vans, Miss Ramirez and the vice-principal, Michelle's angry mom and her mom's drunk boyfriend, the bawling twin sisters, the porch and front yard crowded with people and cameras and lights. This was a major event. A girl had run away from home, had spent the night in the burned house. Michelle would be arrested, taken to jail. The Kid would be shown as an accomplice. The mural would be discovered, broadcast on TV, unfinished before the signal could be sent out, the angel still missing a hand, exposed for everyone to see.

He stopped at *Gift 2000* and bought a few things for Michelle. A box of cereal, a word search book. Finally screwed up enough courage to make his way down the street.

There were no news vans, no police cars. There were no people crowded on the sidewalk. The burned house looked like it always looked, quiet and empty. He couldn't believe it. He couldn't believe that something like this could happen and no one would know.

There seemed to be another candle missing from the ring by the front door. The Kid couldn't be sure, but he thought he remembered more candles the night before.

He opened the security door, moved through the front room quietly, into the hallway, past the bathroom. There was no guarantee that Michelle was even still there. He might find the living room empty, the expired candle, a note that said she'd left for the Twin Cities.

The Kid heard something to his right, a noise in the bedroom. He turned to see a shadow coming fast, swinging something large, a club or a bat, and he was only able to drop the *Gift 2000* bag and put his hands over his face before he was hit hard in the chest. He fell onto his backpack on the floor, rolled and curled, keeping everything close and tight to minimize how much the kicks and punches hurt.

Nothing else happened. He lay curled in a ball, waited. Was it Brian and Razz? Was it the grabbing men from the library lawn? Nothing else happened. He heard heavy breathing from above. He didn't open his eyes, didn't want to see what was coming. He would rather just get through it.

"Fuck."

He knew the voice, but the voice didn't register. He kept his body clenched, his arms and legs drawn in as tight as they could go, his stomach tensed, his eyes closed.

Someone was touching him. A hand on his shoulder. Not punching or scratching or pushing, just a hand on his shoulder. The voice again. "Kid, I'm sorry. Look. It's me. Open your eyes."

He knew the voice, but the voice didn't register. He squeezed tighter into the ball, clenching every muscle, keeping his face hidden away.

"Kid, calm down. It's okay. It's just me."

The hand moved to his elbow, prying his arms off his head. The Kid fought against it, but the hand kept pulling, unfolding his elbows and knees.

He opened his eyes. Someone was crouched beside him, long hair hanging down to brush his cheeks.

"It's okay," Michelle said. "I didn't know it was you."

They sat on the living room floor next to the candles. She'd hit him with a two-by-four she'd pulled from one of the charred hallway walls. She'd been carrying it all day in the house as a weapon, in case the men who stole her backpack came after her again. She kept the two-by-four beside her as she ate the cold chicken and handfuls of cereal straight from the box.

"I have a good swing," she said. "My dad used to tell me I could play for the Dodgers if they let girls play."

The Kid didn't know if her swing was that good, but he knew it was hard. He could feel a bruise forming on his chest, the skin tender and swelling.

She told him that she hadn't left the house. She'd read the comics about a million times and looked at the mural, but other than that it was pretty fucking boring. She picked up the word search book, looked at the cover, put it back down. Dug another handful of cereal out of the box and shoved as much as she could into her mouth.

"Did anybody ask about me at school?"

The Kid shook his head.

"Good," she said, although she didn't sound like she thought it was good. The Kid thought that maybe she sounded disappointed. He wondered if he should have lied, if he should have said that all the kids were asking about her, Miss Ramirez was asking, Mr. Bromwell, everybody. He wondered if maybe she would go back home if he told her this.

*Are you coming back to school?*

"Hell no."

*Someone's going to notice.*

"Who's going to notice?"

*Miss Ramirez.*

"Fuck Miss Ramirez."

*You shouldn't say that.*

"Why not?"

*She's our teacher.*

"So the fuck what?"

*People are going to get worried.*

"Who, Kid? Who's going to get worried?" She looked at him, her face red, her mouth filled with a pink mush of half-chewed cereal. The Kid tried to think of someone besides himself who would be worried that she was sleeping here. Michelle waited for an answer. The only sound in the room was the popping of the dry cereal in her mouth.

"Exactly," she said, chewing again. "Nobody gives a fuck." She poked a straw into the juice box, took a long pull. "You're going to come here soon and I'll be gone. Don't be surprised. You'll come in here and the place will be empty again. I'll leave the candles. That's how you'll know I'm gone. I sent a letter to my dad today. He's going to send a bus ticket right to this address. One-way to Minneapolis."

*When?*

"Soon." She picked up the word search book, flipped it over to look at the instructions on the back cover. "I don't know when exactly, but soon you'll come in here and I'll be gone."

The Kid didn't know if he believed her or not. He knew she wanted it to be true, but he didn't know if it actually was true. She said she hadn't left the burned house all day, so how did she mail the letter? Where did she get the stamp?

"Let me see," she said.

*What?*

"Where I hit you. Lift up your shirt and let me see."

The Kid shook his head.

"Don't be a pussy. I just want to see where I hit you."

The Kid untucked his shirt, lifted it over his belly, up past his head. He couldn't see what Michelle was doing, but he could feel her leaning in, her face in close to his chest. He felt her hand near the sore spot, the warmth of her fingers, not touching him, just hovering close.

"Not bad," she said. "I don't know if it'll make a scar, but it's not a bad bruise."

He sat in the pickup in the parking lot of Lucy's school. He wasn't sure how long he had been there, what time it was. Midafternoon. He hadn't been to the school since Lucy had been gone. He'd had no reason to go back. He hadn't even driven by.

A hefty security guard stood by the front entrance, cleaning his nails with a toothpick. Darby told the man he was a parent. The guard nodded, let him through. Darby stood in the main hallway. The overhead lights shone off the linoleum, the metal lockers, a headache-inducing gleam. The hall empty, the middle of a class period.

He climbed the staircase to the second floor, past the principals' offices, the break room. A day like this, right about this time in the afternoon. Greene carrying Lucy down the hall. He tried to picture it, tried to conjure the moment around him, but now that he was actually there, he couldn't. He couldn't see it.

He stepped into the nurse's office. The nurse was washing her hands at the sink, an older woman with bug-eyed glasses and a short chop of bottle-reddened hair. She looked up when he came in the door.

"Can I help you?"

She didn't recognize him. He was surprised by this. He thought that she'd know exactly who he was. She had seen him many times before, picking Lucy up from school, helping Lucy move things in and out of her classroom in the afternoons, during weekends, summer recess. The nurse shook her hands in the sink, pulled a brown paper towel from the dispenser. She tilted her head a little, walked toward him, drying her hands. She tossed the paper towel in the garbage pail, waited for a response.

"I'm looking for a student," he said.

"Are you a parent?'

"Yes."

"You have a child at this school?"

"No. I have a son in middle school."

"We don't give student information to anyone other than parents or legal guardians."

"I'm not looking for medical information."

"We don't give any information to anyone other than parents. Can I have your name, sir?"

He didn't want to say it. He wanted her to know without him saying it. He wanted her to know, to remember.

"Darby," he said, finally. "My last name is Darby."

She looked at him, eyes swollen through the lenses of her glasses. "Oh," she said. "Oh, Mr. Darby, I'm so sorry. I didn't recognize you for some reason. I'm so sorry. How are you?"

He nodded. The familiar question. He nodded. That was his answer.

"It was Dennis, right? Your name? Dennis, I was so sorry to hear about Lucy. We all were."

He didn't know what that meant. That she'd heard about Lucy. This woman had been there, had called the ambulance. He didn't know what she was talking about, that she'd heard about Lucy.

"How is your son? William?"

"Whitley."

"Whitley. Yes, of course. I remember Whitley. When Lucy was setting up her room in the summers, he'd be running in and out of the empty classes, singing in the loudest voice."

"He's in sixth grade now. Whitley."

"Is he still singing?"

"No, he's not."

He wished he had brought the newspaper clipping. He wanted to show her the name, the blurred face. *Greene, D.* He wanted the nurse to tell him what she knew, what she remembered.

"Mr. Darby?"

The nurse was looking at him, concerned. "Is something wrong with your hand?" she said.

Was something wrong with his hand. His hand was covering his mouth, holding his mouth shut tight, keeping the speck inside. He brought his hand down, hooked his fingers through his belt loop to keep them still.

"Is there a coach here?" Darby said. "A football coach?"

"Mr. Gonzalez. I believe he's with a class at the moment."

"Could I leave my phone number for him? Could I leave him a message?"

She sat behind her desk, opened a message log. She wrote a name in the log, *Dennis Darby*, and he gave her the number of the new cell phone.

She closed the log, looked up at him.

"Dennis, do you need some help?"

He didn't know who she was talking to. Dennis. He shook his head. She didn't know who she was talking to, what she was talking about.

He was halfway down the main staircase when he had to stop. The speck in his mouth, gagging him. He needed to open his mouth but he was afraid to open his mouth.

The bell rang. The classroom doors opened behind him, students emptying into the hallway. The staircase filled, students pushing past, ascending, descending. Darby held on to the center railing, waiting for them to pass, his mouth shut tight. He cleared his throat, waited. The crush of students pushed into him, shoulders and elbows, students his size, larger. He gripped the handrail, closed his eyes, kept his mouth shut. Cleared his throat, waited.

It took forever. He stood there forever, waiting for it to end.

Miss Ramirez made an announcement at the start of the day, even before she took attendance, even before they all stood and put their hands over their hearts for the Pledge of Allegiance.

"Michelle Melendez is missing," she said. "She's been missing for two days, and her mother and father are very worried about her."

Her mother's boyfriend, The Kid thought. Miss Ramirez had her facts wrong. Michelle's mother and her mother's boyfriend.

"Has anyone seen her in the last two days?"

All the kids shook their heads. They hadn't seen her. A couple of the boys in the back laughed at something Razz said.

"This isn't funny," Miss Ramirez said. "This is a serious situation."

The Kid shook his head with everyone else, hoping he wasn't shaking it too much or too little. Hoping he wasn't a bad liar.

"If you see her, or if you hear of anyone else seeing her, you're to tell me immediately," Miss Ramirez said. "Does everyone understand?"

All the kids nodded. They understood. The Kid nodded along with them, not too much, not too little.

He found Matthew sitting by himself at lunch. The Kid needed to tell Matthew about Michelle. He needed someone else to know. It was too much for him to know alone.

*There's something I have to tell you.*

"What?"

*It's a secret.*

"No," Matthew said, shaking his head. "I told you. I don't want to hear any more secrets." He tried to ignore The Kid, tried to watch a kickball game on the other side of the yard, Brian and Razz and a bunch of kids from other classes, running and shouting and laughing.

*This one is important.*

Matthew kept shaking his head. "You shouldn't be here."

*Where?*

"Here. Sitting here. I don't want you to sit here."

*Why not?*

"Because if you're sitting here then no one else will sit here."

*Who else is going to sit here?*

"I don't know. Anybody."

*Who?*

"I don't know who. Anybody." His voice getting louder. "If you're not here, maybe somebody else will sit here." Matthew speared a ravioli with his plastic fork, pushed it around through the tomato sauce on his tray. "Just because people don't like you, you think people don't like me either."

*Who cares what they think?*

"I care," Matthew said. He was shouting now. The muscles around his mouth were trembling. He stared hard at The Kid.

"Aren't you sick of people not liking you?" Matthew said. "I am. I'm sick of it."

The kickball game was breaking up. The other kids started back toward the lunch tables, toward the doors to the school.

"Just get out of here, okay?" Matthew said. He took a sip from his milk carton. "I don't want anybody to see you near me."

The Kid couldn't believe it. Matthew was all The Kid had, he was The Kid's only real friend. And now he was ashamed of The Kid? Now he was better than The Kid, he was worried to be seen near The Kid?

The Kid didn't even know what he was doing, he was so angry. He grabbed Matthew's milk carton and threw it, splashing Matthew's face, the front of his shirt. Matthew jumped up, fell back into the bench. Milk dripped from his nose, his chin. He didn't say anything, just looked at The Kid, his mouth wide with shock. He wiped his eyes, grabbed his backpack and turned from the table, bumping right into Brian as Brian passed behind the table. Matthew's wet shirt and hands pushing into Brian, getting milk all over the front of his track jersey.

"The fuck?" Brian said. He lifted his arms like he was going to take a swing at Matthew, but then the bell rang, the end of the lunch period, and the yard aides moved out across the pavilion to shoo the kids back into their classrooms. Brian looked down at his wet uniform, moved past with a shove to Matthew's back, knocking him into the table.

Matthew wiped the milk from his eyes again. He gave The Kid a last look as he turned back toward the school. It was the same look other kids gave The Kid when they thought he had bad breath or B.O. When they thought he was contagious. The look like Matthew couldn't believe someone that awful was even allowed to exist.

He went back into the garage to get the clipping from the drawer. He wanted it with him, felt he would need it when the football coach called.

The light in the windows was fading. The haze of the day had grown to cloud cover, the gray threat of rain. He opened the workbench drawer and removed the clipping. He pulled the drawer out further, pulled the drawer all the way out of the bench. The wooden rabbit was gone. He looked on the floor, back behind the lower drawers. He tried to think, tried to recall if he'd moved it, if he'd changed things. The tape recorder was gone, too. The Kid's recorder and the cassette Darby had found.

Up in The Kid's bedroom, he searched the dresser drawers, the drawers of The Kid's small wooden desk. He dumped the drawers, spilling socks and underwear across the floor. He pulled clothes out of the closet, The Kid's notebooks from the shelf. He lay on the carpet and reached under the bed. He found the recorder and the cassette. The rabbit was gone. He couldn't find the rabbit. He reached further under the bed and found a calendar, another calendar from the previous year. Arrows in the squares, pointing to the right. Days and weeks filled with arrows. The previous month, the previous, back to the beginning of the year. The other calendar had arrows as well, leading back from the end of the year to the previous fall, to the day Darby had told The Kid what had happened to Lucy.

Darby sat on the floor and looked at the calendars. He couldn't believe there were so many arrows. He couldn't believe that they'd spent so many days without her.

The cell phone jangled on his hip. The number displayed wasn't one he recognized, wasn't the nurse from The Kid's school, wasn't Bromwell's office. The man on the phone introduced himself as Mr.

Gonzalez, Art Gonzalez, the football coach at the high school. He'd received a message that Darby would like to speak with him. Darby asked if they could meet that afternoon. It wouldn't take long, he wouldn't take too much of Gonzalez's time. He knew a bar not too far from the school.

It had started to rain. Fat drops splattering on the street, on Darby's windshield. The rabbit was gone. He had to stop thinking about the rabbit. He had tried to save those things, but it was impossible to save them. He knew that now. He could feel the loss, the failure to protect those things. A blank space within him.

The cell phone rang again. It was Bob's voice on the line, distant and fuzzy.

"David? David, I've got a shitty connection. Can you hear me? I'm on my way north. I couldn't watch any more of it on TV. I know the area. I used to camp up there."

Bob was talking loud and fast. Darby didn't say anything. He had to fight to keep his mouth closed. The speck was in his mouth, threatening to get out.

"Listen to me," Bob said. "I want you to look in on Rhoda, if I'm not back soon. Can you do that? Can you do that for me?"

He wanted to tell Bob to turn around, to stay away from what he'd seen on TV, but he had to keep his mouth shut, had to keep his teeth pressed into his tongue, and then the cell phone connection was lost, the line was dead.

The afternoon sky looked burnt, brown and gray, the sun just a pale blot behind the haze. Rain coming.

There was some commotion in a far corner of the schoolyard. A surge of kids running, breaking up from their recess groups to join the rush flowing back toward the far corner. The Kid had a bad feeling about this. This kind of excitement was never good. He followed the nearest group of kids, walking quickly at first and then breaking into a run, dragging a little behind the wave. A few yard aides noticed all the excitement and started toward the crowd from the opposite side. The Kid knew that it would take them too long to get there, to do anything about whatever was happening inside the growing ring of kids.

The Kid reached the outside of the crowd, started pushing his way through. Just about everyone was taller than he was. The Kid shoved stomachs and chests, trying to make his way into the center. He passed Arizona, who was waving her arms at the yard aides, yelling, *Help, Help.*

The first thing he saw was Matthew, half of Matthew's face, shiny and wet with tears, his eye spinning, white and wild, looking for help, a way out. Brian had him in a headlock, his ropy arm tight around Matthew's neck, the hidden half of Matthew's face squeezed into Brian's ribcage. Brian was punching him with short, hard pops on the top of the head. Matthew was screaming, a high, terrified sound. The Kid had never heard anything like it.

The aides would never get there. Brian was landing those rabbit punches, *bam, bam, bam,* and Matthew was screaming and The Kid thought of this as something more than just another fight, thought of this as an irreversible thing, something that would be around forever. Brian hitting right on the top of Matthew's head. The Kid thought of some kind of brain injury, Matthew with lightning bolts over his head. The Kid thought of this as permanent damage.

He kept pushing, finally through the innermost ring, and then he was out into the middle. It felt like falling, that sudden emergence into the open space at the circle's heart. Brian still had Matthew in the headlock, was still punching the top of his head, both of them turning counterclockwise with the force of the punches, the punches spinning them slowly as if Brian wanted every side of the crowd to get a good look.

The Kid had to move fast. As soon as he got close to them, as soon as someone noticed, another kid would jump in, Razz or one of Brian's other friends. This was how these things worked. Everybody stayed back, everybody observed the rules until somebody didn't and then all bets were off.

Brian's face was set. He looked determined, his eyes straight, his jaw tight. He was trying to do something, there was something he was trying to accomplish. He would keep hitting Matthew until something happened, something that couldn't be taken back. The scream, the sound Matthew made was the most awful sound The Kid had ever heard.

The Kid was in there before he really knew what he was doing, wedged between the two of them, and then he had his arms around Matthew, like a bear hug, his back to Brian, and Brian's punches were wilder now, surprised, and he hit The Kid's backpack and the back of his head, just above his neck. The punches were so hard. The amount of pain was something The Kid had never felt before, ripping up from the base of his skull, over the top, settling in behind his eyes.

He held Matthew in his bear hug and they all fell to the ground, The Kid on top of Matthew, Brian on top of The Kid, punching wildly. The Kid's face pressed right to Matthew's face, Matthew's wet cheek against The Kid's, and The Kid held on as tight as he could until he finally felt Brian's weight pulled off him, heard the aides' voices and P.E. teacher's voice, The Kid's face pressed to Matthew's, his cheek covering Matthew's mouth, trying to muffle that scream.

The bar was dark and humid. The rain beat against a large plate-glass window beside the front door, the window glowing with the dull outdoor light. There was a muted TV mounted up behind the bar showing live shots of the Tehachapi situation, the line of cars on the dirt road that Bob had talked about, all the people trying to get into the compound.

Darby sat on a stool at the middle of the bar. There were two women sitting at the end by the TV, smoking and drinking beer. The women wore pink nurse's scrubs decorated with teddy bears and giraffes. The bartender came by and Darby ordered a shot and a beer. The rainwater was still running from the top of his head down the back of his neck. He could smell the menthol of the women's cigarettes. Bob's brand. He thought of Bob driving north, toward the images on TV. He thought of the things he had lost, the things he had failed to protect. His hands were shaking, so he held the beer bottle, peeled at the label with a fingernail. The bartender brought him another shot.

On the TV, it looked like the authorities were gathering, a sizable police and federal presence assembling at a staging area a good distance from the press tents. The TV cameras switched to long-lens zooms, trying to make out what was going on, men suiting up, helping one another suit up.

Darby took off his jacket and wiped the rain from the top of his head, the sides of his neck. His shirt was stuck to his back. He pulled it free and leaned down the bar, extended his arm across the scarred wood, asked the nurse closest to him for a cigarette. She shook one free from her pack and rolled it to him. The bartender dropped a pack of matches and a tin ashtray beside his shot glass. Darby took the cigarette in his teeth, lit a match, touched the match to the paper.

Twelve years falling away like nothing, like some kind of misguided endurance stunt. He took a slow drag, held it in his chest, let the smoke seep from his nostrils. His body warming, his fingers tingling. Twelve years. How easy. How easy to just stop doing something.

Flack-jacketed SWAT officers ran across the TV screen, helmeted heads kept low. The camera moved erratically, searching for the right shot. The klieg lights were off, the compound was blurry in the dusk, and when the SWAT officers ran past the glow of the TV lights they disappeared, they ceased to be.

A tall, thickset Latino man came in through the front door, shaking out an umbrella. He looked around the room, and when he didn't find who he was looking for he propped his umbrella in the corner and took a seat at the end of the bar near the door. He was wearing a hooded windbreaker with the familiar eagle mascot on the breast. He struggled to pull it off over his head, standing his hair on end, spraying rainwater far enough to land in tiny beads along the edge of Darby's ashtray. The man looked for a place to hang his windbreaker, finally draped it over the stool beside him. The bartender went over and the man ordered a diet soda. He looked at Darby, looked at the women at the other end of the bar. He checked his watch and turned to look at the door behind him. Darby didn't know why Gonzalez didn't say something, didn't introduce himself, and then he realized that Gonzalez was looking for a man who could be Lucy Darby's husband and Gonzalez didn't see that man.

Darby sat in that empty space for a while. His hands were still shaking and he wanted to finish the cigarette before he said anything. Another minute, another two minutes. He wanted to get his twelve years' worth.

On the TV, a reporter stood in front of a satellite truck, looking at the camera and then looking at the sky and then back to the camera again.

Darby pushed the stub of his cigarette out in the ashtray, slid his beer and shot glass down the bar toward Gonzalez. Introduced himself. Gonzalez stood, apologized, blamed the rain, the dark bar, the long day at school. They sat again, an empty stool between them. Darby signaled to the bartender and the bartender refilled his shot glass, brought another beer. Gonzalez seemed uneasy. He said he didn't know Lucy very well, just in passing really, in the halls or at faculty meetings. He said that he'd been surprised to get Darby's message, that he thought it might have been a mistake.

The bar filled gradually. Men mostly, white and Latino, a group of uniformed city bus drivers, a group of construction workers with drywall dust on their hands and boots. The outside light was fading, the window getting dark.

They sat and drank. It seemed like Gonzalez had said what he was going to say. He looked at his watch, moved his windbreaker so a bus driver could sit on the empty stool. Darby had assumed Gonzalez would know why he'd been called, what Darby wanted to know. That he would come to the bar with Greene's name on his lips.

The front of Darby's jeans were still wet from the rain and when he dug the clipping out of his pocket it was damp, the black type smeared on the paper, the photograph blurrier than before. He smoothed it out on the bar, careful not to tear the wet paper. Gonzalez leaned in and looked at the photo, the caption beneath.

"Darian Greene," Gonzalez said, and Darby nodded like he already knew the full name.

There was a crowd around the bar now, two and three deep. The noise level was rising. Darby finished his beer and when the story still didn't come, he asked Gonzalez about Greene, what kind of kid he was, what kind of player. Gonzalez seemed unsure of this, like he didn't know where this conversation was going. He'd said his piece. He shook a few cubes of ice out of his glass and into his mouth, crunched them in his teeth. He said that Greene was a white kid who thought he was a *cholo*. Walked around with his jeans halfway down his ass, his ball cap on crooked, the whole thing. Bragged about his car, his guns. With a kid like that, Gonzalez said, you didn't always know what was real, what was B.S. Gonzalez looked at Darby and when Darby didn't say anything, Gonzalez continued. Greene had a lot of problems, home problems, girl problems, maybe drugs. That was the word on the team anyway, that there may have been a drug problem, a meth problem. Gonzalez didn't know about any of that, it's just what he'd heard. He looked at Darby, crunched more ice.

Last year, Greene had lost a lot of weight as the season had gone on. He'd become paranoid, violent. He got into a fight with a couple other players in the locker room and Gonzalez had to cut him from the team. He dropped out of school not long after. His girlfriend was pregnant, or that was what Gonzalez had heard. She got pregnant and they both dropped out around Christmas.

Orange light in the darkness of the TV picture, pulling the attention in the bar. *Fire,* someone said, and the word began to spread in circles around the room, *Fire, fire.*

Darby asked if Gonzalez knew where Greene was now. Gonzalez crunched ice, looked Darby in the eye for the first time. His gaze flicked down to the ink on Darby's neck, Darby's arms. The scripted letters on his knuckles.

"He owe you something?" Gonzalez said.

Darby looked at his hands, kept his mouth closed, nodded.

Gonzalez shook his head a little, like he was disappointed with himself for what he had said, what he would say.

"Out toward Barstow. Somewhere near there. He had an uncle or a cousin who worked at a factory, could get him a job. Cement factory. Someone told me this. I don't know who. One of the players from last season."

Darby reached over the bar, took a pen from a Lakers mug, wrote the name and the town on a napkin, folded the napkin into the pocket of his jeans. This should have been enough, but it wasn't enough. He had a name, he had a place, but it wasn't enough. He wanted to hear the story. He wanted confirmation that Lucy hadn't been alone. That she'd been carried by Greene, that she'd been surrounded by her students. He wanted to hear the story. He hadn't heard the story in so long. He'd told it, to himself, to The Kid, but he hadn't heard it. He needed to hear it from someone else.

A postal worker was sitting on the stool beside Darby, drinking a frozen margarita. Gonzalez was gone. His windbreaker was gone, his umbrella. Darby didn't know how long he'd been sitting there alone. His shot glass was full again. There was a fresh beer beside it. The bar was packed with refugees from the worsening rain. Bodies pressed

against Darby's back and shoulders. Wet jackets, wet hair. He looked
to the other end of the bar for the nurses. He wanted another cigarette. The Kid would be home from school soon, but Darby didn't
want to go home. He thought of The Kid discovering his bedroom
torn apart, not understanding what had to be done, what Darby had
to do.

The glow on the TV grew bigger, brighter, the outlines of the
compound now visible in the flickering light, gray smoke leaking up
from the roof into the dark sky. *Fire, fire.* People leaned forward on
their stools, pushed in to get a better view. Darby thought of Bob
on his way up north. The bartender held the remote up to raise the
volume. A reporter's voice over the shot of the fire saying, *Conflicting
reports, unconfirmed reports.* Saying, *Unknown source, the cause of the
blaze.*

The newspaper clipping was spread across the bar in soggy
pieces. Hands and elbows had dragged it apart, separated the wet
newsprint into curling bits. Darby could feel the speck in his mouth
so he clenched his teeth, he kept his mouth shut tight.

The flames now filled the TV, the orange light flickering out to
the faces in the bar. People in the bar covered their mouths as they
watched. Darby covered his mouth. A bearded man in the back corner shouted angrily at the TV, *No, no, no.* The speck was rising; the
speck was here. Darby's hands were touching the speck so he pulled
them away from his mouth, held them at his sides. It looked like the
entire compound was on fire. *No, no, no.* Darby was afraid that his
hands might be contaminated by the speck. He tried to rub them
clean on his jeans. The pager buzzed on his hip. He unclipped it
from his belt, tried to focus on the display. A page from Everclean,
one from Roistler's cell phone. Another from Roistler, more from
Everclean, going back to the day before, the day before that. He
clicked through the display. A week of unanswered pages.

The pager was contaminated now. His hands had touched the
speck and now his hands had touched the pager. He tried to wipe
his hands on his jeans but it was no use, it was no good. He left the
pager on the bar, held his hands away from his body, backed out of
the door onto the sidewalk, shaking his hands in the rain.

They stood alone in the waiting room outside the vice-principal's office. There was a row of chairs against the wall, but when someone was waiting in that room because they got in trouble they had to stand, they couldn't sit.

The nurse had shined a light in Matthew's eyes and ears and held up a hand in front of his face and asked him to count the fingers. When she was satisfied that he seemed okay, she sent them both to the V.P.'s office.

They'd been waiting for a long time. It had started to rain, water lashing against the windows behind the secretary's desk. There was a small TV on the desk. The picture showed a long dirt road winding back toward some distant mountains. The road was jammed with cars and trucks and campers, luggage and boxes strapped to the tops of the vehicles, people hanging out the windows, yelling at police officers who were motioning for them to turn back. There was a fire somewhere, off camera, smoke filling the sky above the line of cars.

"Why did you come in there?" Matthew said. The nurse had given him a square of gauze to hold under his nose if it started bleeding again. He had pushed it up into one nostril, really wedging it up there, making his voice pinched and reedy.

The Kid didn't have an answer. The back of his head was pounding from where he'd gotten hit. His eyes were getting blurry, but he didn't want to cry. He wanted to call his dad. He wanted to hear his dad's voice on the other end of the phone.

"You didn't think you were going to beat him up," Matthew said.

The Kid couldn't stop shaking. His hands, his knees. He could hear the vice-principal's voice from behind the closed door, Brian's voice saying something in response.

"Why did you come in there?" Matthew said.

The Kid didn't have an answer. He couldn't stop shaking. The room blurred and then he felt Matthew's hand on his arm, Matthew's hand holding his wrist, and they stood like that and waited for the office door to open.

Steve Rogers was lying in his corner of the porch when The Kid got home. The rain had slowed to a drizzle. The house was empty. His dad must have already left for work. The Kid went through the house, turning on lights, his head and neck still throbbing from where he'd gotten hit.

He found his room torn apart. His room a disaster area. His clothes had been dumped out of his drawers, pulled from his closet. His notebooks had been pulled from the shelf. The cassette recorder and the tape he'd found were pulled out from under the bed. His calendars were out from under the bed. His dad must have found the calendars and gotten mad at what The Kid was keeping track of. His dad so mad that he destroyed The Kid's room.

He took the recorder and the cassette and went back out onto the porch. Steve Rogers was still lying in his corner. The Kid wanted to tell the dog that he knew what was wrong with him, that he'd looked it up at the library. He knew it was stupid, but he wanted to tell the dog that there was a name for what was wrong, that there were books with pictures, and then maybe the dog wouldn't look so wary all the time.

It was quiet on the street. No loud cars, no helicopters, no shouting. The Kid put the tape in the recorder, pressed Play. The gears took a second to start turning, gradually getting up to speed. He heard traffic noises and muffled voices speaking Spanish. He heard dogs barking and looked over to Steve Rogers and Steve's ears perked up at the sound. Then a voice spoke, loud on the tape, the voice too close to the microphone.

"This is Whitley Darby," the voice said. "Also known as The Kid."

It sounded like a little kid on the tape. It sounded like a little kid trying to make his voice deeper. The Kid almost didn't believe it was him on the tape, that he sounded like that. That this was his voice.

"Tonight I'm turning the show over to a very special guest host, a person who needs no introduction."

The Kid switched off the recorder. He couldn't do it fast enough. He knew what show this was. He remembered this show. It was from a year ago, last fall, right around the start of fifth grade.

He'd woken up in the middle of the night to find his mom sitting on the edge of his bed, gently shaking his shoulder. Wake up, she was whispering. I can't sleep. Let's go downstairs and sit, she said. Just for a little while. Not for long, just for a little while.

The Kid didn't know what was going on. His mom acting nervous, afraid. They went down to the living room, the house quiet and dark. His dad away at work. Three-thirty in the morning, according to the clock on the VCR. Even the late-night talk shows were over; even the hosts were in bed.

His tape recorder was sitting on the coffee table. How about an episode of your show? his mom said. How about a special episode? He shook his head, told her that he was tired. He couldn't think of any guests, any questions. He didn't know why she'd woken him up in the middle of the night, why she was acting that way.

I can't sleep, she said. I'm just having some trouble sleeping.

She took his hand and led him out onto the porch. They sat on the top step. She had the recorder in her lap.

What if I'm the host? she said. Just for tonight. What if I fill in for you?

She switched the tape recorder on, handed him the microphone. Her hands were shaking, and when The Kid looked at her hands she stuck them between her knees, clamped her knees tight. He was so tired, but his mom seemed so strange, so afraid. He held the microphone up and she nodded at him to start the show.

He made his introduction and held the microphone out to her. She gave him a weak smile, a forced smile. She pulled her hands from her knees, took the microphone. Cleared her throat.

This is Lucy Darby, she said. Honored to be filling in for Whitley on this installment of his popular and long-running show.

The Kid looked at the dog. Steve Rogers was still in his corner, legs stretched out, watching The Kid. Maybe The Kid didn't want to hear the tape, but maybe the dog would like to hear it. Maybe the dog should hear her voice. Then he wouldn't growl or bark when she came back. Then he'd know her. He wouldn't snarl when she finally turned down the street, when she came up the driveway, scaring her away.

The Kid stood, carried the recorder over toward Steve's corner. Slowly, carefully, no sudden moves, nothing to spook the dog, nothing to make him want to lunge and attack. The dog watched him approach. The Kid placed the recorder on the porch a couple of feet from the dog's outstretched paws. He pressed the Play button and turned and sat back down on the steps, away from the dog, and there was her voice, just like he'd remembered it, his mom's voice on the porch, the dog looking at the recorder, his head cocked to the sound.

He'd taken a pair of latex gloves out of his toolbox and drove wearing the gloves. The gloves would prevent the contamination from spreading any further. It took him longer to get home than it should have. He drove slowly, carefully. He was worried about the contamination and the rain and the alcohol in his system.

He found The Kid sitting on the porch steps, not far from the dog. The Kid didn't ask him where he'd been. Probably figured Darby had been at work. Darby asked The Kid why he was out on the porch and The Kid wrote that he couldn't sleep.

He wanted to ask The Kid about dinner, if he'd eaten, what he'd eaten. He wanted to fix dinner, but the speck was in his mouth and he couldn't open his mouth to eat. He went up to the bathroom, peeled off his gloves, scrubbed his hands and face in the sink. The soap wasn't enough. He could get in the shower, but water wasn't the problem. Soap was the problem. He could go to Everclean, use the showers there, but then he remembered the flames on TV, the unanswered calls on his pager. He scrubbed his hands, he scrubbed his face, but the soap wasn't enough.

He didn't know what time it was. Late. The Kid should be in bed but Darby needed to get himself clean. He steered The Kid back outside to the truck. He wore another pair of gloves as he drove.

The supermarket shone brightly in the night. The electric signs, the floor to ceiling windows at the front of the store. They came through the sliding doors into the fluorescent glare. The store was busy, small lines at four or five checkouts, carts in nearly every aisle.

The Kid went to look at the magazines. That was fine. They wouldn't be there long. Darby found the aisle with the detergents, the cleaning supplies. He moved down the aisle, scanning the packaging,

finding nothing but perfumed hand soaps and body wash, no dis-
infectants, nothing like the industrial-strength powders and sprays
at Everclean. He pulled a boxed bar of soap down from the shelf,
opened the box, shook the bar out into his hand. This soap wouldn't
work. Too soft, too gentle. He shoved the bar back into the box,
dropped the box on the floor. Pushed past a couple of carts to the
household cleaners. Rows of aluminum cans with brightly colored
plastic caps. He scanned the labels, sweating through his shirt. He
found a can in the middle of the aisle, top shelf, something that
looked industrial-grade. A no-nonsense black & white label, a block
of small-type hazards and precautions. He took the can from the
shelf, shook the can. He could feel the speck in his mouth, but he
didn't want to touch his mouth again. There was a list of viruses on
the can, but he didn't need to read the label to know the list. He
knew the list. He shook the can, popped off the cap. Herpes Simplex
Type 1, Herpes Simplex Type 2; Hepatitis A, B, C. He knew the list,
he lived with the list.

He pulled off the gloves and sprayed his hands with the cleanser.
The pain when the disinfectant hit the dog bites was a searing, white
hot thing. A woman shopping a few feet down the aisle turned,
watched. Darby sprayed again, coating his entire hand. He could
still feel the contamination from the speck on his skin. He dropped
the can to the floor. It rolled away, clattering down the aisle.

A woman called out, Someone get a manager, please.

He tried another can, spraying both hands, spraying up his forearms. More people gathering in the aisle, watching from behind their
shopping carts. He dropped that can, picked another off the shelf.
Tried that can. He could no longer feel his hands, had trouble working the nozzle.

The manager entered the aisle, a pear-shaped man in a striped
dress shirt. He made his way toward Darby, squeezing between the
onlookers, the parked shopping carts. He made a face when he
smelled the disinfectant. He looked at Darby's wet hands, the cans of
cleanser scattered on the floor. He asked Darby if he could help with
something, asked if Darby needed some assistance.

"Give me a second," Darby said. "This will only take a second."

The manager cleared his throat. Darby cleared his throat in response. Of course. He knew what to do. He could get rid of the speck once and for all.

A woman waiting with her cart said something to Darby. The manager made a shushing motion to her, and then he said something to Darby, something about blocking the aisle, about having to leave the store.

Darby shook his head. He wasn't finished yet. He shook the can of cleanser, opened his mouth, coughed, spat. It was hard to shake the can when he couldn't feel his hands.

Shoppers were watching from both ends of the aisle now, three and four carts deep. The manager signaled toward the far end of the aisle. A uniformed security guard made his way toward them, squeezing though the tangle of carts.

"Just give me a second," Darby said, his mouth open, fumbling with the spray can, unable to get his numb fingers over the trigger tip.

Someone said, Get him out of here. Get him out of here before he does something.

The manager said, Please, please, everyone take it easy. Please.

"Just give me a second," Darby said. He had his finger on the tip, his mouth open wide, aiming the can.

A woman screamed, Get him out, get him out, get him out.

A hand on Darby's arm. Darby thought it was the manager, the manager had laid a hand on him, or maybe the security guard, attempting to drag him out of the store. Darby forced his hand into a fist, what he thought might be a fist, turned, ready to swing. But it was The Kid. The Kid's hand on Darby's wet forearm. The Kid standing between Darby and the manager and the crowd behind the manager. He'd got in through the crowd and the carts somehow, his eyes wide, scared.

The Kid wrote something in his notebook, big block letters across two facing pages. He turned and held it up for everyone to read.

*EVERYTHING IS OK. THIS IS MY DAD.*

Darby dropped the can. The Kid pulled Darby along with one hand, held his notebook up with the other, showing it to the crowd on each side of the aisle, keeping them at bay, moving forward slowly toward the front of the store. The crowd backed up as they approached, unclogging the aisle. They walked past the checkouts, The Kid showing his notebook to all sides, warding off the crowd, pulling Darby through the front doors and out of the store.

five

They drove home from the supermarket, his dad with no expression on his face, just staring straight through the windshield, not saying a thing. At the house, The Kid got out of the pickup, went on up to the porch. Steve Rogers watched from the corner, wagging his tail, happy to see them. The Kid opened the security door, the front door. His dad hadn't locked either of them in his rush to get to the supermarket. The lights in the house were still on. The Kid turned back and saw his dad sitting in the truck, the engine still running, the dome light on. His dad's head was down, looking at his lap. His dad was sitting on his hands. The Kid went back out and opened his dad's door. Turned the car off, took the keys out of the ignition. His dad said nothing. He took his dad's arm again, led him across the lawn, up onto the porch.

The Kid took him back to the old bedroom. He didn't know where else to take him. The bedroom was cold and dark, smelled like dust and stale air. He sat his dad down on the bed, pulled off his boots, his socks. Tipped his dad back until his head touched the pillow. His dad's eyes were still open, staring at the wall. He tucked the sheet all around his dad, over his feet, in at his sides, pulled it up to his chin. His dad wrapped like a mummy in the cold bed.

He had done this before. This was not a new thing. There had been times when he'd woken up in the middle of the night and heard noises down in the living room, in the kitchen. His dad away at work, the house dark except for the streetlights through the windows. Downstairs, his mom would be standing in the living room, in the kitchen, in front of the desk in her office, unsteady on her feet, swaying in place. Empty bottles and glasses in the sink, sometimes glasses broken in the sink, in sharp pieces on the kitchen floor. Her hands at her face sometimes, holding her face. Her hands up at her ears sometimes, pushing in, like there was something she didn't want to hear.

He'd take his mom back to the bedroom, sit her on the bed. Take off her shoes, lay her back onto her pillow, cover her up. He'd pick up the glass pieces from the kitchen floor, from the sink, careful not to cut his fingers. Sometimes he was careful enough, sometimes he wasn't. Red blood from his fingertips, from a slice across his palm. The soft whirring of the VCR in the living room, taping the last of the late-night talk shows. His mom back in the bedroom, not sleeping, just saying, *oh god oh god oh god.* The Kid picking up glass, looking at the clock on the microwave. How long until morning? How long until sunlight through the living room window? How long until his alarm clock, until breakfast, his mom sitting at the kitchen table, normal again, smiling as he came down the stairs? The night before forgotten, the night before a thing of the past. How long until sitting on the couch with the tape of the talk shows playing, that safest hour before school? The Kid making his mom laugh with his impressions of the hosts, of the guests. On those nights, The Kid picked up glass, looked at the clock, did the math trying to see how long.

He stood in the kitchen listening for sirens. He was sure that the people at the supermarket had called the police, that the police were coming and would take his dad off to jail. He listened for he didn't know how long. He heard plenty of sirens, but the police never came.

He got his backpack and the cassette recorder, the tape he'd taken from the garage. In the kitchen, he packed some cookies and juice boxes. He didn't want to leave his dad, but he had to bring Michelle some food. He was already very late. She was probably starving. He went out onto the front porch. Steve Rogers was lying in the far corner, watching The Kid, his eyes glinting in the streetlight. The Kid thought that maybe he should give Steve Rogers an order, maybe he should tell him to protect his dad, not to let anyone in the house, not to let the police near, but he thought it would be pretty stupid to write the orders in his notepad and show it to the dog. Instead, he stood on the porch and thought of the things he wanted Steve Rogers to do while he looked the dog in the eye. Finally Steve Rogers looked away and The Kid hoped that maybe this meant he had gotten the message.

He stood across the street from the burned house, slowing his breathing, listening for signs of trouble, looking for faces in the windows of the neighboring houses. After he was sure that no one was watching, he ran across the street, up onto the porch, eased open the security door, stepped inside.

He didn't want to get hit with a block of wood again, so he knocked his knuckles on the wall just inside the door, the secret-code knock from all sorts of old movies, the tune of an old-time song that his mom used to sing while his dad was cutting his hair on the front porch, *Shave and a haircut, two bits*. The Kid had no idea what that meant, but it was the well-known secret code knock, and he hoped Michelle would hear it and know it was him, put down her two-by-four.

He made his way through the front room, down the hallway. The living room was pitch black, no light from the candles. He knocked on the wall again. *Shave and a haircut*. No response. He listened for breathing. Maybe Michelle was asleep. He didn't hear anything. He stepped into the room, shuffling his feet across the floor to make noise, to wake her up before he got too close and scared her into action. In the center of the room, he could see some comics and the candles in a ring on the floor. Only one candle was still lit, just barely, the wick burned down to a nub. He expected Michelle to jump out at any moment, knock him to the floor, but nothing happened. The room was empty. He walked back through the house. She wasn't in the dining room, the kitchen, the bathroom. He stood in the doorway to the bedroom, looking at the burned bed, the charred walls. There was nobody in the house. The Kid couldn't believe it. She had gone to Minneapolis. She'd been telling the truth. Her real dad had sent money and now she was sitting on a bus, riding across the night-world of the map, the empty highways from The Kid's dream. Free, away from here.

The word search book was gone. She must have taken it with her, something to do on the bus. He looked across the floor. The rabbit was gone. His dad's rabbit. He'd placed it there as some kind of protection, something to ward off trouble, but he didn't think that she'd take it with her when she left. He didn't really think that she was going to leave.

How long would it take for her to get to Minneapolis? A week? A month? Would she be on the bus when Y2K happened, when the planes fell, when the missiles shot up? Rolling along a farmland highway at night, streaks of white light in the sky, some going up, some coming down. She'd never get a chance to monkey with the computers at school now, to try to convince them that the year 2000 could really exist. The Kid still had her money from that bet, the five dollars she'd taken from her mom's bedroom. The retainer. The Kid guessed that this meant he'd won the bet. He'd lost the rabbit but won the bet.

He blew out the last candle, gathered up his comics and walked back through the dark house.

Darby woke in their bed for the first time in a year. Dusty sunlight streaming around the edges of the blinds, golden slats on his outstretched arm, the sheet beyond.

He thought of arms around her, holding her. Not his arms, but at least she wouldn't have been alone. The alternative was worse. The thought of her not surrounded by something, held and protected in those last moments. The thought was too much, but it would not leave him. He imagined Greene's arms holding her and he wanted to smash Greene, he wanted to thank Greene.

It should have been him. He should have been there, somehow. But it wasn't him. This was the truth, this was something that would not leave him.

He stood in the motel parking lot, the row of orange doors before him. He knew why he was there. He knew why he was there in the way certain essential things were ingrained in his muscles, in his bones. Something so obviously true that he could not let the thought form completely. Knowing that if he let it out, if he tried to release it from his body, then everything, every other certainty, would collapse in its presence.

He didn't know where his pager was. He'd lost it somewhere. The supermarket, maybe. Maybe that hadn't been a dream, the supermarket, cornered in an aisle by angry strangers, The Kid leading him out by the arm.

The newspaper clipping was gone, but there was a napkin in his pocket with a name and a town and he knew that a truth would be there, waiting for him in the desert.

Of course The Kid knew her real name. He'd heard Miss Ramirez say it many times, heard other kids in class call her by it. He'd seen her write it in large blue letters on the dry-erase board, had seen it on the tops of quiz papers. But the name did not stick to The Kid, did not stay with The Kid. When he thought of her, he thought of the name he had given her. It seemed more right, it seemed more true.

Arizona sat alone two lunch tables away. Rhonda Sizemore and some of the girls from Arizona's old table were looking at her and whispering among themselves. Brian was suspended. Matthew was still staying home. The Kid didn't know how long he'd be gone, if maybe his parents had pulled him out of school or something. The Kid chewed his sandwich, watched Arizona, tried not to get caught looking. He'd made his own sandwich that morning, packed his own lunch, his dad still back in the bedroom, sawing logs.

He had to finish the angel. He knew this. Not just before Y2K when the whole world went crazy, but now, before things got any worse with his dad, before the police came and arrested his dad for what he'd done at the mall, what he'd done at the supermarket. He had to get his mom home now. He would finish the angel and she would send the signal and his mom would come back and make things right again. There was no more time to waste. Now Michelle was gone, Matthew was gone.

He looked at Arizona, tried not to get caught looking. He thought about how she had come to visit him and Matthew at their lunch table that first day. How she'd come to be interviewed on Halloween. He thought about her hand on his arm when he'd made those jokes, when he'd made her laugh.

She looked up when he sat across from her and her expression didn't change. He couldn't tell if she was happy for the company or if she wanted to be left alone.

"How do you feel?" she said.

The Kid shrugged. He shrugged again when she asked him how Matthew was feeling.

"I hope he's okay," she said. She looked like she was going to cry. "I really, really hope he's okay."

The Kid opened his notebook, turned to a blank page.

*How long is Brian suspended for?*

"I don't talk to Brian anymore," she said. She looked at Rhonda's table. "I don't talk to anyone over there anymore. I'm sorry I was ever friends with them."

The Kid stared at his lunch bag. When she didn't say anything else, he looked up and saw that she was watching him, waiting for something. He realized finally that she had said that last thing to him, she'd meant it specifically for him.

The Kid nodded. He didn't want her to feel sorry.

She looked back down at the table and The Kid could see her eyes filling, her bottom lip trembling.

"I don't want to be here anymore," she said. "I want to go home. I want to go back to my old school. I was wrong about this place."

The Kid turned back in his notebook, looking for an earlier page. Something she had asked him at lunch, what seemed like years ago now. He finally found it, the blank space between two lines he had written, the time she had asked how long they'd have to be friends before he would tell her his secret.

*I need your help,* he wrote in that space, and then he slid the notebook across the table so she could read.

They planned to meet outside *Gift 2000* right after school. The Kid thought they should meet at night so they wouldn't be followed, but Arizona told him that there was no way she could leave her house after dark. Her father locked the doors at eight o'clock and that was it. The Kid would have to show her whatever he wanted to show her right after school.

The Kid stood in the parking lot, waiting. He was still worried about Brian and Razz. Just because they were suspended didn't mean they had been removed from the world. A long white truck pulled into the parking lot, stopped with a sigh. A man hopped down from the front of the truck, unlocked the big back door, rolled it up. He lifted out a red dolly cart, pulled some boxes down and stacked them on the cart. The Kid wondered what was in the boxes. More word search books, maybe. Y2K supplies, bottled water, batteries, clean underwear.

"I'm here, Whitley." Arizona was standing beside him, wide-eyed, excited, maybe a little scared. They walked across the parking lot, then down through one of The Kid's alternate routes. Arizona talked the whole way, telling The Kid about where she used to live, her old school, her old house. Telling him about her old friends. She said that it was possible they were going back there, her family, that her dad would be transferred back. She said she thought that would be a good thing, she thought she'd prefer that to staying here.

The afternoon was cool and humid after all that rain the day before. They turned down side streets, came back around by way of others, a long, winding route, The Kid trying to throw any pursuers off their trail but also glad just to hear Arizona talk, just to walk and listen. He wanted to walk as long as they could, wanted to make the route as long as possible. He felt like they were in some kind of alternate dimension while they walked, just the two of them, shifted out slightly from everyone else, from the rest of the world, an alternate timeline where everything was different, where everything was okay as long as they walked, as long as he could listen to her talk.

They finally reached the sidewalk across the street from the burned house. Arizona stopped talking, looked at the face of the house, the black-hole eyes, the charred, jagged roof.

"What happened to it?" she said.

*There was a fire.*

"Was anyone hurt?"

The Kid nodded. It was getting late. Arizona would have to go home soon. He looked both ways for traffic then jogged toward the house, motioning for her to follow.

On the porch, he showed her the photos wedged into the security door. The color had faded and the pictures were curling in at the edges. The Kid wondered how much longer they'd be there, how much longer until they just fell out onto the porch and the wind blew them away.

Arizona took some time looking at them, studying the faces. She kept her hands clasped behind her back as she looked, like she was trying to keep herself from touching the photos, like she was looking at something in a museum or an expensive store.

After a while, she said, "Do you know her?"

The Kid wasn't sure how to answer. He'd never seen the red-haired woman while she was alive. He'd never talked to her. But now he saw her quite a bit, now he'd spent quite a bit of time with her.

The Kid nodded. He guessed that he knew her. Guessed that he knew her at least enough to say so.

Arizona looked back at the photos, the picture of the red-haired woman smirking in front of the gas pump. "She's beautiful," she said. "She's not really pretty, but she's beautiful."

He led her into the front room. The glass crunched under their sneakers. He showed her the cracked, blackened walls, the smashed furniture. They started walking again and then he felt her take his hand, felt her fingers laced with his.

He needed to show her everything. He led her into the kitchen, the bathroom. They stood in the bedroom doorway and he watched her eyes following the black trail from the bed up the wall to the ceiling, and he could tell by how she squeezed his hand that she knew what had happened in this room, that she was picturing the red-haired woman and that she was seeing the flames and hearing the screaming.

In the living room, he heard her take a quick breath when she saw the walls. He showed her the pirates on the open water, the school, the other kids in the schoolyard, the streets around The Kid's house, Steve Rogers on the front porch, and then the center of the mural, the angel lifting up toward the hole in the roof.

"Did you draw this?" she said.

The Kid didn't know if she could see him clearly, but he nodded anyway.

"It's beautiful."

He held out his notebook, flipped back to the pages of hand drawings. Michelle, Ms. Ramirez, the lunch lady. He gave her the notebook, then pointed to the angel so she could see what it was missing. She looked at the angel, up at the hole in the ceiling, the sky above. He didn't tell her why he needed to finish the drawing. It seemed like she understood that it was important without him telling her anything. She walked toward the wall, holding The Kid's notepad with one hand, letting her other hand hang at her side, the way that the angel's hands were hanging. The Kid picked a piece of white chalk off the floor, walked over to Arizona and started to draw.

They hadn't exchanged so much as two words since what had happened at the supermarket. The night before they'd eaten dinner in silence, absolute silence, not even the sound of The Kid's pencil in his notebook. Darby had tucked The Kid into bed and then sat in the pickup, waiting for daybreak. When The Kid left for school, Darby filled the dog's food and water bowls, taped a note to the front door. He didn't think he'd be home by dinner and he didn't want The Kid to worry.

He drove out of the city into the uncorrupted desert, north and east, one hour, two hours, the landscape flattening and spreading, going from green to brown, grass to dust, and it felt right, this movement across familiar terrain, it felt like going home.

He stopped at a gas station just inside Barstow and looked for Greene's name in a phone book. He went inside and asked the woman behind the counter for directions to the address. She said it was an apartment complex just off the freeway, just about the last thing you saw before you left town.

The complex parking lot was poorly paved, nearly empty. There were five or six two-story buildings, first floor doors opening onto the lot, second floor doors opening along a narrow walkway. A dry, kidney-shaped pool sat behind a fence in the center of the complex. A boy with shaggy brown hair who looked a little older than The Kid was standing on a skateboard on the rim of the pool. He took a step forward and disappeared down the side, wheels grinding on the concrete, then he reappeared over the opposite wall, up and out, two or three feet into the air, turning in flight, then dropping back down into the pool.

Darby sat in the pickup. It was midafternoon, hot and bright, quiet except for the skateboarder, a familiar long-dead desert time.

He remembered skipping school with friends and this being about the time of day they'd wondered why they'd bothered, the thrill of the morning gone and the afternoon stretching on endlessly, longer even than if they were sitting in a classroom watching the clock.

He was wearing the lucky shirt, the faded yellow date shirt, because he felt that it gave him strength, that it would keep him from turning back. He felt that it would keep him from sitting in the pickup all afternoon and then just driving away, leaving without getting what he'd come for.

The skateboarder disappeared down one side of the pool, came up the other. Darby got out of the pickup, walked to a small building on the other side of the lot. The laundry and mailroom. One of the washers chugged along, filling the room with the smell of hot detergent, soapy water. He pulled the chain on the overhead bulb. There were two rows of mailboxes on the wall above one of the dryers, the last names of the residents embossed on small labels. He found it in the second row: *Greene/Piniero, 23*. Piniero must be the girlfriend with the baby. Darby hadn't even considered the possibility that she could be there, with or without Greene. That she could be home right now. He hadn't even considered her on the drive out, hadn't considered the baby. He'd only thought of Greene.

He walked back across the lot. Twenty-three was the last door on the top deck of the furthest building. There was a passageway that cut through the middle of the building, a couple of vending machines, a cement staircase. Up on the second floor, he could see across the complex to the scrub brush and sand beyond, the glinting asphalt of the freeway in the far distance. He could see down into the pool, where the skater sat beside his deck, rubbing his knee. Darby went down to the end of the walkway, stood beside 23, listened. There was a large window next to the door, thick blackout curtains drawn against the sun. The sound of a television from the apartment next door, a daytime talk show, muffled voices and audience laughter, but nothing from 23. The walkway continued around the corner, where it ended abruptly, the rusted metal railing turning in and bolted to the stucco wall. There was another, smaller window on this side of the apartment, the same blackout curtains drawn. Darby placed his fingers along the sash, pushed gently. The window slid open to the side. He stood, listened. No sound from inside the apartment. He pushed the window further, opening it completely. Still no sound.

The skateboarder started up again, wheels grinding in the empty pool. Darby stood by the open window, touching the blackout curtain. He couldn't wait any longer. He lifted one leg up and into the apartment, ducked his head and pulled the other leg through.

He saw her in the school courtyard and thought she was a ghost. He thought he was seeing things, spirits in the morning light. The Kid wanted to blink to reset his vision. He wanted to rub his eyes like a cartoon character in disbelief.

Michelle Mustache, coming across the courtyard from the back gate, dragging her backpack, her ratty sneakers flapping on the blacktop.

The morning bell rang. He wanted to stay back and wait for Michelle, but Miss Ramirez had been keeping him close since the fight and she led The Kid into the building before all the other kids, losing Michelle back in the crowd.

All morning he kept turning in his seat to look at her, to make sure she was really there. She sat at her desk at the end of the row, head down, doodling in a notebook. No one said anything about her return. Miss Ramirez didn't make any kind of announcement. It was like nothing had happened, except The Kid couldn't stop turning in his seat, looking back at her to make sure what he saw was true.

She wasn't at lunch. The Kid figured she was probably in Mr. Bromwell's office. He sat alone, chewing the sandwich he'd made that morning. Matthew was back, and sat at a table with Miss Ramirez and some of the other teachers. Arizona was absent. The Kid wondered if she'd gotten in trouble for not going straight home yesterday, if she'd gotten caught somehow. Her dad the military man. The Kid wondered about the mural, the completed angel, how long it would take for the signal to go out and reach his mom.

Michelle didn't come back to class after lunch. The Kid didn't know if she was still in Mr. Bromwell's office or if she'd been sent home or what. At the end of the day, he stood out by the front gate as the courtyard emptied, waiting. Matthew walked by and nodded before getting into his father's car at the curb. The last kids were coming through when he finally saw her trudging his way, head down. He stepped in front of her and she moved to walk around him and he stepped in front of her again until she stopped and looked up.

"Get out of the way, Kid. I've got to go."

The Kid shook his head. He opened his notebook, but she was talking again before he could write anything.

"My dad's coming to pick me up and I've got to be out there when he comes. I can't walk home anymore."

The Kid wasn't sure what she was talking about. Her dad had come out from Minneapolis?

She looked past him to the street. There was a line of parents' cars and trucks idling at the curb. Michelle was anxious, chewing skin from her lower lip.

"The cops found me that last night," she said. "They just kicked in the door like they thought they were tough shit. They said neighbors had seen the candles the past few nights and called. They didn't handcuff me, which was pretty dumb. They just put me in the back of the police car and drove me home."

She didn't look at The Kid as she talked. She watched the street, chewing her lip.

"I didn't snitch you out, don't worry. I didn't tell them anything. I said I didn't know anything about the drawing you made. I said it was already there when I found the house."

She unzipped her backpack, dug around inside. Came up with something in her fist, held it out to The Kid.

"Here's your rabbit. See? I didn't lose it."

The Kid took the rabbit, pressed his thumb into the worn wood.

Michelle saw something she recognized on the street. The Kid turned to see a monster of a truck pull up to the curb, beetle-black and shining in the sun. The passenger window rolled down and The Kid could see Michelle's mom's boyfriend stretching across the seat, looking out at the kids on the sidewalk. He started calling into the crowd, barking Michelle's name.

*Where's your dad?*

"He's here to pick me up, Kid, I told you."

The Kid didn't know what to write. The Kid didn't know what was going on.

"I'm a fucking liar, Kid, okay? I'm a liar about everything."

Michelle's dad was still scanning the crowd, barking her name. He hadn't seen them yet. It seemed like Michelle's feet were stuck to the sidewalk, like she was unable to move. She watched her dad and her face started to fold in on itself, her cheeks and her chin and her eyebrows all pulling in to meet in the middle.

"I want to be able to go back, Kid," she said. "Even if they tear it down, even if your drawing is gone. Okay?"

The Kid didn't know what she meant. Tear it down? He couldn't write fast enough. He was reduced pairs of words, fragments of sentences.

*Tear it*

*What do you*

She wasn't looking at his notebook anyway. She was looking at her dad and then she was looking at The Kid and she was crying.

"They're going to tear down the house. That's what my dad said. But you can just draw it again in your notebook, right? You can just draw it again and we can look at it whenever we want. You have to promise, okay?"

The Kid couldn't believe it. They were going to tear down the house?

"You have to promise, Kid. You have to promise."

He could barely understand her, she was talking so fast.

"You have to promise."

The Kid couldn't believe it. What about the angel? What about the signal? But Michelle was still waiting for an answer, watching him, crying hard now, her face wet with snot and tears. He turned to a new page in his notebook.

*I promise.*

Her dad called her name again and she turned to go. The Kid grabbed onto her shirtsleeve. When she turned back to him, he handed her the rabbit. She looked at the rabbit and shoved it down deep into her backpack. Then she was moving again, hurrying past The Kid to the passenger door of the truck, climbing up and in, disappearing behind the rising tinted window.

The Kid stood on the sidewalk, stuck in his spot like Michelle had been stuck, his notebook still open in his hand. The sidewalk emptied slowly, the rest of the cars and trucks pulling away from the curb. He didn't know what to think. He didn't know what to do.

They were going to tear down the house.

Darby stood in the dark apartment. He kept the curtain closed behind him, the edges glowing with the exiled outside light. One main room with a double bed and a crib, a dresser with a TV and a boom box against the wall. Baby toys spread across the carpet, blocks and a rubber ball and a pair of plastic dolls. There was a kitchenette built into the wall leading to the bathroom, a half-fridge and microwave and hotplate. There were clothes on the floor, on the unmade bed. Toothbrushes and coffee mugs around the kitchenette sink.

He moved into the room. Loose change and haphazard piles of rap CDs covered the top of the dresser. Posturing men on the covers with tattoos and jewelry and firearms. A starburst of unframed pictures was thumb tacked to the wall by the TV. Greene flashing gang signs, a joint burning between his fingers. Piniero, hugely pregnant, her face defiant with dark slashes of eyeliner. Then a newer picture, Greene and Piniero standing by the empty pool of the apartment complex, holding their baby.

In the earlier pictures, the L.A. pictures, Greene was tall and well-built, athletic, but he grew thinner as the photos became more recent. There was a hollowness to his eyes, the deep-socketed haunt of an addict, a young man wasting away.

Darby opened the drawers of the dresser. T-shirts, socks, bras, underwear. He opened the drawer of the bedside table. More photographs, and underneath those a square of cardboard, a divider of some kind, and underneath that a gun, a thick, blunt thing, black plastic and metal.

There were newspaper clippings tacked to the wall along the other side of the TV, the paper dry and brittle from the heat. Team photos, game recaps. *Greene Goes the Distance* was there, the familiar photo, the familiar blur. It was a shock to see it. Something Darby had carried with him, something he'd looked at countless times. He'd thought of it as something that had existed only in his pocket, in his hand. Something that had been destroyed in the bar, torn into wet shreds. Seeing it tacked to the wall felt like a betrayal. It existed apart from him, without him. Here it signified something unknown to him. Here it had a meaning that he didn't recognize.

He pulled the thumbtack, the clipping from the wall. He thought of Lucy cutting the same photo from the newspaper, losing it between the boards of the porch. He thought of Lucy falling in her classroom, the sudden noise of desk chairs pushed back, commotion of students rising. He thought of Greene coming forward, kneeling beside her. It was hard to picture him, now that Darby had seen his face. It no longer fit. The story no longer came readily.

He thought of Bob opening a closet door in the back room of a dark house. He thought of all the doors he'd stood beside while Bob opened them. He thought of two cops opening the orange door of a motel room. Thought of two cops on his porch in the late morning, hats in hands, showing him something, a driver's license, holding the picture up for him to identify, to confirm. Darby squinting in the sunlight, the cops looking at their caps, their hands, the floor of the porch, anywhere but at him.

The speck pressed at his lips, but he kept his mouth closed, bit his tongue until he tasted salt.

He pictured opening the front door and the cops on the porch telling him something about a motel room, something about Lucy. He didn't want to think about this but he couldn't stop it now. Now that he was in this man's room, now that he had seen Greene and the girl and the baby he couldn't stop this thought. He had opened the front door of the house and the cops on the porch held her license up for him to confirm and he looked at the picture on the license and it broke his heart, the name on the license, his name, the name she had taken, the name they had shared. He thought of standing on the porch long after the cops had gone, standing in the living room, standing in the kitchen, that endless afternoon, waiting for The Kid to get home from school, not knowing what he was going to tell The Kid, what he'd be able to tell The Kid, what he'd be able to say at all. Knowing he couldn't say it, that it couldn't be spoken. Fighting with it, tearing at it with his hands, the day progressing, the truth shrinking as the day ground on, receding slowly inside his body until something else appeared. A picture in his head of Lucy at the front of her class, falling, a student rushing to her side. Lucy carried down the school hallway. Not alone but comforted by her students. Not alone but held in someone's arms.

He didn't want to think about this but he couldn't stop it now.

The sound of a key in the lock and Darby turned to see the front door of the apartment open, a figure in the doorway and blinding white sunlight beyond.

There was no time for an alternate route. It was the wormhole alleyway or nothing. There was no telling when they'd tear the house down, if they'd torn it down already. He had to get there, stop them, give the angel time to escape. He ran as fast as he could, backpack bouncing painfully, textbooks kicking against his spine.

Here he comes, Whitley Earl Darby, commonly known as The Kid, running as fast and as hard as he's ever run.

Halfway there, three-quarters there, legs burning, lungs screaming, daylight at the other end closer with each stride, and then he was hit hard from the back, the wind flying from him, his feet leaving the ground and his body landing and then they were on top of him, their hands on The Kid's face, on his neck, Razz's weight pinning The Kid while Brian dug for something in the pocket of his jeans.

"We told you, pig," Brian said.

Brian was gathering all the spit in his mouth and so The Kid clenched his own mouth tight, but Brian turned his head and spat on The Kid's forearm, spat again, pressed something into the wet spot on The Kid's arm, gripping The Kid's arm hard.

"We told you, but you wouldn't listen."

He was afraid they were going to pee on him. All at once this thought came to him. He was afraid they were going to pee on him like they'd peed on the clothes in his gym locker, and then what would his dad do? His dad would throw him away like they'd thrown away the wet clothes. The Kid started to shake. He moved the parts of his body that he could still feel. He started to flop and shake. He had to keep them away. He had to get to the burned house. He lifted his hands toward them. He shook and lifted his hands.

This was called the aura phase. Also called the prodrome phase.

He stiffened his arms and legs. He made gagging noises in his throat. He snapped his jaw, his teeth cracking together. He stuck out his tongue, made his tongue as big as he could make it, flopped and shook and gagged until the weight lifted, Brian and Razz off of him, backing away, running away, and The Kid rolled onto his side and looked at his arm and saw his skin shiny with Brian's spit and smeared ink, the tattoo he'd left there, the dark blue star.

Greene was upon him, suddenly, tearing at Darby's face, his eyes, his mouth. He was even thinner than in the pictures on the wall, all sinew and bone, but brutally strong, his hands at Darby's throat, long fingers pressing into Darby's windpipe, ragged nails tearing at his skin.

Darby couldn't breathe. He stumbled and fell and Greene was on top of him, swinging and connecting solidly, shouting as he swung, punches to the face releasing bright white explosions in the dark room, breaking Darby's nose, the pain flattening his whole head numb. Darby fell flat on his back, a rainbow-colored plastic ball next to his head, a baby's toy. He tried to speak, to explain himself, but then Greene's boots were on him, kicking him in the stomach, the ribs. Darby tried to roll out of the way but there was no room, the bed was in one direction and the crib was in the other. He grabbed the leg of the crib and pulled himself to his knees and there was another blow to the back of his head, felt like the heel of a boot, and he slammed into the crib, breaking the railing, hanging over the jagged wood. Greene still shouting, Darby spitting fluid into the crib, and then Greene was off him and Darby knew where he was going, what he was after, but Darby was between Greene and the bedside table and he lunged for it, falling to his knees again but grabbing hold of the drawer, his hand inside the drawer and then the gun was in his hand and he was turning, he was wheeling on Greene and then he had the muzzle of the gun pressed hard to Greene's chest.

The Kid ran, expecting to find a crowd around the burned house, the street full of police cars, news vans, a bulldozer pushing in the walls, the house folding in on itself, burying the mural, the angel, trapping her before she'd had a chance to escape. The call that was going out to his mom cut off, leaving her out there alone. He didn't know what he'd do when he got there, if he'd try to run in front of the bulldozer, waving his arms, the bulldozer plowing right through him, knocking him aside as its shovel burst through the house's charred walls.

The blue star burned on his arm. The Kid tried to ignore it, hoped his sweat would wash it away before it infected him with whatever it was made of.

The burned house's street looked normal. He was shocked to see this. The street looked and sounded like the street. Cars parked at the curbs, dogs barking in backyards. No police cars, no sign of a bulldozer. But there was something new, The Kid could see it as he ran down the sidewalk. A plywood wall had been put up around the burned house, six or seven feet tall. There were new paper signs on the wall, *No Trespassing! No Traspasar!* He could see the jagged roof of the house sticking up over the wall, but that was it. He couldn't see if anything else had been done to the house, if the walls had been torn out, if the porch had been ripped off.

He looked along the wall for a way in, a hole or a door. There was nothing. The wall was impenetrable. He reached up and jumped, thinking that maybe if he could get a hold of the top he could pull himself up and over. But he couldn't reach, and he doubted he was strong enough to pull himself up even if he could.

He went back around to the front of the house, unstrapped his backpack, dropped it to the ground. Stood on the backpack. He still couldn't reach the top of the wall. He looked around for something else. Saw the half-melted garbage bin still sitting by the curb, filled with burned junk from the house. He pulled it up across the yard to the plywood wall. Strapped his backpack on and climbed on top of the bin. He could see the house. The house looked the same, the house looked intact. They hadn't torn anything down yet, they'd just built the wall to keep people out. He lifted a leg over the wall, then the other, sat on the top. It was a long drop to the ground. The Kid wondered if he would break a leg or a foot if he jumped. If he'd be stuck there, lying on the ground between the wall and the porch steps, unknown to everyone until the bulldozers came and plowed through the wall and buried him forever under plywood and dirt.

He couldn't take too long to decide what to do. Anyone could see him sitting up there and call the cops again. Brian and Razz could have followed him. He decided to attempt a maneuver. He'd scoot around on the top of the wall so he was facing the other way, out toward the street, and then he'd hold onto the top of the wall and lower himself down, hanging by his arms, dropping the last few feet to the ground. It seemed like a good plan. The Kid twisted himself so he was facing away from the house, then he grabbed the wall, took a deep breath and pushed himself backwards, off into the air, but his pants caught on the wood and he lost his grip and fell all the way down into a heap on the ground a foot or so from the front porch.

He got up, dusted himself off. His wrist ached and his legs hurt where he'd landed. There was a rip in his pants where they'd gotten caught on the wall, but nothing seemed broken. He turned to the house. The window holes were boarded up. The boards looked like wooden eye-patches on the house. He climbed up onto the porch and saw that the pictures were gone from the security door. The Kid looked all over the porch, but he couldn't find them. He pulled at the door, but it wouldn't move, wouldn't even open an inch. He saw that a couple of two-by-fours had been screwed across the top of the doorjamb, sealing it shut. He walked around the side of the house, squeezed through the narrow space between the plywood wall and the house, looking for some way in, an unboarded window, something. He found it at the back of the house, the slim kitchen window, still unsealed. The Kid grabbed onto the bottom of the window, pulled as hard as he could, lifted a bruised leg up and over, shifted his weight until he rolled over the sill, through the window onto the blasted countertop, one sneaker landing in the glass-filled sink.

He lay there for a second, breathing hard, watching the dust swirl in the afternoon light, listening to his breath, the creaking sounds of the house, distant dogs and sirens.

His sneakers crunched through the kitchen, out into the hallway, back into the living room. The angel was there, the mural was there. The whole thing was intact, the drawing was untouched. He walked over to the angel, looked closely. She seemed higher on the wall. She was moving closer to the hole in the roof. How much longer would it take her to get there? The Kid would have to stay and wait. It might take the rest of the afternoon; it might take all night. His dad would get worried, but The Kid had no choice. He would stay and wait until the angel was up and out of the roof, until she was off telling his mom that she was needed, that she needed to come home.

He emptied his backpack, sat in a corner across from the angel. Put the cassette into the tape recorder, rewound, pressed *Play*. He listened to the sound of his own voice, his mom's voice, watched the angel. The light drained from the hole in the roof and the cuts in the walls until it was dark in the house, the only light in the room the glowing blue star on The Kid's arm.

He pushed the gun into Greene's chest, backing him away, moving them both through the room. Fluid leaking from Darby's nose, soaking the front of his lucky shirt. Greene lifted his arms, eyes wide. Darby pushed the gun into his chest. Darby wanting to pull the trigger once, twice, because neither of them had been there when she fell.

The Kid woke to a familiar voice. It took him a few seconds to realize who it belonged to. It was Smooshie Smith, Talk Show Host of the Future. Smooshie was conducting an interview somewhere in the room. The Kid kept his eyes closed, listened.

"Where are you?" Smooshie said. "Can you tell our audience where you are right now?"

There was the sound of cassette-tape hiss and crackle, and then his mom's voice was there in the room.

"I'm close. I'm nearby," she said.

"Where have you been all this time?" Smooshie said. "What have you been up to?"

"I've been all over the map. I've been visiting people. My mother. Old friends, people I used to know."

"And now what?" Smooshie said. "What do you have lined up next?"

The Kid opened his eyes. The room was dark except for the glow of the blue star. He couldn't quite tell where they were, Smooshie and his mom. He thought he saw shapes, moving shadows and shapes, but it was hard to tell for sure. His head felt like a beach ball, big and floaty. He heard the hiss and crackle of the cassette, and then he heard nothing.

"Please," Greene said. "Please. I've got a little girl." His voice high and scared, his hands up and out, shaking, fingers flexing. "Take whatever you want," he said, "just, please."

Darby stepped to his left, the gun still pressed to Greene's chest, moving them both, the gun the hinge on which the room turned, and then he backed away slowly toward the open door, the gun still trained on Greene, the center of his chest, and then he was out into the sunlight, he was back out into the parking lot, into the pickup and away.

The mural was moving. The Kid opened his eyes again after he didn't know how long and in the murky blue light he could see the mural shifting, the sea waves churning, the dingy tossed on the waves, the pirate ship bearing down on the two doomed figures in the little boat. Water rushed around the slanted streetlights and telephone poles. The houses and buildings were burning, his own house was burning, red and orange woodcut flames sprouting out of the roofs of the neighborhood, licking at the ceiling of the room.

Darby drove with the gun on the seat beside him, the pain in his nose and the back of his head, his face wet, his shirt wet. He drove out of town, bypassing the freeway entrance, asphalt to dirt road to desert, the sunlight fading, fluid in his mouth, the gun a possibility, the gun an option on the seat beside him.

She was there, standing over him, his mom, looking just like he'd remembered, her crooked smile, her glasses, and all of a sudden The Kid was scared and embarrassed, worried about his smell, his bad breath and B.O., all the disgusting things that had driven her away in the first place, but she kept her smile and shook her head and when she spoke he could hear the tape hiss, the cassette-tape crackle behind her voice.

Darby walked from the truck, from what was left of the road, out into the dust and scrub brush, the sky purple as a plum, his shirt red and ruined, the gun in his hand.

He had wanted to make an even exchange, but there was nothing to give. He had wanted to hear Greene's story, but there was no story, or no story he would recognize. When he met the real Greene, the Greene he had created fell away into dust.

Greene's gun in his hand, hard and cool within his fingers, like a thing taken from a dream.

The cops stood on the front porch, hats in their hands. They showed him her license, her picture. He had the license at home, he remembered this now. He kept it in an envelope in a drawer in the garage. He hadn't looked at it in over a year.

He was crying and he was grunting to keep from crying, to push it back into his throat. Moving like a wounded animal, dragging himself across the desert. Every few feet the sobs forced him to stop and kneel and gather his strength before he could walk again.

They had lost the things she'd left. Whoever had cleaned the motel room where she'd been found. She'd taken two pictures from the bulletin board over her desk back in the house that last morning, a picture of Darby, a picture of The Kid, and these things had been lost, the last things she'd looked at, the last things she'd seen. These things had been misplaced, thrown away, burned. There were blank spaces on the bulletin board now, the things she'd taken with her that they never got back.

He'd thought he could keep them safe. The things he'd taken from the rooms. But those things were gone, those things were lost now too.

He stopped and looked around. Nothing but sand, the outline of the truck in the far distance, the black hills beyond. He missed her so much he wanted to leave his body behind. He missed her so much he wanted to fade back into the desert.

The gun in his right hand, The Kid's initials on the knuckles of his left. Their son, home alone now, maybe. Their son and his talk show. Their son and his notebooks. Every day he would look more like her. Darby knew this. Every day he would see her more and more in his son's face.

Greene's gun in his hand. It would only take a second. It would only take a moment, the same moment in all of those rooms.

A man in an apartment, a girl in her bedroom. A woman alone in a motel room with an orange door. Her son at school. Her husband at home, in bed, asleep.

He missed her so much. But there was something else, there was something more. He knew this now and it was like a blow, it was like a fist to his chest.

He missed his son, too. He missed The Kid.

He left the gun for the wind to bury, for the desert to devour. He walked back toward the truck, his hands heavy, his feet heavy, his nose leaking fluid that he called by its true name, the word entering his head for the first time in years.

The Kid was standing in the room. He'd been in some kind of

achy not-quite-sleep and now he was standing in the room looking up at the angel. She was almost to the hole in the roof, up and away from the burning city. He could see the inky black sky above, the woodcut stars turning in the night. The angel stuck her head up through the hole and breathed deeply, sighed. Her cowboy boots dangled down into the room. Her skin glowed, her wings glowed. Her hands rested at her sides.

She spoke and he had never heard anything like the sound of her voice, would never hear anything like the sound of her voice, a thousand brass bands, TV talk-show bands, the fanfare of a million charged moments before the host steps through the curtain to greet the audience and the camera.

"An angel is someone who is gone, someone who is dead," she said. "An angel is someone who is not coming back."

And then she was gone, up through the hole in the roof, out into the sky, gone.

It is a cool, clear morning. The heat broke overnight, finally, leaving an autumnal snap in the air. She stands at the kitchen counter, making a peanut butter sandwich for Whitley's lunch. David sits at the table, back from a job, drinking coffee to wind down. His pale bare feet stick out of the bottoms of his jeans. She asks him what she always asks him, where the job was. Not what it was, how it went, but where. Hawaiian Gardens, he says, down by the casino. He looks overtired, over-worried. He rubs his eyes, tries to block a yawn. He looks like a little boy.

She hasn't slept in she doesn't know how long. She has lost track of the time since she last slept peacefully. She and David have been up late for the last few nights, talking on the front porch, at the kitchen table. Crying, arguing, compromising. David pleading with her, offering to do whatever he needs to do to get her help.

She cuts the sandwich in half, wraps it in wax paper, packs it in a brown paper bag. She is surprised by how well she is able to do this, how well she is able to function. She is amazed by how normal it all seems, this day of all days. David finishes his coffee, puts his mug in the sink, shuffles back to the bedroom. Upstairs, Whitley's alarm blares to life.

She rinses the dishes, walks back into the dark bedroom. David is already in bed, sheet pulled up tight to his neck, eyes at half mast. His jeans and undershirt lie in a heap on the floor. She sits on the edge of the bed, lays a hand on his cheek. Her hand is shaking, and he looks up at her, so she takes her hand away. She leans in and kisses him on the forehead, on the lips. She closes the door behind her when she leaves.

They walk the three blocks to the corner, she and Whitley. He totes his oversized backpack, she pulls her plastic rolling cart full of textbooks and notebooks and ungraded essays. He says a few things, not much. He is still chastened by her outburst, when she dropped the olive oil. She asks him questions, and when he replies with one- and two- word answers, she just talks anyway, she fills the space with sound. She finds herself telling him about her students, the kids in her classes, the questions they ask, the progress they've made. She tells him their names, their interests. She wants him to know them. She feels it is important that these things don't get lost, that he know these things about them.

They stand at the corner. He looks out at the street, the swelling traffic. Goodbye, Mom, he says, and turns away, starts toward his school. Hey, she says, stopping him, turning him around. She wants to run to him, touch him, his hair, his face. But she says nothing when he looks back, she just forces a smile, a wave with her free hand. She lets him go, lets him turn and keep walking.

She waits for the bus at the corner. She takes it as far as the drug store. She buys what she needs, stuffs the bag into her rolling cart. She waits for the bus again, takes it as far as the motel. She has seen the motel a hundred times from the window of the bus on her way to school. The low, tidy brick building with a row of orange doors.

The manager sits behind the counter in the office, an older black woman, her thin hair graying at the temples. A younger black woman in a maid's uniform is dusting the desks and tables, spraying surfaces with lemon-scented cleaner and wiping them dry with a blue cloth.

Lucy pays for a room, asks that someone come by around 3 or 4 o'clock to do a quick cleaning, to change the sheets on the bed. The manager tells her that the room has already been cleaned, and Lucy says that sure that it has but that she's just particular. The manager frowns, but the maid gives her a little smile and nod from behind the manager's back.

She measures her life by fear, blocks of fear, their severity and duration. A block when she was six, a block when she was ten. A block from thirteen to fifteen, from seventeen to twenty. A block at twenty-three, a block at twenty-five. A block from twenty-nine to thirty-three. A block last year, the worst yet, a six month block

starting when she received the call from her mother, telling her what
had happened to her father, what her father had done. Her life as
a checkerboard, black-red, black-red, alternating blocks of fear and
anticipation of the next block of fear.

When she was a girl, she would lay in the backyard in Chicago
and press her hands against her ears, squeezing her head, trying to
keep it away. That dark thing that she thought came in through her
ears. In through her ears and into her head. She lay in the grass and
squeezed as tight as she could, writhing with the effort. The blue sky
shaking above. Her mother came out the back door, across the grass
toward her. Embarrassed, looking back and forth into the neighbors'
yards, worried that someone would see. Her mother grabbing her
elbows and lifting her off the grass, hissing, *What are you doing? What
are you doing to yourself?* Her hands came away from her ears and that
dark thing crawled in through the opening. She wanted to scream at
her mother for pulling her hands away, but it was too late. She shook
her head as hard as she could, trying to shake the thing out, but it
was too late. It was inside, again, and another black block had begun.

For years she covered her ears when she felt it approaching, but
she never succeeded in keeping it out. It always came, through any
opening it could find. Lucy in her bedroom, Lucy on the school bus.
Lucy in her dorm room, in her car, in her apartment on the night
of her first date with David. Lucy in the old house she and David
bought, one of the things she thought would help keep it away. Lucy
locked in the upstairs bathroom reverting to her old tricks, sitting
against the toilet with her hands pressed to her ears.

This is no way to live. She knows this. This is not how people
live.

The air in the motel room is still, lemon-scented. There are two
double beds with white bedspreads, a small round table with two
wooden chairs, a TV on a dresser. A sink stands at the far end of
the room beside the door to the bathroom. She parks her cart in a
corner, empties the drug store bag onto the second bed. Two bottles
of vodka, a bottle of orange juice, a roll of scotch tape, a package of
razor blades. A curled receipt for her purchase. She opens the curtain

on the front window, stands in the early morning sunlight. The parking lot is empty. The light is warm on her face, on her neck. Dust swirls around her hands. She wants to sit on the edge of the bed, turn on the TV, watch the morning news shows. The comfort and company of familiar voices. She can see herself sitting here all morning, until the game shows come on, then leaving the room, leaving the things on the bed, taking the bus home, crawling into bed beside David. She can see stopping this, going no further with this.

She has dreams where she's not afraid. She has dreams where she loves her husband, her son, her job, and that is enough, that is all she needs. In the dreams, she lives a life washed with relief. She is happy, she is free. When she wakes, the disappointment is crushing, the sense of loss for that other life. When she wakes, the fear doubles back on her, bears down on her with a vengeance, even stronger than before.

She closes the curtain. She takes a bottle of sleeping pills from her purse, sets it on the bed. She locks the front door.

The bathroom is small and clean. White tile on the floor and walls. She runs hot water in the tub. In the bedroom, she takes her wallet out of her purse, her license out of her wallet, sets it on the bedside table. She takes a plastic cup from the counter by the sink, peels off the cellophane wrapper. Pours orange juice into the cup, vodka. Spills much of it onto the counter, into the sink. She takes a drink. The warmth spreads down her chest, through her limbs. She opens the pill bottle, shakes the pills into her hand, swallows them two at a time, emptying her plastic cup. Pours herself another drink, less juice this time.

She checks the level of water in the tub. She tears a blank page out of her planner and takes a pen out of her purse and looks at the blank page. She sits at the table by the front window, the closed curtain. She writes across the page, *Call the police. Please do not open the bathroom door. Please call a cleaning service, but please do not call Everclean Industrials in Glendale.* She holds the pen over the page, reads what she's written. Thinks of the maid back in the motel office, her smile and nod. *I'm sorry*, she writes. *I'm sorry*, again. One more time, a third instance at the bottom of the page. Something to break up the blank space. She feels that she can't write it enough. She pulls strips of scotch tape from the roll, tapes the note to the front of the chair. Sets the chair in the middle of the room, facing the front door, where it can't be missed. She finishes her drink. She takes her cell phone out of her purse, turns it off, sets it next to her license on the bedside table. She smoothes out the spot on the bedspread where the vodka and juice bottles sat. She does not want to disturb anything that she doesn't have to disturb.

She turns off the faucet in the tub. Steam swirls across the surface of the water. She undresses, folds her clothes and sets them on the toilet seat cover. She does not look at herself in the mirror as she passes back into the bedroom. The rough carpeting under her feet. She takes the package of razors from the bed. She takes two photographs out of her purse. Before she left the house, she'd pulled them from the bulletin board above her desk. She sets the pictures on the rim of the tub. The first is of Whitley, standing on the porch the previous Halloween in a costume she'd made, an overstuffed bag of groceries. The second is of David in the booth at that all-night diner on their first date.

She'd barely made it through that evening, the beginning of another black block. The fear had been so great. But there was something about him, a physical presence, an internal solidity that made her feel safe. A kindness in his light green eyes. She looked at the tattoos running up his arms, disappearing under his short sleeves. Two days before, she would have clutched her purse if he'd passed her on the street. Now she couldn't stop looking at him.

At one point he got up from the booth to use the restroom and she almost called out to him, she almost said his name, just to hear it in the diner, just to ensure that he was coming back. A few minutes later, when he sat back across from her, she was so relieved that she took his hand on the table and held it tight, smiling like a fool, rambling nonstop again, making noise to block out the fear.

She'd pulled her camera out of her purse and snapped a picture before he could even register what she was doing. She'd smiled like it was no big deal, like it was just an impulsive act, but this was an important thing, recording this moment, his face in the booth. If she never saw him again, or if she saw him for a few weeks or months and then never saw him again, she knew it was important that she have some physical proof, that she could always see his face in this moment and remember when she felt safe.

She opens the package of razors, takes one out, wraps the rest in toilet paper and places them in the wastebasket. She pours herself another drink. No juice this time. She closes the bathroom door. She steps into the tub. The heat passes up her legs, the tiny hairs standing to attention. The room is rubbery, inexact. The pills and vodka rushing through her system. She sits slowly, carefully, easing herself into the water.

She rests her head back against the tile wall. The tops of her knees, her toes break the surface of the steaming water. The two pictures sit down by her feet. She leaves her glasses on so she can see their faces. Her glasses fog in the steam and she wipes them with her thumbs. She lets her arms slip under the water, her skin warming, softening. She looks at their faces. She is sure that she is crying, but she can't feel anything anymore. Everything is numb. She sees David sitting at the kitchen table, his bare feet sticking out of his jeans, looking like a lost little boy. She sees Whitley at the street corner, looking back when she called to him, and she sees him as he will be in a few years, as a teenager, as a man.

She wishes that she were stronger. She wishes that she were someone stronger. She is so scared and so tired of being scared. She is so sorry. She could have covered that note with apologies, she could have filled the page, but there was nothing more to say.

The razor cuts cleanly and quickly and she takes off her glasses and closes her eyes and submerges herself in the water and lets go.

The Kid felt a hand on his arm. He opened his eyes and saw Matthew's face hovering above him.

"I thought you were dead," Matthew said.

Matthew led him out of the burned house, over the wall, onto the sidewalk. He carried The Kid's backpack over his shoulders. Matthew said that he'd seen The Kid talking to Michelle after school and then running in the direction of the burned house. He was worried, so he'd snuck out of his house just before dinner to look for The Kid. He said he'd probably be in big trouble when he got home, but there wasn't too much he could do about that one way or the other.

They walked out of the neighborhood, The Kid feeling nauseous and unsteady. He threw up in a row of bushes near *Gift 2000* and felt a little better. Not great, but better. He didn't know what time it was. Looked like prime-time TV time, televisions flickering in the windows of the houses and apartments they passed. Matthew said that they should go back to his house so Matthew's father could take The Kid to the hospital but The Kid just wanted to go home. His hands and feet tingled, like they had been asleep for a long time. Matthew held onto his shoulder as they walked. The blue star on The Kid's arm was now just a dark, sweaty smudge.

The house was dark, no lights in the windows, on the porch. Maybe his dad was out looking for him. Maybe his dad had been taken away by the cops.

Matthew opened the gate and they started up the front yard. There was something happening in the darkness on the porch, movement and noise. The Kid heard snuffling and snapping, choking noises, and then they were close enough to see Steve Rogers flopping around on the porch. A real seizure, not fake like The Kid's. Steve Rogers snarfing and gagging, rolling across the porch in jerky spasms.

The Kid didn't know what to do. Matthew was walking backwards, eyes wide at the thrashing dog on the porch. And then The Kid remembered, he had it all written down, his dad's instructions, the things he was supposed to do in case this ever happened again. He turned Matthew around and got his notebook out of the backpack. He turned back through the book, looking for the right page, but it was too dark to read anything. He remembered the first thing his dad had done. He ran up onto the porch, stepped around the convulsing dog, unlocked the security screen, the front door, reached inside the house and turned on the porch light. Steve Rogers's face shone twisted, jaws biting, his eyes searching for help.

Matthew stayed put halfway down the lawn, mouth open, feet frozen in place. "What do we do, what do we do?" he said.

The Kid was scared, too, but there was no time to be scared. The Kid was sick, but there was no time to be sick. The dog gagged and sputtered on the porch. The Kid found the right page in the notebook. His dad had gotten into a good position and held Steve Rogers down, one hand on his ribs, one hand on the side of his head. This was after his dad had gotten bitten and yelled Fuck. The Kid figured he could skip that part. The dog thrashed at his feet. The Kid was afraid, he didn't want to get down on the floor, put his hands on the dog, get bitten, but the dog needed help and his dad wasn't there and he couldn't let Steve Rogers flop around like that. He figured that Steve Rogers was maybe more scared than he was.

The Kid dropped his backpack, knelt on the porch, walked on his knees, slowly, keeping his notebook in one hand, reaching out with his other hand. Matthew stayed put on the front lawn, saying *Oh geez oh geez oh geez.* The Kid touched Steve Rogers's fur and the dog jerked away, jackknifing around in almost a complete circle. The Kid was scared but he reached in again, grabbed the fur near the dog's ribs, holding on when the dog flopped and bucked. The Kid dropped the notebook, left it open on the porch to the right page, reached in with his other hand, the really dangerous part, reaching for Steve Rogers's head, the flashing teeth just inches from The Kid's fingers, and then he had it, one of Steve Rogers's ears, and he flattened both of his hands and pressed down, moved in closer to use all the weight and strength he had, pushing the dog down to the floorboards, the dog jerking and bucking and The Kid pushing and looking over at his notebook. There was something he was supposed to do that he was forgetting, something he was missing, and then he saw it, the thing his dad had said to Steve Rogers, the thing that had finally calmed the dog down. He wanted to get Matthew's attention, maybe Matthew could read what was written in the notebook, but Matthew was standing in the yard with his eyes closed and Steve Rogers was still bucking so The Kid opened his mouth and tried but nothing came out but air, nothing but a pitiful squeak, the dog thrashing under his hands, all the weight and strength The Kid could muster not quite enough, the dog working itself loose, and The Kid tried again and this time it happened, a strange scratchy sound, an unknown sound of some kind, a secret loose in the world.

"It's okay, Steve," The Kid said. "This is fine, this is okay."

Steve Rogers flopped and bucked and The Kid held tight, held him down, kept repeating what he'd said, his dad's words, his throat scratched and burning, and slowly the dog moved less and less and then not at all, just lay under The Kid's hands, panting, his sides heaving, snout against the floor, eyes looking out into nothing. It was over, and The Kid sat with his dog and kept his hands on his dog and felt it all gone, the angel, the Covenant, an unbelievable loss.

"Holy cow," Matthew said.

The Kid pet the dog, stroked his fur gently. "It's okay, Steve," The Kid said. He didn't need to look at the notebook to remember his dad's words. "We did it. It's going to be all right now."

Bob in a message on the cell phone:

"I got there too late, David. I was in that long line of cars when the fire started, when the feds rushed in. Everyone was screaming and honking their horns. Some guys in the pickup in front of me had hunting rifles and they started firing shots in the air, but no one was moving. It was a one-lane road and nobody could go anywhere. I finally turned back, found a motel a couple of miles away and spent the night. I didn't sleep much. I couldn't understand why I came up here. What I had planned to do. It didn't make any sense.

"This morning I got up and drove back out to the compound. The road was mostly empty, just some fire trucks and news vans. The feds had set up a tent about a hundred yards from the press area. There were a bunch of folding chairs, a coffee pot, some bottled water. Nobody there. I sat and watched the recovery workers, the smoke from the compound. Pretty soon, people started coming. Friends and family of the Realists. They went right to the press area and the press pointed them to where I was sitting. These people came over and they were crying or they were raging or they just looked numb, they just looked blank, and I'm sitting there with a cup of coffee and some of them just started talking to me. They must have thought I belonged there, that I was there with the tent. Someone would talk for a while and then they would stop and someone else would talk. There were fifteen, twenty people in the tent at one point. They sat and talked to me all morning. I never told them I didn't belong there. I didn't say much of anything. I just sat and nodded, got people coffee."

Bob coughed away from the receiver, sucked on his cigarette.

"I'm back at the motel now. I'm going to get some sleep, maybe, something to eat. Then I'll go back to the tent. More people are probably coming and I think someone should be there when they do."

The Kid was sitting on the porch with Steve Rogers when Darby got home. There was a rip in The Kid's pants and most of the color was drained from his cheeks and he sat with his hands on the dog, holding the dog like something had come and passed.

Darby got out of the pickup and walked up the front yard. As he got closer to the porch light he saw The Kid's eyes widen at the sight of the dark stain on his shirt, his nose stuffed with gauze from the old first aid kit in the pickup.

Darby sat next to The Kid and held The Kid's head to his chest, held him close and tight and then he heard it, quiet at first but gaining strength and volume, The Kid's sobs, rising up from the porch, coming faster and harder, the beautiful sound returning to the house.

six

They drove east out of the city, past sand hills and turning white windmills, The Kid leaning his head against the window of the pickup, watching the wisps of clouds in the sky, the reflection of the dog in the side mirror. Steve Rogers sat in the bed of the truck, ears blown back, eyes closed, snout to the wind.

About an hour out of traffic they pulled over for a few minutes. His dad stood back by the gate of the truck, away from The Kid, scratching the dog's neck while he smoked a cigarette.

What had happened in the time since the angel had left? A month and a half. His dad had a new job now, at a hotel out by the ocean, fixing things in the rooms, bathroom sinks and toilets and busted TVs. He worked during the day, leaving for the hotel when The Kid went to school, coming home not too much longer after The Kid got home. They still ate fast food most nights, or got takeout, but once a week a woman from his dad's new job came by and left dinner in Tupperware containers for his dad to heat up in the microwave, meatballs and boiled potatoes and some kind of pancakes that were supposed to be for desert but that The Kid ate for breakfast. A kind of food The Kid had never heard of. Croatian, his dad said. The woman came by once a week and talked to his dad for a few minutes on the porch and then left the dinner. The Kid wasn't crazy about the food, except for the pancakes, but his dad said they should eat it. This woman had gone to all the trouble of making it and bringing it over.

The burned house was gone. Trucks from the city had come and bulldozed it one afternoon, pushing the walls in on themselves, collapsing what was left of the roof. The Kid and Matthew and Michelle had stood on the sidewalk across the street and watched until it got dark and the streetlights came on and they all had to go home.

Arizona was gone, too. Her father had packed the family up and moved back to their old town, her old school. The Kid had gotten a letter from her the week before. She said she was happy to be back where she belonged. She said she thought he'd make a great talk show host someday. On the bottom of the page she'd drawn a red-haired angel with both hands flying up into the sky.

It was dinnertime when he and his dad entered the desert city. New, clean shopping centers, gas stations, restaurants. Palm trees like the palm trees in movies, in TV shows, tall and straight, the dead fronds cut away. Neighborhoods with nice cars in the driveways, neat houses with trimmed green lawns. No traffic, no one on the sidewalks.

They parked on a quiet side street, leaving the dog in the back of the truck. The pink stucco wall was at the end of the block and his dad boosted him up and over and then climbed over after, both of them jumping down, landing on the grass on the other side, *bump, bump,* one after the other.

The place was just like his dad had described it. The Kid looked around, amazed by the exactness of the vision. Like a memory he never knew he'd had. The colors sharp even in the fading light, green and gold and flamingo pink. The winding streets were quiet, the bungalows quiet, everyone eating dinner, maybe, yellow lights in the windows, the sky getting dark. New Year's Eve. The clocks would strike midnight in a few hours and then who knew what would happen.

They found a swimming pool, the water bright and blue, rippling slowly with shadows from the palms stretching overhead. They stripped down to their swim trunks and his dad slid into the pool, turning over onto his back, wincing when the chlorinated water rolled over the red lines on his nose, the place where it had been broken and was still trying to heal. Sounds of people laughing in the far distance, one of the bungalows on the golf course, the sound of someone clapping, pop of a champagne bottle. The air warm and dry, the wide sky going orange and red in the sunset. The Kid stood beside the pool. The pebbled cement was rough under his bare feet. He didn't know if they were going to get caught or what. What would happen if they did. His dad floated on his back in the pool, looking up at the blinking lights of a plane passing slowly overhead. The Kid watched the plane, thought of the weight in that machine, the magic of how it stayed up in the air. He said the word, all three syllables, *aeroplane*, just loud enough that only he could hear. He wondered if his voice had changed while he hadn't used it, if it had gotten deeper in the time it was away.

His dad was standing chest deep in the water, neck back, watching the plane. The Kid said his dad's name, realized as soon as he said it that he wasn't loud enough. He said it again, "Dad," louder this time, and this time his dad turned and saw The Kid and opened his arms. The Kid took a step toward the pool, then another, plugging his nose, one foot off the ground, the other off the ground, a moment in the air, rising over the pool, the purple hills in the distance, the plane overhead and his dad waiting in the water below.

Scott O'Connor was born in Syracuse, New York. *Among Wolves,* his 2004 novella, about a boy who believes his parents have been replaced by imposters, was praised by the Los Angeles Times Book Review for its "crisp, take-no-prisoners style." Untouchable is his first novel. He lives with his family in Los Angeles.